FLESH
OF THE
BLOOD

DEVASTATION

BY E.A. CHANNON

Flesh of the Blood

As we fight against the wind together,
thank you Paulette for being there for me!

Prologue

The tower rose high into the morning clouds like it did each day. This morning it broke the sun's light apart, making beams of soft but pure light shine down across the city below, highlighting the temples, buildings, public places and green areas where trees pushed themselves high into the sky. The light reflected off the two rivers rushing through the canyon that lay at the end of a deep glen, creating a picturesque scene for the pair of eyes that watched from above.

The high minister, Halashii, of the city of Manhattoria, capital city of the Empire of Pendore'em and Edlaii, a place of stability and military might that had stood for many cycles south of the Sernga Mountains, stood on the highest balcony of the tallest tower within the city so he could look over the incredible populace and buildings that lay upon these lands.

Pendore'em and Edlaii had once been two kingdoms — Pendore'em one of men and Edlaii one of elves — when a war between the two ripped the southern lands apart, almost igniting even the rivers and lakes as the two fought over who would rule the lands. The fighting continued until, after over 250 cycles of constant war, a peaceful agreement was made. Slowly over the next 60 cycles, the once separate kingdoms were joined together, bringing lasting peace that has kept the land together, even bringing the two beings together to grow a new race never seen on Marn before.

Laying his hands on the rail, he scanned down over the city streets and buildings, as he did every day before he began his duties, watching the city wake up and begin its day. He understood and knew that this city was built for peace. "Let it stand for peace, and peace will reign throughout the lands," was the motto of its founders, and he loved this place. The wind blew into his face softly, making him smile slightly as his long, dark brown hair pushed over his eyes, tickling his nose slightly. Standing at only about five and a half feet in height with a slim but healthy body, the minister was not one built for battle like many others, and with his robes covering him, he looked even smaller to many.

The tower on which he stood, known as the Moon Tower, stood across from its cousin towers. There were five in all throughout the city and glen beyond — the Night, the Sun, the Wind and the Tower of Stars — each a mighty tower unto itself, and each provided the inhabitants of the city a place to rest, pray, think, and be joyful within and, if needed, a place to feel secure if the city was ever attacked. While peace was the motto, the city's founders were not naive. Whereas one tower was built along high cliffs cut out over the cycles by the rushing river below it, another lay within fields of grass to look over the plains beyond, and one stood within the river itself, built on an island that burst out of the river, to provide the best vision for those within. Being the tallest, the Sun Tower stood over the rest on top of the mountain that rose on the eastern edge of the city to look over the lands in peace.

The River Vete, the river that divided the city in half, roared from the eastern mountains towards the western seas many miles away. Its turbulent waves of water gave the city the ability to power its mills and even helped with its defenses and with the placement of the city's royal castle in the south, which was protected by high cliffs along the southern border of the city and by the river to the north.

Within its walls, this city held at times over 125,000, and even up to 155,000, citizens, travelers, such as merchants, and more. All were striving to live their lives in peace and to build their own rewards selling goods brought in from the western seas and eastern oceans as well as the southern fields, where animals were plentiful, bringing in food and more to the citizens. Life in the city was one all in the empire wanted to be part of.

As the minister thought of the history of this city and its people, he heard a slight cough behind him, making him turn slightly to see one of the other lesser city ministers standing with a halfsmile by the door that led into the chamber.

"Morning, my friend. Another glorious day I think it will be," the high minister said as he walked in smiling, but then the smile disappeared when he saw the look on the other minister's face. "Problem?"

He watched as the minister swallowed, giving him a look that seemed to say, "Yes, there is a problem."

"You could say that, sir." He pulled a parchment from underneath his robe, lifting it up to read it. "I received a report that Brigin'i City has been destroyed by a large force of orcs and other creatures."

"Brigin'i ... interesting. That place is well fortified ... and how could orcs? ..." His voice quieted down as he started to read the report himself.

First there was a report that Stych Castle and its village had been sacked by a large force of orcs and goblins that had landed from the eastern sea, raiding it in the middle of the night, catching the guard defending it completely by surprise. Hence they were able to destroy it within a day.

"And what of the royal family? Are they alive? What of the princess? And the elven nations up there ... are they helping ... resisting?" the high minister asked as he looked over the report.

The other minister continued his report, explaining, "The orcish army split into two arms, one attacking Brigin'i whilst the other has been able to fight off and keep the army of Bru Edin cornered. A report says that the princess has been kidnapped. By whom, we do not know, nor where she has been taken, but King Dia sent those competitors from his games after her instead of on the usual quest to complete the competition he was holding. There was no word on the king and queen themselves."

Lowering the parchment, the high minister turned and walked to look back out over the city below, thinking about the other reports that his spies had told him of black clouds covering the sky and whispers of something rising in the eastern seas months ago.

Turning, he looked directly at the minister, who returned his gaze.

"Have the Red Guard placed on alert. Send word to our people in Blath 'Na City, and find out if they have seen, heard or even smelled anything of the happenings in the north."

"Yes, Minister!" The man turned but then stopped when the high minister's movement indicated he wasn't done speaking.

The high minister crossed his arms as he thought for a moment, looking over the map that had been painted along the wall, giving a wide view of the lands they lived on. Then he turned his head towards the other minister and finally continued. "I want the guard at the Father Gate doubled, and have their commander ready a force to move into the northern lands if needed."

The other minister bowed. "Yes, Minister Halashii!"

The minister turned and left the room, leaving Minister Halashii to his thoughts as he walked back out onto the balcony to try to figure out what might be going on in the north. For while he believed this might be the beginning of what the legend foretold, he was not sure how to ensure it had come to pass.

"The orcish army has landed, sacking Stych as easily as it did. They won't stay after destroying Brigin'i. ... Orcs don't just sit around. ... They roam and attack. ... So where would they move next?" Halashii spoke quietly to himself as he stared down, watching the people of his city walk below along the streets.

A knock on his door brought him back from his thoughts. He called for whoever it was to come in as he walked over to his desk. The door opened, and an elf covered in polished armor walked in.

"Ahhhh, General Vana, please ... sit down." Halashii sat down as General Vana walked up to stand at the other end of the desk. The elven features of the general shined under the warrior's bright green robes and cloak. His long silverish hair hung along his back, but today the elf had put it in two tiedup tails. This made his face seem a bit tighter and longer, the minister thought quickly when he saw him. "You heard?" he asked quietly.

"Yes ... first Stych, now Brigin'i ... and by orcs of all creatures." Vana crossed his arms as he spoke. "And the kingdom of Sawla'Mor, that principality southwest of Blath 'Na, has turned, siding with whoever is leading that army of orcs." Vana spoke quietly, without any sense of anger or surprise.

Upon hearing that the small kingdom would do such a thing, Halashii rose up and stared at the elf standing across from him.

"Why would they choose to do that?" he asked.

"The orcs number in the thousands, and according to a report, there are many goblinkind, giants and creatures never seen before, and hard for those making the reports to describe, moving within their ranks."

"How did you get this information, Vana? Minister Wampol just told me about the sacking of Brigin'i."

Interrupting Halashii, the general informed him that his Red Guard had been on patrol when they encountered people fleeing Stych who told of what had happened.

"There were survivors?" Halashii considered why orcs would leave survivors in such a battle. There must be a reason behind it.

"Yes, but not many, sir. ..." Vana turned and walked over to the wall that had the painted map of the empire and beyond. Halashii walked over and joined his general to look over region the warrior was speaking of.

Pointing at the dot that said "Stych," south of Blath 'Na, the largest port city in the northern areas, the general quietly spoke of what they had seen.

"The survivors, sir, were farmers and others living in the near countryside and had been able to get away just in time. The reports that have been put together from various accounts tell of an army seen moving north by northeast, moving through Sawla'Mor, which opened its borders to this army and let them move freely through. Much of its populace was even seen joining."

Halashii crossed his arms and thought about what the general had just said. Then he asked a simple question.

"So this orc arm has traveled from Stych, which it destroyed, through Sawla'Mor, who joined them, and then headed northeast, splitting to attack Brigin'i' and Bru Edin?"

Not wanting to sound more depressing, Vana piped in. "There have also been signs of another army north of Brigin'i that has moved through and destroyed a place named Castle Bahn."

"Nakalor is the mightiest elven kingdom in the north. Why haven't they reached out and helped Brigin'i' or the other smaller places?" Halashii cut in.

"They did, sir ... but the orcs and their allies were able to move right through them."

"The Vaca'nor fortress city of Bru Edin I would consider too strong and capable of easily holding off anything orcs could throw at it, but now I wonder. Maybe that is where this army is heading and not Blath 'Na City and Brigin'i. ... That could be ..." his voice trailed off as he looked at the general, who stared back, holding his hands together across his stomach and listening to his lord speak while nodding slowly when the minister looked at him.

"Yes, my lord ... I believe who or whatever is leading these creatures plans, and it's just an idea, but he might be working on destroying the northern kingdoms completely. From what I've read, King Dia's people have already been slaughtered along with the Levenori, leaving Bru Edin and Blath 'Na City, which are now in danger, if the report is true," Vana calmly explained.

"Is there a way to find out what happened to Dia and his

queen?" Halashii knew the answer even as the last words left his mouth.

"No, my lord ... all we can do is prepare to either hold off what might be coming or send an army north of the Sernga Mountains to help as per our treaty with Nakalor and Brigin'i, but ..." Vana left the last words to trail off as both knew that doing so would weaken the empire.

Turning, the high minister walked back to his desk. Vana watched his minister as he heard the words almost at a whisper. "A darkness from the east will come and make a queen ... and she will become a queen of the mightiest of empires upon all our lands."

Vana scratched his chin, thinking of the legend that had been told only as children's bedtime tales. "That is only legend, sir. ... You don't believe in stories, do you?" Vana asked.

Halashii stared at his elven general, swallowing slightly as he gathered his thoughts and spoke quietly, leaning in as he did. "I want you personally to be on guard with your warriors at the Father Gate. Give me your eyes when you report there, my friend," Halashii said, not answering the question that Vana had asked moments before.

Vana nodded slowly as he turned to look at the map once again. Then, bowing, he left the chambers to carry out his newest orders as Halashii stood over his desk, watching his empire's greatest warrior leave while a shadow crossed the minister's face.

"Everything is going the way Methnorick knew it would. Let us hope everything goes the way he said it would, or all will be lost now." Quickly he called for his assistant to order the ministers of the empire to gather.

Chapter One

The branches slapped against his face as trees and bushes rushed past on both sides of his eyes. Heavy breathing was pumping into his ears. A deer flew into view and quickly screamed as it fell under his claws. Blood flew everywhere, and then the rush of trees and bushes took him over again. Howls and roars could be heard coming from him as the dream moved on.

Soon he entered a clearing where he observed a group of creatures sitting around a fire, eating and laughing. His breathing slowed down as he slowly crept along the edge of the trees. The laughing creatures didn't notice that they were being stalked as their voices echoed through the trees.

Suddenly he burst from the trees, claws ripping apart bodies, creatures screaming in panic as they were showered with blood. The party ended in screams and death.

Howling erupted into the night as he looked over the dead, ripped bodies and quickly turned and rushed into the trees. The image of forest animals dying underneath the claws remained as the trees rushed past.

The morning sun hit his face, warming it up to wake him from sleep, ending the dream. He noticed he was lying on the ground between a large tree's roots. Looking around, he saw a carcass of a deer lying nearby with blood everywhere as the dream came quickly back to his memory.

"By the lords!" he shouted, quickly shaking his head, thinking how real everything seemed in the dream. He wondered where he was as he continued to look around when he heard yells in the distance. He quickly got up and started to move towards the sounds. He entered the clearing, where his friends seemed to be enjoying a small breakfast by the campfire, smiling at him, not really caring that he seemed out of sorts. "That's what happens when you sleep under the stars," Kikor had once joked.

* * *

Within the forest, while out patrolling the area, the small orc party returned to their camp to find all of those they had left behind drinking the night before massacred. Gasping and grunting in anger as they walked through the camp, seeing the massacre, the orcs were hushed by their leader. He walked around the outside of the camp, looking at the ground, stopping suddenly when he found what he was looking for. Looking at the others, he grunted orders, and they ran off in the direction in which the creature had left the night before. It did not take them long to find the trail of those of the creature had just joined.

Out looking for wood for the morning fire, Kalion and Meradoth quietly joked about the journey and lack of excitement when suddenly they could make out the sounds of metal upon metal and blasts coming from the direction of their camp. Screams could also be heard both from orcs and their friends, making both nod at the other and rush forward to where they knew the camp sat.

Bennak, who was not far from the other two, was doing the same thing when he heard the same noises. Dropping the wood he held, he pulled out his sword and went crashing down the path and through the bushes to find right in front of him three orcs with their backs to him fighting Whelor, who himself had just found these creatures charging at him moments earlier. Seeing the large halforc emerge from the forest made Whelor grunt loudly.

"Any help would be grand!" the large man said, deflecting an axe blade from one of the orcs as they screamed something, thinking he was speaking to them.

Bennak swiped his huge sword from the left to the right, taking the head of one orc cleanly off and making another scream when its back was sliced open. One of the others saw this and quickly turned to confront Bennak, giving Whelor a chance to strike and dig his weapon deep into the left side of the orc, killing it instantly. Another orc not far away moved to charge at Whelor but didn't have a chance to do anything as an arrow flew past Whelor and Bennak and struck the orc in the chest, slamming it back to hit the ground hard a few feet away from Whelor. Both looked to where the arrow had flown from and saw Kikor, who was hiding behind a dead fallen tree, nod back to them as she looked for others to kill with her bow.

Just as Whelor turned to confront the newest attacking orc warrior, Kalion came flying out from the forest, pulling out the two short blades that he carried. Quickly he fought back the attack from three orcs who were running in just to the left of the encampment, killing two quickly and scaring the other away by screaming madly at it, making it drop its rusted sword and run away, screaming in terror.

Hrliger and Niallee had both been sitting next to Zahnz, enjoying the warmth from the fire. The mage had been preparing a spell to heat up the rocks, explaining that a fire would cause smoke to rise and might alert any orc patrols, just as the orcs had entered the camp. All three grabbed their staves and, as one, sent a wave of energy towards the first group of orcs they saw crashing out of the brush, each using their skills to throw a massive blast of energy at the creatures.

The druids made the ground underneath the orcs instantly go from being hard dirt to a muddy mess as the bushes and trees around them looked like they had woken up in anger and moved to attack the orcs, who were now struggling to escape the mud. The trees with their large branches reached down to grab the now screaming orcs who had able to escape the mud and threw them back into the mud to keep them closer.

Zahnz threw a burst of fire bolts hard into one of the large orcs, making him fall back into the mud, screaming from the pain of the fire and being put into the mud.

Up above on the rocks, Holan was dealing with a few other orcs he had followed up a rock face that stood nearby.

"Uggg, is tha' all yea got, you ugly beast?" Holan yelled out, hoping in its anger it would mess up and give him an opening.

"You dwarf ... you dead!" it snarled back, almost spitting in Holan's face as it did.

Holan hated these creatures, as all dwarves did, but it was the smell that bothered Holan the most. "Do'na take a bath, orc?" Holan quickly smirked, ducking under another sword swipe at his head.

So far he wasn't making any headway with this orc, and he was starting to get tired and could hear the battle below in the camp going on. Hoping his weakness wouldn't show on his face and that his speed was not slowing slightly, Holan did his best to attack and defend against these orcs. Just as he was trying to come up with a move of attack, he saw his chance and was able to knock one orc off balance by swinging his axe at its legs, catching the orc's cloak and pulling it towards the dwarf. In return, the orc had to jump back so it wouldn't lose its legs. Quickly seeing its problem as it jumped back, it slammed into a tree that Holan had slowly been working the orcs back into. Holan's axe catching its cloak made the orc fall forward off balance, giving Holan the chance to knock its sword away. Then, swinging it in one large circle, Holan dug his axe into the orc as it bounced off the tree.

"You orcs ar' getting bettr, I can say tha'" Holan commented, taking in deep breaths. Raising his axe up, he waited to see if any other orcs would attack, as he could hear more screams, metal clashes and even explosions coming from the camp below. "Come on, yea nasty orc, come on!" Holan screamed out as he turned to charge down to help his friends, but he was stopped when another orc stepped out of the forest. Observing the orc for a moment, Holan was able to see that this creature wore armor and cloth that he had never seen before. Most of the orc tribes in these areas wore blue or green-styled cloth with grayish armor, but this one wore red cloth with black armor, as did his now dead companions, Holan suddenly observed out of the corner of his eye.

"Where yea from, orc?" Holan finally asked, wondering.

Seeing the face of the orc get angry as he looked at the ground and saw the orcs that the dwarf had just dispatched, Holan prepared himself for it to attack, but it didn't. Instead it took something out from behind its armor and poured it into its mouth, almost laughing at the same time. Instantly the orc began to quiver and shake, dropping its sword to the ground and falling to its knees at the same time, letting out a high-pitched scream.

Holan was confused. He had never in his long life seen an orc take its own life like this before. "What is going on," he thought as he looked around, wondering if it was a trap of some kind. He stepped forward and looked down at the quivering orc, who was foaming at its mouth, looking back at him with its black eyes. As Holan moved closer, it laughed at him, making foam leak out as it finally spoke, though Holan could hardly make out what it said.

"Dwarf, you ar'yea goin' to die when me master finds yea hav'a killed me a' me brothua's. ... I die for me master." At that, the shaking orc slowed down its shaking and lay still for a moment. Foam stopped coming out of its mouth. Holan was even more puzzled at what the orc had said. Bending down, he looked at something that was sticking out of the armor when an explosion down below at the camp made him remember that the camp was under attack.

Standing back up, Holan kicked the orc just to make sure it was dead and ran over the rise and into the camp to surprise a large orc from behind by slamming his axe hard into its back. Holan could almost hear the crack of the orc's backbone as the axe struck hard. In one motion, the arms of the orc came up, and it fell forward with a loud groan, taking Holan's axe along with it, of course. Seeing the orc falling down with the dwarf's axe, another two orcs turned their attention from fighting Amlora, who was keeping them back using a large staff that she had pulled from her horse moments earlier, using it in a well-executed defensive move. Around her lay three dead orcs, two blackened by mage fire from that very staff.

When the fighting ended a while later, Kalion and the others looked around the camp, which was littered with blackish statues and bodies of orcs everywhere.

Jebba was pulling his blade out of the body of an orc when he noticed Bennak, who was now resting on a log not far away. Wiping the blood off using the rags from his dead orc, he walked over. Bennak was covered in orcish blood from head to toe. Jebba didn't ask, but he knew that the halforc was all right but also angered that the orcs had caught them unaware and that it had taken so long to dispatch such a small group.

Niallee and Hrliger came walking over. Niallee was helping the gnome walk, as he had some type of limp. It turned out he had taken on an orc but had fallen backwards over a tree root. The fall had somehow twisted his ankle, but it did save him in the end, for one orc would have chopped him in half if not for that tree root getting in its way.

Kikor had run out of arrows during the fight and was now gathering arrows from the fallen orcs as she walked over to join the group. Amlora had gone over to check on Harbin and was working on healing him since he had been wounded by something that flew into his shoulder. The others could hear him grunting from her healing.

As they recovered from the attack, Kalion looked around worriedly, causing Kikor to ask, "What is wrong?"

Kalion looked around once more. "Where's the thief? And where is Zahnz?"

Chapter Two

*C*hansor had disappeared long before the battle or before the sun was even up. He had heard something in the forest while lying on his blanket and thought that it couldn't be an animal. Since the others had still been asleep, he quietly got up and snuck into the dark when he saw what must have been what he had heard: two black figures almost blending in with the trees and brush. Moving so he couldn't be seen, he watched and wondered what they were; he studied them for what seemed hours, so when the screams and sounds of battle erupted behind Chansor, he knew they had to be part of it. The black-clothed creatures just watched the battle rage on, which he thought was odd. Were they with the orcs, he wondered, or something else?

He stayed hidden and continued to watch them for what seemed like an hour. He winced when he thought a friend had been killed or hurt, but he could see the clearing well and saw that the battle his friends were waging was leaning in their favor. Finally, he got a view of the two figures, and what he saw made him gasp. It turned out they weren't orcs or even men but two dark elves standing there, watching, observing ... maybe taking notes, the thief thought.

When the battle began to turn against the orcs, Chansor observed the two dark elves whispering quietly to each other and nodding, almost smiling as they did, before turning around slowly and walking deeper into the forest and disappearing.

Chansor looked back at his group, wondering if they needed his help, but then he took the opportunity to follow these suspicious dark elves to see where they might be going. It didn't take him long to find out, as the two walked over the hill away from the group's encampment and up to some very large-looking animals. Quietly hiding behind a fallen tree, Chansor couldn't tell what these animals were due to the shadows and darkness, but he could see large fangs protruding from their mouths, and their breathing was loud. Even from where Chansor hid he could hear them breathing, and as the figures drew near, the animals almost got excited to see them as the elves jumped on their backs.

Chansor could just hear their whispers but couldn't make out any useful information as they sat and waited for a few more moments until they turned their mounts and rode quickly down a deer path, away from the group and towards the west.

Chansor watched them disappear into the forest. Knowing he couldn't keep up with those animals, he turned and ran back to the camp. As he came into the clearing, he saw orc bodies everywhere and then looked at the others innocently.

Niallee, Hrliger, Holan and Kalion were standing next to Amlora as she was talking about something. Bennak and Jebba were off to the side, speaking quietly to each other. Meradoth, Birkita and Kikor were also talking to each other as they walked around the campground, checking the dead bodies.

Niallee was speaking to the group. "Where did they come from?"

"And the next question is, how did they find us?" Amlora asked.

"I thought we had fooled the ones following us. Do we think these are some of that same group or a new group that just happened upon us?" Hrliger asked.

Just then Chansor walked up behind Meradoth and said, "Hi," making Meradoth drop a bag he had found on a orc moments before. All conversation stopped as everyone looked at the little thief.

"Where in the deepest hells have you gone to?" the mage asked, leaning down and picking the bag back up.

"What ... I ... well ... mmmmm ..." Chansor stammered, looking over to Amlora, who was talking softly to Kikor and Birkita. "I heard something in the forest and went to investigate."

"And what did you find?" Amlora asked Chansor. He was about to answer as he looked around the campground but got distracted from answering Amlora when he noticed something.

"Where is Zahnz?" Chansor asked, curious about his whereabouts, but then he started to notice the goodies that the orcs had left around him and went to see what he could find. "Ohhhh, what's in here?"

It didn't take long for the group to find the missing mage, as he was still resting up against a tree. When Chansor saw the mage's robes — always dirty, he thought — he called out and quickened his stride, seeing that the mage was close by.

"Zahnz, the orcs have all been slaughtered." When Zahnz didn't answer, Chansor called another time but slowed down his stride as he did so. He called to the others, "I have found him. Over here!" He slowly walked around the tree to see why the mage hadn't answered.

Chansor understood why Zahnz couldn't say a word when he saw the large spear sticking out of his chest. The mage must have died instantly, the thief thought quickly, being surprised by the orcs as he moved through the woods.

Chansor had been positive that Amlora and Zahnz were getting personal with each other after seeing signs on the trail like them walking side by side and being in close conversations while walking and around the fire at night. He knew this would kill the cleric, so he moved to block the view as the others in the group hurried up to him. This was going to drive her over the hill, Chansor thought, just as Whelor walked around the tree slowly, moaning quietly when he also observed the dead mage. Chansor was right, for as soon as Amlora rounded the tree, she slowed her stride as if she knew something was wrong.

Whelor looked down at the thief and then back at Zahnz, stopping his moan when he noticed something wrong with what he was seeing. Not only was the mage stuck to a tree by the orcish spear embedded in his chest but his throat had been cut as well. Whelor leaned closer to see the cut and saw that it wasn't a cut of an orc blade, nor had it been done hastily. It was done smoothly, as if by an expert with a clean blade.

"I saw black-clothed elves, I think, out there in the woods during the battle, watching you all," Chansor whispered, looking directly at Whelor and then at the others. Amlora stood back, away from the others, not venturing any closer.

Leaning back the man looked down at the thief. "You saw what?" Whelor wanted to make sure he had heard the man right.

"They were two dark elves ... just watching you!" Chansor answered.

"Dark elves, like Zahnz?" Kikor asked.

"Yes, but they wore black cloaks, much like the ones the orcs wear. ..."

"That might explain what has happened here." Whelor pointed to Zahnz's throat. "Our mage here must have known them, or at the very least seen them, but wasn't fast enough."

Chansor was intrigued by what Whelor was talking about now. Zahnz killed by ... ? He started to get excited as he remembered something. "The elves — they left on ... I think they were animals, but I couldn't get a good look. I did see something very unusual, though. ... I thought I saw fangs."

"Fangs? Anything else that might identify what kind of animals they were?" Kalion asked, speaking in a slightly angered voice.

"How did they leave? Did they fly or ride them away?" Meradoth asked Chansor.

"They rode down a path through the forest, and all I can say is they weren't horses. They were bigger and lumpier — no wings though."

The sound of metal clanking came up behind Chansor, and even before turning his head, he knew it was Holan coming to see what they had found.

He stopped and looked closer. Seeing the mage's throat cut and blood splashed across his robes, he said, "Stupid mage."

As Holan said this, Chansor looked over at Amlora and saw her cringe at the dwarf's words. "Sorry, my lady," Holan whispered then.

Shaking his head, he realized that whoever killed him must have done it before the battle, for the blood was dry. "Bastard," Holan said under his breath, and at that, the dwarf turned around and walked back to camp, leaving the others to watch him go.

Chansor looked up to see Whelor staring out into the forest, seemingly not listening to Holan or the others. Whelor was looking out towards the dark of the forest, and he was bent over a bit with his hand over his stomach. Chansor thought that was concerning, so he walked over.

Walking up, he looked up at the big man's face. "Whelor, are you ok?" Chansor asked, thinking the man had been wounded.

Whelor turned quickly at Chansor's question and smiled suddenly. "No, no, I'm fine. I'm fine." Whelor answered so fast that Chansor was taken aback at the answer.

Raising his eyebrows, Chansor was about to ask him another question, but Whelor didn't give him a chance. Whelor walked past the thief and their dead friend and walked back directly to the camp.

Chansor's curiosity with regard to Whelor was piqued, but of course, this was the man who had disappeared before with no word, returning the next morning looking both tired and stressed.

Amlora stood at the back of the group. Looking at Zahnz and then to the others, she finally said, "Well, what do we do? We can't just leave him here."

"What would you like us to do — bury him?" Hrliger asked.

"Does anyone know the customs of the dark elves?"

"Out of respect we need to bury our friend before we leave!" Chansor piped in.

Amlora suddenly spoke again. "He once told me that death is just the spirit leaving the body to travel the world. It becomes an empty shell, so it is common to burn that empty shell." She said this in such a way, like she was channeling him, that as she looked up, she found the others all watching her intensely, so she hastily continued, "I mean that it really doesn't matter what we do to his body now."

Quickly Bennak and Jebba walked over, and as one they pulled the mage's limp body from the tree and laid him on the ground. Kikor and Birkita moved over to take care of Zahnz's body. Birkita looked up at Amlora, who just stood over them, watching. Birkita said, "He may not have the same beliefs as my people, but once dark elves and elves were one. We will bury him the way our people would. Amlora, do you want to help?"

Amlora looked her in the eye and nodded her head "yes." As the three women cleaned the body of Zahnz, Niallee and Hrliger used their skills to open the ground. After a few of the others in the group placed Zahnz's body in the freshly dug area, the two replaced the dirt. When they finished, each bowed their head and quietly said their best to their friend. Then they turned and slowly walked away, leaving Amlora alone to say her goodbyes. Chansor, who stood not far away, trying to understand what had happened, observed a tear going down her face and knew Zahnz's loss was going to be hard on her.

When she turned and saw the thief standing there, staring at her, both smiled and nodded to each other before each returned to the camp, where everyone was packing what was left of their trampled belongings in silence, giving their last thoughts for their friend.

With only two horses left — it seemed a number had run off during the battle — Holan and Chansor jumped on one and Hrliger

14

and Niallee on the other.

Whelor and Bennak decided that they could walk behind the group as a rear guard, not speaking a word to each other as they did. The mages, as always, quickly came up with an interesting way of traveling. Grabbing their bed rolls, they made the things lift up to fly into the air and through the woods, and they were soon flying in front of the group. They heard Chansor moan that it wasn't fair, making Meradoth giggle as he flew past.

The group slowly made its way along the deer path that took them back towards the eastern road. It didn't take them long to get out of the forest and into the wide, clear grasslands.

The group stopped when they cleared the forest to observe what was before and around them. Standing high and strong to the north was the easternmost arm of the Pilo'ach Mountains range, the largest group of mountains in the northern reaches.

To the south was nothing but rolling hills and grass with heavy clouds above them from a storm that was approaching. Heavy amounts of rain and lightning could be seen falling onto the grasslands. A small river they needed to cross was growing in size from the amount of rain coming down.

Kalion soon found the road that the orc army had used about half a mile south of their current location. It wasn't hard for the rest to see it from their observation point.

Hrliger quickly pointed out, "This army seems larger than what we saw at Dagonor." Kalion mentioned, "The dwarven fortress of Chai'sell is not that far, nor is Bru Edin." Looking back, the ranger cocked his head up to look at the mages. "Any chance you two can transport yourselves to either of those places and let us know if they are even there?" Kalion asked the two mages sitting on their flying bed rolls, listening to the ranger. Seeing Amlora's sad face, he was trying to think beyond their quest and not of those who had been lost.

Harbin and Meradoth looked at each other as Meradoth pulled something out of his pack. Whispering to each other for a few moments, they looked up and, as one, nodded their heads "yes."

"I think Meradoth has a better chance than I to do this. The main components that make this bed roll fly take up a bit of my energy, so I'm a bit too tired to do any hard traveling," Harbin said as he looked from the group to the other mage.

Meradoth looked at his friend, smiling for a moment, and then looked at the rest. "Where should I go, then?" he asked.

Everyone looked at Kalion, as he was most informed about the area. He pulled out a small rolled parchment from his pack and tossed it over to the mage. "Try Bru Edin first. ... A bit easier to get to, I would imagine. Tell us what you find," Kalion stated. Meradoth unrolled the parchment and checked out the information. Though not the best map, it at least gave him an idea of where he was compared to Brigin'i City and other known places, so he nodded back at Kalion. Then, holding the map in his hand, he looked over to the group.

"Ready, my friend?" Harbin looked over at Meradoth, who only nodded back, not saying anything as the others wished him safe travels.

"I don't think we should stay here until you get back, Meradoth," Hrliger piped up. "Look for us on the road." The gnome smiled up at the mage.

Everyone looked at the gnome sitting with Holan on the horse. Holan quickly said back to the gnome, "And why not? I do na see a problem sitt'in hera for a while, yea?"

Hrliger smiled a bit at the dwarf and looked back to the forest at that moment. Niallee, Birkita and Kikor each turned to look at the forest as they began to hear something in the far distance that sounded like heavy footfalls of horses coming their way.

When they heard the all-too-familiar sounds of orc battle cries a bit clearer and a bit closer, Jebba looked back to Meradoth. "I believe we will be riding hard from here, so if you have the ability to move, I'd hurry!" Jebba pointed towards the north and east.

Meradoth nodded and, saying a few words, moved his fingers to cast a spell. The area around the mage turned slightly orange and then blue as the others watched his body warp and then disappear in a flash.

Harbin adjusted himself on his bed roll and rose up higher into the sky to look down onto the forest, from where the sounds were approaching. Whispering something, he closed his eyes quickly to see through the heavy foliage of the trees, spotting what looked like at least a hundred orcs and even a few giants marching down the road they had used.

"ORCS ... MANY OF THEM ... AND THEY HAVE MANY GIANTS!" he yelled down as he quickly lowered his flying bed roll, making the remainder of the group quickly move into action. The two horses started to gallop while those on foot started to run at full speed to keep up. As he watched the others leave the area, the mage whispered to the bed roll he sat on to slowly lift up into the leaves, moving in the direction of his friends at a slower pace. Since this was the first time he was using a bed roll to carry his weight a great distance, he was learning the speed with which the bed roll could move was much slower than expected, but better than walking or, as was the case now, running, he thought.

Quickly the group vacated the area, following the mage as they did, leaving nothing but foot and hoof prints in the dirt and grass as they escaped. If they had stayed and seen what was following them, they would have witnessed about half an hour later orcs and other creatures following the group burst out of the forest's edge, screaming as they did so. Only stopping to gather themselves and look around, they quickly saw the group riding hard away from them in the far distance, giving way to screams of anger as they saw their victims getting away.

Instantly, a small orcish creature burst forward and ran to catch their victims, and another saw the flying bed roll above and started releasing arrows at it. Harbin chose to dodge the arrows rather than fly out of range, for he wanted to stay close to his friends; however, he was not quick enough, and the bed roll took two arrows before he could maneuver out of range. One was close enough for him to feel the wind as it flew past his face, causing him to look down angrily, only to be surprised at what he saw.

He saw a giant grab a tree right out of the ground, its back tightening as its muscles worked hard to pull the tree out of the ground, and then hurl the tree in his direction.

"Oh, lords!" he yelled, watching the massive tree fly up into the air and towards him. Luckily he had enough time to maneuver himself out of the way, but it in doing so, he gave the giant's comrades enough time to get themselves close enough to release more arrows at the flying bed roll above them.

Harbin started throwing bolts of lightning and a few other nasty objects at the orcs as he looked back, catching the sight of his friends getting farther away by the second. He knew that slowing the pace of these creatures was the only way for his friends to get away, and so far, it was working.

Chapter Three

*A*s the city's populace walked around doing their business, buying and selling goods brought in from the regions of the south, they began to notice the warriors gathering and marching from the garrisons that were positioned around Manhattoria.

At first the ministers didn't want to scare the populace with the news that the north was under the threat of total war, but rumors spread, and soon there was a parade of children and women saying their goodbyes to their sons, fathers, brothers and even lovers as the hundreds of warriors marched north towards the gate known as Hakan'nor, or the Father Gate.

The Father Gate, the oldest of the four massive gates in north, had an enormous bridge crossing the Great Canyon that lay just south of the Sernga Mountains. This gate stood high between two mountains, blocking the way north and south. For many cycles, this gate had been an imposing sight.

The gate stood as a testament to both dwarven and elven engineering from when they relied on each other for survival cycles before when these lands were first settled. Between the two massive towers that made up the defenses of the gate lay the gate itself, which could be opened fully to allow a huge army to get through quickly or could be locked down to allow only smaller entries to ensure security. This is how the gate remained most days. Only once in recent memory had the gate been fully opened to let through eight massive war machines that the city of Blath 'Na had purchased from merchants in the south over 20 cycles earlier.

As groups of troops arrived at the Father Gate, many for the first time, they all stood in awe as they were given their orders to fall out. To open the gate fully required using the strength of four mages who lived within the four towers around the city, and they took some time in doing so. The sound it produced told everyone in the region and beyond that the gates were opening — the noise it produced was called the "Lion's Roar." There was no need to open the gate fully often because the noise, although it had not been heard in cycles, deterred many creatures from venturing south. Using sound saved lives, the empire found.

On this day the Father Gate held an outpouring of activity as the warriors gathered there to reinforce the gate's warriors who had been stationed there and began preparing themselves as reports that armies of orcs and more had been seen in the north and could be moving to where they stood at any moment reached them.

The activity was moving well, Commander Tevanic thought, as he stood, arms crossed, watching everything going on around him. He didn't need to tell anyone what needed to be done. Everyone had trained well to get to this point. He had made sure of it.

Tevanic's long, blondish hair exemplified his elfish features from his mother while his body showed his man side, with bulging muscles in his arms and chest, which even under the chain mail showed his body's strength.

When a new warrior came to this gate, they were trained hard for six months before being tested. Those who didn't make it were sent on to another post in the south. He wanted only the best to be here with him as this was the only crossing from the Sernga Mountains into the southern region on the eastern edge of the empire. Over the cycles no army, orc or other creature had been able to pass the gate, and he wanted to make sure he wouldn't be the commander who changed that history.

Turning slowly, he walked towards a gathering group of people when he saw the smiling face of a farmer he had known for a while.

"Kramnier, my friend, how are you doing this day?" The farmer, an older man with a long white beard pulled on the reins, stopping the wagon that he was driving. As the horses whimpered slightly, he pulled back the hat he wore since it was a bright day.

"Well, my friend ... good to see you, sir. ... Not too bad, just glad to get away from the wife today!" Both laughed hard, knowing what he meant.

"Hitting you hard again is she?" Tevanic asked, patting one of the horses' heads, calming it down, as he listened to the farmer's words about how she had woken up and yelled at him until he left the farm about three hours ago and he was sure he could hear her voice still yelling at him as he made his way into the glen.

"You know, Sir Tevanic, I'm sure she used to be an orc or something in a past life." Again both laughed as Tevanic walked closer, looking up at the older man.

"I'm sure she was." He laughed and smiled. Seeing the concern on the man's face as he looked around at the commotion, the warrior answered the question before the old man asked.

"We have been given reports that there is orc activity in the north, and we are just making sure everything here is at the ready in case they decide to attack the empire." Tevanic wanted to say more, but ...

"Orcs ... I heard the rumor that the north is about to fall. ... That's why she was mad at me. She wanted to go south where her sister is living near Lake Ralk'k. She wanted to keep the supplies that I bring in weekly for the garrison for ourselves ... and head to the capital or somewhere! The fact that I left anyway really had her mad." The farmer grunted, thinking of her face.

Hearing the man speak, the commander suddenly became worried, for with rumors come discord and fright among the people. *How does a farmer who lives in the country know what is going on in the north? Have the rumors reached that far?* he wondered. He pulled himself up so they were face to face, making the farmer suddenly

21

lean back, showing his slight uneasiness. The farmer had been bringing food supplies to the garrison for many cycles now, and Tevanic knew he could not tell him anything; he was not good at keeping secrets of any kind.

"Where did you get news that the north was falling apart, Kramnier?" Tevanic whispered as a few farmers rode past slowly, looking over at them. A few nodded, seeing that it was the gate commander.

The old man swallowed. "I ... mmm ... I ... well ... mmm ... I heard from a friend who's a fisherman. He was fishing off the shore near Stych when he saw it fall. He said that he saw hundreds, even thousands, of orcs and other dark creatures land there and begin destroying the area. He watched them march away after burning the place to the ground." Kramnier's voice shook as he spoke.

Stepping back, the warrior looked around as the last of the morning's wagons came in with food and supplies. Looking south, he saw nothing except for a herd of deer that was feeding on some food that had fallen to the ground from the wagons a mile or so away.

"It is true, my friend," he said in a whispered voice. "The north is falling apart. I do not know how bad ... but it is, and we could be attacked by a heavy force of orcs very soon." Looking back up at the shocked face of the farmer, he continued, "Get these supplies out of the wagon, get home as quickly as you can, and get that wife of yours to the capital or her sister's. If this gate falls ..." He didn't need to say anything else. Both knew what would happen if it did. Tevanic thought to himself, *At least the capital is far enough south in the Empire that it may be safe.*

Without saying a word, the farmer yelped as he cracked the reins, and quickly his horses moved as he looked back at his friend, knowing this might be the last he would see of him.

Stepping away from his farmer friend's wagon, Tevanic again looked at the herd of deer, silently wishing he was one. None cared about what was going on around them. They were just eating their way through life. What a life that was, he thought, as he slowly made his way back to the easternmost tower of the gate, where his sleeping area was.

* * *

Brigin'i lay in ruins as the orcs moved through the streets, catching those people left inside to quickly die under their blades. Screams echoed everywhere as building after building fell under the heat from the fire storms that rushed down the streets and many people burned to death.

Many of those who did escape the dead city were found easily in the eastern and northern forests and cut down by many dark elves who waited there after fighting off their cousins the elves from Levenori. The elves had retreated deeper into the forests after seeing that their relief to the city had come too late to help.

Everywhere around the once proud city became a killing ground as the forest soon also caught on fire, causing smoke to rise even higher and making it hard for those escaping, but many did use the cover of the smoke to get away and made their way south.

General Kaligor walked through the fallen northern gate, surveying the damage that his army had done, including the bodies littering the ground everywhere, with a proud smile on his face. Smoke moved past the general as he stepped over body after body to move down into the city, making his way towards the castle that overlooked the city.

Placing his hands on his hips, Kaligor pulled in a deep breath as he spoke to his army. "Spread the word. ... You have one day within these walls to do what you will. Tomorrow we march for Bru Edin!" Kaligor's raspy voice echoed his master's orders as the creatures he led cheered and roared at what he had just said. He made his way up the main road, seeing giants far above rip the imposing gates that had once protected the castle, only stopping when their general walked by, nodding at them as he did.

As he moved into the courtyard, he found himself face-to-face with a few prisoners being knocked to their knees by their captors. Seeing their general walk in, they quickly stepped to the side and waited for the general to inform them of what to do with the prisoners.

The prisoners, many bloodied and bruised from the fighting, all stared up at the Cyclops as he walked up. None of them believed what they saw, each thinking that this giant of a creature only existed in children's tales. The sight of him caused many to shake and tear up in fear.

When Kaligor stopped before them, they each watched as he crossed his massive muscular arms and looked down with his eye, making a few shake their heads in disbelief and look away rather than meet his gaze, knowing that soon they would be with their gods.

"Which of you is a leader? Where is King Dia?" Kaligor's voice boomed.

"Methinks this one is, my lord!" a giant orc standing behind the prisoners piped in, kicking the back of the man in front of him, making him groan as he fell forward slightly. "This ones killed many of our warriors before we caughts him!"

The eye squinted slightly as Kaligor looked down at the man who had once worn bright armor, which was now ripped and covered in blood from orcs.

"Name!" the general called out as his voice echoed slightly in the courtyard.

When the man didn't respond, the orc who had spoken up moments before kicked the man hard in the back, making him cry out in pain as he fell forward again, smashing his face hard on a stone.

As he lay there, Kaligor smiled at the man's resistance in trying not to answer his question. He nodded at one of the orcs standing behind the prisoners, who, in turn, grabbed the prisoner by the hair, pulling his head back.

"Name!" Kaligor demanded again. "You don't answer, and I will kill each one here!" His words made the others kneeling close their eyes and take a deep breath to steady themselves.

"Marbod ... my name is Marbod," the man spoke, though having to spit blood out of his mouth as he did.

Leaning his head back slightly, the general thought about the name, trying to remember if he knew it. "Ahhhh, Captain Marbod is it? Mmmmm."

Again the captain spit hard to clear his mouth as an orc grabbed his hair tighter, pulling his head back farther to look up at the general, who watched the man as he struggled, the pain showing in his face.

"Your city is mine, Captain. ... Do tell me where your king and his queen are, and I will make sure your life will not be more painful."

Spitting another glob of blood from his mouth, Marbod, whose face was slightly swollen now from hitting the ground, looked up and smiled slightly, knowing that this creature didn't have the king yet. As he smiled, Kaligor leaned down so that their faces were directly looking at each other.

"I know not where the king is ... nor would I tell you if I could ... but I'm sure Dia and his queen escaped here before the city fell," Marbod stated in defiance.

Kaligor smiled back. He respected the man's resistance in not telling his captor what he wanted to know. Kaligor turned, looking over as, one by one, the other prisoners, who moments before had been right beside Marbod, were pulled away. Their screams for mercy echoed in the courtyard, where they watched as other orcs dug holes and then dragged each prisoner, one after another, and tied them up and onto a pole with sharpened points, which they then placed into the hole.

As Marbod watched, many screamed and died quickly from the shock of their bodies sliding down the poles. Others screamed for their mothers or their gods to take them quickly as they struggled to get off the poles. Their struggles only made things worse, pushing the poles deeper into their bodies as they slid down, making their screams harsher by the moment.

Turning around, the general looked down at the shocked face of the captain as he watched his people die in front of him. "Tell me, Marbod, and I will stop this." Kaligor saw defeat in the man's eyes as Marbod looked down at the ground.

Marbod knew his life was at its end. Even if he did tell this creature what he wanted, he was going to be killed. So gathering his courage, he looked back at the other prisoners who were pleading and then back up at Kaligor.

"I fought for these people!" Marbod's own anger rose at seeing his people like this as he looked up at the Cyclops standing before him.

"Tell me, Captain, or I will do this to everyone still alive within this city!" Kaligor's anger rose now as he knew the man was not going to answer.

As Marbod breathed in a huge breath of smoky air, his chest pushed out under his ripped clothing, and he stared up into the eye of the general who had conquered his city without answering him further.

Seeing the resistance, the Cyclops leaned back. "Kill them ... kill them all!" Kaligor screamed. The pleas for mercy were heard as Marbod looked at the ground, grimacing. Then all suddenly was silent. When an orc's hot breath hit his neck, he knew it would be over soon. As his head was pulled back, he saw the ugly face of his killer smiling down at him and placing his rusty, bloodcovered sword at his throat.

"No ... not him!" Kaligor's voice made the orc let Marbod's hair go, causing Marbod to fall back as he saw the general walk over to stand in front of the orc behind him.

"Put the captain over there. I want him to watch the others die first. ... He will be last!" The orc laughed hard, obeying his master. He grabbed Marbod by the hair again and started pulling him as he moved forward. The orc pulled the captain up on his feet and in one motion threw him at a group of orcs, who quickly grabbed the man and dragged him off. Kaligor didn't care now. The city was nothing to him. He was only carrying out his master's orders.

Kaligor stood, watching Marbod get lifted high into the air, screaming and struggling to get away. His arms were roped and tied behind him as he struggled more to get free. The orcs holding him only laughed as two others pushed the point of the pole between Marbod's legs. He screamed in pain as the pole was pushed into him, ripping his pants as it did. Kaligor crossed his arms, and his smile grew as his warriors lifted the pole.

"There will be blood ... for what you've done here, Cyclops!" Marbod's screams echoed loudly within the courtyard, making everyone stop what they were doing to watch the warrior slide slowly down the pole. When Marbod's screams quieted down, the Cyclops turned to the orc captain, who was waiting for orders.

"Find me Dia. ... Now!" Kaligor grunted loudly as he stormed further into the castle to look for his prize.

* * *

The group had been able to get distance between themselves and the pursuing orcs. As they ran towards the open plains in the far distance, Harbin flew past the group to scout the area before them and to ensure the safe return of Meradoth when he finally returned to the group.

The mage could see the road far ahead split. One way went back into a forest, and the other stayed in the open. Yelling down for them to hurry and get moving towards the forest road and not the other, he looked up and noticed movement far in the distance flying in the air towards him from the same direction as the orcs.

Waving his hand over his face, he whispered some faint words. In order to get a better view, he used his special sight to focus in on what he was seeing. Flying just above the treetops, he watched as the beasts started to come into view. They looked just like those they had encountered days before outside of the Dagonor Castle ruins ... the same ones who had killed Winsto!

"No ..." was all that came out his mouth. Harbin's sight ability showed him four of these flying beasts coming his way. They were large with bat-like wings and heads with huge fangs hanging out of their mouths. What were they? he wondered, trying to think of creatures he'd seen in the past.

Then he noticed the riders on top, and that sent a slight chill up his back. Each wore a black cloak with a red lining that covered each of their faces. He could see what looked like burnt armor underneath the flapping cloaks and what looked like blades of some type hanging along their thighs. He was sure they knew he and others were here, for they were flying straight at them.

Quickly flipping around, the mage flew down hard to catch up with his friends, who had moved quicker than he thought and had made it to the forest's edge. He could see Kikor waving at him to follow her as they entered it.

Niallee and Hrliger stood before him when he flew into the forest opening. As he flew past them, they started chanting a few words. Kikor ran inside the forest as Harbin turned to see the trees that surrounded the entrance quickly glow bright blue and then start to move and intertwine themselves, completely blocking the road behind the group, almost like the entrance had never been there before.

"Thank you, my friends. Now climb aboard so we can catch the others!" Harbin stated to Niallee and Hrliger. Smiling, Kikor refused and ran down the trail without a word. The others quickly jumped on as he turned the roll around and flew down the dark path, quickly catching up with his companions, but not before they whispered their thanks to the trees. Moving past the rear stragglers, he moved to the front of the group and slowed down so both Jebba and Kalion could hear him and to let Niallee and Hrliger jump off.

"We're going to have company. Four of those flying things we encountered a few days ago are moving this way. I think Niallee and Hrliger slowed them down, though, closing off the forest entrance."

Jebba nodded, motioning for the group to stop and listen to the mage, who lowered himself down to look directly at the group.

"Could they just be moving this way because it was our last direction?" Birkita asked, looking at Harbin, who shrugged his shoulders.

"I know not, but it isn't all of them of course, like what we saw outside of Dagonor. ... Only four this time."

"What about the orcs following us?" Kikor asked, looking back where they all had just traveled from. "Did you see any signs?"

"They were far behind but still on our trail. These flying creatures were closer," Harbin stated as he lifted his head to look behind them, seeing nothing coming down the trail yet.

"How far to that dwarven city?" Jebba's question made all look at the warrior and then to Holan. Seeing that he, and not the flying mage, was the center of their attention suddenly, Holan cleared his throat.

"Well ... we do not have far to travel until we are out of these trees, but then we are in open fields until we get to the valley that the city looks over."

"How long, Holan?" Jebba pressed again. The others could hear the slight frustra-tion in his voice.

Returning the stare, Holan took a moment to think. "Maybe a day the way we are moving, but since we cannot keep that up much longer ... I'd say a night's bed and we should be in the valley. Another half day to cross the valley."

All groaned then, thinking that they would have to spend another night in the forest ... and with a large band of orcs behind them. All turned to look at the trail where they knew the orcs could be crashing through any moment.

"We have to remember Meradoth should be joining us soon," Harbin reminded the group as he looked through his pack for anything he could use to help them move faster.

Suddenly, as if the mention of his name had summoned him, the group could hear the now-familiar sound of Meradoth's travel portal. With a flash of blue light, he appeared a bit up the trail from the group.

The group rushed up to see how he was and what he had found out. All started to ask questions at once when Jebba whispered, "We best not stay here for long. We know that the orcs can work through anything if they try hard enough." Suddenly a noise cut the mage off, making everyone look to where they had just been.

An explosion could be heard echoing through the forest, making the group quickly pull weapons out as they all heard screams of pain, terror and more coming down the trail. Hrliger and Niallee looked at each other, knowing what was happening. Quickly they explained the trap that the trees had helped them set.

"We druids have a way to speak to the forests, and these trees are no different when it comes to their hatred of the orcs. It turns out that by us giving them the slight advantage of a spell I had been working on before the games, the trees could crush the orcs as they tried to pass them and fight the giantkind without being harmed by blade ... but this will only last for a small amount of time," Niallee explained as the group continued to watch the forest behind them.

The screams lasted for a long time. Meradoth moaned for them to get moving as he and Harbin stepped onto their flying bed rolls. As one, the group quickly turned and followed the mages, soon leaving the screaming in the distance as they ran at a steady pace, finding this part of the trail softer than the others.

Quickly Kalion had gone ahead, running quietly with Birkita, who ran along his left side under the low-lying trees to scout the trail, as Harbin, now with Meradoth, who was tired from his travel spell, traveled slower on his flying bed roll, making him unable to scout ahead as he had before.

After riding for a few hours with no sign of orcs or the flying creatures, the group decided that they needed to rest for a while and to give the horses a break as well. The poor beasts were sweaty and showed their exhaustion. Doing their best to give the poor horses room to rest, the group broke up and leaned against trees to rest themselves, pulling out water pouches and bits of food they had left. Whelor and Bennak scouted back the way they had come to see how their pursuers faired and if any had been able to follow them.

It didn't take long for the two to find the orcs that were following them. Like Jebba had said, orcs will do whatever they must to work through a trap, even sacrificing their own to do it.

Both came back, quietly telling the others they could hear screams again, so Harbin, now standing on the ground again, waved his hand across his face. Using his vision spell, he looked behind and saw dust rising again through the trees. Quietly informing everyone else of what had just happened, he and Meradoth decided to try something more powerful. But this time he was going to try to kill as many as he could, asking Niallee and Hrliger to assist them with their druidic skills of talking to the trees.

The four moved off to an area more open but along the trail, not far from the group that was resting.

"What can you both do together?" Harbin asked as Meradoth walked up beside his mage companion.

Smiling, Hrliger looked up at his elfish friend. "I'm sure we can do something." The gnome clapped his hands and began to rub them together, speaking words that made Niallee smile and nod, knowing what he was planning. She began to repeat what he was doing with her hands.

As the two druids did their thing, both Meradoth and Harbin turned to each other and placed their hands on each other's heads to think together, almost like looking deep within one another. The two mages brought up some ideas without speaking aloud.

As Niallee and Hrliger made the sky turn dark above the trees, they called the winds, heavy rain, thunder and lightning to strike and slow down the orcs while Harbin and Meradoth enacted spells to reduce their numbers in the confusion.

As orcs came screaming over the hill not far away, Harbin could just make out that they wore what looked like armor under their robes. Getting a hint of silver or gray when the sun shined through the clouds, Harbin smiled at the thought that came to him.

"Heat!" he mumbled to Meradoth, who returned a smile.

He and Meredith started to wave their hands and arms in motions that would start the process of the spell, not hearing the sudden screams and battle cries erupting from the orcs at seeing their prey before them.

Harbin and Meradoth stopped their arm movements when the orcs got within an arrow shot. Then, as one, they both extended their hands like they were pushing something towards the orcs, and as red fire burst from their hands, both said the last word of the spell, releasing its effects.

Almost immediately, the orcs stopped running and began looking at each other as their armor began to glow, first turning a light red and then quickly moving to a deep, dark red color. Harbin and Meradoth stood and watched as the orcs began screaming as their armor began to melt on their bodies.

Harbin and Meradoth smiled at the effect of their spell. The forest erupted as flashes of lightening burst through the forest trees and struck the giants as they moved over the hill in the distance, instantly dropping them to the ground.

Seeing that the spell was stopping the orcs and the other creatures in their ranks, Harbin was considering another spell they had used in the past. But from what he could tell, though at least 50 orcs were still alive, they were not following the trail or them as fear had taken them over. None looked like they wanted to follow their prey.

Turning, the four smiled at what they had done together but

did not speak as they walked to rejoin the group. Seeing Jebba lying against a tree, sleeping heavily, they walked over to find Kalion and the others resting as well.

"So what happened?" Kikor asked as the four fell to the ground to rest next to the others, who all looked at the four, interested in what they had done.

Taking a deep breath, Meradoth leaned back against a tree and looked up to the sky. "Oh, we took care of the orcs that were chasing us." He closed his eyes as he talked. He reached his arm over to his pack, pulled out a water bag and took large swig of fresh, cold water.

"I wish I could have seen that. What did you do?" Chansor piped in.

"Just gave their armor a bit of a warm-up." He looked over to stare directly into the thief's eyes.

Kikor raised an eyebrow and then asked, "Any sign of those flying beasts seen earlier?"

Harbin blew out a breath as he relaxed slightly. "No, I believe I was wrong. I guess they didn't see me or our group, and with the luck of the gods, I hope they turned to the north when the clouds moved in to cover this forest."

Kikor looked over at Kalion, who nodded at the mage's answer and lifted his forehead as he looked over at Meradoth, who still hadn't told them what he had found.

Kikor, sensing what he was going to ask, spoke first. "Meradoth, tell us what you found."

As the others waited for the mage to speak, Whelor came walking into the area quietly and woke up Amlora, asking her to take his place as sentry. Meradoth watched the exchange for a moment and then looked at the group that was looking back at him.

"Hmmmm, well, there is a small village near here at the southeast edge of this forest. The dwarven citadel is at least a half day away, and we have to cross an open field to get to its gates ... but we are very close to the edge of the forest, so we could make the village easily."

"Bru Edin ... Meradoth, what of Bru Edin?" Kalion whispered.

Meradoth's face told the ranger the worst. "I saw a large army of orcs massing near Bru Edin. The fortress looks like it is preparing for a siege."

Kalion leaned back, looking up at the sky as he thought about what to do. As Kikor and Chansor quietly talked to Meradoth about what he had seen, Kalion's thoughts were on where they should travel now.

A few feet away, Harbin saw that a few were falling asleep, so he decided to sleep as well. The horses were so tried that both had fallen down and slept on the ground next to their riders. The chase had been hard on everyone, so it didn't take long for most to fall asleep.

Not far away, Amlora stood, watching over the forest around them. The weather was getting cold, with winds coming in from the east and south, but she didn't care. Whatever the mage had done to the orcs who had been pursuing them for the last few hours had definitely stopped them from chasing them for the moment, as she couldn't hear or see any signs of them.

As rain started to come down again, Whelor moved to lay himself underneath a larger tree to keep dry. For the next three hours, he slept, awaking to see a small deer quietly move by. He watched it for a moment, but nothing happened and he got bored, so he closed his eyes again. They quickly shot back open when a snap of a small branch from behind made Whelor jump, pulling his sword out to attack, when he saw Amlora walking quietly behind.

"Sorry, Whelor," she whispered as she came up alongside the human.

Nodding that he understood, he was glad that she was there

anyway. Amlora said quietly that she had come over since he had been making noises like he was dreaming that might alert the orcs to their position.

"Oh, gods ... I am sorry ... not enough food or sleep, I guess," Whelor whispered, making Amlora smile as she patted his shoulder and turned to walk back to where she watched over the camp and the forest around them.

Not far away, Jebba, who had been able to keep himself awake, was sitting against a bush under a tree, watching the group sleep where they lay. Turning, he looked at the one person in this group he trusted now. He hoped that his decision to reveal his plans to Bennak wouldn't cause the half-orc to push him away or even tell the others, but he had to take the chance.

"It seems like we are continually on the run, and I'm tired of running. Kalion is only showing how scared he is by doing this, do you not think, my friend?"

Bennak, hearing that Jebba was not happy about the way things were going, nodded slightly at the warrior's words, indicating he felt the same way. ... He wanted to fight.

"I joined this group to find some little girl ... to find this spoiled princess ... and the riches that came with it. I joined to help my family live. If we flee this group, I will fight, my friend ... but let us fight with them until we cannot!" Jebba placed his hand on Bennak's shoulder as the big man spoke, letting him know that he understood.

Bennak's blood boiled slightly, wanting a fight to happen. He saw the smile on Jebba's face as the warrior whispered that the two of them were unstoppable in battle and would prove it very soon.

Turning to face Jebba, Bennak said, "Now is not the right time. We can't go back and fight now in Brigin'i. We are too far past the point of return. The orcs that followed us are no more, so what do you propose?"

"When we get to Bru Edin, we leave this group, as I believe

the riches in that place will take care of us both, and I am sure the army there would love to have us both in their ranks."

Bennak thought about the place his friend was speaking of. He had never been to Bru Edin, but he had heard of its massive walls and the strong army protecting it ... and the riches — if anything, Bru Edin was known to have caves full of coin and more.

"Bru Edin, then!" Bennak turned and whispered to his friend, seeing the warrior smile and nod, leaning back against the tree to watch the group sleep before them.

Chapter Four

The haze was hard to get through, but slowly her eyelids opened as the muffled sounds of screaming and yelling that seemed almost like a dream became clearer.

"Get a move on there. ... That rope, yes. Pull it, you lazy slave!"

The snap of the whip rang. "I said move along here! Out of the way!"

Shaking her head slightly to get the final haze out of her vision, Shermee looked slowly around to see where she was now. She was inside the same carriage that she had been in for a while now, but for how long, she wondered.

Groaning as she moved herself to get the blood flowing again and feeling her back stiffen up from being in an odd position, she struggled to get comfortable when she quickly discovered her hands were still held together by rope, making her wrists hurt.

Stopping her struggle, she looked at the sides of the carriage and saw that the two small windows that the carriage had were covered by black drapes, giving her no view of the area they traveled through but only providing dim light through the sides. Leaning closer to the closest window, she caught familiar sounds. She could tell they were somewhere within a city or town, as she could hear people talking and other sounds that made up a town.

As the carriage bounced, she noticed that it seemed to be riding on cobblestones as well, which she knew only a city have. Maybe they were back in Brigin'i, she suddenly thought. However, she knew that would be unrealistic.

"Why would my kidnappers take me back home?" she whispered to herself.

A throat being cleared made her jump back in the seat and blink her eyes quickly as they adjusted to the sight of a black-covered man sitting in the shadows, staring back at her with a slight smile on his face.

"Who ... who are you?" she nervously asked, feeling the man's powerful presence as he sat there, staring back at her.

"My name is Quinor, Princess. You need not worry. I will not harm you in any way. I am more ... your protector on your journey."

As Quinor spoke, Shermee could see from the clothing he was wearing and the way he looked at her that this powerful man had been in many battles, and the way he spoke made it sound like he had cycles of experience. He seemed calm, and while she wasn't, somehow his words seemed to calm her slowly as she tried to comprehend what was going on. But this man reminded her of someone she was really beginning to miss.

"Then why are my hands tied?" she questioned quietly.

Ignoring her question, he just smiled at the lady, understanding that she was just trying to figure out what this was all about. Quinor leaned forward slightly, making the leather armor he wore over the grayish black shirt groan a little.

"Princess, you remember being kidnapped by elves ... dark elves, I mean?" Shermee looked at the ground for a moment and then nodded "yes" slightly, so he continued even as the carriage jumped over a rock of some kind, making someone outside yell hard to slow it down.

"I and my ... my friends outside this carriage got you away from them. ... Do you remember that?"

Shermee's face registered the memory of being woken up during a skirmish, but she shrugged her shoulders, which told him she remembered it slightly.

"Well, Princess, my master, the one I saved you for, wants

you to be kept safe, and those creatures could not be trusted to do such a thing, so I had to clear the plate of them."

Shermee swallowed, wondering who this master was he spoke of. Just as she was about to ask, Quinor smiled, seeing her ask the question in her head. "Methnorick is my master, Princess, and you're to be taken to his island fortress to become ... to become his bride." Quinor swallowed at those last words as he stared at the girl in front of him.

At that Shermee let out a weak whimper as her mouth dropped open. Her thoughts raced back to when she and her secret love stood in the courtyard within the castle of Brigin'i, which seemed a lifetime ago now.

"*I promise, my love, your father will know about us soon. I just need to get through these games of his. Then I will speak to him.*" His hand moved up her face, making her close her eyes.

"Ohhh, Kalion." She whispered the name again and again as she thought back to their last time together.

Quinor leaned back, not saying a word, and stared off into the nothingness. The princess curled up on the seat and cried silently, now scared that her life was at an end, knowing that this man she was being taken to was the most evil of men. She had heard some warriors back in Brigin'i as well as the dark elves speaking of him as they dragged her away from her father.

Quinor swallowed again as he slowly looked at the girl, seeing her body shake from the horror he was about to put into her. Not wanting to deal with it, he looked away from her beautiful face as he pushed the drape next to him open slightly, bringing bright light into the carriage that almost blinded him for a moment as he checked on their progress. Hearing the young lady's whimpers and crying brought pain to his chest, as he knew that once she landed on that isle, this young lady would never be the same.

Quickly, to distract himself from her whimpers, he said, "Welcome to Blath 'Na City, my princess."

* * *

Chansor made his way through the forest, trying to check on the damage done by his friends earlier. He couldn't believe the number of dead and burnt orcs he found lying on the forest floor. He also explored the size of the three giant creatures, trying to see if any of these bodies held anything of value, like information, only to come up with nothing, which made the thief slightly angry. Turning, he finally saw what he was looking for as he knelt down and began patting down the corpse that he thought might hold the message he wanted. Finally, he found a tiny pouch he wanted, but as he grabbed it, he cursed as it deteriorated in his hands from the fire, and he saw the parchment within it fall to the ground. Grabbing a pouch of silver coin he found on what he thought must have been the orc leader, based on the armor it was wearing, Chansor angrily turned and walked back to find his companions waking up and packing their things.

Walking through the camp, Chansor grabbed his small pack and continued walking down the deer trail they were using to get through the forest until he came to the edge of the forest. He found the sky here was bright but very cloudy as well. Meradoth had been correct that the group had not been far from the edge of the forest when they feel asleep the night before. Looking around, he saw far away to the east the mountain on top of which, according to Kalion, stood the huge castle of men called Bru Edin. Between that mountain and Chansor lay the large open grass fields known as the Edin Plains.

From what Kalion and Holan had told the group during their travels, the mountain used to be a massive volcano that had exploded many, many cycles ago when the gods ruled and fought each other over these lands. According to the legend, it was during a battle that a giant was killed by the gods and pushed into the mountain itself, causing it to fall onto itself and collapse, resulting in the formation of a lake many cycles later. Chansor smiled to himself,

40

hoping that he would be able to see this fortress and the lake, as Kalion had told him the lake was one of the beauties from the cycles of being that had been kept natural by the inhabitants of Bru Edin.

Chansor remembered Harbin piping in to say that when men migrated to this area from the eastern seas, they found these fields lush for growing grain and roving with live-stock, but when the orcs moved into the area cycles later and began their attacks, the men living in this area lacked a defendable area where their people could be safe. So with the help of dwarven smiths who were living nearby, they began to build a wooden fortress wall at the bottom of the extinct mountain to surround their largest village.

However, attacks from orcs soon proved too much for the wooden wall protecting the village, causing it to catch fire and collapse after a few battles. So from within their underground kingdom of Chai'sell, the largest dwarven citadel that lay far to the north of Bru Edin, dwarves and men worked hard together over the next 100 cycles to enlarge and strengthen the fortress, but this time they built on the side of the rock face and along the top of the mountain. Soon the place began to take shape, turning into a fortress which was given the name of Bru Edin, or "Shield of Edin" in the human language.

To protect the castle and its people, two massive doors were made of the hardest wood and metal found deep within the Dwarven Mountains. The name of "Shakra'boraden" was placed on them in remembrance of the first known king of men, who, according to the legend, brought their people out of the darkness. These doors held, chiseled within the metal, the arms of each human king who had ruled their people, giving them power to defend those inside.

Behind this gate and along the road stood even mightier, larger and more defendable gates, known as "Netfor'aden," named after a warrior queen who, during the first recorded war between men and the orc races, had been able to prevent an entire orcish army from taking over the kingdom in the east after her husband

— a king whose name has been lost in time — had been killed during a battle with a creature of legend known today as a dragon, its true name lost in time.

The leaders of this new city asked those elves living in the east and north to enhance this gate with some type of magic that could stop anything that tried to break through it. It was told that nothing, with the exception of dragons, could penetrate the gate, and since dragons were only a legend and hadn't been seen or heard of except in children's stories, men had never worried since. "Watch out for dragon fire" was a common saying parents in Bru Edin told their children at night.

The magic of the elves also gave these gates the ability to glow when someone or something evil approached. Both doors were so large and heavy they had to use trains of horses to open and close them, so they were kept open and only closed in times of war, which had not been seen since a small orc army had tried to assault the city as it rampaged across the plains over 200 cycles ago.

Water was pumped in by the dwarven engineers, who had found a flowing river just under the base of the dead volcano. Using an ingenious idea, the dwarves used pulleys and tunnels to bring water to both the castle and its surrounding town, and from there it was spread out into the fields around the mountain to give the wheat and grain fields needed water when the rain was poor, which it rarely was.

These waterways were also built to give the fortress an extra line of defense, if needed. If an attacker were able to break through the defensive walls, then the water could flow out, causing the fields to flood and making it hard for warriors to operate their equipment.

Outside, built next to the town, were stables for the over 5,000 horses that resided next to the barracks for soldiers and warriors of Bru Edin. Though the stables were new, only just built with stone, they were always expanding with the help of gnomes who also lived nearby within the northern mountains.

Along the walls of the fortress and inside the huge curtain

wall that stood along the southern edge of the mountain, huge war machines had been built, giving the fortress a huge defensive force. Towering in size, each was 50 feet in height and made use of an ingenious network of pulleys and ropes to place stones in their cradles. Each machine housed its own company of warriors and engineers — a total of around 30 could work each machine, if needed.

People worshipping the gods soon built temples within the castle walls as well. Each of these temples was built using coin raised by each religious order that had lived and worked in the north over the cycles. Over the cycles their temples grew in size to show their devotion to their gods, each becoming itself a small fortress within the fortress to protect its own orders and needs.

Over the cycles Bru Edin grew to become the strongest fortress city in the region — a place where men held power over the lands it watched over.

This is what Chansor was thinking about as he stood behind a tree, looking over the fields towards the high mountain in the distance. Heavy rain began to fall, but the thief didn't care, as his sharp eyes soon picked up movement to the south of where he stood, and it was movement he didn't rejoice in either.

Chapter Five

*S*taring at the parchment in his hand, Minister Halashii read the reports of orcs and goblinkind seen moving along the northern edge of the Father Gate, which had been ordered closed by him earlier.

A slight lift came to the corner of his mouth as he read on that Brigin'i had fallen to the orcish armies that had destroyed Stych Castle and conquered the lands along the eastern shores. Looking up at the map painted on the wall, he could see that the only parts that were really left to resist this orcish onslaught were the elven kingdoms and that sore of a city fortress Bru Edin.

Another report that he had been given during the night informed him that Blath 'Na City would soon fall as well, which brought his mouth more into a full smile as he saw on the map that the north would soon fall completely.

Leaning over to his desk, he lifted another parchment given to him earlier that made his smile quickly disappear, though. Per an agreement he had made with Methnorick secretly, he was to close the Father Gate to trap anyone trying to escape south from the north, but Methnorick had also ordered him to send his armies through the gate that lay to its west, the Mother Gate, to attack the small dwarven city that lay just beyond its opening.

This agreement with Methnorick caused the minister concern as he considered the new report his spies had informed him about of Brigin'i's princess being taken by dark elfish mercenaries. He considered whether this was Methnorick's doing or a ruse to confuse him about what the dark leader was planning.

As he stared at the map, trying to figure out what to do,

suddenly the map began to change right before his eyes, making him blink a few times and wonder what was going on. He leaned back and gasped slightly as he watched.

Stepping back from his desk, he watched as lines that showed mountains, cities, valleys and more moved slowly to form the dark shape of a cloaked figure staring back at him: Methnorick.

Halashii's jaw began to clench and then shake within his head as he watched Methnorick's face continue to become clearer. Then he heard the deep, haunting voice of Methnorick. "Halashii ... your people ... are they ready?"

Halashii gasped and his body shook upon hearing the voice from the map. He considered the voice almost smug as he looked at the red eyes that stared at him. He knew he had to respond soon, so taking a deep breath, he cleared his throat as he bowed deeply, hoping he could make Methnorick believe that he was his servant.

"Ye– ... yes ... my lord ... my people have done what you have asked of me. The Father Ga– ... Gate is shut. My ... my armies march as we speak north ... just as you ordered." His voice began to shake as he considered what Methnorick would do if he figured out his hesitations.

"Good, the plan is moving just as I predicted. With Brigin'i and King Dia dead and gone, I will soon rule the lands to the north completely." Methnorick's voice echoed in the chamber.

"What of this report I have heard of his daughter ... his princess? Do you know anything about that, my lord?" Halashii dared to ask, hoping his lie about marching his armies north would go unnoticed. He thought back to the attempt that failed to get the princess during a quiet raid on Brigin'i last cycle. He had sent two of his best warriors there to bring her south, only to have them die along the way, encountering a large group of trollkind.

"She is not your concern, Halashii!" Methnorick hissed, making his eyes turn redder. "My armies are moving to destroy Bru Edin, like they have done to the others that have resisted me. Be ready for my order to attack Cruachator!" Halashii quickly nodded, hearing the voice get louder on the last word.

"I do as I'm commanded to the glory of your name, my lord, Methnorick!" Halashii bowed deeply, still shaking under his robes from his lord's presence. When no answer came, he lifted his head to stare at the map, only to see that it was the same as it had been before, showing the lands in the north and the south; the form and image were gone.

Taking a deep and slow breath, Halashii knew he was playing a dangerous game with Lord Methnorick. His pact would let him keep the empire whilst Methnorick would control the north, but down deep the minister knew that this evil creature wouldn't stop there. He just knew he needed to set his plan in motion to ensure the empire's safety, but how could he do so without his lord finding out? So far Methnorick had known everything.

Turning away from the wall, he collapsed on a soft chair as he considered his next steps.

* * *

The carriage had stopped a while earlier, and the princess had been brought out into the light, making her eyes scream in pain as she tried to cover them with her arms. Quietly, she was brought into a building where she saw a few warriors standing to watch her as she was thrown on a chair and offered some food and drink.

Quinor, the warrior who rode inside with her, walked over to another man and whispered as she ate the food like it was the first she had eaten in cycles. As she overheard the two speak about her and the situation, she stuffed the food down quickly, not caring what she was eating, and drank what she could before they might take it away.

Looking at the princess and then back to the man who stood before him, Quinor whispered, "What of the news from the west?" not realizing his voice carried in the room.

"Brigin'i has fallen ... but no news on the royal couple."

Hearing this news that her beloved city had been destroyed and her parents had disappeared made Shermee's heart jump. She started to tear up, but she resisted, for she would not give all these warriors the satisfaction. She continued to listen, using the food to block her sad thoughts of her mother and father.

"Where are the dark ones? ... Did they stay within the forest? ... Why am I not speaking to them now?" the other warrior asked as Shermee quickly looked him over.

Black in face and armor, the man looked like he could take on 20 of Brigin'i's best, but it was the scar that went down his face that startled the princess the most. It looked as if it almost showed his brain when he moved in the light.

"They were planning on killing her before they got here and telling you she resisted during the capture, so my men and I had to kill them instead," Quinor quietly answered truthfully.

The dark man's face showed some concern, Shermee thought, as he looked over at her and then back at Quinor. He slowly shook his head in disbelief, mumbling that he had never trusted dark elves in the first place.

"Well, problem solved, then ... and I'm surprised you did it without any loss to your men. Fighting those dark elves, I have found, is almost impossible. I would love to hear about how you did it, but our master is in need of getting the princess quickly."

Quinor nodded, smiling at his feat of killing dark elves, but he understood things needed to get moving to stay on target. As he looked at his prize and then back at the dark man, he asked, "What is the plan?"

"A ship will be coming in on the morrow. You and your men are to place her on the ship and leave her to the crew. The trip shall take a week of sailing, but by week's end, she shall be presented to our master."

Quinor listened, but his feelings were presenting a problem

for him. He had to follow his orders and bring the princess to his lord soon, but he also wanted to ensure her safety at any cost. For now he would do what he was told, but he knew he had to think of what to do, and soon.

* * *

Kalion and Birkita hid underneath the large bush. Having moved to the edge of the forest that lay at the western parts of the Edin Plains, they sat under the wet, dripping leaves of the bush, watching as the long line of heavily armed orcs marched by. For the past hour at least, the two had watched these ugly creatures tramp through the rain, marching eastwards.

Without talking, the two slid backwards and scrambled across the ground until they were clear and then ran quickly back over another hill to find their group waiting in the clearing.

Hearing the rustling in the bushes, Bennak and Whelor pulled out their swords, but Kalion waved them off when he saw them.

"It's ok. The orcs did not follow," he said after grabbing a drink from the water pouch that Holan threw him.

"What did you see, ranger?" Jebba asked, waiting for Kalion to catch his breath as the warrior crossed his arms, wondering what was going on.

"We saw at least ten score orcs march by. They were taking their time, and they did not seem on alert." Birkita nodded as Kalion finished the water he was drinking.

"They are no longer in the plains area, so I believe we can move on," Birkita piped in.

"Where do you think the orcs are headed?" Kikor asked.

"They could be headed towards Bru Edin or farther east towards Blath 'Na City. It is unclear right now, but they are not here, which is the best news."

"We should move quietly, though, do you not think?" Hrliger said. "Orcs are loud when they march, but they can pick up our scent if the wind moves in the right direction."

"Well, then, let's not get scented, haha," Chansor said, giggling as he came through the brush, catching the others by surprise. He quietly said that he had scouted forward and could see the mountain that Kalion spoke of and what looked like signs of a village between where they were and the mountain.

They all looked at the thief, nodding in agreement at his comment as the little man sloshed some water down his throat. The group slowly started to move out of the forest onto the plains, with Kalion leading the way.

"Might be where the orcs are marching, too," Kalion whispered to Kikor as they walked.

After an hour of walking, they came over a small hill, from the top of which they could make out a small village ahead. "Skynburgh, I believe," Kalion whispered. This village lay at the western edge of the kingdom of Bru Edin, which was still a few hours' travel away but could be easily seen in the distance.

Quietly moving down the hill, all hoped for a slight repeat of the rain and a bit of warm food before reaching Bru Edin; however, this thought died instantly as they moved closer. It was Kikor and Birkita who noticed things were not right with Skynburgh. Birkita raised her hand, stopping everyone as she squinted her eyes and then nodded to Niallee, who had moved up to kneel next to her. Kikor had moved off to the side, kneeling down to check out the village, which made the group pull out their weapons, knowing something was amiss in Skynburgh.

Niallee looked to where Birkita was focusing her attention: on the ground of what could have been the main street were what looked like two bodies lying on the ground. Smoke seemed to be coming not from the normal fire pits, as they had thought when watching from the distance, but from houses burning with fires that were slowly dying under the heavy rain. Niallee looked over to

Jebba, who stood not far behind her, and motioned him over.

Turning to the rest of the group, Niallee whispered what she had seen, and within a moment all agreed that they should go into the village and help any survivors that they could find.

As the group moved into the village, they spread out to cover more area, leaving Meradoth and Birkita at the top of the hill to cover them. Harbin, who had jumped off his bed roll moments earlier, now walked near Kalion as he prepared himself for what they might be in for in this village.

Holan was the first to move into the village and saw the signs of what had happened to Skynburgh. Scores of bodies lay everywhere. Women, men and even children were dead. Many were burning, and many had been hacked to pieces and left along the ground for the birds.

"By the gods," Niallee gasped as she came, moving up behind the dwarf. Holan didn't turn around but kept looking at the bodies before them. Seeing the rest of the group move into the village, Holan slowly walked forward with the druid following him quietly. He gripped his axe tightly, expecting anything to jump out.

"There must have been at least a few hundred villagers here," Niallee mentioned quietly. Holan didn't answer, only nodding his head, as the group continued to see signs of carnage throughout the village.

As Birkita walked around the front of one of the cottages, she looked at the ground and noticed footprints in the mud. She saw that many were of orc origin, but then she noticed the light prints that could only be from a dark cousin.

"Qlorfana!" she whispered out loud, speaking the ancient name of dark elves. As her eyes tracked where the prints went, she saw a few of the others coming down the main road.

Then a smell hit Birkita's nose. Looking around, she couldn't understand where it was coming from. Then she turned, and Kikor got her attention as she felt one of Kikor's arrows fly by her face, slamming into something behind her. Quickly turning as she lifted her sword up, Birkita observed an orc now with an arrow deep in its chest. Kikor's feet could be heard racing up as she called out to make sure her friend was ok.

"There must be more; one would not stay behind to scrounge around for prizes." Both watched as the shocked orc gasped from the arrow embedded in its chest and slowly fell forward to splash into the pool of water in front of it.

Running past the two elves, Whelor knelt next to the gasping creature, seeing that the thing wasn't going to live long with the arrow sticking out of its chest. Whelor looked at the ugly beast, leaning over a little to look directly into its eyes. Then he kicked the orc and began to ask it questions.

The orc opened its eyes but couldn't say much as it spit up blackish blood. But it did smile when it saw that it was Whelor looking down at him.

"You … we have already destroyed Brigin'i … and now we surround Bru Edin. You will not get far. Your kind ... will ... not ... survive ... long ..." It couldn't finish as it coughed up more blood and then died. Whelor kicked the body again, looking over as Kikor came walking up to him. Whelor looked up at her, seeing the rest of the group moving up behind her.

"Did it say anything?" Kikor asked, looking down at the orc and then over to Whelor. Whelor's face told her the answer.

"Yes, a lot, actually!" Whelor repeated what the orc had told him as he pushed his sword back into the scabbard. But his eyes got wide as he looked past the elf's head, and he started to pull his sword back out to address the new threat coming at them from behind one of the huts. Holan and Hrliger's screams made everyone react quickly. Kikor pulled out an arrow from her quiver and began releasing one after another at the oncoming group of screaming orcs as Kalion looked around for an avenue of escape. However, as he looked over to see Harbin shaking his head "no," the warrior turned to face the attack force. Kalion nodded back and, replacing his blade, he pulled out his bow and made it ready. "If you all want to fight, I am with you," Kalion quietly called out to the others as he observed Chansor pulling Amlora over to a hut not far away, hopefully to keep the cleric safe.

"Revenge for the people of Skynburgh!" Holan piped in as he lifted his axe and tightened his grip on it as a group of four orcs advanced on him.

"For Winsto!" Birkita quietly said as she gripped her bow stave, releasing an arrow at the same four orcs who were attacking Holan.

"For Brigin'i!" Whelor cried, spotting another orc come around the side of a hut at the edge of the village.

"For Fulox and Zahnz!" Niallee said as she began to move her hands in small circles, quietly speaking to the roots underneath the ground, calling on them to move to her words.

Kalion, Jebba, Birkita and Kikor, as one, released their arrows as the others dug their feet into the mud and rushed forward, screaming at the tops of their voices. Hearing the screams, Chansor peered out of the building and watched with wide eyes as he saw his friends move forward.

Chapter Six

The damp tunnels that led underneath the castle and city of Brigin'i hadn't been used in so many cycles that some parts of the walls had collapsed due to water, roots and more pushing on the stones. This made it hard for the warriors moving through, using their swords to cut through roots, to get their captive out safely, knowing that the orcs above would kill their prisoner instantly if discovered. The only light they had was the one torch of the man who led the group through the tunnels.

Grunting and grumbling about how terribly the tunnels were kept, Baron Parnland hated the fact that he had to work hard to get Dia out of the city like this, knowing General Kaligor was now in the city above, destroying it. The loud screams of the populace stuck inside the falling buildings echoed down the tunnel. He did not understand why he was choosing to bring King Dia to Methnorick himself rather than letting Kaligor take him, but he knew Kaligor could not be trusted with his own life. He just felt that he stood a better chance with Methnorick than Kaligor. He knew Kaligor was working for Methnorick, but for some reason, he still did not trust the creature.

He was glad he didn't have to face the Cyclops; the baron's greed for Methnorick's promise of wealth and power in the north pushed him now.

Parnland pushed Dia hard to keep him moving, but instead, the king collapsed to the ground, as he was deep in thought about his people and his queen. Seeing his once proud king now defeated like a child, Parnland walked over and slapped the man hard, bringing a large red welt to his face just as Dia looked up defiantly at the fat man standing over him.

"You're a child, Dia. Always have been, always will be. Lord Methnorick is going to crush you. You will bend and kneel before his strength and be made a servant to his power."

Coughing up some blood from the cut inside his mouth, Dia spat it out onto the floor and looked up at the baron, now smiling at him in the torch light.

"Only the weak believe in his strength. He will destroy everything. Even you, Baron, will die at his hand!" Dia said defiantly. "Only by fighting together can we defeat him. You must join me."

Smiling, Parnland leaned a bit closer so that only the two of them could hear each other. "Dia, your city is lost. ... Your lands are gone. ... Your people are all dead. ... Why fight? Who or what do you have to fight with?"

"I may not have my people, but I will continue to fight for those who can't fight for themselves!" Dia finally declared in a stronger voice, feeling his anger rise as the visions of his wife moved through his mind. "If you are so sure about this Methnorick of yours, why do we escape this way? Surely Methnorick has control of my city. Why not turn me over to his generals?" Dia taunted.

Parnland laughed, causing the others to laugh as well as the sounds echoed through the tunnels. He struck the king again hard, making the man grunt. The baron knew he had just broken the king's nose, for he heard bone crack under his fist, which put a smile on his face.

Looking at his men, he said, "Let's move!" before turning and making his way to the hidden entry to the tunnel that opened up about a mile outside the city walls.

Grabbing the fallen king, the others pulled the man up as he grunted from his pain. Blood leaked onto the floor as they continued moving.

Pushing and cutting through roots, they finally broke through to find that they were indeed in the forest outside of the city. Parnland slowly pushed himself out of the tunnel, not knowing what might be waiting.

As he looked around, his ears caught the sounds of the city's death throes but nothing else — no sounds of battle or voices of any kind. Lowering himself back down, he waved to two of the warriors who were with him to move out and make sure the area was clear as he stared at Dia, who had been pushed against the wall by one of the other men.

Looking up to see one of the men signaling that it was all clear, he motioned to the others to move Dia out. Parnland waited for the others to get free of the tunnel entry before he started to move out, but as he looked back down the tunnel, he suddenly felt like he was being watched. Pushing the feeling away, he called out for help to the others and was quickly pulled up by two grunting warriors, who grumbled about his weight.

"Which way?" one quietly called over to the baron, who breathed hard from the substantial amount of exercise they had been doing.

Looking over to the man who worked for him, the baron blinked hard to get rid of the sweat now pouring into his eyes and looked around to make sure of where he was. Then he pointed in the direction he knew they had to travel, hoping that the carriage had not been destroyed and would be waiting.

"East ... we must travel east!"

Quickly, without a word, the group stood up and moved from the area. One grabbed Dia, making sure his mouth was quickly gagged. They dragged the man until, finally, the screams and sounds of his beloved city disappeared behind them.

✳ ✳ ✳

Harbin launched a huge ball of flame, which exploded in the midst of four orcs, causing them all to instantly disappear under the bright red and orange colors.

Whelor and Bennak used their powerful frames to knock a

few of the orcs down as they pushed through, chopping heads off and screaming at their victims and using their shields to break the face of another orc together.

Holan, following not far behind due to his short legs, used his axe to cut through orc armor. He also cut a few exposed legs, causing several others to die under his edge as the dwarf laughed and yelled insulting words at the black-cloaked creatures.

Seeing that the group wouldn't take long to dispatch this group of orcs, Kalion and Jebba quickly dropped their bows and charged forward, both wanting to feel the dying breaths of the orcs. Jebba stabbed the first orc that turned to face him, causing black blood to cover him as his blade broke through the creature's skin. Pulling it out, he ducked quickly as another tried to cut his head off. As he bent down, he stabbed the orc in the stomach, making the creature scream and fall back. This gave Jebba a moment to look around and see Kalion with his two short blades sweep left and right, blocking a few blades from cutting into him and allowing Jebba to deliver a cutting blow to his right to take out Kalion's attacker and then another one to his left to take out his own attacker.

The two elven warriors, Birkita and Kikor, stood side by side as they released two more arrows each before they moved to join the battle as well. Kikor made sure her arrows were aimed at a large orc that had somehow been missed by the others. The creature's height was about the same as hers, but its body was as large as Bennak's.

She watched her arrow burrow deep into the orc's chest, causing it to stop for a moment before continuing to charge on. She pulled out her blade and ran forward, sweeping her blade across the face of the orc, cutting through its helmet and slicing the creature's face in half.

Bennak, in his anger at not being to kill enough orcs as quickly as he had hoped, swung his sword around to push three orcs away as he grabbed one by its throat, lifting it up as he squeezed, making the creature drop its own axe to grab at the hands around its throat.

"Bastardsssssss!" Bennak screamed as he turned and showed the others orcs what waited for them. In one move, he snapped the neck of his victim and threw it at the orcs that had stopped to watch, causing them to fall over when their comrade fell onto them.

As Birkita released her last arrow, she dropped her bow and instantly saw that a few remaining orcs were trying to move to her group's left side, using a building to cover their movement. Not being able to get any of the group's attention, she turned and moved around another building to see if she could maneuver herself behind this group of orcs trying to get behind her friends.

Moving around the cottage, she stopped and slowly peeked around the corner, catching sight of the orcs she had seen moments earlier. Taking a deep breath, she stepped around the corner. The orcs had stopped for a moment to see where they were going, giving Birkita the opportunity she needed. Lifting her right boot up, she grabbed a small blade she kept there, looking at what she could aim it at.

She could just make out them grunting about what to do as she pulled her arm back and threw the small blade at the back of the largest in the group. Then she ran forward, hoping the surprise killing might cause the others to hesitate.

She instantly found herself to be correct. As her blade hit the back of the neck of the orc, causing it to grunt as it fell forward, the others stopped to look at their companion, wondering what he was doing down there. Birkita charged up behind them.

As she moved up, she used a shoulder to push one orc into the wall hard. It fell to the ground as she pushed her blade deep into the back of another, causing it to look down in total surprise to now see something sticking out of itself. Only a groan came from its mouth.

Pulling her blade out fast, not waiting to watch the orc fall, Birkita turned completely around, swiping the blade across the neck of another orc, cutting its head off. Turning, she faced the one orc left, who, even though he was surprised at seeing an elf this close, raised his sword to attack. She moved in to finish him, a quick deflection of the orc's blade giving her the time to slice hers across his chest, killing him instantly.

Coming around the corner of the building to join the group, Birkita smiled, seeing that all her friends were alive. The rest of the group had finished off the remaining orcs, and now as she looked, she saw that Whelor and Bennak were covered in black blood. Jebba was pulling his sword out of the chest of the last orc with Kalion looking at him. He nodded to the ranger that he was fine as he pushed the now dead body of the orc to the ground. Hrliger and Meradoth were talking to each other as Harbin and Niallee walked up to join them. Kikor was standing beside a pile of orc bodies just as Chansor and Amlora came out of one of the huts with bright smiles on their faces.

Holan's voice suddenly screamed for help, making all look around to see where the dwarf was. Then they heard Kikor laugh as she walked over to a mound of dead orcs and pulled the grumpy warrior out as he screamed at Whelor for throwing them on top of him during the skirmish.

Kikor patted Holan's shoulder, saying that he was fine. Smiling, she turned around and walked over to stand next to Kalion as they looked over what was before them all.

"We need to move quickly!" The voice made everyone turn, expecting it to be another orc or something, when they saw Birkita. "Whelor found out some information earlier that we need to address."

As Whelor shared the information the orc had told him earlier about Brigin'i and Bru Edin, the others slowly came to understand the impact of what they were hearing. Now they just needed to decide what to do with this information.

* * *

On the Black Isle, Methnorick walked himself down the dark stairwell that led down into the deepest parts of the island to speak to an old man about his next plans for conquering the lands in the east.

"I am sure, my lord, that these creatures will be able to do what you desire, sir." The old man, bent over and shaking in his clothing, almost whimpered as he answered the question of the man standing over him.

The two stood in an enormous room full of bodies — many hanging from hooks attached to chains that dropped from the ceiling — which for many cycles had been used for experiments by the old man. He had told anyone who asked that they were being used for medical and religious purposes.

When Methnorick had conquered this island, he had heard about what the old man had been doing for the previous ruler. Instead of making him a prisoner or killing him like all the others, Methnorick felt he needed this man who had good ideas and made him continue his work.

The man worked hard for this new lord. His experiments so far had worked, reanimating the dead using the corpses of the populace that used to live on the Black Isle and using them to attack a small village in the northernmost reaches of the land just west of the island. Without incurring any losses of their own, his warriors had killed everything there quickly.

"How many do you have?" The voice was answered by a tiny whimper, but Methnorick waited, knowing the old man was weak from his long hours of working nonstop.

"M– ... my ... my lord, I have over 500 here for your army ... all ready whenever you need them, my lor– ... my lord!" The voice trembled as he spoke, knowing that if he made one mistake, Methnorick would make him suffer.

Leaning down slightly, Methnorick reached out and grabbed the old man, smiling as the man cried out for mercy. He held him by the neck, lifting him up slightly to look him directly in his old eyes.

"Then send them out this night!"

Nodding quickly, the man cried out as Methnorick released him, crumbling to the ground as he hit the floor hard. As he looked up, readying himself for another question, he saw that suddenly he was the only one in the room, besides his experiments that lay not far away.

Pulling himself up slowly, the man looked around. Seeing that he truly was alone now, he swallowed hard, and making his way over to the table, he began to pull a metal switch that released the bodies that lay on the tables. As he looked around at the number of tables with bodies lying atop, he started shaking in his clothing again. He could even hear his jaw rattle as he watched his experiments move, slowly rising from the tables and beginning to move off them. Seeing the old man, they walked slowly towards him, making the man shake as he wondered if he had done something wrong.

The man swallowed, backing up to a large door he knew would lead to the docks beyond. He didn't dare turn his back on these experiments, not knowing what might happen. He pulled on another switch, and the door cried as the metal bolt opened the huge door quickly.

Looking behind him, he hurried, seeing that the bodies were closing in on him. He rushed through the doorway and made his way down the large hallway towards the other end, where he could see moonlight.

He listened to the scraping footfalls as he reached the end of the hallway, where he pulled another switch to open the gate that stood there. On the other side, he saw two men standing guard turn quickly around, surprised to see the gate opening and an old man wearing dirty clothing covered in blood and chemicals move through.

"What are you doing, old man?" the first guard moaned. As the old man walked past him, the guard grabbed his shoulder, finding it frail and small.

"I ... I'm doing our master's bidding, sir: getting his army to the ships!" he said, looking up at the young man and seeing the man's patience wasn't there. The other guard starting laughing, saying what a waste of a man he was, when both guards heard movement behind them.

Releasing the old man, they turned, pulling out their swords as suddenly, out of the dark, hands reached out and grabbed the guards. Trying their best to defend themselves, they hacked off a few arms, but soon the men screamed as they were overwhelmed by sheer numbers.

Screaming himself, the old man backed away quickly and continued to the large ship that waited at the dock not far away. As he moved down the small road, the screams of the two men died quickly away, as he knew they would. He considered what was about to happen, knowing he had started something that he couldn't stop. He knew if he had more time he could control them, but Methnorick wanted them now.

Running as best as he could on his frail legs, he saw a sailor standing by the ship. He cried out for the man to get the ship ready as he got closer. When the sailor opened his mouth to ask why, the old man turned and pointed to what was moving up behind him.

Cursing quickly, the sailor moved and opened the massive hatch doors that led to the ship's cargo area. After ensuring the creatures behind him saw where he was headed and were following, the old man walked quickly onto the ship and called out for the sailor to hurry inside.

As soon as the hatch hit the ground, the sailor cried out as he turned the corner of the boat's hull, almost being caught by one of the creatures reaching for him. He ran over to where the old man was standing at another hatch inside, this one smaller and at the far end of the boat, as the creatures began to fill the boat up, trying to reach the two men.

"What the hell are they?" the young sailor asked. The old

man could see the sailor was showing signs of running, so he grabbed his shoulder.

"Do not run until I tell you, boy. They will only chase you down!"

Seeing that the hull was filling quickly, the old man turned and opened the hatch letting both himself and the sailor through. Waiting for the boy to get through, he closed the hatch and leaned on it, breathing hard. He looked at the sailor, who stared at him, eyes wide with fear.

"Those things are ... are already dead!"

Chapter Seven

$\mathcal{A}$s the group left the village, they started to discuss what they had heard about Brigin'i and what that meant for them.

"We do not have any confirmation that what the orc said is true or, if it is, that the king is not alive," Kalion said.

Jebba fired back, "But what if it is true? Then everything we are doing is for nothing. The fortune and lands we were promised? Nothing!"

"The princess still needs our help," Kikor said. "We can't overlook that."

Jebba replied, "Yes, but …"

Meradoth interrupted, "I agree with Kikor. We have no way of verifying what has happened back in Brigin'i, and we made a commitment to help the princess." As he looked around the group, the others were nodding their agreement — all except Jebba.

After walking for a few hours, Birkita turned to Kikor and said, "Tell me about your people."

"I was born of the Eagle People. My clan, Bright Spear, was not a powerful clan, nor did it have much influence. My father was the healer of the clan and wanted me to follow in his path …" As she trailed off, she looked at Birkita and asked, "And what of your clan?"

Birkita thought for a moment before answering, "My mother was the chieftain of our … well, I wouldn't call them a clan like you have. I would say they were more like wanderers from the southern edge of the Levenori forest."

"Why is that? I have never heard of elves not tied to a clan."

"Well, it is difficult to explain, but my mother had different ideas after the death of my father, who was the leader of the clan.

She thought she should rule the clan by right of marriage and breading, I guess. The males of the clan did not agree and wanted to place one of themselves as clan leader and voted against her."

"Ouch!" Kikor exclaimed.

"Yes. She was so upset that she even talked a number of the women of the clan into leaving their partners to join her. She took me and those few and moved into the southern part of the forest."

"How old were you when this happened?"

"Oh, I think I must have been about two or three because I don't really remember much about the clan. She has been training me to take her place one day ..."

"Do you think you will?"

"At this moment, I just don't know. She is the only reason I am here."

"What do you mean?"

"Well, Mom thought that the games would give us more standing in the world. Like you said, you had never heard of a group not tied to a clan. She thought that winning the prize and the overall games would bring notice to our people and potentially bring more women to join us."

"What? There are no male elves within your ... ah ... group?" Kikor asked, surprised.

"Nope, not a single one. My mother felt that men had betrayed her, so ..."

"But how do you ...grow your ranks?"

"Only by bringing in new elves. We have only had one actual birth, and that was an elf who came to us with child already. Thank the gods she had a girl. I am not sure what my mother would have done otherwise."

They continued walking for a bit, and then Birkita turned to Kikor. "So why are you on this ... quest?"

"For the honor of my clan and my people, really."

Both remained silent for a while, and then, suddenly,

Chansor appeared out of what seemed like nowhere.

"Where did you come from?" Birkita quietly asked.

Chansor shrugged his shoulders, smiling. "Nowhere, why do you ask?"

"It is not nice to listen in on others' conversations, Chansor," Kikor stated with a sideways glance at Chansor.

"I wasn't. ... Honest!!" Chansor pleaded, but when both Kikor and Birkita looked at him with raised eyebrows, he admitted, "Well, I might have heard a bit."

"So then, tell us. What did you hear?" both said at the same time.

As Chansor started to repeat, word for word, everything the two had just said, the two elves looked at each other and shook their heads.

The group walked over a high-rising hill to look across at what used to be some type of a stone circle. Many of the stones had fallen over and lay just beyond the towering shadow of the high mountain that held Bru Edin. The road they left behind wound itself far to the south and could be seen disappearing in the high grasses.

"That's an old druid's circle," Niallee stated as she came over the hill, seeing the stones. She recognized the patterns of the stone placement and the markings that were on a few of them. As the group made its way up the hill and into the circle, she moved up to one of them, nodding that she was right. "Yes, this was once a place of peace and harmony for the religious order that was known as 'Claw Bear' hundreds of cycles ago but is now a dead sect!"

"Claw Bear, huh?" Whelor said, looking at the druid, who was touching one of the stones. "Unusual name for druids." He found the name quite funny. Where he was from, any name mentioning bears meant warriors.

"They believed that the bear was the most intelligent creature of the forest. Their symbol was a bear's claw." She didn't look at Whelor as she said this but stared at the stone.

"I was just commenting, Niallee. I did not mean any offense to you or your people," the big man whispered as he walked slowly away, looking at the other stones. He walked over to the closest stone and looked at the markings she was speaking about. "Interesting markings, though. What do they mean?"

Niallee didn't say anything for a few moments. Her fingers traced a few of the markings as she tried to remember some of old teachings. "I am not sure I remember. Hmmm ... I believe these marks might have been ones of protection." She continued looking at the stone, trying to remember more.

Whelor looked at the stones a moment longer and then felt pain within his stomach, making him grip his gut. Looking over at the rest, hoping they didn't notice, he smiled at Niallee, giving her a look like he had business to do. Smiling back, she nodded and looked back at the stone as Whelor quietly disappeared into the forest just beyond the stones.

Not far away, Bennak and Jebba made their way to the other side of the circle and looked over the Edin Plains before them as drops of rain began to hit their faces. Bennak leaned his face back, hoping the rain would clean the dry orc blood off his face, as Jebba shook his head, suddenly hating rain.

"What do you think, my friend?" Jebba asked, pulling his hood farther forward to keep his face out of the rain. Looking out into fog that was beginning to move in, the bowman couldn't make out much now. Bennak huffed for a moment as he looked out into the haze himself.

"I do not know, Jebba. Whatever the druids find here, I do not believe it will help us much, and why ... those orcs could come over the hill behind us at any time." The half-orc was right, and Jebba knew it. Niallee finding the reason stones were here wouldn't help them in a battle.

He turned around to look at the druid, who was kneeling to look over the stone. He shook his head in disbelief as he saw Amlora and Hrliger kneeling down to see if they could help Niallee figure what the marking were. The others had pulled their packs off and tried to rest next to other stones but kept eyes looking outwards. Who knew what might be hiding out there, watching them? Kalion knew little of these stones, yet having traveled past them many times before, he knew that these stones would at least give him a bit of cover for a while, as they had left the road far behind.

Niallee walked over to stand next to the ranger as his eyes scanned the grounds behind and around them. Looking out herself, she moved closer to him and, after a long while, finally spoke to him.

"These grounds are sacred, you know, my friend," she stated. Looking at Kalion's face, she wondered something. "Do you know the story of the Claw Bear people?" She crossed her arms under her robe to warm herself up from a chill.

"Not much of it ... only that they were known as some of the first or ancient ones." His voice got the attention of Chansor and Kikor, who were sitting nearby. Both looked up to listen to the druid's answer.

"Ancient, yes ... but not the first ones. Other druids speak of these druids as though they were, but these markings say they were not."

"Why is this place so sacred to your people?" Harbin called over, making the two look back at the mage, who, even though it was raining, was lying on the ground with his hands clasped behind his head like it was a nice summer day.

Niallee looked at Harbin and then back to Kalion. She smiled gently at both, saying, "The Claw Bear people, according to my elders, were the first ones — the ones known as the gods that came from the sky and once ruled beyond our world."

Jebba, hearing her speak, couldn't believe it. Shaking his head under his hood, he looked at the half-orc, who seemed not to be listening, as his face and eyes were concentrating hard, looking out into the rain.

"And how ... how does this help us now in our situation?"

Jebba turned and asked, looking at the druid. "Beyond heading towards Bru Edin, we don't know where we go from here. We don't know where the princess we are supposed to be finding is or what lies ahead."

Looking at Jebba, Niallee could feel the anger in his question. She replied, "Well ... it doesn't really help us in our situation. ... It's just that this circle holds an important place in our tales, and as you can tell, the orcs have never touched it, fearing that it does hold power of some kind against them." She placed her hand on the stone nearest to her. Looking up at the top of the stone, she closed her eyes as the rain drops hit her face.

"I do not care if orcs have never been here nor that this place is ancient. ... All I care about is how far it is to the city," Jebba answered, looking back at Bennak, who now looked like he could see something far away.

"What do you see, my friend?" he whispered to him, looking out himself and wondering what the big half-orc was seeing. Bennak didn't answer as he concentrated on looking out into the mist.

"Not far, my friend ... not far!" Kalion answered quietly, seeing Bennak's stare and wondering if the half-orc was feeling the same thing he was.

Birkita, who had crossed her legs much earlier to rest, suddenly jumped up to look out into the rain, grabbing her bow stave that was leaning against the stone behind her.

Out in the twilight erupted a scream, which brought the group to arms quickly and prompted them to assemble. Kikor moved up to stand next to Kalion and Niallee. They all looked out into the thick fog, seeing nothing out there.

"What ... what is it?" Chansor asked quickly, trying to see what they had begun to point at.

"Orcs ... and lots of them coming this way," Kikor whispered, seeing the shadows in the rain.

"By the gods ... they found us!" Amlora whispered, seeing the same movement.

"How far?" Jebba asked as he and Bennak quickly moved themselves behind a large stone next to them when another scream sounded off. "How did they find us?" he whispered to Kikor while looking at the half-orc, wondering how Bennak had known something was coming.

Kikor squinted harder and saw that they had at least a few moments until the beasts got close enough. Turning to look straight into Jebba's eyes, she said, "Very soon, Jebba. Our leaving the road did not fool them, it seems." The elf cocked an arrow and made herself ready.

Kalion nodded, angered that the orcs had found their trail and that they could be trapped here. Cursing himself for his stupidity, he quietly gave orders for the rest to get to positions that could give them the best cover. The group knew what to do and did their best to get ready. Birkita got her bow at the ready and waited next to him as both pulled their bows to their tightest points and waited for the word to send an arrow of pain into the orcs charging towards them.

Holan, Chansor and Amlora got themselves ready as well. Harbin moved his hand in circles and said quiet words, getting a spell to form just at the edge of his tongue, knowing that fire might not work the best with this rain now pouring even harder. Meradoth did the same, bringing up something that could cause the most damage.

Chansor watched Amlora as she did her best to get her tools ready to care for any wounded, and he wondered if she should just hide since she didn't look well.

Hrliger knelt down, touched the ground, closed his eyes and began to speak to the creatures living within it as he tried to find out more information.

"How many, my friend?" he heard Amlora, who was closest to him, whisper as she observed what he was doing. Slowly he began to make out the number of orcs that were approaching.

71

"We have got at least four ... maybe five score orcs and goblinkind approaching," he called out to everyone so they heard. The rest instantly planned out in their minds how to combat the charging orcs.

"There are maybe four giantkind from the northern hills with them, and some creature ... I cannot tell what it is, but ... it seems to be in charge." His voice trailed off as he concentrated on that creature, wondering what it was as information came to him from the creatures living within the ground that rushed to talk to him.

Pulling his hand off the ground when he had gathered what he could, he started to form the words of a druid spell in his mind. Looking up into the sky, he saw that the heavy rain clouds would give him the best attack, so he raised his hands, and just as he spoke the final words of the spell, both of his hands started to glow with a blueish fire that caused the clouds above to stop moving, as if time had stopped.

The group looked up at the sky, watching with open mouths as the clouds stopped their movement and turned darker, soon blocking out the light and causing the area around the stones to be shrouded in darkness as well.

Instantly the rain came down hard and thick, almost forming a wall directly between the group and the oncoming orcs. The rain quickly turned from heavy rain to heavy sleet, making it hard for each side to see the other, but it would give his group a chance, he thought.

* * *

As the old man and the sailor stood on the pier, they watched the ship, now filled with his experiments, quickly sail. Both wondered who would, or could, operate it when suddenly chills rushed up their backs as they heard what sounded like feet scraping wood moving behind them. They considered the possibility that they had missed a few of the creatures.

Swallowing, both turned together, expecting to die within moments, but as their eyes adjusted to the darkness and began to make out the figure walking towards them, they felt a slight relief ... for a moment.

"Thought it was one of them!" the sailor whispered, looking at the old man, who didn't respond but just stared at the figure moving closer.

"Did you do what our master wanted?" the old man and the sailor both heard the creature that walked toward them whisper. The sailor gasped as he saw the creature move out of the shadow and come towards them.

"Yes ... I did. All creatures are on that ship. ... No, I do not believe it will have a problem on its trip to the mainland ... unless the weather changes for the worse, sir," the old man quickly stated.

The sailor looked at the creature standing before him and then glanced back at the old man, wondering what he was talking about. He opened his mouth to ask a question when suddenly his mind was filled with such a roar of screams that he grabbed his head and screamed out himself, falling to his knees.

"The boy doesn't understand, sir. Please don't hurt him. He was just doing what I told him, sir!" The man reached over, grabbing the boy's shoulder and trying to comfort him as the boy held his head, trying to get the screams out of his mind.

"Please, sir ... please ... no!" The old man suddenly felt the enormous weight of what felt like thousands dying in his head as he also reached up to cover his ears and screamed out, falling down next to the sailor, who now stopped his own screaming and fell forward.

"I'm sorry, sirrrrr!" The old man was trying desperately to stop the pain when he felt one last shove of yells in his mind erupt, causing him to stop his own screams and fall down dead at the feet of the creature looking down at them both with its huge black eyes.

"No witness!" a voice echoed in the wind just then as the

grey-skinned creature moved to stand at the end of the pier and watch the ship it was controlling cut through the waves and move west towards its destination.

Chapter Eight

The City of Ports, Blath 'Na City, was the largest known city in the lands, where ships sailed in and out from lands near and far. It was built so long in the past that a legend had arisen that a god of the seas had built this place so he could place his head on it as he rested.

Along the outer edge of the city stood a massive, thick wall, about four to six feet in depth, that was strong enough, it was said, to stop the largest of giants. Along the north, west and south stood large gates that never closed, as the populace and travelers moved through them so much that if they closed, the congestion would back up instantly and cause profits to sink.

The port itself was the heart of this city, with enough docks to hold at least 30 ships, large and small, as well as warehouses alongside each to hold wares and markets nearby to sell everything brought in, from clothing and jewels to weapons. Blath 'Na was famous for being an open city for all.

To protect this legend of a city stood a moving army of thousands of cavalry that rode each day around the large open fields that surrounded the city. Having never lost a battle or even encountered an enemy worth fighting, this cavalry never stopped training.

Within the walls of the city stood temples dedicated to the gods, council towers that rose high into the sky, and buildings for the rich and the poor to live, breathe and work in. The streets were never dirty, as workers were always cleaning up trash and other debris everywhere. Rumors developed that the secret to Blath 'Na's success was not the grand wishes of the gods but the riches that the markets gained from buying and selling. The rest of the city shined in the glow of every night, which was reflected in the creatures that stumbled out of the forest and towards the wall.

* * *

Everyone saw what Hrliger did as they began to feel the ground rumble under their feet from the orcs rushing forward.

Kikor saw the orcs get close enough, so without a word she released her string, sending her arrow straight on to hopefully strike a large-looking orc she saw emerge out of the ice. As she did this, Kalion, Jebba and Birkita did the same, watching their arrows also fly into the dark rain and sleet.

Knowing this ice wall was confusing the orcs, the group heard screams of pain that confirmed they were hitting flesh. Quickly replacing arrows on the strings, the archers released another round of arrows into the rain when suddenly the arrows they were sending through the air burst into blueish white and glowed brightly as they left their bows, causing the archers to look at their bows for a moment.

Not caring when they heard more screams coming out of the dark, they continued, but Kikor and Birkita both gasped as they could see through the rain their arrows striking an orc, who stopped where he was and looked down at his chest, screaming in anger at the pain or something else.

Reaching up, he tried to pull the arrow out but stopped when his chest quickly turned white as the ice effect shot across his whole body, covering him within a second.

Two orcs next to him watched this happen and got even angrier and ran as fast they could towards the group in front of them, screaming, but they suddenly stopped as they were hit by arrows and turned white as ice formed around them.

Quickly the field before the group was covered in dead orcs

and goblins and even one giantkind who had been shot dead, but the screaming continued as the others got riled up more and made their way as best as they could through the heavy sleet towards the stone circle.

Kikor was able to release three more arrows at the orcs, as did Jebba from where he was. Within a few moments Kikor had killed ten orcs, who were now lying either dead on the wet ground or withering, frozen in ice.

This didn't seem to scare the orcs off as much as Harbin had hoped, as he watched them begin running up the small hill that led to the stone circle, screaming even louder at the loss of their comrades.

As the orcs got close to the first stone, a burst of light exploded from within the stone circle, and instantly, a greenish fog appeared around a large group of orcs, who in response began screaming as at least ten or twelve of them dropped their weapons and began itching and pulling their armor off, trying to stop something underneath it.

This gave the quest group's archers easy targets to kill as a few more orcs ran into the fog and got affected. Slowly, the orcs stopped screaming as they fell down quivering and died from arrows or the greenish fog encircling them.

Niallee, kneeling not far from Hrliger, held her hand on the ground as she also spoke to the creatures under their feet, smiling at what she had planned, when she looked up, hearing a terrible scream not far from her.

As she looked with wide eyes, she saw an orc move around the stone and rush in to find the elf Birkita standing there, just waiting for him. Birkita pulled her sword out quickly and raised it above her head, waiting for the orc to rush her, which he did, screaming upon seeing the elf warrior. He didn't even get close to the elf, though, because as the orc passed the first stone, Bennak jumped out and, in a massive swing of his sword, cut the head off the surprised orc. Birkita watched as the orc's head tumbled past her feet and looked up at her for a moment, blinking.

Bennak didn't even stop to see what happened to the orc, as he roared loudly and rushed at a second orc coming up directly behind the one he had just killed. That orc, seeing the huge half-breed charging him, screamed and raised his blade up in the hopes of stopping Bennak's sword as the massive blade swung down. He wasn't able to, as Bennak's blade, being a well-made piece of weaponry, sliced through the orc's sword like it wasn't even there and plunged into the orc's head, cutting it in half and causing the orc's black brain matter to burst onto his armored shoulders.

Bennak tried pulling it out, but his blade was stuck in the head of the orc, so he lifted his leg, and using it, he pushed the dead creature off his sword. When it came out, even more blood and internal organs of the orc came with it.

Meradoth, seeing that the ice wall and green mist were stopping the onslaught, maneuvered his hands around quickly, pushing his palms out. He whispered a word, and at least 12 orcs screamed out instantly, disappearing a moment later. If it hadn't been raining, everyone would have seen the dust where the orcs had been moments earlier, but as it was, it just added to the mud.

Niallee stood up as the rush of orcs moved up the hill, getting closer than she liked, but seeing the half-orc and elves fighting them off, she was amazed at the power of their group.

Meanwhile Amlora, who was waiting for any injuries to happen, seeing that the number of orcs charging in was such that someone was bound to get hurt, decided that an open space to the side of the group was just too easy for the orcs to get through, so she quickly reached into her pack and pulled out two potions that, if combined the right way, would give her what she wanted. Shaking the potions in their bottles, she threw the tops open, poured the liquids out on the standing stone next to her, and watched as the two liquids combined, instantly creating the effect she had hoped for. Each in its own way healed certain injuries, but if mixed together, they did the opposite. Soon the stone began to disintegrate and fell over, landing to make a large wall of stones in between two of the huge standing stones. She smiled when an orc got caught under it, dying instantly and leaving behind only a quivering hand.

This now gave the group better focus in three areas instead of four, letting the green mist stop the orcs from entering another opening. Holan thanked Amlora for what she had just done as he ran past her to confront an orc who was trying to get over the now downed stone. Holan stood in front of the orc and blocked its sword with his axe's blade, countering it by quickly pushing the orc back as he yelled at him.

"That all yea got, you ugly beast?" Holan yelled, almost spitting in the orc's face.

The orc snarled and spat back at the dwarf as he swung his rusted sword in a downward swing. Hoping his strength would weaken the dwarf, the orc put everything he had into the swing, but when the dwarf's axe again stopped his blade, the orc screamed in anger.

The orc took two more swings as Holan seemed to just laugh at the orc's weakness in not being able to kill him. This, of course, did exactly what the dwarf wanted; the orc just seemed to lose control of himself as he swung his blade almost like a mad creature.

Holan found his opportunity and, in a quick shot, slammed his axe into the side of the orc, severing his arm completely. The orc screamed in shock as he saw his arm and sword fall to the ground, blood spurting everywhere. At the same time, Holan laughed at the withering orc, who had just moments earlier said he would kill the little dwarf.

"And you thought you'd kill me," Holan leaned over and said directly into the orc's face as the orc fell to his knees, knowing that he would be dead in a few moments.

The orc spat at the dwarf, at which point Holan's axe swung down hard and hit the orc's shoulder, severing it completely from the rest of the body and letting both parts of the orc fall to the ground.

Turning around just in time, Holan deflected a blade from a heavy pole axe that came out of nowhere. Holan knocked it away again and stepped to the side as the pole axe came down hard a second time. It just missed Holan's boot and dug deep into the ground. The large orc who was holding the staff cursed loudly but didn't get a chance to pull the pole axe out of the ground, as Holan's axe came swinging down and, in one stroke, took both arms of the orc off just below the elbows. He fell back, screaming madly, now with stumps throwing greenish-black blood everywhere instead of hands. Holan didn't even blink an eye and, turning all the way around to get the heaviest swing of his axe, he slammed it into the middle torso area, almost cutting the orc in half.

Screaming a dwarfish battle cry of triumph, Holan turned to face the next orc who would challenge him. None came towards him after seeing what had happened to their friend; a few even turned and went after others in the group or ran away into the dark rain.

"Come on, yea ugly beasts. Come an' get me!" he yelled as loud as he could. He decided he wouldn't wait and ran over to plant his axe into the back of an orc fighting with the thief, Chansor, who stupidly decided to join the battle, thinking he could fight the orcs like the others.

"Get out of here, you stupid boy!" Holan yelled into Chansor's face after the orc fell over and Holan pulled his axe out of the orc's back.

"I want to help!" Chansor yelled, challenging Holan's warning. Holan smiled at the thief's strength in the midst of what was going on.

"I know you do ..." Holan called back as he saw another orc running up the hill towards them. Swinging his axe around, Holan killed it instantly.

"Go protect Amlora, then. She needs your help, boy!" the dwarf grunted as he faced a green-skinned goblin who burst out of the rain.

Chansor didn't want to argue anymore. The dwarf was

stubborn and, at that moment, very mad. So the thief turned and ran over to stand next to the druid, who was ducking a spear that had been thrown at her. Seeing Chansor running up, Amlora thought at first that the thief was coming to protect her or something. *I don't need protection,* she thought quickly.

Holding another potion, one she used to get ingredients from deep within the dirt to help with healing bones, she opened the top and threw it with one big toss of her hand at five orcs coming over the crest of the hill. As the potion hit the ground, it instantly opened up the earth underneath their feet, causing the orcs to scream loud as they fell into the open hole and a standing stone that was next to the hole collapsed hard onto them.

"By the gods, how did you do that?" Chansor asked, almost like an excited child seeing a new toy.

Amlora smiled and was about to answer the question but didn't get a chance to as she saw an arrow fly out of the dark rain towards her. She fell forward and to the left as the arrow just missed her shoulder. Chansor moved over and helped the woman back up.

"Amlora?" Making sure that she was well, Chansor decided that he needed to do something as a loud roar came from far away, causing Chansor to feel a little shaky in his knees. Amlora looked over the thief's shoulder in the direction of the sound, and being taller than Chansor, she could see what it was as she stood up.

"What is it?" he asked. Amlora still didn't answer as she squinted her eyes to look harder.

Then all at once, Amlora saw what had made the sound. Her eyes widened as she quickly grabbed Chansor, pushing him down to the ground despite the thief's grumbles, which stopped instantly as a huge spear came flying over their heads a moment later and slammed into the stone standing behind them. The spear was large enough to crack the large stone in half as the top half fell backwards.

Amlora got up, not looking to see if Chansor was well. Harbin moved to stand in front of the two, arching his arms around, and in one big motion, a huge fireball soon leaped away from his hands to shoot back outwards towards the creature that had thrown the spear moments earlier.

Chansor got up. Jumping up and down, he tried to see what the mage had sent, but he couldn't see the fireball, as the rise of the hill and the bodies of both the orcs and his friends, fighting now hand to hand, were in the way. A moment later, though, he heard a terrible scream, not like the one he heard earlier, but one of pain, which meant that the fire had hit something and was hurting whatever it was.

"What do you see out there, Harbin?" Chansor was getting impatient, wondering what was there. Harbin just stood there and watched a moment longer. Then he turned and looked down at the little thief, saying, "Giant of some kind." He smiled for a moment and then turned to enact another spell.

"Ahhhh," was all that Chansor said as both he and the mage noticed that more orcs were running up the hill now.

"I thought Hrliger said there were only three or four score of them. ... I think this is more than that!" Harbin grunted. The fireball had drained him badly. As he felt his body weaken, he had to use a stone to hold himself up for a moment. He only had a few smaller tricks up his sleeve, nothing that could stop the onslaught of orcs coming in, he realized then.

"I think you should hide, my friend. It's going to get very bloody very soon. Get Amlora and yourself to safety if you can," the mage stated, looking to Chansor. He knew that the thief couldn't defend himself against that many of the ugly things.

Nodding to the mage, Chansor grabbed Amlora, who argued for a moment, but then quickly, both ran over to the far eastern side of the stone circle and ran around the first stone they came to, which happened to be huge but cracked.

"We need to get ready to run if this battle turns against us, I think!" he said as he breathed hard on the druid, who nodded back as they both heard the screams, steel and explosions on the other side of the stone they now knelt behind.

Chansor wanted to help out, but he was getting very afraid and didn't know what to do now.

Who knows what is going to happen and if these are the only orcs in the area? Yes, Hrliger said that there were only about three score of them, but ... the thief thought as he looked at the huge number of screaming, black-cloaked creatures charging in.

The fighting began to build up to an almost enormous roar of screams of pain, battle cries, explosions and steel hitting steel.

Chansor and Amlora looked at each other, as they both knew that the stupid orcs would not just keep charging up that one side of the hill. Sooner or later, they were going to find other ways into the stone circle.

Both were hiding as close as they could against the stone, and with the high unkempt grass in front of and around them, it would be very hard for anyone to find them without looking hard. Chansor pulled the druid as close he could, hoping that the heavy rain would cover their hiding spot.

"Oh, gods," Chansor said out loud, noticing movement coming up on his left at the bottom of the hill, which really wasn't that far away from where he was. "I hate it when I am right!" he said, and realizing that he had spoken louder than he had intended, he quickly put his hand over his mouth.

The movement had to be orcs, but the rain and sleet coming down and the grass in front of him made it a bit hard for him to see clearly. The thief knew that his friends were all looking other ways and probably wouldn't see the orcs coming up behind them. He had to do something, but he was still very scared, and really, what could a small thief do against orcs?

Then he saw them come into the light as a fire ignited up above, probably due to a spell or something, and he saw the reflection of what was coming. "Hmm, make that a few orcs," he whispered to himself. "Many!"

He felt he had to do something, but he was just a thief and couldn't really stop an orc. Besides, he was, in the end, a scared young man who had thought this was just going to be an adventure like a treasure hunt or something, not a fight against some of the scariest creatures in this world. He rifled through his side pouch, though, just to see if he had something of use.

The first object he found was a bottle of some potion he had found back in the city. Another was a parchment he had borrowed from Meradoth just before he left. Actually, Meradoth had asked him to hold on to it. The third was a small crossbow that he had taken from a dark elf he had found on the battlefield after passing through the Hathorwic Forest. No, seeing that it only held a small bolt of some kind, the crossbow wouldn't do anything except make the orc he shot very mad.

So he decided that he would just wait and see what happened. His group was skilled enough to know what he knew would happen, so he was sure they could fight their way out of this.

So Chansor just sat there and listened, thinking about how and why things happened in this world of his. Then he noticed something: those orcs came up fast and out of nowhere like they were waiting for something. Looking closely at the orcs moving towards him, he made a mental note to talk to the group about his thoughts.

As he watched the orcs quietly signal to each other to spread out along the back hill, Chansor could see they were going to attack all at once from different points along the stones, probably hoping that the large attack would confuse his friends, which it probably would.

Hering what sounded like a roar from Bennak or something else large within the stone circle, he saw the orcs stop and then get themselves ready to launch their surprise attack.

"They are sure taking their time, letting their comrades sacrifice themselves while they ..." Chansor cut himself short when he noticed an orc standing only a few feet from him. It was the smell of the orc that first caught Chansor's attention. The smell was disgusting, almost making the thief sick to his stomach.

Chansor placed his hand over his mouth, trying not to get sick, which saved him at first, as the orc who was near him thought he heard something but decided it must have been from the battle up above and kept slowly moving past Chansor.

Amlora watched with wide eyes, herself feeling sick from the smell coming from the orcs, but she had nothing left to use on the orcs, so she kept still and quiet.

Chansor breathed short breaths, not believing how terrible the smell was, as he watched the orcs all raise their hands into the air as one; the one next to him then lowered his quickly. Not believing what he was seeing, he watched the orcs, begin to move up the hill when suddenly a scream burst from behind the stone he had been hiding under. Whelor burst out of the forest and attacked a giantkind at the northern end of the circle, quickly dispatching it with a hard blow to its head.

Looking around, trying to see what he could kill next, Whelor saw the others fighting hard where they stood when flames showed him that his people were being surrounded.

Screaming out a warning to the group, he rushed forward, falling and slamming into the orc standing next to Chansor's hiding spot, knocking the orc back before he could raise his rusty sword.

Listening and watching the two grunt and growl at each other, Chansor saw the strong man quickly cut down the orc with a hard swipe of his sword. Turning quickly, Whelor charged at the others trying to move up the hill to get behind the group.

Amlora saw what was going on around her, so seeing that the boy wanted to help out, she grabbed the thief's arm and held on to him for support, shaking her head "no" at him. Chansor could tell the cleric wanted to run away, so he slowly leaned out of their hiding spot to look when he saw their horse not far away, trying to get its reins to loosen from the stone that he had attached it to earlier.

He looked from the horse to the big warrior, watching Whelor, who in the past had always been the quiet one, erupt in bloodcurdling screams that almost sounded like they came from an animal. The warrior used his hands, his sword and even his mouth to kill the orcs now trying to encircle him.

It didn't take long for the stone circle, so sacred a place to Niallee, to become a deadly battleground as the group fought hard to hold back the orcs, who now seemed to be coming out of the ground to attack them.

As Whelor moved the fight away from where they hid, Chansor grabbed Amlora under her arms, pulling her up, and they moved around the dead and dying orcs now littering the ground and reached the horse. Calming it down just enough, he grabbed its nose, whispering to it to calm itself, as he released the ropes he held and swung Amlora up on the horse's saddle.

Turning around, he gasped, seeing Whelor reach out with a hand that Chansor was sure now held long knives instead of fingers and, in one quick move of his hand, completely rip out the throat of an orc who tried to move up. The orc grabbed his wound and fell back, gasping for air.

Whelor then turned his attention to the other orc and killed it with a downward strike that almost cut the orc in half. Chansor watched the big man lean his body back slightly and let out a scream as though he were celebrating the deaths of the two orcs, whose bodies fell to the ground next to him.

Mobilizing the moles underneath, Niallee had been able to open up the ground, causing many orcs to fall forward and break their ankles and other body parts as they ran. But now she and Holan worked together as she sprang a trap by having the ground implode to create another huge hole, which caught orcs charging towards the dwarf. Holan watched them fall downwards and scream, as Niallee had also called some animal friends to come out of the ground to attack the orcs as they scrambled to get out. Snakes and other creatures, from spiders to beetles, attacked and bit the orcs in as many places as they could. Those orcs bit by poisonous creatures soon slowed down as the poison took over. Holan yelled at Niallee to keep it up as he turned and charged another group of orcs trying to run up behind.

Not far away, Birkita was using her best skills to fight the orcs off as well, whipping her blade hard left and right and even jumping over some heads to stab the orcs in the back. When she saw Harbin fall suddenly against a stone, thinking that the mage had been hit, she ran over to check on him, only to find that he was just exhausted from his attacks. But now he needed some protection fast, as an orc got through the ring that the group had been able to make and past the others. Seeing a defenseless mage leaning against a stone and what looked like a weak little elf, the orc charged towards them, thinking they would be an easy target and kill.

In two swipes of her sword, Birkita severed the orc's arm and then its head, which fell down in front of the mage, who smiled and thanked the elf. He had done all he could, so he was grateful that the elf was there. He was missing Zahnz a lot now, thinking the three would be a good match right now as Meradoth charged at a group of orc warriors, throwing an orc's head into the crowd like an exploding bomb, causing those caught in it to scream in pain as fire, metal, bone and more exploded outwards.

As Birkita fought back another few orcs who had made it through, she did her best to quickly end their lives until she saw an ugly and large giant, not caring that its skin was almost melting away, come bursting through the poison cloud that was still hanging near the ground.

A few arrows stuck out of its chest and legs and half of its body was black and burnt, undoubtedly from the fireball Harbin had released earlier.

Birkita didn't even think much about the giant as she quickly charged the beast, hoping to kill it because its eyes — or eye since it had only one that had been split in half — were looking directly at Jebba, who was only a few feet away, fighting with his back turned to it. She ran as quickly as her feet would carry her, jumping up onto a few dead bodies of orcs so she could leap onto the back of the giant. As she landed, she took her sword and drove it as hard as she could into the back of the giant.

Of course, the beast wouldn't let her stay long, as it roared in pain, and reaching up, it tried to grab Birkita and throw her far away. Birkita was just able to keep out of its reach as she again and again drove her sword deeper into the giant's back.

After the fourth thrust into its back, the giant stopped trying to grab her and finally fell down to its knees. Birkita took this opportunity, and grabbing the hair on the head of the giant, she reached around and swiped her sword across its throat, cutting deep enough to kill it quickly.

When she finished her cut, she jumped off as it fell forward, landing on an orc that was running by, squashing it. As she landed on the ground, she drove her blade deep into the face of the orc, pushing the blade hard into the orc and leaving it to die underneath the giant.

Cursing the gods, Birkita looked around quickly for a sword and saw one lying not far away. She ran towards it, grabbing the sword as she turned and waited for the next orc to challenge her, which didn't take long.

Off to the other side of the area, the other elf, Kikor, had run out of arrows, as she had been releasing and shooting them as quickly as she could. Her bow, which was given to her, along with whatever magical powers it had, by Harbin, was causing an enormous amount of death for the orcs. All over the place along the hill and in the field stood ice statues of her victims.

As she released the last arrow directly into the face of a surprised orc that had run around the stone in front of her, icing it quickly, she immediately reached down and pulled her sword out of the sheath on her hip. Laying her bow on the ground, she charged a second orc that was following the first, now frozen, orc, slicing through its chest quickly with a fast swipe of her blade.

The orcs, seeing a thin, small elf with blond hair standing alone, had thought she would be an easy kill. They were not thinking that long, though, as she quickly killed five orcs within a few moments.

Hrliger's scream erupted out of the mist when he received a terrible wound as a large orc slashed the druid's leg, making him fall back. The small gnome almost lost the leg, being surprised by this orc who had been able to get past the others. But Niallee, who moved quickly over to the small gnome, wrapped a ripped piece of cloth around the gash, making sure it stopped the bleeding. Then she knocked the orc back, using her staff to push it off balance.

Jebba, fighting hard a few feet away, had received a few wounds from a sword and a few arrows that had found their marks. The warrior stood, fighting an ugly-looking orc that seemed to be the leader of this orcish contingent.

The two were locked, fighting hard against each other and striking hard and quick. Neither gave the other a chance to rest or back away, even when the orc's sword bent and broke. Using its huge size, the orc pushed Jebba away so it could bend down and grab another sword lying on the ground near it.

Jebba, grunting from the sudden push, noticed that this orc wore what could be considered a crown of some kind on its ugly head. He heard it swear that it was going to kill the human, but Jebba didn't respond in kind as he deflected the orc's new sword to the right with his own, getting himself back up to stand firm on the ground again.

They began to move around each other, each striking the other with several hits, but it was the orc that was winning this small battle, and the orc knew it. Jebba began slowing down as he suffered from the amount of blood he was losing, and he could tell he didn't have much longer.

Yelling to the orc that it would never win, Jebba took this chance to fake a downward slash of his sword. The orc raised its sword up to deflect it, but Jebba turned completely around, and moving just inside the orc's arm and sword with his back to the orc, he pushed his sword back under his left arm and into the orc's chest. Caught off guard by the surprise move, the orc's face showed nothing as it realized what had just happened. Looking down and seeing Jebba's sword in its side and the human standing right up against its chest, the orc spat both blood and saliva onto Jebba's face as the man turned to look, making Jebba close his eyes.

Cursing something that Jebba couldn't understand, it fell down and landed on its back with a loud huff of wind and lay still.

"Stupid orc!" Jebba said as he spat hard at the orc's body and turned around weakly to see how the rest were faring.

The fight was taking its toll on the group, as Bennak, who had taken a spear in the arm, fought off three goblins that had rushed through the green mist, not caring that it burned their skin, and staggered back to see Jebba kill the leader.

"We need to run, my friend!" Bennak grunted loudly over to the man, who looked as tired as he was now.

Nodding in response, Jebba looked around to see where everyone was standing.

"I do believe we should leave this place!" he yelled loudly when he saw that the orc numbers seemed to continue on through the darkness.

Noting that the thief and the cleric, along with their one and only horse, were gone, he cursed the little man for leaving as a few more arrows came flying out of the rain, hitting the stones near his head.

Jebba knelt down to duck under them as Kalion ran over and placed his hand on the warrior's shoulder, breathing hard as he did.

"Get Bennak and Harbin and make your way to Bru Edin, now!" Kalion almost yelled at the other as more screams erupted from the rain wall.

Birkita came running over, and almost slapping Kalion, she

swung her blade around to block a sword that was coming down on the ranger's head.

"Wake up!" she screamed, running away after cutting the creature down.

Suddenly the scene around him slowed as Kalion looked down to see the face of the orc and its anger at not being able to kill the ranger. His ears rang as Whelor's blood-curdling scream made him look over and watch as the big man swung his sword around, covering the ground around him with bodies. The man almost howled in triumph, bending his back slightly, spreading his arms wide and screaming after killing another orc. Kalion's eyes moved over to see the dwarf get knocked down hard by a large orc that had pushed itself over the fallen stone. Holan seemed to lie there for a moment and then quickly got up to fight back.

Kalion could tell his people wouldn't last long with all these openings. Turning his head, he looked at Jebba and could see the archer was thinking the same thing. Both nodded as Jebba ran over and grabbed Bennak's shoulder, telling him to grab the mage, and Kalion cried over to Kikor and Birkita to cover their retreat as he ran over, pushing his sword deep into the back of the orc that was about to kill the fallen dwarf. Killing the orc as he moved by, he grabbed and lifted Holan as the dwarf struggled to get up.

"We are moving from here, now!" Kalion told the grumpy dwarf as the ranger turned to see what the others were doing.

Meradoth used his staff to deflect blows from and knock out orc after orc as he swung it around. The mage, when he found an opening, used it to send a blast of loud horns, causing orc and giant alike to scream and fall down, covering their ears and giving the mage time to turn and run.

Kalion watched as Bennak and Jebba, holding Harbin between them, moved past and down the other side as Whelor finished off a giant that had tried to crush the big man under its large club.

Amazed at the sudden strength and anger coming from the

quiet man, Kalion shook his head, thinking he'd have to ask him later about it, but for now he yelled hard to the man to move to Bru Edin.

Whelor, breathing hard as his chest rose up and down under his armor, looked through blood-caked eyes at the ranger, who was crying for him to move and retreat. At first he couldn't believe what he was hearing. Blood was moving hard through his head, causing him to shake it a bit as he looked at the ranger, who was mouthing words he didn't think he believed were being spoken.

"Retreat?" he mumbled. How could they do that when he knew they were winning? But then he noticed that Bennak and Jebba had left with the mage and that only he, Kalion and the two elves were left. He knew they would not have much of a chance to fight, as he saw more of his enemy move through the ice wall and up the sides of the hill.

"We are not done with these beasts, I think," Whelor yelled between breaths. The huge man was, like Bennak and the others, covered in orcish blood and guts, but he was also as wounded as the others, too. He had taken a deep cut in his side when an orc had used an arrowhead to stab the human in a lastditch effort to kill him. The pain wasn't there, but he knew he had been wounded.

"Whelor, we cannot fight them all. We need to leave this place, NOW!" Kalion almost screamed as the ranger turned and deflected an arrow that came out of the rain, aimed at his head.

Hrliger and Niallee, having heard the ranger's call to retreat moments earlier, grabbed themselves and, doing their best, struggled to move. The woman had to pick the gnome up and carry him on her shoulder as they moved down the hill and into the open field. They stepped hard to keep up with Bennak and Jebba, who were not far ahead, carrying the mage between them.

"Best, my friends, that we ... run!" Kalion pointed towards where Bru Edin lay, far away in the distance. "We must make Bru Edin castle if we are to survive." Seeing the two elves fighting hard to do what he had asked, Kalion ran over and, grabbing the bags that he had thrown down, he quickly pulled out what he needed to protect their retreat.

As Whelor moved past the ranger to cover him, the big man could see that, for the moment, the orcs had stopped their attack, probably taken aback by the group's sudden retreat, he thought. But he could see through the ice shield that they were arranging another attack, and soon.

Kalion, meanwhile, pulled out a pouch and parchment he needed and, throwing his pack to the ground, he cried over for them to move as Kikor, nodding, yelled over for Birkita to move.

Kikor grabbed her bow lying not far away as she turned and followed the ranger. Birkita, likewise, knocked a goblin down hard with her sword hilt and turned to follow, reaching for her bow as she ran past where she had dropped it earlier.

As the group ran down the hill, out of the stone circle and onto the high-grassed field, moving hard to get to the safety of the mountain, they could make out the roars, screams and even a few curses from the orcs watching them retreat.

Hearing the curses, Kalion whispered that he hoped these orcs would do the same as orcs he'd fought in the past and stop to search the group's packs and belongings left on the ground instead of chasing their prey. He knew that at least those goblins that seemed to be moving with the orcs would stop. Kalion and the rest — some slowly, some quickly — disappeared into the heavy rain and mist that had moved in as Kalion prayed for his people to run faster!

Chapter Nine

Methnorick sat upon his large stone throne, looking at a tapestry that was in front of him, when the large but weak-looking human came walking to stand near him without saying a word. The king of the Black Isle, the largest island that lay off the mainland to the north and east, called Black due to the heavy rain and storms that always covered it, making it look black to those sailing by, waited, looking at the tapestry to see the scene that unfolded on it until he laughed, quickly turning his head and seeing the human standing there with his head down, looking at the floor.

"Ahhhhhh, welcome, my dear King Bogamul," Methnorick said, turning and continuing to watch the tapestry as the man spoke up quietly.

"My Lord Methnorick ... I came as you asked." The king looked at the floor, not wanting for Methnorick to see him looking up. The rags that once were clothing full of color and stature were now covered in dust, mud and even worse things, making the once proud king look like a slave.

Still looking away from the king, Methnorick smiled as the scene unfolded in front of him, showing the lands outside of Bru Edin as his army massed. Methnorick slammed his hands together, seemingly congratulating himself that his plans were coming together nicely. As he moved his hand over the tapestry, the scene finally disappeared, and then Methnorick turned his head and looked at the king before him.

"You, king, are to do nothing. Nothing means nothing, do you understand?" Not waiting for him to answer, Methnorick continued, "Are your armies ready to follow mine?"

The tone of Methnorick's voice brought a fear the king could barely endure. His knees started to shake within his clothing, and without looking up, he nodded his head "yes" and quietly answered that his armies were at Methnorick's command.

"Good, King," Methnorick said with a snear. "When this is done, if you obey, you will be rewarded handsomely, or at least I will allow you and your daughter to live." Looking over to a young slave who stood nearby, Methnorick motioned her over and then looked back to the king.

"You may go, King, but just remember: I am watching." He pointed to the tapestry before him. "Be warned, King!"

The slave walked up to Methnorick as he spoke. He reached for her hair, pulling her over to sit on his lap he stared at the king. As the king left the room, he took the opportunity to look over his shoulder to observe his new lord ravaging the slave who sat upon him.

"Someday, my lord ... someday I will be there when you fall. It will come, I promise, and I will save you some way, my baby girl," the king whispered as he quietly walked down the hall and away from Methnorick.

* * *

Days earlier a ship that had crashed just north of the city on the sharp rocks lying about ten miles away had been found, but with no survivors. The council, believing help was needed, sent a search party of cavalry to see who it might be and to help if needed. When no report came back, a young mage decided to venture outside the walls and investigate. When he returned moments later, all he could say was that of the four villages he had visited were all now dead and only what he thought to be the undead moved within them.

"All life was dead," he whispered, making the others around him gasp in shock. Many of his order had been wondering what could be moving out there before another group of cavalry was to be sent to find out, but they were too late; the council had already sent out another group of cavalry. Upon hearing what the mage shared, the council quickly ordered the main gates to be closed after the battalion marched out to protect the city.

Before the army could march more than a mile outside the city, creatures were spotted moving slowly south out of the forest. Quickly the ranks of men formed, making ready for what was heading toward them.

Now, as the sounds of battle echoed everywhere within the city, many scrambled to figure out what to do. As screams from the warriors raged outside, the northern gate finally opened, letting the army back in. Of the 9,000 men sent out to protect the city, only 4,237 were able to make it back in safely before those who had opened the gate saw the creatures walking towards them and pushed it shut again.

As the creatures slowly moved towards the city with no weapons of any kind, those who made it in stated quickly that these creatures couldn't be damaged by arrows or even swords. They were only interested in massacring the men-at-arms of the army, taking them down by sheer force and using their teeth to inflict damage. Warriors on the wall watched in horror as soldiers who had just minutes before gotten attacked and killed slowly got up and started moving with the other creatures like they had forgotten who and what they were. They stumbled over and attacked other warriors, who were now fighting even harder.

Many wounded, all screaming that they had been bitten or scratched by the creatures attacking outside, were pulled into large barns to be cared for. An unimaginable number of lives were lost in the battle outside as the leaders of Blath 'Na themselves looked at each other, uncertain about what to do. All clerics and healers were to be sent to the northern section of the city to help the wounded who had made it inside the gates. These clerics were quickly hard-pressed to take care of the large number of individuals wounded while fighting outside the walls.

Having used a needle thread to close the terrible wound

the young warrior had and wrapping it up tightly, the young cleric worked feverishly to get him into the barn that lay near the gate. Moments before having done these things, the cleric had used a potion to calm the man down, as he had been screaming in pain, almost having lost his arm in the battle waging outside the walls of Blath 'Na City.

As the potion calmed the man down, Espa pulled the cloth from his shirt and did what he could to close the wound up. As he did, he saw many others with the same type of wound being rushed around. It was almost like a bite; many of the clerics moaned while they did what they could to care for the wounded.

As Espa tightened the cloth over the wound, getting himself ready to move on to the next wounded warrior, the man woke up suddenly and grabbed the shocked cleric by the wrist as he looked at him with wide and scared eyes.

"Get out of here! You need to leave!" the man gasped hard.

Smiling slightly, Espa nodded. "It's fine, my friend. You're inside the city, so nothing can get in from out there. I've ..."

Shaking his head, the wounded warrior interrupted Espa quickly. "No, no, you don't understand. They can't be stopped. No matter what we did ... they kept coming!" the man's voice rasped hard as he tried to breathe through the pain of his wound. He gripped Espa's wrist so tightly that the cleric had to let go of the cloth to grab the warrior's hand and try to break the grip that was hurting him.

"Sir ... I'm sure what you might have seen out there was just an illusion or something. Nothing dies and comes back!" Espa smiled again as he tried to calm down the warrior, who violently shook his head in disagreement.

"If I die ... I will kill you!" the man whispered. Espa believed the man was fainting from the pain, making him frown as the warrior's eyes closed and he let go of Espa's wrist.

"Sir ... sir ...?" he whispered back. Then, shaking his head, he finished his job of tightening the cloth around the man's arm.

As he lifted himself up to move to the next warrior, who had just been placed on the ground near him, he heard a loud gasp behind him. He lifted his bag of medical supplies to look over at where the gasp came from and saw another cleric standing up with his arms stretched out, shaking them like he was trying to push something back.

Espa was about to ask what the man was doing when he turned to see the warrior he had been caring for just moments before slowly get up from the bed roll on the ground and begin to struggle to move towards the cleric.

"What is going ..." Espa whispered when suddenly another scream erupted from the far end of the barn. Espa looked that way to see a warrior, who had probably moments before been cared for, attack the cleric by reaching out and grabbing the older man and pushing him to the ground as the man screamed for help.

Espa looked over and saw the wounded man, trying to get up quickly like he had rabbit within him, jump a few feet and grab the now screaming cleric, who tried to turn and run away.

As the warrior fell on the cleric, Espa gasped hard, dropping his bag quickly, suddenly scared for his life. Looking over at the open door, Espa began to run that way, hoping when he got there he could close the door and shut whatever this sickness was within it, but as he took three steps, he heard a loud groan behind him. Joining with the others in the screaming, he saw the man he had been caring for now standing before him, almost red-eyed with a gasping mouth, hands reaching out towards him.

Espa didn't get more than two more feet away before the warrior rammed hard into him, causing him to lose his breath as the weight of the man made both collapse hard onto the stone floor.

Espa screamed, reaching out to another cleric who was struggling to get two of these creatures off his back as he screamed for help as well. *Help* was his last thought to his gods when he felt a terrible pain like he had never felt in his life erupt from his shoulder as hands moved across his back to grab his arm and neck.

He quietly gasped when he felt his shoulder and neck being ripped apart and saw his blood pool on the floor next to him as darkness covered his eyes and all became quiet.

"I've been told that soldiers posted near where the wounded are cared for, sir ... they can hear screams from the barns being used to house the wounded," one of the council members declared through the yells and cries as the rest of his council moaned.

"What do we do?" screamed a woman council member looking over a report describing the losses on the battlefield.

"We need to accept that the bitten must be left on the field or isolated. We can't leave them in the streets!"

Most couldn't believe what was happening, nor that it was happening so quickly. Soon reports from the northern gates stopped coming back, causing the council to fear that now the soldiers guarding the barns had also been attacked.

When a small explosion sent up a fireball into the sky, the council ran over to the large balcony to look out and watch it as a few whimpered out of fear of losing their city so suddenly.

Further inside the city, people started to hear the battle that had erupted. Much of the city's population was terrified of what was attacking them. The screams from the warriors fighting did not help and were loud enough that those within feared the worst.

From where the council stood above the city, they could watch as word quickly spread that the plague had made it inside and the population scrambled to get away and make their way to the ports.

Chaos suddenly erupted. Many people fell into the water as they were pushed and herded along by the city guards trying to keep the peace and order within the port area. Someone among the council whispered, "We never considered this in our plans to protect the city."

The city as a whole was seen retreating from the outer walls, abandoning their houses and market carts that lined the street and other buildings. Wagons were littering the roads, blocking cavalry horses from moving through to get to the main gates. Supply trains could not make it through either; many fell victim to theft by civilians trying to get food. Fires could be seen from the council tower as the creatures began moving from the north into the city proper.

Temples tried to keep order in their own areas, but even they quickly fell to the rush of people trying to get to safety, many pushing their ways into the temples, believing their gods would protect them.

As ships slowly left the port, a few were dragging people who tried to swim to the ships out in the open seas.

* * *

Kalion led the way as the group moved across the field and away from the army, back into the forest and towards the passageway into Bru Edin. Their trick had worked for the most part. Meradoth had thrown up a rain of burning rocks that fell hard on the ground, causing the orcs that tried to follow to turn away and stay to try to find out what was left behind, but he was sure that the rocks and their packs wouldn't keep the orcs long.

Birkita was doing her best to disrupt the few remaining groups of orcs on their side of the rock storm that were still pursuing them. Releasing three arrows quickly, she killed two orcs at once and caused the third to stumble in its pursuit of the group. Not far behind Birkita, Kikor hid behind a small bush and waited until the other elf ran past her and brought the orcs close enough for her to use her blade. Birkita knew that Kikor was using her as bait, which was fine for the moment, as Birkita knew that she would do the same. Birkita taunted the orcs even more as she ran in the direction of the rest of the group, turning once in a while and yelling insults at the orcs to get them to run directly at her.

A few moments later, the grunting of the orcs chasing Birkita and the sounds of their armor clacking could be heard as they yelled back at her. As the group got within a sword's length, Kikor jumped in front of them, surprising them. The shock of seeing an elf in their faces made the three orcs instantly forget what to do for a moment as they stared at the blond elf. That moment was all Kikor needed, as she cut quickly and deeply into two of the orcs within seconds, killing them. The third, coming to its senses, tried to stab at Kikor, but she was faster, deflecting the rusty orc sword to her left and, in a quick twist of her body, taking that orc's head off in one swift motion.

Checking to make sure the first two orcs were dead, Kikor also looked to see if more orcs might be running up. Seeing none moving through the tall grass, she turned and gave chase to the small number of orcs that were now chasing Birkita, catching up to them easily.

One of the orcs giving chase watched the lead elf running away, taunting him. When he had finally had enough, he pulled out a small throwing axe and, in one quick motion, threw it as hard as he could, hoping it would find its mark. Then he ran after the axe as it flew through the air towards the blond elf.

Kikor watched with wide eyes as the orc threw its axe, cursing that she hadn't killed those orcs earlier. She ran as fast as she could past the orc that moments before had thrown the axe. Ducking to let the axe to miss her, she quickly turned to face a slower orc trying to chase Birkita, and with a quick strike of her sword, she took out one of the orc's legs causing it to fall over heavily into the soft growth on the ground, screaming in pain and yelling orcish curses.

Birkita paused in her run, hearing the orcs' screams of pain, which made her smile. Thinking that Kikor had done the job for the moment, Birkita turned around to see the last remaining orc fall, but just as she did so, the small axe that had been thrown a few moments before struck her hard in the chest. Instantly Birkita was thrown back hard to the ground, causing her breath to be pushed out hard from the force of the hit. She stared at the dark skies above her, blinking hard as she mouthed her surprise and her vision turned dark.

Kikor ran over and, in a quick motion, took her blade's edge and cut the neck of the orc, quickly silencing it. She screamed her friend's name and ran up to where Birkita's body lay.

"Birkitaaaa!!!"

As she ran up, falling to her knees, she knew that Birkita probably wasn't alive. The axe had struck her hard in the center of her chest, instantly killing the elf. Kikor's eyes watered quickly as she cradled her friend in her arms, crying loudly as she did. She couldn't believe that Birkita, a friend she felt closer to than any other in this adventure besides Kalion, was gone. As the rain came down and cascaded over her face, Kikor vowed that all orcs would pay for her death as she watched the ring of stones far away, seeing her enemy cheering its victory there.

As the rest of the group stumbled through the tall grass, grunting hard from the uneven ground, Chansor, who had stopped to grab a pack that had fallen on the ground, heard Kikor's scream echo not far away.

"Birkita ... Kikor ... hey, everyone ... come help me!" he screamed, dropping the pack and running back.

As the others heard him yell back, Kalion, who was directing the group from the front to follow a dried stream bed that would be easier for them to escape through, stopped what he was doing to run back. Quickly, the rest did the same.

As the group burst out of the grass, they saw Kikor cradling Birkita in her arms. Gasps and moans erupted from the group as Amlora checked on their friend to confirm that she had passed.

The others in the group slowly gathered around. The rain let up suddenly as Kikor held her friend's head in her chest, whispering an old elven prayer that she knew Birkita might laugh at but would love at the same time. Not wanting to leave Birkita but knowing they had to get into the city before they were discovered, she looked up at the others.

"I'll carry her, Kikor!" Bennak reached down and picked up Birkita as Kikor looked to the east towards the mountain and noticed Birkita's bow stave lying near some small bushes. Standing up slightly and grabbing the bow stave, she pulled it around her body as her eyes became wet from her tears, her body already soaking wet from the rain. She finally noticed that the rain, which had been coming down for a long time, had now completely stopped.

Chapter Ten

*N*iallee stood, looking through the bushes to see the walls of Bru Edin before them. The journey from that stone circle had taken a major toll on their group, even though it had been a short distance. Bennak still carried Birkita's body without saying a word to the others. The loss of Birkita had caused all to make this part of the journey silently, as each thought about the losses they had suffered so far.

Whelor reflected on the time the group had first met and Birkita had come up and introduced herself to the group around the campfire. He thought, *She seemed so strong and independent. How could we have lost her so soon?* He considered this and remembered times along the trail when she had laughed at something Chansor had done or comforted Whelor when he had returned, never questioning where he had been, just offering comfort. She had told him once, "I know something is up with you. You have a secret." Putting a hand up to stop him from saying anything, she continued, "Whatever it is, when you are ready to tell us, we will listen and not judge." He remembered her putting a hand on his shoulder, smiling and then walking away, not waiting for him to say anything else. He considered his secret, wishing he knew what was happening to himself and wishing he had spoken to her about his problems before.

Kalion, who led the group, again moved through the grass with a tight face, being both sad at Birkita's death and angry that this journey was taking so long. He also considered the path they were on and the friends he had made as he led the group quietly to the secret pathway that led under the city walls, the one only he and a few other rangers knew about.

This passageway was used sometimes by the council at Bru Edin to get messages into and out of the city without having to bother with the guards.

As Kalion passed a corner, he reflected on the time he had brought Shermee on one of these missions, sneaking her out of the castle so her father would not know. He recalled how she had gone once on a diplomatic trip with her entire family years before for a summit with the Empire in the south and how she had begged him to show her the massive fortress.

She had a way of getting anything she wanted from him. Luckily, he had been able to convince her that going to Bru Edin would be noticed by her father and probably by others since it was at least a normal week's travel away. As the others quietly walked past where he stood, not wanting to bother him as he thought, he stared into the corner, thinking of her. He thought, *She has to be ok, and I will find her.* Then he stopped and looked at the others in his group and wondered, *What would they think if they knew why I was really on this mission?* He looked over to see Jebba and Amlora walking together. Jebba was leaning on her slightly, as he had injured himself by tripping over a tree root not long after they had discovered Birkita.

Amlora looked over at Harbin on his flying bed roll. He had also been injured during the battle, but no one had known about it as they left the stone circle. As the group slowly snuck under the wall, Amlora checked on each member of the team as they passed her. The mage smiled slightly, telling her it was only minor and that it could wait. However, just as he passed her, he groaned and quickly fell over. Running up to grab the mage before he could fall off the rug, Amlora found that the wound was very bad, indeed, and that he had lost a lot of blood. She did everything in her power to stay the bleeding. However, as she now looked over at him lying there on the bed roll, she worried that it was not enough.

As she considered how far away help might be, Chansor, who had been leaning nearby, cursed as he stepped on his ankle again, sending a shooting pain up his leg and causing him to lean even more on the wall just as Jebba walked by, believing he didn't need the woman's help now. Jebba's mood had darkened since the loss of Birkita, but no more than anyone else's. It did not help that he had injured himself by not watching where he was going.

Kikor was not doing well either. Her hard run to escape from the orcs and the loss of her friend were straining her body and her soul. Her body had taken a beating, suffering many cuts and bruises, but her mood was far worse, for as they continued down the trail, she thought deeply about her friend and the many talks they had had. She looked over at Bennak, who was still carrying Birkita's body, and thanked the gods they had not left her behind. She also considered in her dark mood how close they were to Bru Edin now and hoped it would provide them safety.

The group had not encountered orcs for a while on their journey to Bru Edin. However, as the walls of the city loomed before them, they soon heard the sounds of metal and horse hooves clapping near them. Before they could hide, a horse patrol from Bru Edin burst out of the grass and came towards the group.

"Cavalry!" Jebba screamed, pulling his bloody sword out as Kikor, with tear-covered eyes, pulled hers out as well. The group quickly stopped to confront what was coming at them.

"It's, ok, my friends. They're on our side!" Kalion declared, smiling and signaling to them as he stepped to the front of the group. He watched them rein their horses towards him and gallop over, pointing their spears at him as he sheathed his own sword, showing that he wasn't a threat to them. He motioned to the others to do the same.

"Wa 'ou dou'g 'ear ra'gr?" one of the cavalrymen asked as he jumped off his own horse and walked over to stand in front of Kalion. As the cavalryman looked Kalion over, he saw black and red blood crusted all over the ranger's armor and clothes.

"I'm from Brigin'i, sir," Kalion began. "I have people within my group who are in need of help, and I need to get them to your castle." Kalion pointed behind him to the rest of the group.

"Wounded, huh? ... Why are you out here when the orcs are about?" another warrior asked from on top his horse. He hushed when the one standing raised his hand to quiet him.

"Aye ... and do you know, lad, that this field is covered in orc patrols?" he asked, placing his sword back into its sheath.

"Yes, we are very aware of that, sir; we have encountered a very large group along the trail from Brigin'i. Is there a way we can discuss this more inside the walls, maybe? My friends need attention." Kalion waved his hand to show the riders his companions again as he looked at the six horsemen staring back down at him.

After looking over the group, the lead rider turned to his second, ordering him to go to the castle and inform them of the news of finding the group. The second stood, looking at Kalion just a moment longer. Then, turning his mount around and kicking it hard, the man rode off without a word.

"So let's see to yea friends, ra'gr," the rider stated, smiling as he walked past Kalion to look at the group.

"Luckily orckind doesn't venture here for some reason. We heard from prisoners that they find this grove area haunting or something," the man said, smiling at Kalion like it was a joke that orcs were scared of something like the dark.

Kalion slightly smiled upon hearing that orcs didn't venture into this area, and he watched his friends become more comfortable now.

Meradoth pulled his hood back as the rider walked up. Meradoth reached out and shook the man's hand as the mage coughed a little to clear his throat.

"When I arrived at Bru Edin, the place was preparing for a siege, but they added patrols with men and arms, I see. Are your leaders believing that the armies of orcs that were to the west were the only numbers they were facing and the city was not ready?" he asked through a scratchy voice.

The man shut his mouth tightly and stared back at the mage before stating, "The orcs made a surprise attack last night. The orcs and their allies moving out of the south and east took the village that lay just outside the walls of the fortress, ransacking it and killing most who lived within it before we could counter them and get them to retreat."

Kalion saw a few of the riders shift in their saddles upon hearing of the killing, making him understand that a few here must have lost friends or family. Looking back up at the rider, he listened as the man continued.

"They came in hard, bringing with them large numbers. Many of our people were stuck outside without help, as the gates were closed before they could get inside. They were trapped and were ... were killed."

"How many are there in your group?" one of the others asked, seeing Holan move out of the high grass and appear shocked to suddenly see horsemen.

Kalion looked up at the man who asked the question and said, "Fewer than we started with."

One of the men moved up to Bennak, who was still carrying Birkita's body. When the man quietly asked if he could help, Bennak pushed him away, saying, "I got her."

"Currently we have twelve in our party," Kalion said, quickly looking back like everyone else as they heard screams of orcs out in the distance, all knowing that the orcs were moving closer each moment. The patrol riders shifted again in their saddles as Kalion continued, "I think we best get inside the walls."

"Agreed. Get your wounded onto the horses, and the rest of you continue moving down this trail. You're within the border of the fortress, my friends. You're safe." The rider walked over to his horse, pulling himself up in one quick jump as his companions pulled up those in the group who needed help.

The riders turned their mounts and the group followed

the cavalry patrol while Kalion, looking around at the group that walked with him, blew out a breath of relief, as finally they would be able to rest and get well. As he looked at Whelor's face, Kalion saw something different in the man — fury, or madness maybe? — something that made the man look different from how he appeared not long before ... something Kalion didn't have time to talk to him about, for they needed to keep moving into the city.

* * *

The black-winged creature flew steadily over the large, dark castle that lay below. No scream came from the animal. There was no sound except from the wind being made by its large wings. Chenush sat on its back and motioned for the creature to land in the large courtyard that at that moment was still full of orcs and goblins practicing.

As the bat-like creature with long leathery wings flapped hard, coming into view, it screamed at the orcs and others on the ground to get out of its way and fast as it landed, taking out a few orcs that were too slow to move. In one motion Chenush jumped down from his saddle, patting the creature's head as he walked past. Then he strode over, walking past the scared orcs and other creatures, many kneeling as he passed them, to the entrance, where his master was attending to matters of the army.

Chenush walked up the stairs, passing a few sentries and guards who stood, protecting their leader. Seeing what was coming towards them, they fell to their knees, quickly squirming and hoping he wouldn't harm them as a pain within their minds erupted suddenly. Seeing their weakness as he passed them only made him stronger. Slowly each rose up a moment later as the pain they were feeling disappeared, leaving them feeling weak. Each wondered what that thing was that had just moved by them.

As Chenush moved through the corridors, orders were issued quickly, and soon the hallways were cleared of any guards.

He ascended the stairs and moved down the hallway. Seeing where he needed to enter, he pushed the massive doors and walked into Methnorick's chambers.

As the doors opened, Methnorick himself was standing over a large table, observing a large map. Looking up, thinking some stupid orc was intruding, he quickly smiled when Chenush moved into the room. Methnorick motioned for Chenush to approach him.

Bowing his head slightly, Chenush said, "I have the greatest of news to report to you, Master!" His voice sent shivers up Methnorick's back from the excitement at the prospect of hearing anything good. These creatures always made him smile; he loved how they sent fear to those they were near. He knew they fed off fear and strong emotions, and he considered the moment that he had enlisted the help of the vampires, knowing it was worth everything to have them at his side.

Smiling, he said, "Hmm, and what news do you bring, my friend?" Even though his spies had already told him this message, the vampire would confirm everything now.

"As you are aware, Brigin'i City has fallen, my lord. All humans captured have been taken care of. A few defenders left have either scattered to the forests or were massacred trying to get away." The news made Methnorick forget every fear he had as he almost laughed out loud, looking down at the map and staring at the dot that represented Brigin'i City.

"Ha! Dia, you thought your city would protect you in the end. My armies have proven that ..." Looking back at the creature, he asked, "What of Dia, my friend? Have you seen what became of him ... and Baron Parnland?"

"No, my lord. Though small parts in Brigin'i Castle are still holding out, they are being quickly squashed as we speak, I would believe, knowing Kaligor's mind. And the last word was that the baron was moving the prisoner through some secret tunnels under the city and they are now making their way east."

Turning back over to the table and the map, Methnorick

leaned over and traced the movement it displayed to confirm where his armies were. Not looking up, Methnorick whispered, "The queen ... what of Shermeena? Is she also a prisoner?" He pointed at a mark that represented another army, thinking to himself that this army should not be there as he waited for the answer.

"I have plans to use her, along with Dia, in my battles beyond!" Methnorick quietly stated, looking at the ancient creature standing before him.

"The queen, my lord ... was killed by the baron's men. How, I know not, but she was. My spy confirmed that her body was left within the castle's private chambers used by her." Chenush stopped and waited for Methnorick to respond to the news.

Quickly, the dark lord slammed his fist hard on the map and table, causing it to groan.

"Why was the queen killed? That stupid fat baron was told not to do any harm to that family." Methnorick had plans for both Dia and Queen Shermeena. He also had plans to marry and use Dia's daughter, Shermee, as part of his plans that led south. At least he knew the princess was on her way to him now as he looked up at the vampire who stared back, not moving.

"Where is the princess now?" he rasped, slamming his fists hard on the table again, making it crack. His eyes poured over the map, and then he looked at Chenush again for an answer.

"I believe they have boarded the ship in Blath 'Na and are on their way here, sir," Chenush responded, not fearing the man who stood before him.

Methnorick was unusual, Chenush had found. All men, elves and other creatures feared Chenush ... but not Methnorick. He stood toe to toe with the creature that had lived longer than anything that stood on the Black Isle ... and that made Chenush wonder.

Chapter Eleven

A number of the group members rested quietly in the large room on the soft beds provided by the high council that ruled Bru Edin. Kalion had slept well that night, and as he lay there in bed, he kept thinking of the news he had been told as they approached the fortress gates. A gate captain named Captain PoPicor told the group when asked that the princess had not been seen within the lands of Bru Edin but that movement of orc armies could be seen as far as the Edla Forest, which lay maybe ten miles southwest of the Edin Plains. He continued to explain that an even larger army of the creatures was at least three to five days east and moving fast with large numbers. Kalion considered this army as he lay there now. *These must be the ones that we heard attacked Brigin'i,* he thought.

The captain told Kalion that orc raids from the south had destroyed almost everything on the fields lying beyond the castle, but somehow as the team had come through the city, the people seemed positive, as if nothing were going on outside their walls. So far the orc raiders had only attacked the walls' defenses with minor skirmishes; the city even left one gate open, which was the gate the team had come through. This seemed very unusual to Kalion. *Why haven't the orcs attacked in full force? What are they waiting for?* he wondered to himself as he lay there holding his hands together over his chest.

He had also been told that so far every town, village, hamlet and other settlement had been destroyed by these raiders. When a band of hill elves, believing that they were next, tried to attack the orcs, the orcs had been able to stop the elves by using the villagers captured in their raids as shields until they were dead and then throwing them to the ground to be trampled over as the orcs marched on.

He heard the rumors spread throughout the fortress that humans were being used for food as well. Kalion couldn't believe how much the lands were turning upside down as he closed his eyes to sleep.

When he woke up a while later, Kalion raised himself up in his bed and leaned back against the wall. He continued to think about this new turn of events and what this meant for their mission. Would the others want to stay and help out here and fight with the people of Bru Edin or continue on? Especially after losing Winsto, Zahnz and now Birkita, the ranger didn't know what they were thinking.

Jebba was stable after receiving the help of a cleric but was still in need of rest. Whelor and Bennak just needed a good cleaning, according to a few ladies who cared for the group.

It was Hrliger who was in the most need of the clerics. His leg wound was deep, and it took many of them to care for the gnome. The clerics having taken him to another room, the others worried about him as they fell asleep from exhaustion.

After thinking for a while, Kalion decided just to quietly walk outside for a breath of fresh air. As he walked away, he failed to notice a shadow move away from the beds and follow the ranger out of the room.

Kalion walked down the hallway, looking at some of the artwork that was on the wall and admiring how the artist imagined the lands around Bru Edin. He continued down some stairs to a small courtyard. As it had started to rain, he walked over and leaned against a wall with a small awning covered in beautiful greengage. Even though he was just wearing a robe and trousers, not his usual leather jacket and gloves, having taken them to be cleaned by someone, at least he had pulled his boots on. He was a bit cold as the rain slowly dropped down, but Kalion still liked it. The air was good to breathe, and that was all he cared about at that moment.

After a little while, Kalion realized he had his smoking pipe in a pocket, so pulling it out and lighting it up, he closed his eyes to relax for a few moments and think.

Kalion began to think of the best course of action and the right plan to ensure the quest group continued on in their search for the princess of Brigin'i. As he considered the options the team could come up with that would delay this course of action, he thought of ways to counter anything they would come up with.

Going back west to Brigin'i was out of the question now. The orcs were by now covering the western forests and glens between Bru Edin and the city. He could easily dissuade that course. And who knew if the populace of Brigin'i was still alive? Was Dia alive? Staying and helping Bru Edin, however, would take a bit more convincing, especially since the promise of riches from King Dia was now in question too. He had to find a way to assure them that the promise still held. He knew that the group still questioned the information that the orc had given them, but he wondered if any convincing would work.

"I must try!" he said to himself.

Then he considered that, once he had them completely on his side again, he would have to decide in which direction they needed to travel. The mountains in the north were under Frost Giant control. Even though Kalion knew that Dia had made a treaty many cycles ago with the large creatures (there had even been one within the games — he remembered seeing the massive creature walking the streets of Brigin'i), the treaty between Dia and the white giants was shaky and could break anytime. Plus going through the mountains would be treacherous climbing and take more time, and he was sure the princess wouldn't have been taken that way.

Going south was certainly way out of the question for them now with the news he'd heard recently about armies being seen coming from that direction. So that left moving east, which was the easiest way, of course, to the coastline, and according to the most recent information they had received, the princess was still heading towards Blath 'Na City. So that was the way he intended to go until he heard differently.

Earlier he had asked the command here at Bru Edin to send word to Blath 'Na to see if anyone matching her description had been seen. No word had come back to the Bru Edin commander as to whether they knew of any sightings of her in Blath 'Na or along the road leading there. Probably not. Kalion smirked at that thought, but he had to continue to try. Whoever took the girl had been doing a good job of keeping themselves low and unseen by anyone.

Making their way along the Great North Road and then proceeding up it to Blath 'Na would be the fastest way to travel. However, considering what they had encountered so far in their journey just from Brigin'i, to here, traveling along open roads was not their best option.

Then it hit him as he drew in a breath from his pipe. The dwarven kingdom of Chai'sell: he knew traveling through it would cut maybe four days of travel, bringing them right to the edge of the elven high kingdom of Fuunidor, which lay at the easternmost spur of the mountain range surrounding the Edin Plains in the north and just outside of the border of Blath 'Na's region.

The only thing though that bothered the ranger was a rumor he had just heard from a cleric that Chai'sell's gates were open and no sign or word had come out of it for days now. This was unusual for the dwarves, but the thought of traveling through Chai'sell to get to Blath 'Na sooner made the thought of going there enticing.

He opened his eyes quickly and came back from his deep thoughts when he heard a slight scuffle to his right. Kalion scanned the courtyard around him, but not seeing anything, he closed his eyes again and kept thinking of their travel plans, taking a small puff of smoke from his father's pipe to keep him awake in the cold.

When he heard the sound again, he opened his eyes, slower this time, and looked around slowly, squinting in the moonlight as best he could to see where the sound might be coming from. Then he saw something move off to his right and go down an alleyway away from him. Kalion got the sense that he knew this person but didn't know why he was there, so knocking his pipe against the wall to put it out, he decided he needed to find out who this shadow was.

He walked over to the alleyway slowly as he stuffed his pipe away and peered around the last corner. At first he didn't see any movement, but then he saw the shadow again move past a doorway out of the corner of his eye and continue down the small walkway. As quietly as he could, he gritted his teeth and moved around the corner and towards a hallway.

Coming around a corner, Kalion was watching where he placed his feet as he made his way down the alleyway and onto the small walkway at the end. Still watching for the shadow but only seeing an actual form once, Kalion squinted hard to make out who or what it might be.

When he got to a doorway, he ducked in quickly and peered slowly around the edge to watch as the form disappeared into a corner and then walked under a torch that hung under a large doorway. What he saw didn't surprise him much: a small figure, maybe a child or even a gnome, but a form he knew. As he looked closer, he shook his head slightly as he saw that it was Chansor. Not wanting to talk to the boy, Kalion stepped out of the doorway and continued following Chansor to see what he was up to.

Trying to stay in the shadows as he walked what seemed like several streets, Kalion finally saw Chansor come to a building that held no torch light within it. Stopping at a doorway, he leaned back against it and observed Chansor's movement as he began to feel something coming from the building.

The thief had walked up to the door to knock on it quietly, and it quickly opened. No light came out through the open door, and this puzzled Kalion even more. Then he looked around as he discovered something else. There were no guards, no foot patrols, no one walking around like he had seen before. The city fortress seemed to have gone quiet, at least here.

Interesting, Kalion thought to himself. He stood in the shadows, watching the building and looking for any sign of what it might be, when he saw behind him down the road a foot patrol walking by finally. The two warriors were talking to each other quietly; one was holding a torch to give them light, not noticing the movement to their left as Kalion made his way up to them.

"You there ..." Kalion whispered. Both jumped a bit at the sound of the ranger's voice. Turning to look his way, they saw a man in robes standing half in the shadow of the doorway, his hand raised up showing he meant no harm.

"Sir ... what are you doing out here at this wee hour?" the older of the two warriors asked as he stepped closer to Kalion.

Kalion looked back towards the dark building and motioned the warriors to be quiet as he walked around the corner to hide himself. "I was having a smoke when I heard something and had to follow it. You know who I am, right?" Both nodded slightly in the affirmative. "Tell me about that building if you can." Kalion motioned to the building he had just seen Chansor go into.

Both warriors peered around the corner and saw what the ranger was talking about. The older turned back with a slight smile to confirm he knew the building that Kalion was talking about.

"That's the thieves' house, known around here as 'the Hole.' Why? You're not thinking of going in there, my lord, are you? The council says they serve a purpose for our city, so we do not interfere in their daily business. They respect the council's orders and stay in for the night, unlike you, sir."

The image of Chansor popped into Kalion's mind and gave him more questions. "Thieves, you say? Well that explains a bit," he whispered.

He peered around the corner again and watched the building for a moment. Leaning back against the wall, he took in a deep breath and then looked over to the sentries.

"I thank you, friends, for the information about that place." He nodded and then walked around the corner as quietly as he could. The two watched the man, their mouths open, about to ask him why he was out, but then they shook their heads and pulled their cloaks in from the cold rain falling on them both as they continued on their patrol, moving away from where they knew Kalion was going.

Kalion meanwhile had moved down the street, staying in the shadows that he noticed now were darker than before and even seemed to be moving with him. He stopped to step inside a doorway of what used to be a warehouse of some kind and watched the shadows for a moment. Then he looked at the thieves' house to see if he could see anything. He could see nothing moving in the windows or around the building, but the shadows seemed to keep moving slightly even though the moon wasn't, which confused the ranger.

As he squinted to see what he could, he started to get a funny feeling inside. He leaned back to hide in the doorway and steady himself, but the feeling kept getting worse. He didn't know what was happening until his legs started to feel weak and he collapsed to his knees.

"Oh, gods ..." was all that came out of his mouth as suddenly his whole body slumped down and he fell into the street. His vision started to fog up, but just when he was about to pass out, he saw a figure walk up and stand over him.

Blinking his eyes, trying not to pass out, he tried to see who it was. Hearing the figure laugh quietly down at him, he opened his eyes one last time and saw who it was.

"You!" Kalion shouted and then quickly slumped down onto the ground and fell into a deep sleep as the figure bent down and picked up Kalion's body. Turning around, the figure walked back towards the thieves' house, walking through the front door and disappearing as it closed behind him.

* * *

Captain PoPicor stood along the wall that surrounded Bru

Edin, watching the fields beyond and the forest and observing the campfires of the raiders now surrounding most of the city.

Being a warrior of some 30 summers, he was an experienced member of Bru Edin's army. He knew what was coming towards them, for he had fought against these creatures for most of his life. However, he had not seen orcs in a number of cycles, so seeing them now made him wonder. Many of his men were new and young, so they were scared. He both saw and heard the fear in their voices when they spoke and when they moved around him.

A few last patrols that had been sent out before the gates had closed returned and reported that the fields, hills and roads were littered with burnt bodies, tortured prisoners and destruction. From the smoke PoPicor could just make out in the far distance, rising out of the forests in the south, he knew more orc reinforcements were closer than many thought. Letting out a long breath, Po knew things were not the best.

Walking around the floor of the tower that stood along the wall, he turned when he heard the footsteps of armored feet coming up behind him. He nodded as the soldier came up, huffing from the hard walk up the stairs. The young man took a breath and blew it out hard for a moment and then walked over and placed his bow and spear against the wall. Taking in a drink of water from the pouch that hung from the ceiling, he turned, saying, "I am sorry, sir, that I am late."

"You are actually right on time. It is a good thing you ran." He smiled at the young man, trying to calm the nervousness Po could hear in the man's voice.

The soldier smiled back and walked over to stand next to the wall and look out the window. The sun to his right was going down, so the landscape was creating shadows that made it a bit hard for him to see. He looked over the woods and the fields beyond and saw nothing except a few birds flying over them and the campfires. So far he saw that it was still peaceful and silent, and he smiled at that thought.

Seeing the young man smile, Po-Picor said, "Do not let the silence make you think that the orcs are not preparing for an all-out attack, my lad." The young man turned upon hearing Po-Picor's voice.

"What do you know, sir?" The voice was a bit shaky. Walking up, Po-Picor smiled, placing his hand on the shoulder of the young man.

"There is smoke beyond the forest, and a group of warriors brought in by our cavalry out on patrol earlier spoke of heavy orc movement coming in from the west and south. The minor skirmishes we have had are nothing compared to what I believe might be coming." Po-Picor looked out over the other's shoulder when he thought he saw movement at the base of a massive tree but blinked it away as he saw that it was a deer moving along the edge, probably trying to get away from what was coming.

The boy gulped roughly as they looked out. His face showed it: he was scared to death. Po-Picor's grip on his shoulder made him feel a bit better though. The captain knew what he was doing, and the boy was sure that Po-Picor would protect him and the others as best as he could.

They stood like that for a while, looking south at the campfires of the orcs below. Their voices echoed up to the warriors patrolling the wall nearby, making everyone inside nervous upon hearing Po's words about what had been seen.

As darkness covered the tower, the young man went over to start a fire that was used to keep the sentries warm during the cold night, but Po-Picor ordered him not to do it. Whispering, Po-Picor pointed out that he could see orcs moving out and along the edge of the forest now.

"I do not want them to see us moving along the wall if I can help it!" he whispered, pointing to the boy's armor. The boy nodded and moved as quietly as he could in the armor around the pillar to see what the captain could see.

Looking out, he saw that, indeed, his captain was right. He

could just make out three large orcs moving along the edge of the forest, looking around themselves — for what, he couldn't tell. None of them carried a torch or light of any kind, but they were armed very well. Each held horrible-looking spears and shields as well as some type of weird-looking sword. The orcs' armor wasn't as good as theirs, but it was good enough, the boy thought. Just seeing these orcs for the first time in his life made the young man shake a little again.

Po saw the young man shaking and whispered, "They looked like a small scavenging patrol and nothing else, so it will be fine as soon as they leave." Seeing the young man heartened by his words, Po-Picor looked out again and watched them, using just one eye to help with his night vision. Scavenging ... these orcs were up to something, and he knew it. Orcs only scavenged after they attacked something. Looking around the woods, he thought he could see a few more orcs hiding behind some heavy bushes and large trees. But these orcs weren't looking for something; they looked like they were waiting for something.

"What are you waiting for?" he said quietly to himself.

The boy quietly asked his captain if he should raise the alarm or go send word to the other towers. Po-Picor said, "No, we will wait. All towers should be on full alert anyway."

Just as the soldier was about to say something, Po-Picor saw what the orcs were up to. He could make out them maneuvering a huge piece of equipment out of the forest edge. It seemed to be a crossbow, but its size was triple that of a normal bow — the size of one a giant would use. Alongside it came two giants pushing it forward.

Just as the captain made out the huge crossbow being pushed, an arrow bolt shot out of it and flew towards their tower with tremendous speed.

Screaming quickly for the boy to get down, Po-Picor threw himself down and away from the wall just as the bolt flew into it. The whole tower shook terribly when the bolt hit the stones, sending shards of rock that were once the wall everywhere. The tower rocked for a while as stones that had held the wall up cracked and slowly began to fall apart, many turning into dust as they fell apart.

The captain, lying on the ground, shook his head to clear it of the explosion. He looked up to find the boy but instead saw along the floor a crack forming from the tremendous hit the tower had just taken. Scrambling up quickly, he saw the boy lying unconscious at the edge of the stairs, so he grabbed the young boy's collar and pulled him down the stairwell.

As he began to pull the boy, his ears picked up loud screams from behind. Letting the boy down, he turned to look out towards the forest and saw what everyone feared but expected: a huge wave of orcs exploding from the forest towards them.

Cursing himself for not sounding an all-out alarm sooner, he saw another two arrow bolts heading towards the tower, so he grabbed the boy's collar again, quickly pulling the young man down the stairs. He even made the boy fall and roll down the last few stairs as the heavy bolts again slammed into the walls around them, making the floor shake so hard that he almost fell over. A few smaller fire arrows shot at the tower flew just past his head to slam into the wall behind him and ricocheted onto the ground.

As he made it to the ground behind the tower, the captain reached out and pulled the large rope that would ring the bell the engineers had placed on each tower many cycles before to alert Bru Edin of attack. He pulled it hard again and again, making it ring as loud as he could. Quickly he heard the echoes of the other towers doing the same as those sentries saw what was moving towards them. As he did this, he screamed orders to men near the tower to get to arms and quickly.

The young man moaned loudly as Po-Picor continued pulling the cord. He turned to look at the boy and saw that he hadn't moved much since the tower had gotten hit moments earlier.

He screamed for the boy to get up and move to the safety of the castle itself, and his concern increased when he saw that the boy still didn't move. Letting go of the bell rope, he ran over and turned the boy over and saw that a large piece of rock had hit the boy in the back of his head. Dark blood was flowing down his neck and into the back of his armor now. He saw that the boy wouldn't make it much longer when the boy's eyes slowly opened up.

"Ca– ... Captain ... I ... I am so ... sorrryy." As he spoke, some blood gurgled out of his mouth, and he started to convulse. Po-Picor tried to calm the boy down, as he could now hear the screams of the orcs outside the walls getting louder and closer.

"May your gods protect you, my boy. I am sorry," he whispered into the boy's ear as the boy's eyes slowly closed for the last time. Shaking his head, thinking that he should have done more, he lowered the boy down as he reached over and grabbed the sword that had fallen out of his hand earlier. Getting up, he knew that they didn't have much of a chance if the orcs moved into the tower, so he would keep them from the tower with everything he had.

"Move, you men. Orcs are approaching!" he screamed loudly, his words matching those of others echoing along the wall.

He moved then to line up forces to repel any orcs attempting to get into the now damaged portion of the tower. As he surveyed the area, looking for the best place to position men, he saw that, even though the tower he was just in stood, it was heavily damaged. He also noticed that a few of these bolts had ropes attached to them, and he was sure orcs were now crawling up the lines toward the tower wall. As he screamed orders to his men to take out the lines before the orcs could reach the wall, the bells rang from the other towers, signaling to the Bru Edin council and the people inside the approaching attack.

He ran over to the edge and saw that no orc had made it to the tower walls yet, but their screams were loud anyway, and he saw their bright torches illuminating their ugly faces under their black cloaks as they got close to the tower edge, running hard out of the forest beyond.

Cursing again, Po looked over the field quickly to see what

126

must have been hundreds upon hundreds of orcs moving quickly towards the walls as their arrows dropped out of the sky onto the Bru Edin defenders. He saw his men were losing, as several lay on the ground, killed by arrows as they moved to repel the orcs. He knew that he had to get those lines released, so he jumped up and screamed as loud as he could with sword drawn to hack at the lines, releasing the orcs to fall to their deaths.

* * *

Screams erupted around the wagon as it moved down the crowded road, bouncing hard as it rolled over those caught by its wheels. The driver maneuvered it towards the pier, where he knew their ship waited for them.

Inside the wagon Princess Shermee, her hands still tied in front of her but her mouth not gagged this time, sat across from Quinor. Both held onto the walls, trying not to fall over as the wagon bounced along the road.

Quinor looked over at the princess, amazed at her composure. He had thought she was a spoiled king's daughter, but she didn't seem bothered by the screams outside or the movement of the wagon. Instead, she sat there staring back at him with eyes filled with hate and anger.

Since leaving the warehouse an hour before when the word came that the city was going to fall and that the ship was ready to depart, she had been quiet, which made Quinor a bit nervous, for he wondered what she was plotting, if she was, of course. Even though he thought he knew her, he wasn't taking any chances. Hence, her hands were still tied. His companions had grabbed her and placed her back into the wagon when it was time to leave. Quinor jumped in and closed the door as the driver jumped up and grabbed the whip to move the four horses. The other men in the warehouse ran over and pulled the warehouse's giant doors open, letting the screams outside echo in

As the wagon moved out of the warehouse, Quinor heard the men opening the door screaming to those beyond to get out of the way. More moans and screams came back from outside the wagon, begging to be let in, so he pulled out his short sword in case any tried to get in. The wagon didn't stop as the sides echoed with what sounded like scraping — like nails of animals scraping to get in. The pounding and the screams of the helpless finally made the girl wince.

Quinor was about to ask the driver what was going on when he looked outside the small window and got his answer. Whatever had made it to the middle of the city was now scrapping to get inside of his wagon. Luckily they did not have the mobility to grab onto the wagon as it quickly sped past, keeping those inside and on top safe.

The driver outside, earlier having seen his companions die as the creatures surrounded them, cracked his whip hard, yelling for his beasts to move and get the wagon out onto the road quickly, even though it was filled with undying creatures and the populace trying to get away now. He rolled over them as they tried to get at him or grab the horses, maneuvering the wagon down the road and towards the port that lay to the east. He quickly got away from them, clearing the road as the horses pulled the wagon hard.

He got to a main road that was crowded now with the people of Blath 'Na trying to get to the port, but he didn't stop and soon ran over them, as he knew he was on a mission that couldn't wait. A few jumped onto the wagon to get away, but Quinor, getting himself outside quickly, was able to dispose of those trying to get a free ride from him.

"Don't stop for anything!" he screamed to the driver, who only nodded back as he whipped the horses again to get them to move faster.

Leaning back in, Quinor breathed out as he saw his prisoner look at him sternly. "You know we cannot stop, Princess. If we do, we won't make it out of this dying city," Quinor said quietly, making Shermee squint a little at him.

"Did you have anything to do with what is going on outside?" Hearing her finally say something surprised him. He noted her voice, so soft and almost beautiful, like the voice of the daughter he had lost so many cycles earlier.

Shaking his head, he answered, "No, but I have a good idea who brought it here." He grabbed the wall as the wagon rolled over a large man outside, making him scream in pain.

"Methnorick?" she said with hate in her words. Quinor nodded back as he remembered meeting with Methnorick's spokesmen months earlier, who told him that the dark man was using something called technology.

"And this is the man I am being taken to marry?" Shermee asked, trying to hold on herself as the wagon lurched everywhere and trying not to hear the screams outside as the driver continued to whip the horses forward. "Why would he do this?" she asked Quinor.

Shaking his head, Quinor breathed in a huge breath and looked directly at the girl. "I know not. He has his reasons for everything that happens. Methnorick is all about the old magic, so I would guess it has something to do with that."

"What magic?"

Swallowing, Quinor was puzzled by her question at first, but then he remembered that many did not know the true history of magic. "Do you not know where the mages, the clerics, and the druids get their powers from?"

Just then the wagon ran over something large, making both hit their heads on the ceiling as they bounced hard into it. They both groaned loudly as the driver yelled outside that they were at the port and he could see the ship.

Quinor looked at the princess, who was rubbing her head with her tied-up hands as the wagon lurched hard and stopped. As he moved to open the door, it flung open hard, the driver standing there looking in.

"Come. ... Hurry, before the people get here and take our boat," he said as Quinor moved over, grabbing the princess and pulling her outside.

As she was pulled out of the wagon, she looked around, for she remembered her father telling her Blath 'Na City was a massive port city with a circular wall of immense stones that had protected it from outside armies for many cycles, along with huge towers where minds of knowledge worked and lived, houses where many rich and well-off lived, bright-colored banners flying everywhere, and glorious foods and treasures. Now, however, all she saw was chaos and destruction, everything falling apart and burning in the distance. Quinor moved to make her sit down in a small craft, which one of Quinor's men untied. The three other men with her, using oars, maneuvered the boat out into the water.

Smoke rose up into the air like heavy clouds as she could see fires erupting in one part of the city. Each time a fire exploded, she could hear screams as she watched people scrambling to get to the ships that were docked at the piers.

"Gods help them!" she gasped, making Quinor look back and think the same thing as the boat they rowed moved slowly to the black-sailed ship waiting for them.

Chapter Twelve

*D*reams ... dreams ... dreams are good ways for the mind to relax, and it was said that the gods talked to you through dreams. However, some dreams are brought on by the dark or evil gods, and this dream was a terrible one. It spoke of death, torture and a tremendous amount of destruction for the cultures that were around him.

A voice, the voice of someone he knew, spoke to him quietly through his dream, almost reassuring him that things were well and he should not be troubled by the dreams he saw. The voice told him that the orcs, the dark beings and the other creatures he saw, like those that flew in the air, were not what he thought. For some reason he felt more relaxed listening to the voice, though he wondered who or what was speaking to him.

Opening his eyes, he shook his head as the voice spoke to him soothingly, attempting to wake him up. Looking through the fog that lay over his eyes, Kalion shook his head again, trying to bring his senses back.

"Are you well, my friend?" the familiar voice quietly asked him. Kalion rubbed his face and eyes, continuing to try to wake up quickly. Looking around, he saw that he was in a small, dark room with only two candles burning on a small table not far from him. Next to him, though, he could just make out the form of someone sitting there watching him.

"Who ... where am I?" Kalion asked, realizing his voice was dry. "Who speaks to me?" Kalion tried to raise himself up, swinging his legs around so he could sit up. It was hard, as his head was still foggy when he tried it, so he gave up for the moment. Looking over to the figure sitting nearby, he could just make out a smile looking back at him underneath a hood.

"You are fine, friend. Here you are well and cannot be harmed."

Kalion searched through his memory quickly for whose voice it could be. When it came to him, he looked directly at the covered face with a surprised look. "Harbin?"

He saw a smile form under the hood, and then the figure nodded as his hands came up and pulled back the hood, showing the mage's face. Kalion looked around when he saw the mage's face. "What ... what happened? Why am I here, friend?" he asked again, having a little trouble speaking with a dry throat. The mage laughed quietly at his question.

"What is so funny, mage? I left that room with you sleeping in it, and now you are here. What are you playing at?" Kalion's voice rose slightly from the anger he felt.

Seeing no response from Harbin, Kalion continued, "Are you the one who knocked me out?" The questions were pouring out of Kalion's mind and only stopped when Harbin raised a hand to quiet the ranger.

"I will tell you what happened, my friend, but first, drink something. I believe you need it." Harbin waved his hand at the table in front of him, which was instantly covered with a cloth, a candle and a goblet of wine. Kalion looked at the table and then back to the mage with a look of concern.

Smiling, Harbin understood Kalion's hesitation, so Harbin lifted his other arm and opened his hand. The goblet in front of Kalion flew slowly towards Harbin and into his hand. Taking a drink, Harbin nodded to show that nothing was poisoned and that it would not hurt the ranger.

"You have ... you are more powerful than I thought, Harbin," Kalion whispered as he reached out and took the goblet with wine to soothe his dry throat, but with hesitation.

Hearing the comment, Harbin finished his wine and then leaned back against the wall, staring at the ranger.

"When I fell asleep tonight, I traveled within my mind to Blath 'Na City, where I was surprised."

Kalion gave the mage a questioning glance and then said, "Interesting ... and what did you find in the City of Ports?" Harbin raised a hand, letting the ranger know he needed to speak as he leaned closer.

"I found it in disarray, Kalion. That city was being attacked. By what, I couldn't tell, but many of its citizens were escaping by sea, and many were dying trying to escape whatever was attacking it." Harbin spoke quietly as Kalion stared at him.

The ranger stared at the mage as he remembered Blath 'Na City, its huge walls, and its massive army of cavalry and warriors. Hearing the mage speak of it being almost a shattered form of what it had been before made him hesitate slightly and lean his head back.

"Outside its walls ... well, let's just say that nothing alive walks there. I saw it, my friend. Believe me." Harbin took a drink from the goblet and then continued. Kalion couldn't believe what he was hearing, but he let the mage finish.

"Harbin, you talk as if this were really happening. Did you talk to any leaders of the city or its people?" Kalion asked, not being pulled into Harbin's story. He knew that Harbin was powerful and he could do amazing things, so hearing that he could move his mind from one place to another was not really a surprise to the ranger.

"Their leaders ... let's just say that city no longer has leaders. Those I did try to speak to did not know who or what it was that was attacking them, but they spoke of heavy losses to their people and stated that they were rising after dying."

"How many?" Kalion asked.

"I could not give a number or percentage, but many of their people have been killed. Those who die seem to come back — alive in some way — and attack those around them. Many buildings and a few cleric towers had been destroyed, and even the mages' tower was under siege, as people believed they were places of safety. Many people who were just trying to survive were sabotaging or ransacking everything, trying to find safe places to hide from the danger. Though I believe some were just trying to steal, a larger portion of the population was trying to get to the port to escape."

As Kalion listened, he believed what he was hearing and knew that things were worse than King Dia could ever have thought when he had spoken to the ranger before he left. The whole of the north seemed to be imploding.

As Kalion tried to come up with a way to put it all together, Harbin spoke of large fleets of ships coming from the eastern seas that he believed had to be Methnorick's.

Kalion's hope that the team might be able to complete the quest began to disappear. "Is there a way you can find out about those ships?"

"Maybe ... but they are very far away, and I can only travel so far from my body. But when I left Blath 'Na, I decided to venture to the one place where mages go to rest and reflect and gain knowledge."

Kalion gave him a questioning look, having never heard of such a place, and asked, "Where would that be?"

Harbin smiled, "I wish I could tell you, but both Meradoth and I are sworn to secrecy and cannot reveal its location, my friend. I am sorry."

Kalion started to ask other questions, but Harbin raised his hand again to quiet him down, seeing that the ranger was starting to get slightly frustrated, as the mage was speaking too slowly of what was happening across the lands which Harbin could see in his eyes.

"I went to this place for a number of reasons. First, to ensure the safety of my kind, but also to determine if what I was seeing was Methnorick's work ... or something beyond even him. What I also found out, Kalion, is that the empire is on the move as well.

So not only are we being attacked from the east but also, I believe, from the south. My superiors felt the movement from the south, as they sometimes can feel emotions, and they felt the anger, sadness and more caused by the armies moving to the gorge and mountains in the south. They were marching east towards the coast and the northern gates."

"What do you mean 'felt movement,' Harbin?" Kalion asked, taking another drink and feeling his voice coming back.

"Well, that is hard to explain, but we can feel a difference in the energy of the world sometimes — kind of like a pulling of our minds. It is hard to explain, but those who lead have more powerful emotions than do those who are led."

Kalion leaned back against the wall and thought of a hundred more questions that came to his mind about everything his friend had just spoken about. *So Bru Edin is becoming surrounded. Brigin'i has fallen, and those armies are moving east towards Bru Edin as we sit here. Who knows what this Methnorick has planned beyond the destruction of the north? Marching south beyond the mountains or taking on the empire maybe? Are they coming to help us or him? If Blath 'Na has truly fallen, the north doesn't have a major port that could hold large ships like those we might need to find the princess if she has left Blath 'Na. But if she is in Blath 'Na, how can we get there quickly to save her if she is stuck there, hidden, trying to escape as well? Or has she already left the City of Ports before this assaulting enemy of death?* Kalion looked over and smiled at his friend.

"Why did you attack me, Harbin?" Kalion lifted a hand to rub his neck where someone or something had hit him earlier, knocking him out.

Harbin gently smiled and nodded his head slightly. Pushing himself up, he got up and walked over to a door behind where the mage was sitting that Kalion just noticed. "I believe there is a spy in the group, Kalion," Harbin said, not turning around. "I found this information while at the sanctuary."

Thinking for a moment, Kalion asked, "Who?" and

135

continued to consider the question. *I know I am not a spy and never have been, even for King Dia. Harbin's abilities have grown. Does he plan to kill me?*

Harbin turned as Kalion moved. "If it was you, my friend, I would have killed you before you woke up, but it was not I who knocked you out. I found you in the alleyway. No, my friend, I know it is not you. You might be the only true warrior in our group. No, it is someone else ... someone I have not found yet."

"How did you find me anyway?" Kalion's question made Harbin grunt a slight laugh. "After I returned to the group earlier from grabbing a pie to eat, I found that you and another were missing, so I used my power to locate you. You both seemed to be in the same location. I came here to find you and Chansor but only found you."

"I saw Chansor go into a thieves' den or house here in the city. I was following him, trying to see where he was going. But how do you know there is a spy?" Kalion asked again.

"Let's say that I just know." Harbin leaned back against the door and crossed his arms, looking at the ranger as both thought about their situation.

Kalion got up and walked to stand opposite his friend. "Harbin, you have left me with a lot of unanswered questions, but I think we need to get back to the group. Let's not speak of the part about the spy around the group until we get more facts, yea?" Kalion put a hand on Harbin's shoulder. Harbin smiled and returned a few quick nods.

Turning around, the mage opened the door, letting in the cool wind from the night's air, and began walking down the cobbled road with Kalion in tow.

Neither spoke, but Kalion looked directly at his friend's head as the ranger continued to think about this news that there was a spy in the group.

Who could it be? ... Why? ... And Harbin, even with all your power, are you telling me lies to gain something?

＊ ＊ ＊

While the two were talking in the small room, outside Chansor peered around the corner of the building, seeing nothing except shadows and mice. Chansor, who knew that Kalion had followed him earlier, had been waiting now for at least an hour. When he left the thieves' house after conducting his business, he walked outside and saw that the ranger was no longer there, but he noticed along the ground a pouch that used to be Kalion's. He had noticed it a long time ago when they first started out on this journey.

The sun, he noticed, was slowly rising above the mountains to the northeast, giving him the ability to see more of the courtyard he was in, but so far there was nothing to see. Not feeling rushed, he put the pouch into his pocket and walked over and leaned against the wall in a dark corner, believing that sooner rather than later his friend would return to get his pouch.

It wasn't long before Chansor saw the ranger leave the building not far away with Harbin. Curious about what the man was doing, he quietly got up himself and quickly left the corner. Using his cat-like thieving abilities, he was able to catch up to the ranger within a few moments.

The three walked down a few roads, and soon Chansor began to recognize that they were returning to where the group was probably still sleeping. He also noticed that neither man had spoken to the other while they walked.

Chansor, being the curious one, thought that was a bit odd since he thought both were friends. But it was nighttime ... or at least morning since he began to hear people waking up from their sleep. A few times he had to dash hard to avoid being drenched by someone's morning pee pot being thrown out of a window. Luckily neither man turned his head to look back. If they had, Chansor might have been seen.

As the two men returned to the house the group was using to recover, Kalion quietly took a slow drink from a goblet of water he found as he thought more about what to do now. "Who might be the spy?" Kalion finally asked out loud, but in a whisper. He saw the mage react to his voice, but it was not a question to Harbin. Leaning over, he grabbed the handle of the blade he carried along his side. Given to him by his father many cycles be-fore, it held his family's emblem along the blade and much more within it

"I know not, my friend, but be warned that there is one traveling with us." At that Harbin turned and walked to go back outside. He opened the door but stopped in the doorway and turned to look back at Kalion. "Know this, Kalion: he or she — whoever they might be — must be found!" Harbin turned back around and took a step forward, only to be quickly stopped when the small figure of Chansor popped in his way.

"What the ... ?" Harbin asked, slightly angered.

"Oh, sorry, Harbin. I ... mmm ... I was just out getting some air ... by the central courtyard ... you know, the one with that huge fountain?" Chansor hoped his lie wouldn't be noticed as Harbin smiled and pushed his way past, leaving the thief and Kalion looking at each other.

Suddenly a soldier appeared in the doorway. "Sirs, you are wanted. Please come with me."

Chapter Thirteen

Bru Edin had always been proud of its army and cavalry, and it showed as the general reflected on how earlier that morning he had watched proudly as his men marched and rode by with proud looks on their faces.

'Who could stop the Mountain Fortress?" many voiced loudly.

Later that morning, Kalion and Meradoth were standing next to General Nafanor, the head of Bru Edin defenses. As he stood there holding the reins of his prized war horse, known by everyone as "Beam," Nafanor saluted his captains who marched by. The general was a large man, his physique reflecting cycles of lifting heavy weapons in battle and pushing war machines on the field of battle. His hair was short, unlike that of most who stood around him; cycles of fighting and the stress of leading had also turned most of his hair white, leaving just a single a black line going down one side, which made it easy for others to find him on the field.

Sitting next to him on his grey mount was his second in command, Marshal Ekror, a cavalryman with over 30 summers of experience riding in the wilds, fighting against orcs and other darker creatures.

Nafanor considered now as he stood in his chambers, looking over the maps of the city with Kalion and Meradoth, the news that Kalion had brought him that Skynburgh had fallen without a survivor. He had also received reports that four border towers had been overtaken; two, he was told, fell without even a fight as all living within were lost in each. His army had never lost a battle before, but this time he was worried. He considered the training he had given his men and knew they were prepared for what was to come, but he was still surprised at the positive nature of his men. Even knowing that heavy orcish war machines had been seen being moved from the west, his men were sure that they would win.

A report lay nearby, so lifting it up, he read that those elves of Levenori, which lay just east of Brigin'i, had been attacked heavily and their forest had been torched. Dagonor Castle, which stood northeast of the Levenori forest, had sent out its army in hopes of countering the orcs' assault on the elves, but no reports had come of what happened to them or the castle until Kalion and his team arrived.

Just then a messenger came running in. A small attack had occurred just outside the wall to the south, and a few goblins had been captured. The goblins revealed that they were there to keep Bru Edin pinned down until the main army moved in.

Considering this information, Nafanor ran back over to the maps of the northern kingdoms and slammed his fist down on the table when he saw what the orcs might be up to.

"Send word to redirect our troops along the walls to the south and west," he commanded, for he saw what he thought might be the plan that the orcs were trying here as well as their overall plan: to divide the north in half.

"Who in all the heavens is commanding those orcs?" he whispered as Kalion and Meradoth spoke quietly in the back to a few captains and leaders, wanting to know information about Brigin'i and what they had seen.

A little while later, a report came to him that wave upon wave of orcs had been seen marching into the small valley that lay between two large hills with watchtowers built so long ago that they had fallen into disuse over time.

The small number of cavalry that Nafanor had placed there retreated quickly when they saw the overwhelming number of orcs moving in. News came that, instead of giving chase, the orcs had just stopped, giving his forces time to make themselves ready.

Since it was built on a mountain, Bru Edin, like any citadel, had many layers of walls for defense and protection. Nafanor was looking at these layers of walls now as he considered that three quarters of his army was out between the second and first layers of the city, waiting for the oncoming army of orcs.

He reread the report that the outer border towers had fallen, which meant that the outer defense of the city had been breached, but this was in keeping with the plans of Bru Edin. The fifth layer was not as strong as the other walls of the city; it was only meant to be a show of force and power, not to hold up a real defense. However, he was concerned about the orcs in the valley and their purpose for being there.

Bru Edin's walls were a system of safety walls that made it hard for an attacking army to just walk in; they would have to work almost through a maze of gates to finally get into the main fortress and city beyond.

He directed over 2,000 warriors to wait just inside the massive gates of Netfor'aden, the main gates of the fortress. He hoped that if it came to it and the outer walls fell, and if the orcs were able to press his army back, these warriors could charge out and repel the orcs. A massive reinforcement of these men would hopefully break their momentum and make the orcs retreat to the southern forests that lay miles away. The cavalry that he had hidden in the north would pinch the retreating orcs by charging around the mountain.

The huge machines were supplied with a large number of rocks and boulders taken from the mountain itself and brought up by clever mechanisms built by gnomes cycles earlier along the innermost walls. Standing next to each machine was a team of gnome engineers and men ready to move as quickly as possible to launch a rock when ordered. Archers were positioned behind the walls and were ordered to assault the orcs as much as possible when the order came.

He knew that all of these plans were based on what the orcs had done in the past to different castles beyond Bru Edin. Even though he had received the news just moments before that these orcs were being led by some new creature, he wished to his gods that his plan would work.

Kalion and Meradoth both watched Nafanor pore over reports and maps and send out orders and commands to others. Nafanor nodded when he saw returning his gaze the ranger and mage he had been told were searching for Brigin'i's Princess Shermee. Motioning them over, he calmly informed them both that he had not heard of her passing through, but with everything going on he had not paid much attention. He probably would have known if some princess had come in, though — it was his duty to know when a royal was making their way in — and since she had not come into the city itself ...

He walked over, placing his hand on the ranger's shoulder. "I am sorry that you got stuck here, my friends. I'm sure your search can continue when we are done with these orcs. They never take that long to deal with." He spoke quietly, with confidence in his words.

Meradoth smiled gently. He knew what was coming at this fortress wasn't a mere army of orcs. "General, you are aware that you are not going against just some simple fighting orcs, but it's an army that contains goblins, giants, hill men and war machines?" Meradoth looked around as he spoke. "Really, everything needed to destroy this place."

The general looked over at Meradoth. "Well, we will see."

"We need to find her, sir. We must continue our mission," Kalion said, not looking at the general but out at the field beyond.

Nodding slowly, Nafanor dropped his hand, crossing his arms as he thought for a moment before responding to the ranger. "There is a way off this mountain that only I and a few members of the council know about."

Kalion and Meradoth looked at each other as the general spoke. Hearing that there might be a way off surprised them both.

"Is it hard to get to?" Meradoth asked for them both.

"Hard to get to, no. To travel on, yes," Nafanor explained.

"How long would we have to travel on it?" Kalion moved to stand in front of the general to get his full attention.

"She must be special for you both to leave us," Nafanor said quietly as a few of his men moved past the three. "I would love to have you fight with us."

"Special ..." Kalion looked down at the ground, thinking of the blond girl they had been sent out to rescue and retrieve, as his heart told him something different just then.

"Yes, she is special ... but in ways I can't really explain here. But we cannot stop looking for her," Kalion whispered back as Nafanor tilted his head back, wondering what this girl meant to the ranger.

Nafanor smiled gently. If it was love for the princess, he understood. He had met the girl two cycles earlier when he was in Brigin'i for the games, and she was beautiful beyond any human he had seen; even the elves had a hard time surpassing her beauty.

Turning, he called over his assistant, an older man of about 45 cycles, who turned and ran over quickly upon hearing his name.

"This is Bosstu. He and I go back almost to the beginning, isn't that right, my friend?"

The man looked over the two rugged-looking warriors in front of him but then smiled and nodded, hearing the general's words.

"Since you and I ran into that cave trying to trap that ice wolf, sir."

Tilting his head back slightly, the general let out a laugh. The other three smiled at seeing the general finally smiling himself.

"I do remember that. You almost fell into that cave, thinking it was flat inside, only to find that it wasn't."

"I almost broke my leg falling down the hole there, sir." Bosstu smiled, thinking back to when they were both 13 cycles old.

Nafanor quickly huffed a breath, smiling as he remembered. Then remembering the other two standing there, he placed his hand on Bosstu's shoulder.

"These two and their group are on a mission. ... One that I do hope one day they will tell me all the details of," Nafanor stated as he looked at Kalion. "But they need to get out of the city quickly." He looked at his assistant's face, the man nodding as he heard his new orders.

"Take them by way of the Cinders and get them to the northern trail."

Hearing where he was taking them, Bosstu looked over at the general and nodded.

"Gather your people and wait for Bosstu by the central square, where he will meet you to take you out of here." Reaching out, he took Kalion's outstretched hand and gave it a tight grip.

"I hope whatever you're doing is worth it, sir. With everything going on around here, we could use some more good warriors!" Nafanor said quietly to Kalion.

"This quest is one of honor for us, sir," Meradoth declared quickly before Kalion could get a word in.

Turning to his friend, Nafanor gave the man a large hug, whispering something to him as a warrior nearby interrupted the conversation, calling out that something was happening.

"Move ... now!" Nafanor nodded to Kalion as he rushed over to see what the warrior was pointing out, leaving the three men alone to look over the wall. Instantly all three gasped at what they saw.

✳ ✳ ✳

A few days earlier, Kaligor had begun marching east, moving hard through the elven forest so that he could catch up with his army. He wanted to enter the Edin Fields on his beast in front of his army; he wanted to make a statement: Kaligor, general of Methnorick's army, was here! He laughed loudly at what his army had already done: the forest was burnt everywhere, animals lay dead on the ground, and once in a while, the body of a slain elf lay ripped apart.

Giving the standing orders as he left for Brigin'i to be burned to the ground, leaving no one to survive and tell a tale, the Cyclops quickly moved with his mount as he left the area. He heard screams echoing everywhere, which gave him a tiny smile.

Not long after he entered the Levenori Forest, or what was left of it, scouts catching up to him told him that they were chasing a group that had escaped the city days before it fell. So far the group had escaped their attacks and had been able to make it to Bru Edin, which didn't surprise the Cyclops. Orcs were fast but not smart creatures, but he had plenty of them, and he was going to use them to the brink of losing the battle.

The scouts informed him that three of this escaping group had fallen in battle. One of them was a dark elf mage, his scout mentioned. Hearing this made Kaligor squint his eye at the messenger, wondering why one of his allies, a Buwan Amnach, was with a group of men and elves.

Dismissing the goblin, he kicked the side of the black furry beast, making it roar, but quickly he was moving. The creature he rode on huffed hard under its black leather armor as cloudy mists rose from its mouth, and its breathing echoed as they traveled down the road at a tremendous speed. Its hooves slammed on the ground, leaving deep imprints from its heavy weight. No creature could get close to it unless its rider let it. All remembered the last time a goblin did — the general's mount had lunch that day.

Kaligor had cared for and groomed his mount since its first day of life many cycles before, and now it was what he had hoped it would become: a black, furry creature larger than any regular horse that a man or elf would ride. Standing over seven feet from its shoulder to the ground, this mount was bred to kill and eat its prey.

Sharp teeth lined its mouth as its eyes constantly scanned the area for dangers to its master above, who called for it to quickly ride.

Pushing his massive chest out, he thought of the battle yet to come. He knew it could be the hardest yet for him, but he didn't care; he was enjoying this now. He had the biggest mass of orcs and other creatures under his command — the biggest, he was told, since the ancient beginnings when the gods arrived from the skies.

Bru Edin was by far the hardest fortress Kaligor had ever tried to assault, but the Cyclops had a plan. This plan made the giant creature smile as he listened to his army sing of their triumphs as they marched, getting closer by the moment to finally ridding the lands of men.

* * *

Far away the large trees that had stood for as long as the elves could remember began to move back and forth as a high wind moved through their branches. Birds within the trees erupted and flew away, making the sky quickly darken as they flew over Bru Edin's defenders, who only looked up briefly.

Horns could be heard coming in the wind as Nafanor's men waited around him. Bru Edin's banners fluttered in the same wind. The only sounds coming from the Bru Edin area were the horses grunting. The rest of his people kept quiet, not wanting to make a sound.

"My lord, if I may?" Marshal Ekror piped up quietly near him. Nafanor jumped a little in his saddle upon hearing Ekror's voice interrupt the silence. "Sir, why not bring the fight to them: advance the first sections forward and bring a show of force towards the orcs?"

General Nafanor smiled, turning around and patting the head of Beam, who nosed him in the face. "Not yet, my friend, not yet. I want the orcs to get close enough for our machines to hit them, and hard, along with our archers." Nafanor looked up at the fortress and could just make out the tops of the war machines over the ramparts of Bru Edin, each of their arms being pulled back.

Ekror grumbled at being made to wait. All he could see was his hatred of what was marching towards his city. He had been told just a while earlier that his family had been killed when a large group of orcs had attacked the village at the bottom of the mountain a few days before. Ekror couldn't think of them after that; it hurt too much to.

The horses around them began to feel nervous now as horns and orcish screams of battle could be heard. Even the ground began to make noise as the feet trampled the ground, making its shake. This was all becoming too much for a few horses, so their owners gave them to their servants, who, in turn, took them back to the rear or into the fortress.

Over the yelling of captains and sergeants working to get their men stabilized, General Nafanor sent word for the war machines to prepare their assault and waved over to his captain of archers to make ready. The man nodded and ran over, yelling his own orders to be ready. Nafanor saw the hundreds of archers checking their bow staves and strings, pulling arrows out as the bags of arrows were placed next to each archer by servants and runners.

The frontline archers stood behind walls built to protect them from return fire. With four sections strung out just behind the main sections, over 1,000 arrows would be released at one time. He hoped it would do enough to at least slow them down. Pulling his reins, he turned his mount around and looked at each man who stood around him to make sure everything was ready.

"My friends, we might be the only thing between us and these orcs getting into Bru Edin. If we fail ..."

"We will not fail, my lord," Marshal Ekror piped in quickly, speaking for the warriors around them as they nodded and cheered for their leader. General Nafanor, feeling pride in their calls, smiled. Kicking his horse softly, he rode Beam forward until he was standing just behind the back line of archers, watching the oncoming orc army.

Marshal Ekror glanced over to one of the captains and quickly ordered him to make sure that the elven archers marching in were placed in the right area. The captain nodded and turned his horse to ride back to meet the elves who had arrived overnight, coming from the elven king who lived due east of the fortress.

When a cry erupted from someone in the line, Marshal Ekror quickly turned his head, pulling the reins of his horse around as he saw that the orcs had stopped marching forward. Their own spear points glinted in the firelight from torches many carried as the sunlight slowly disappeared in the west.

As everyone standing on the ramparts watched, they quickly, as one, raised their weapons up and slammed them on their shields, causing the sound of metal to echo loudly across the field and up to the walls to echo within the city. Soon the noise was joined by their screams and yells.

Yells and calls for order were heard everywhere. General Nafanor continued to watch the orcs when he heard moans from his warriors. He squinted hard and scanned the land to see what they were up to. Were they waiting for something — reinforcements? They must still be moving their army into place behind, within the forest, where he couldn't see.

Just then he felt the familiar rumble of heavy equipment being moved along the ground and heard the screech of metal and wood moving against each other. He pushed himself up from his saddle and then could just make out trees being shaken and pushed out of the way by huge giant-looking creatures he couldn't see clearly as war machines began to move through the openings to be placed just inside the edge of the forest.

"Let's begin this," he said to himself quietly, for he had anticipated that they would have war machines, but the number surprised him.

Pulling in a deep breath, he nodded to his captain, who, in turn, yelled out orders. Nafanor lifted his head and watched the first volley of arrows released by his archers fly into the sky.

The captain quickly lowered his hand, screaming "RELEASE!" The sound of strings being released echoed again in Nafanor's ears, and he and the army watched the sky turn black suddenly as the second volley of arrows flew across the sky and towards the orc army.

Quickly he turned and yelled back for their own war machines to be launched. The signal was sent up to the first line of machines, and their crews moved quickly to release their own rocks to join in with the arrows.

The screams, even from where Nafanor sat on Beam, could be heard as the orcs screamed warnings about the arrows coming down onto them. He could see many scramble and lift their shields up to cover their heads as the arrows flew into their lines, and he smiled as many fell down with arrows sticking out of their heads and backs.

He then watched, trying to figure out what the orcs were going to do to with their war machines, as he could see their crews quickly moving heavy rocks and such and preparing them to be released, but not all were pointed directly at where he sat.

Moving his eyes, Nafanor observed what could have been hundreds of orcs screaming and dying as arrows dug deep into them. Almost as one they fell, dying, as the cheers from his army gave him and Bru Edin a bit of confidence.

When one of his captains yelled something from the distance, pointing out towards the fields beyond, Nafanor pushed his head slightly forward. He squinted to see orcs scramble to open a path for a large orc. This orc held up not a sword but what looked like a large axe behind the main lines of the orcs, screaming something.

Almost as soon as his arrows all found their targets, huge rocks released from Bru Edin created shadows below as they also flew over the ramparts and towards the orcish lines. Everyone stood still and watched, and many cheered, as they soon landed, causing even more havoc among the orc army. Screams and yells combined with the humans' cheers made Nafanor almost deaf, but he still wondered upon seeing the number of orcs his men were killing if this was all the orcs had. Looking around, he continued to watch as his men around him prepared themselves and the archers waited for his order to release another volley.

Yells from below told him the orcs were not returning a volley of arrows, which surprised him.

"Normally you return ..." he whispered to himself as he watched those who survived the first release of arrows from Bru Edin suddenly begin to spread out so far that he couldn't even see the edges of their ranks after a while. Shaking his head slightly so no one could see him, he watched more creatures move out of the forest to fill in for those that had been killed.

This army is here to stay! he knew then.

Looking down to the archery captain, he nodded again, and again the sky turned black from arrows flying towards the orcs as the captain repeated his hand movements. Again screams sounded as hundreds of arrowheads dug deep into the orc ranks.

The human screams erupted again at their slaughter of the orcs, but Nafanor noticed that this didn't stop their march, only slowing them down slightly as they climbed over their comrades that had been killed moments earlier like they were rocks or something.

He shook his head. *So many dying ... for what?* He could only ...

"Oh gods!" he moaned when he caught the movement.

He just caught the sight of the trees moving as hundreds — no thousands — of arrows flew out of the forest towards his men, blacked out so his men couldn't see them.

"EVERYONE DOWN!" he screamed.

Many of his warriors hid under shields and horses as the orc arrows flew into their ranks. The screams of pain were released by the hundreds as Nafanor, gritting his teeth, saw his men getting slaughtered as the heavy orc arrows slammed into shields and armor, causing many to fall to the ground with only a grunt.

The orcs' assault was heavier than anything he'd ever seen. Nafanor could see this as he watched man after man drop around him.

Seeing a captain move out from behind a small wall after the arrows had finally stopped, Nafanor screamed at the man, "Captain, send out word: the orcs are about to charge."

The captain nodded and turned and yelled the order out as Nafanor jumped off Beam, tying the reins to the pillar, knowing she would be safe where she stood. He quickly checked her over, seeing that, luckily, she hadn't been hit. Then he ran around the pillar and over to the edge of the wall, where he could finally see that the orc with the big axe could only be their general. He was whipping his weapon over his head and screaming what had to be either curses or commands.

As he was watching this, the lines of the orcs screamed suddenly and burst forward, each screaming for the blood of the humans they were about to devour. Nafanor looked to his left and right and quickly saw that it was just the front sections of orcs that were moving towards him, not their whole army. At the same time, he saw another volley of their arrows fly over their lines towards his men.

"RELEASE AND COVER!!!!" he yelled, falling to his knees behind the wall. Off to his right, he could see a section of his archers pulling their strings back again and again as they released their own arrows towards the orcs when the sound of orcish arrows came flying through the air as hundreds, if not thousands, of arrows came down on his men.

For those within Bru Edin, the slaughter was terrible to watch, as orc after orc was hit in the chest, stomach or head. Falling down, they were instantly trampled by fellow orcs from behind. The men watched as their machines snapped time and time again, releasing huge rocks to roll over many orcs, killing them instantly. Many cringed, though, when they saw the same thing happen within their own fortress as black arrows flew into many who hadn't made it to cover, and soon the ramparts were covered in their own dead, who screamed for help as they died.

Nafanor scanned the scene around him, shaking his head. When he saw that the orcs' arrows had slowed, he raised himself back up and looked at the forest.

"Why haven't you released your war machines?" he mumbled out loud, seeing giants, hill and other types that he couldn't identify, carrying a few rocks or boulders to be placed in the baskets that were quickly pulled back tight by large orcs.

Quickly wondering if they could, he screamed for the archers to raise their arrows up higher to try to take out the giantkind. Quickly the archers responded and released another volley towards the orcs and giantkind. Then lowering their arms, they continued to release what they could towards the oncoming orcs still charging at the wall as Nafanor yelled for his front lines of warriors to prepare, seeing ladders being brought up among the orcs.

Those warriors that were alive and able lifted up their large shields and planted them heavily on the ground in front of them to form a small wall. Heavy spears quickly shot out from in between each shield gap, making an instant barrier between them and the orcs. As they waited for the orcs to climb the wall, each warrior behind a shield stood ready for what was coming towards them.

It didn't take the orcs long to reach the wall as ladders were brought up and slammed hard on the rock. Like a wave of water, the orcs, still screaming, began to climb quickly up the walls, seeing no resistance except for those archers brave enough to come out from cover to release an arrow at an orc here and there.

Nafanor moved himself to stand behind the shield wall that was formed now at the top of the wall, knowing that if it fell, then all that was left was the main wall of the city fortress that lay up behind them.

"This is it, my friends. Let them know who they are fighting!" he screamed out hard, pulling his sword out and waiting, as did every warrior around him, watching the tops of the orcs' ladders move under the weight as orcs climbed up.

When the first orc came over the wall, snarling under its black hood, warriors along Bru Edin's line gripped their spears tightly. Nafanor lifted his sword up, ready to give his orders as more came over the wall, all screaming hard as they charged his men.

With nothing to stop them at the crest of the wall since their archers had pushed the men off it, orc after orc quickly slammed into the shield wall as many were pinned by the spears that were pointed at them, killing them like fish. Those that made it past the spears slammed hard into the shields, pushing them back slightly, only to be killed by swords from the men behind the front shields.

"Hold!" Nafanor screamed as he saw more orcs climb over the wall to join those that were now trying to push his wall apart and get at his warriors.

"Hold!" He repeated the order, knowing that more orcs would be coming soon; he had to wait until there were enough to push over the wall.

When the top of the wall was covered by enough orcs, he looked down the wall to the left and right, seeing that it was time.

"NOW!" he yelled. As one, his men pushed hard forward, chopping with their swords whenever an orc was able to get close enough. But many were squashed by the shields and walked over by the men, only to be killed by those moving behind. Those that weren't as lucky plunged into the waiting spears, pinning themselves on them, only to be pushed back again. Soon the wave that had looked like water became a waterfall, as the men were able to push the orcs back over the top to fall hard, screaming as they fell onto their comrades trying to climb the ladders from below, killing many of them.

Along the ground those that couldn't get out of the way were also squashed and killed as orc upon orc fell hard onto them.

Quickly the orcs fell back from the wall as their ladders were pushed off the wall by the warriors, who were now at the edge.

Their screams of triumph made Nafanor smile wide as he reached the wall and saw what his men had done. His archers were doing a great job, he noticed, of ending the lives of these orcs as they turned their backs to run away. Clapping the backs of a few men near him, the general yelled over for Marshal Ekror to ready his cavalry when a man near him got his leader's attention and pointed out towards the forest.

He looked up, still with a huge smile on his face. However it disappeared quickly as he watched the giants standing next to the machines in the forest pull the levers back, releasing their rocks towards Bru Edin. He lifted his head and watched the rocks rise up into the sky, as did everyone else around him.

"EVERYONE MOVE!" he screamed, leaving the rampart to get ready for what was coming. He watched the massive rocks fly towards his walls, but quickly he saw something interesting as the objects got closer. His army was well out of their range for the moment, and the rocks landed hard on the ground, instantly killing many of the orcs' own comrades trying to retreat from Bru Edin. Seeing the mistake, the warriors rushed to the wall and cheered as they saw the orcs being killed by their own kind.

Nafanor, seeing the opportunity, yelled out for those wounded to be pulled back, as he knew the orcs wouldn't stay still for long. The orcs still alive were quickly dispatched. The number of men wounded or killed by the few dirty creatures that were able to reach through the shield wall was small. These losses were something Nafanor could take as he saw hundreds, maybe thousands, of orcs being slaughtered in the first assault that the orcs had decided to try.

Smiling but still watching, he observed the giants moving behind their huge machines and pushing them. His archers hadn't been able to kill any of those huge creatures earlier since they were out of range, but as he scanned the orcs' lines and watched their confusion now, he saw that they seemed to be angry that these giants had killed their allies.

"Letting your own get killed for what?" Nafanor whispered to himself as he continued to watch the orcs crash into their lines as their second lines stood still. Then he noticed something riding in from the west along with a large number of orcs, and he knew, seeing this creature that could only be from a nightmare, that this battle had taken a different turn.

* * *

"You know a battle rages outside now, do you not, Kalion?" the little thief spoke up as the ranger walked past the small man. Kalion didn't even stop as he quickly grabbed his pack, making sure it was tight as he turned and watched the others gathering their belongings.

Niallee told the ranger that everyone had recovered from their wounds and had slept enough as well. Whelor and she had gathered enough food and materials to last for at least two weeks. Kalion only nodded to her as he watched Meradoth walk by looking ready as well. He looked over and saw both Bennak and Whelor, the two biggest members of their group, quietly whispering to each other as Jebba leaned against the wall, showing no sign that he was concerned about what was happening, just cleaning his nails.

Moving his eyes around, he saw that Hrliger was the only one in their group that was questionable now. His leg still hadn't healed enough that he could walk. Even with the clerics within Bru Edin working on it, the gnome was told that he had at least another week before he could possibly use it, with an emphasis on the AT LEAST.

Knowing what to say to his friend, Kalion walked over and knelt down on one knee to look at the little gnome, whom he could tell was frustrated about having to be left behind.

"Hrliger, you know we need to get going now. It will be hard for you to follow." He tried to calm the druid down as Hrliger began to protest their leaving, but it didn't work.

"I've been told that you're traveling to Chai'sell now ... a dwarven city, where my skills might be needed!" he spoke through his teeth.

"Ohhhh, and what am I then ... a worm?" Holan, standing not far away, tying up his pack, burst out laughing as he overheard the comments from the gnome. Hrliger could indeed help them in the dark if they ran into trouble there, but Kalion told them all that their travels within the dwarven kingdom would be on well-traveled roads.

Kalion stood up slowly, tilting his head when he heard the orcish horns blaring again, which quieted the group as they listened as well. Leaning back down to Hrliger, he told the druid that he would be fine, but they needed to move soon in case this trail he had told them about was blocked.

Hrliger just nodded as Amlora leaned down, kissing his forehead and wishing the gnome the best, as did Kikor and Niallee. Holan just smiled slightly as his friend. Lifting his pack onto his back, the dwarf turned as the rest began to pour out of the room, leaving only Whelor, who stood in the corner and stared down at the grey-skinned member of their group.

"Whatever happens to this group, my friend ... if I hear that you have hurt them, I will find you and kill you!" Hrliger grunted through a shot of pain from his leg as he looked at the big man, who only returned a look of sadness.

"How long have you known?" Whelor whispered.

Hrliger thought back to when he saw the big man's face change in battle.

"Anger lives deep within, Whelor. I know not what lives in you, but I fear that soon it could come to be a battle within you that I fear you might lose.

Whelor lowered his head as he slowly walked to the door but stopped when Hrliger's voice caught up to his ears.

"When the time comes, Niallee will know what to do."

Before Whelor had a chance to answer, Kalion's voice echoed into the room for him to hurry.

Looking back, Whelor gave the gnome a tiny smile and nodded his head. Turning, he walked out of the room, leaving Hrliger to himself.

"Whatever curses you, my friend ... let you find it soon!" he whispered as he closed his eyes, only hearing horns in the distance.

Chapter Fourteen

The group stood waiting in the square for the one who would lead them out of the city as Jebba confronted Kalion by pulling him off to one side.

Jebba waited for a moment, looking to Kalion and the rest of the group, who were walking away, not noticing that the two had stopped behind them, as all were in conversation about what they were going to do or what they had seen back in the city.

When the group was far enough away, Jebba turned and looked directly into Kalion's eyes. "You, sir, are a chicken ... a chicken for leaving that city when you know we are needed. Why?" he asked, almost rasping through his teeth.

Kalion's face showed that he knew he had to answer, as he could see Jebba's hand holding the pummel that lay on his right side as he looked at him.

"We are a mission, and I'm taking us on it. You know this," he answered quickly.

"It looks to me like you're not taking us on a mission but something else." Jebba gripped his sword tighter as the anger rose up a bit more.

"What are you talking about?"

"This princess ... she is so beautiful that even Kikor over there would be jealous."

"Of course she is beautiful ... but where is your anger coming from, Jebba?"

"I'm on this mission to get a reward that will help care for my family and fight. It seems to me that you're on a journey to find a girl you love and duck away from everything we encounter out there."

"First, staying and fighting is not going to give you the reward you want. It may only leave your family without you to support them. Only by finishing our mission can you get the reward you desire."

Kalion looked up and saw that Bennak and Whelor, who were walking together, had stopped when they noticed that he and Jebba hadn't joined the others.

"Jebba, I do not understand why you, a man who wants coin the most in this group, is angry that we are ducking the battlefield, where you could die and not get that coin. You should be the happiest about not fighting."

"I want the glory of killing the orcs, Kalion. You do not understand that if the orcs are not stopped, they will continue pushing our people to the edge of the land and out into the seas to die there."

Bennak turned and began to walk back. His face showed Kalion, who looked up, that he was worried about what they were talking about. "Listen, Jebba, every moment we delay she gets farther away from us and harder for us to track. We need to keep moving."

Jebba's anger was not at the fact that they were leaving Bru Edin to fight for its life or that they were running away each time they saw orcs or other creatures. No, they had had their fill of fights with the dark creatures. His anger was that Kalion wasn't showing any remorse for the loss of Birkita, and that he didn't seem to think much of Hrliger's wound either.

Turning quickly, Jebba made his way to follow the others, not responding to Kalion's statement about the princess but letting his anger stop his mouth from working for a moment.

As he walked past Bennak, the half-orc looked down at his friend and was about to say something but noticed that Jebba didn't want to talk, so he just stood there for a moment, watching the warrior walk past and then turning his head to look back at the ranger following Jebba. Kalion just smiled up at him as he approached.

"What were you two speaking about?" Bennak asked quietly.

As Kalion walked up and stopped for just a moment to answer the half-orc's question, he looked up the trail to watch the warrior push past a few others, who quickly stopped wondering why the man was pushing as they looked back to see Kalion and now Bennak standing behind the group.

"Nothing you need to worry about, my friend. Jebba just had some questions for me, and he was not happy about leaving the city," Kalion quietly stated, hoping his voice would make the big man feel like nothing was really wrong.

"Ohhh, I understand Jebba is not happy, Kalion. He has been telling me that for a while ... but I follow where you go." Kalion smiled, placing his hand on the man's forearm, thanking him. As one, they both turned and followed the group, which turned and continued to follow Bosstu up the trail.

As they made their way up the trail, only Kikor could hear the screams and sounds of battle echoing up from the city behind their heads, and she knew from the sound of it all that Bru Edin was fighting for its life.

✳ ✳ ✳

Whelor and Bennak were the last to walk through the heavy door and walk down the dark hallway, following Bosstu, who was helping them get out of the city. As they walked through the threshold and into the dark, Bosstu closed the heavy door and locked it, making the hallway echo loudly as he finished the bolt. Turning, the man skipped a little to catch up to the group as the torch he held lit up the hallway. The hallway was narrow, too narrow for the group to do anything but follow single-file behind Bosstu. Bennak's large frame completely filled the entire space, forcing him to hunch over and curse that the hallway was too small for normal people.

No one spoke during their hike until Holan realized that the hall was going downward slightly, whispering what he saw to Kikor, who nodded back to him. They had been traveling this way for some time, but no one knew how long, until after a while the cold, moldy stone that they had been getting used to slowly turned a bit warmer, and soon all were sweating as they walked. Finally Kalion, not wanting to ask their escort anything but knowing he should at least ask something, turned to look directly at Bosstu's face, who, he could see, was sweating as much as the rest of them.

"Where are you taking us?" he whispered, realizing as he spoke that his voice echoed, making the rest stop as well to look at the two.

"I'm taking you all the way that Nafanor, myself and a limited number of the council know is the only way out of the city to the north without being seen." Bosstu looked over the rest of the group and saw Kalion's head nod "fine."

Knowing that sometimes warriors are superstitious and don't trust those they have not met before, Bosstu smiled as he whispered, "I can assure you, sir, I'm not taking you anywhere except to the north of the mountain. We only have to walk not much farther to the end of this hallway, and then we will be outside."

Holan could barely hear what the old man was saying but could feel fresh air coming down a small passage they had just passed off to the left that also led back up. He got the attention of Kikor and motioned that he felt fresh air. She quickly turned and motioned to the next in the group as Holan turned up the unknown path, leaving the rest of the group, for something in his senses told him that this was a way out.

After motioning to Bennak and then down the line what Holan had done, she started to follow when Bosstu turned and yelled, "Be careful when you exit! Sometimes this mountain has left rocks at the entrance!" His voice echoed through the mountain hallway, but it was too late; the dwarf felt the freshness of air hitting his face. Turning around, Kikor placed her hands to her face and called out that they were at the end.

Cheers of joy came from a few in the group, who then whispered. Not wanting to be underground much and not seeing any dangers, they turned to follow Holan's lead just as Holan broke out to find himself standing on a ledge looking over what used to be one of the largest volcanoes in the northern reaches.

Gasping as he breathed hard, he scanned the landscape. Seeing no life such as orcs made the man a bit happy, but he noticed that no other real life, such as trees or bushes, lived here either.

As the others walked out, everyone just stood and looked in amazement. Bosstu made his way past the group. "Welcome to the interior of our mountain!" he whispered.

The caldera of Edin Mountain was a massive landscape that spanned beyond the sight of man. Only the elves in the group could see the other side. Smoke and mist rose from the bowl of the caldera, making visibility hard, but if they all could, they would have seen two small towers that were at the end of the trail that they would have to walk through to get to the north.

Waiting for the rest to get used to the sight of his mountain, Bosstu stepped forward and began the journey on this trail that would take this group away from the city. If they turned their heads south, they would see the top of the city's tallest towers peeking over the rim of the old volcano.

The group continued to follow Bosstu as they descended some rock steps and began to walk north in twos. The trail wasn't large enough for more, but at least they were out in the fresh air.

* * *

The lull that followed the orcs' sudden charge and subsequent retreat from the wall bothered Nafanor as he observed the giants pushing the massive war machines closer and closer to the walls. When they didn't release rocks at his position, he wondered if that creature he had seen riding in earlier had something to do it.

The orcs had been able to retreat to their original lines, but even the orcs seemed to be calming down a bit: no more yelling or screaming, no more smashing their weapons on shields. It was like the two armies were just standing and watching each other now, waiting for the other to make a move.

Word came to Nafanor that the elves were positioned where he wanted them. He nodded to the sergeant who gave him the news of the added archers, who then smiled in return. Nafanor turned and looked again at the orcs. Even from his position, he could see things were going on in their lines, but he just couldn't see what they were doing. He wished he had wings just then so he could fly up and get a look at what they were doing.

"My lord, I was told you needed me." Nafanor looked at the man's right hand, which held a weird-looking staff, bent and twisted, that told him the man was a mage but still used the staff to walk.

"I … mmmmm … I do, yes. I need something powerful thrown at the orcs, anything to slow them down … and news … news on what the orcs are planning. Can you assist?" Nafanor asked the mage, finally looking at the mage's face and seeing his dark lips.

The mage looked at Nafanor and nodded his head "yes."

"I will do what I can, my lord." The mage smiled, showing off his ragged teeth under the dark lips, which sent a chill up the general's back.

The mage raised his weird-looking staff and his other arm, yelling out words that Nafanor didn't understand. Instantly light came from the staff like a torch of some kind, almost blinding Nafanor and making him cover his face for a moment. As he noticed that the light was reaching out towards the orcish lines across the field, he lowered his hand to watch.

When the light crossed the field, a human-looking figure, almost a mirror image of the mage, appeared in the crowd of orcs. The orcs reacted first by scattering, believing that the humans were launching another type of attack on them, but then, seeing this strange man in their own ranks, some started to cheer, for the orcs knew something that Nafanor did not: this mage was on their side. This caused the orcs to snarl where they stood, and across the field and from behind the walls, many heard the familiar sound of swords pounding on shields. A few even started to clatter their axes, and some slammed their shields on the ground.

Nafanor could just make out that the mirror image in the orcs' ranks didn't hold a staff. Instead it was using only its hands as far as he could tell. Within the light of that man, he saw many orc archers releasing their arrows in response to the mage's move.

"COVER!" he yelled out to his warriors. As he looked back, he watched the man's movement for a moment.

The mage raised his hands and clapped them together. Instantly the mage standing next to Nafanor exploded as his staff erupted into shards of wood and light, knocking down every single warrior that was standing close to him. Nafanor was just able to make out what had happened before the explosion slammed into him.

Nafanor was thrown off Beam, and he almost plunged into the spear of a warrior who stood nearby as he rolled to the ground, moaning from the sharp pain in his shoulder.

Picking himself up, Nafanor looked up as a few of his men ran over and helped him up. A few orcish arrows fell around them. Luckily none killed his warriors, but many shook their heads as they couldn't believe what had just happened.

Realizing that a high-pitched sound had made it impossible for him to hear, he shook his head and looked around, seeing people yelling and talking to him. He hit the side of his helm a few times and was finally able to hear the screams from his warriors. Still shaking his head, he moved up to the wall and looked over. Quickly his eyes grew large; the orcs were screaming and charging the wall again. Above, he could see fire arrows rising up into the air behind their lines. Gasping at the barrage that was approaching, he caught sight of their machines snapping forward, releasing huge boulders towards his men.

"COVER!" he screamed instantly, coughing as his throat made it hard for him to speak. The first of the arrows began raining down hard onto his men, instantly killing a few that were too slow to get under something. Screams from his officers and sergeants for everyone to move echoed everywhere.

He turned and noticed that it wasn't just the men near the mage that had been killed but many in the front lines as well. He noticed then how many had been knocked down and that his prized horse, Beam, had been hurt, but luckily its strong armor had saved it and him from a lot of damage.

He cursed himself loudly for trusting a mage, especially one he didn't know. He had never been one who trusted magic, and now this. ... Forgetting about the mage's attempt to kill him, he pushed men for cover as arrow after arrow landed on the stones, bouncing off and hitting a few in the sides but luckily not causing many injuries.

"ROCKSSSS!" someone screamed out loudly, making Nafanor lift his head up to see the massive objects falling down onto his position. A few had hit the ground just outside the walls, but now they were finally hitting their mark.

Instantly these rocks caught many men under them, crushing them without a sound. As the rocks hit the ramparts, many were thrown into the air as the wall that they had stood on quickly exploded under the assaulting rocks. Screams of the dying and wounded were everywhere as many warriors were killed by shrapnel flying into them. This, in turn, instantly opened the wall section for the orcs to climb up.

Nafanor, standing behind the pillar, looked over to where a few rocks had hit the wall and noticed the opening now available to the orcs. He could see many wounded and ones shaken by the explosion standing around, shaking their heads like they were in a daze and trying to figure out where they were, only to be killed by arrows hitting them in the back as they staggered about, making the general curse again.

Nafanor yelled at his archers to return fire, but as the number of his archers was dwindling, he was not sure he had enough for a heavy assault to stop the orcs, which would mean this would quickly become a hand-to-hand fight. The first orcs reached the top of the rampart and climbed over, moving towards his warriors, and charged into them, slicing into their armor as they did. The screams of pain and agony from his men echoed in his ears as he screamed orders to his captains to get things into order.

The archery captain, now wounded by rock shrapnel, saw the front line of orcs climb over the wall and decided to give the order to those archers he had left not to launch a barrage of arrows into the field but at those orcs coming over the wall.

Soon their arrows fell onto orc after orc, knocking them off the wall, but it wasn't enough, as just then another explosion occurred. Covering his head with his one good arm, the archery captain turned his head, only to find that his men near where the explosion occurred were all gone, leaving a huge hole in the wall where moments before his archers had stood.

His mouth fell open as he screamed for his men and ran to the edge to see if any were alive. But before he could do anything, an arrow slammed into his chest, causing the man to gasp in surprise as he looked down at it. Before he could think about what to do, another slammed hard into his chest, causing him to collapse to his knees. Reaching up, he tried to pull the arrow out, only to stop as the pain shot through him. He gasped as he could feel the life draining from the hole now in his chest.

Shaking his head, he knew his life might be at an end. He just knelt there until all life had left his body and his arms fell to his sides. The orcs, seeing the opening, used it to climb the wall and pulled themselves up and through it to rush past the captain, many roaring in victory.

Marshal Ekror, who sat upon his horse not far from the wall, saw the archery captain get killed. Looking around the wall, he couldn't see General Nafanor, and he knew that the wall would soon fall as rocks slammed into it. Even from where he sat, he could see the massive cracks in it.

Pulling out his blade, he ordered all men around him to be ready. They might be the only defense left, he thought, as orc after orc pushed past the warriors on the wall, killing them as they did, and began moving down the steps to charge his cavalry. Turning his head right and left, he checked on the warriors around him when his eye caught the sight of huge giants, goblins and other creatures he couldn't recognize in the masses of orcs moving over the wall and through the holes made by the rock assaults.

Cries for a retreat echoed along the wall as men who could turned and ran backwards behind the safe line of cavalry that was forming. Quickly many who heard the call turned and ran, jumped or even fell off the wall to escape the orcs moving against them.

Knowing that he was out of the range of the arrows of the orcs on the other side, Ekror yelled at his men to position themselves to protect the warriors retreating from the wall. Lowering their heavy spears, they waited for the creatures to charge them, but to Ekror's surprise, the orcs lingered just inside the wall, which gave those retreating time to move through and make their way to the gateway that had only one door open.

As the last of the survivors moved past, Ekror cried out a challenge to those that were attacking his city, but none charged. Above on the ramparts, everyone watched the orcs celebrate that they had taken the first main wall of Bru Edin by jumping up and down, slamming their ugly swords on their shields. Many dispatched wounded warriors hadn't been able to retreat. A few men were made into trophies by the creatures, which brought screams from the cavalry watching.

As Ekror sat on his mount, he could see that if the orcs charged, with the help of the giants he could see gathering in the collapsed areas, his cavalry wouldn't be able stop them for long, so he quieted himself and any others who brought challenges.

"Make sure the gate is ready for us when I call for retreat!" he called over to a sergeant who was standing not far behind. Nodding, the sergeant turned to another warrior and told him to spread the word that the gate was to be left open until the last moment.

Just then a commotion to his left made the marshal turn and instantly feel relief when he saw the rough-looking smile of the leader of the armies of Bru Edin move up on top of his prized horse, Beam.

Nafanor moved up to sit next to Ekror, who saw that the general had taken a beating upon the wall. Half of his face was covered in black blood, and his helm had been knocked off by an arrow, giving another orc the opportunity to hit him with a club, causing the general to lose an ear. His shirt and neck were covered in blood, and his left eye was swelling up.

"Well ... shall we fight or leave the field, my friend, and retreat into the inner walls?" Nafanor grunted through his pain as he tried to smile at the marshal.

Both spoke about the scene before them, knowing that the army had taken a beating, but they kept an eye on the orcs, watching them gather just inside the wall.

Ekror stated, "Well, all the population has been moved into the inner city. Only the tower section remains manned along this section of the wall. With the outside walls breached and with what I see now massing inside the walls just there, I think it best to defend the inner walls at this point."

Nafanor agreed, saying, "The rocks that destroyed the outer walls will not reach the inner walls from their location, so we stand a chance."

Suddenly the two towers to their right that held the outside gates exploded, getting everyone's attention and causing the horses to jump and make the lines collapse.

Everyone heard and saw those men still within the towers

scream and die as both cracked open and collapsed. A few men trying to escape jumped out, only to fall to the ground and die as the towers fell onto them.

"By the gods, man!" Nafanor cried out, holding the reins of his mount as Beam whined under him.

"Time to leave, I think, sir. They are massing together, and it looks like they are moving towards us," Ekror cried out as the orcs upon the wall screamed in victory and both giants pushed the gate down, causing the last of the towers to collapse.

"Send the word: all sections still manned are to make their way to the inner city!" Nafanor grunted, feeling the quick and sudden pain in his face as he looked at the marshal.

Suddenly Beam reared back on its hind legs, screaming out and making the general grip the reins tightly, trying not to fall off the saddle. He saw embedded in the horse's chest a black arrow's staff and feather. Gasping that his beloved horse was going to die, Nafanor looked down at the wicked-looking arrow embedded in Beam's chest and then up to the wall to see who had released the arrow. Scanning the ramparts, he saw an ugly orc not far away lowering its bow and staring at him with a large smile, revealing its ragged teeth. Seeing that it had hit its mark, it let out a bloodcurdling scream that made Nafanor's only ear ring.

Jumping from the saddle as other warriors around him turned their own horses around and made their ways quickly through the open gate, Nafanor had heavy tears in his eyes as Beam fell down on its side, whining in pain as it collapsed.

"Sir ... sir ... you need to leave quickly!" a warrior yelled as he ran up, only to be pushed away by the general as he placed his hand on Beam's now dead body. Seeing that he wouldn't leave, the man looked up and saw that orcs were gathering to charge off the wall. Cursing the general, the warrior turned and retreated to the city, leaving only Nafanor and a few others on the field, who, having been wounded, were slow to leave.

As the man ran away, Ekror's voice finally got into Nafanor's mind, bringing him back to what was happening. Standing up, the general pulled out his sword and looked up at Ekror, who was leaning down from his horse with an outstretched hand.

"Hurry, my friend!" the marshal cried out as the sound around them of screaming orcs and their allies made each man wince. The sound was louder than any had ever heard before.

Looking up, Ekror showed concern. Nafanor reached out and gripped Ekror's hand, and Ekror quickly pulled the warrior up onto his saddle.

Ekror looked directly into the eyes of his friend as he pulled the man up, seeing the anger in his eyes turn to sudden pain. Ekror saw his expression of misery, and then he watched as his friend looked at the sky as he fell backwards.

The marshal was about to say something when he noticed an arrow, black now, sticking out of the left side of the general. As his mind caught up to the present moment, he was about to do something, but he saw that Nafanor, the general of Bru Edin was dead, lying on the ground. There was no time, so before he was killed in the same way, the marshal of Bru Edin's cavalry reined his horse around, and kicking the horse under him, he rode hard towards the gate he saw was beginning to close.

He could see archers upon the inner wall that was currently the last defense left for Bru Edin release arrow after arrow down on the streets of the outer city, killing orcs, goblins and even some giants that were trying to reach the marshal, who rode hard to get to safety.

* * *

Dia was thrown to the ground hard when the explosion hit the tree next to his head, almost knocking him unconscious when it did. All he heard were screams and steel hitting steel around him as he lay there, shaking his head, wondering what had just happened.

His captors had been moving through the trees of Levenori

quickly, passing by groups of orcs and a few goblins that were in the forest. *Probably looking for stragglers that are trying to escape Brigin'i, Dia thought.*

When they had to stop and wait, Dia had a knife placed around his throat and was told not to even whisper. Each time it was Parnland who personally stood behind Dia with the blade to his throat, more out of a sense of power than out of fear that Dia would call out to the orcs. Each time this happened, Dia would relive what had happened to his city and think if he could have done anything differently to save his people, his queen or even his daughter. His daughter was now the only thing he had left in this world, and he wondered where she was now and if the team that he had sent after her had succeeded yet in finding her safe.

When Baron Parnland finally whispered that they were almost to the eastern edge of the forest, the explosion happened. That was the last thing Dia remembered before he found himself looking up at the sky above pushing itself through the trees.

Shaking his head, he looked over and saw one of the men who had been dragging him through the muck and dirt of the forest fall back hard to the ground with an arrow deep in his chest.

Gasping, as his first thoughts were that the orcs had somehow found them, Dia turned and pushed himself up with his elbows. As his hands were still tied up with rope, he pushed himself up against a tree that was nearby and considered his options.

Looking around, he saw that each man who had been with him since leaving the city lay on the ground, all with arrows in their bodies, but he noticed quickly that the baron was not one of them. The once proud Dia felt a chill go down his back, wondering where that fat man was, when he heard a rustling of branches nearby, making him stay still and swallow hard.

Taking in a deep breath and holding it, he felt himself shaking a little, knowing that the orcs would do even worse to him, when he heard a snap of a stick to his right, making him look over to see a pair of boots not far away.

He could hear his heart beating as his eyes slowly moved up to the legs, but then he stopped when his eyes adjusted to the sight of not an orc or a dark elf but a blond-haired elf smiling slightly at the corner of his mouth.

"Soooo, King Dia is it? I didn't expect I would find you out here or that I would find you alive at all," the elf whispered as it stepped forward and knelt down next to Dia, bringing out a small knife, which made Dia suck in a sudden breath, wondering if this elf was playing a mind trick on him. This, in turn, made the elf shake his head as he cut through the rope that held Dia's hands together.

"You're safe ... for the moment, King Dia." The elf stood up and helped the king to his feet when he saw the question on Dia's face.

"I was searching for a few of my warriors when I saw your group moving through the forest, so I tracked you all, waiting for the right time to free you."

Smiling slightly, Dia breathed a sigh of relief that his terror was over. As he looked around the forest, his ears started to hear sounds of orcs and other nasty creatures out there.

"Yes, we've got to get out of here now, King." The elf turned and started to move back into the bushes as Dia followed, but reaching out, he gripped the elf's shoulder, making the warrior turn around and look back with a face full of concern.

"Who are you, friend?" Dia whispered, finding that his throat was dry and sore from lack of water.

Looking around a few more times, the elf said, "I was the captain of the guard of this forest. But since there is no longer a guard, you can call me Caed. Now we must get out of here, sir!" At that Caed turned and began making his way into the foliage of the forest.

As Dia followed, he asked, "What do you mean 'was'?"

"My guards have all been killed and massacred. We must keep moving."

They moved into the forest a ways when Dia grunted that he had to stop and rest, making Caed grumble that they had to move quickly.

Pulling out a pouch, he gave Dia some liquid, which made the man's throat burn suddenly, almost making him scream in pain, but before he could, the pain disappeared, and he felt like he was 18 cycles old.

He looked at the elf, who smiled, nodding at what had just happened to Dia. "I know. ... It's something my people drink all the time. But, sir, we must move now."

"Where are we going, Caed?" Dia asked, amazed that his voice sounded stronger by the moment.

"We go north!" Caed whispered in return, and both moved as quietly as they could, not saying a word until they made it to the foot of the mountains that lay at the northern edge of the forest.

* * *

Not far from the main wall of Bru Edin, Marshal Tassalii was leaning over a table when he got word that General Nafanor had fallen in battle. Cursing, he grabbed his sword that lay not far away, and strapping it quickly to his waist, he ran out of the building and saw the confusion of those in the inner city trying to find a place to go.

He saw the wounded being dragged, walked and wheeled by as the marshal called out for those who could to help the wounded. He and three of his men pushed past them down the road to the inner wall to find out what was going on when, moving through the gate, he saw Marshal Ekror fall off his horse with an arrow embedded in his leg and get quickly carried off by two men.

Now that he was in charge, Marshal Tassalii, who for cycles had been the reserve commander, swallowed hard and cleared his throat as warriors everywhere looked to the man for orders on what to do.

Seeing their fear that they might not survive this, he turned his head around to look at the warriors nearest to him, swallowed and took command.

"Bar the gates. Make sure nothing can get them open!" he screamed, pointing to the heavy gates and watching as warriors moved to do his orders quickly.

"Sir ... sir ... those gates can hold off the worst that the orcs can give us!" a warrior nearby said to the Marshal.

"You just saw the outer two walls fall, son. General Nafanor is dead ... and Marshal Ekror is wounded ... add the addition bars to that gate now!" he answered as anger rose within him at this young man who thought that just locking the gate would stop the orcs from getting in.

Turning, he saw that many were showing signs of defeat, and he knew he had to do something — and soon — or this final defense might collapse like everything else had outside.

As the new commander of Bru Edin screamed out orders, an archer who stood on the gate towers of the inner city saw the Cyclops coming down the main street towards his gate. He and others who were watching and releasing arrows as fast as they could gasped as orcs rushed over Nafanor's still body and towards the walls. A few stopped when they saw who it was and began to carve the man's body up.

Quickly the archer ordered the others to lower their aim and release everything they had.

"Kill anything that moves, NOW!!!" he screamed.

Quickly arrows shot out at the charging orcs, slamming into them and knocking down the orcs in front. And just like before, their comrades just ran over the dead and dying orcs to get to the humans, but unlike when they were in the open field outside the city walls, they now found themselves in narrowing streets, so they were boxed in, making it easier for the archers above to kill them.

Wave after wave of arrows flew out from the towers and the mighty wall of Bru Edin as the defenders dropped orcs, goblins and even a giant or two, all knowing that, if this wall fell, Bru Edin would be finished.

"Of course the outer wall has fallen. Bru Edin will be ours soon!" Kaligor turned his head and saw the creature he wanted to speak to. As Kaligor motioned for him to come forward, the dark-armored creature quietly stepped forward and stood at the foot of Kaligor, looking up and waiting as the Cyclops observed Bru Edin for a few moments more.

Kaligor looked down at the warrior waiting for him. The black armor almost shined in the firelight, as did the white, silvery hair now tied behind his head. The almost-white eyes of the elf looked up at Kaligor, making the general wonder ... if on even grounds, would he want to fight this dark elf? Could he win?

"That inner wall will be the hardest to take, but your people can help finish this for me, yea?" He nodded at the battle before them both. "Your people have ways of getting under the walls while my orcs will just continue to throw themselves at the gate, which will take time, but it should occupy the defenders inside so they will not notice your people. We need to finish this soon and take this city. Our lord, I'm sure, is becoming impatient."

"My lord, it will be my pleasure!" The almost singing voice coming out of its mouth made Kaligor smile, as he knew that this voice came from a killer who was a legend in his world.

Even as he spoke, a message came up, giving word that a large group of cavalry was moving in from the east and west in addition to a large army of dwarves that was marching in from the west, which made the Cyclops smile.

"Wait!" he called to the elf before he got too far away. "Instead, I want half of your people to charge these dwarves coming in to try to relieve Bru Edin. Show them that you are the real masters of the dark!"

The elf smiled wide and only nodded in answer as he turned and cried out in his dark language to a few others of his kind, who nodded quickly, and ran back over a wall to get his people ready. The one nearest Kaligor followed quickly, jumping over the wall like it was a twig, and disappeared into the crowd of orcs and goblins that were trying to rush the wall and fortress of Bru Edin.

Captain Mossi of the Bru Edin Heavy Cavalry sat his units of cavalry when the signal came for them to ride south. He saluted Captain Utina, who led the other section of cavalry. They were both surprised that the signal came so fast, as everyone always believed that Bru Edin was unbeatable. Their sections hadn't been there for long. Horses were still being watered as grooms ran about, getting them ready to ride.

Quickly screams and orders rang everywhere to move out as the sections broke into two halves. As the cavalry rode around the mountain, the first sign of the battle that Mossi saw wasn't the battle itself, or even the sounds of the battle — it was the sky. Blacker than black itself, he thought when he saw it. He heard a few warriors near him yell out about it, but he kept going, kicking his horse to move faster. According to General Nafanor, when the signal was given, it meant that their lines were either in need of support or were collapsing quickly and needed a counterattack, or hopefully, his cavalry was needed to mop up retreating orcs.

Soon rain began to hit Mossi's face as they made their final turn along the road that they were using as a guide. The ground, he saw, was beginning to become sodden with the rain, but it didn't matter to him. They needed to get there as fast as his section could — all 5,000 of his warriors.

As the cavalry rode over the final large rise in the road, he finally saw the battle itself before him. He saw that the orcs had amassed a very large army that somehow was still standing and fighting. *General Nafanor must be hard-pressed to get the orcs back,* Mossi thought as he got closer and was able to observe more of the situation. As he took in more and more of the battle, he realized that Bru Edin could be lost soon, for he could see that the outer walls had fallen.

Screaming out for his men to be ready, he kicked his mount

hard, as did those around him, as everyone could see what was before them.

Mossi hoped that Utina had made it to the same point as he on the opposite road east of the mountain. Hitting the orcs on both ends at the same time would cause panic in their ranks. This was the plan that Nafanor had outlined to them, even hoping it could cause a total retreat of the orcs and their allies, but now all they could hope for was that it would distract the orcs and bide some time for the units within Bru Edin to attack.

Turning slightly in his saddle, he yelled back so the announcement of their section could be heard by the orcs. Turning his head back, he held the reins tight and lowered himself down to the rough ground, gritting his teeth and wiping water away from his face as the rain continued to pound down harder now.

The 20 horn players who rode near the back blew their horns at the same time, playing a Bru Edin battle tune. In the past this same tune would scare off any potential enemies, and Mossi saw that it was distracting the orcs and catching their attention now, for he saw orcs, goblins and the few giants in their lines look over upon hearing the horns' echoing across the Edin fields.

Smiling, he saw the perfect area for his section to ride into; a gap had opened up as a few giants had turned to face him. He pulled out his sword and lifted himself in his saddle slightly as those around him lowered the heavy spears each was carrying to slam into their victims soon.

His men were within an arrow's length of the orcs when, just as Mossi passed a patch of rocks that lay on the ground, it suddenly imploded and collapsed underneath the riders, causing everyone to fall into the newly opened up tunnel below as screams echoed everywhere.

Rider and horse screamed in panic and pain as they landed hard at the bottom, many dying from the fall or from being crushed by others. The huge hole that had collapsed was larger than anyone could comprehend, but the riders didn't get a chance to think much more about it, for the walls of the hole exploded and huge arm-like tentacles shot of out these holes, grabbing screaming rider and horse and sucking them quickly into the holes, where the screams went silent.

The hundreds of riders and horses caught in the massive hole screamed in panic as the hole soon became their grave, the creatures filling themselves with human and horse alike.

Captain Mossi was one of the lucky ones, though. As the hole opened up, he was just able to get his horse, Koozaa, over the edge as the ground disappeared underneath his hooves. He saw his comrades, many his friends for many cycles, fall into the hole and die as he watched what happened to them, not being able to help. Turning his head when he heard movement behind him, he saw that the orcs and their other dark allies had continued their momentum at the walls of Bru Edin and were charging the final wall hard.

Turning his head left and right, he saw that his cavalry who survived the fall into the hole were being killed by a creature that looked like a worm with octopus arms. This creature was reaching out and attacking his men and dragging survivors of the fall off into the depths.

Turning around, he pulled back on the reins of his horse, making the horse pull back and kick his front legs out. Mossi screamed curses at the orcs and then, kicking his horse's side, pointed his mount towards the largest orc he could see. Lowering his sword, he pointed it at the orc's face and charged at it.

"FOR EDIN!!!!!"

Anyone above looking down at the scene would have seen the cavalry captain die as he charged into the thousands of orcs, who quickly cut him and his horse up.

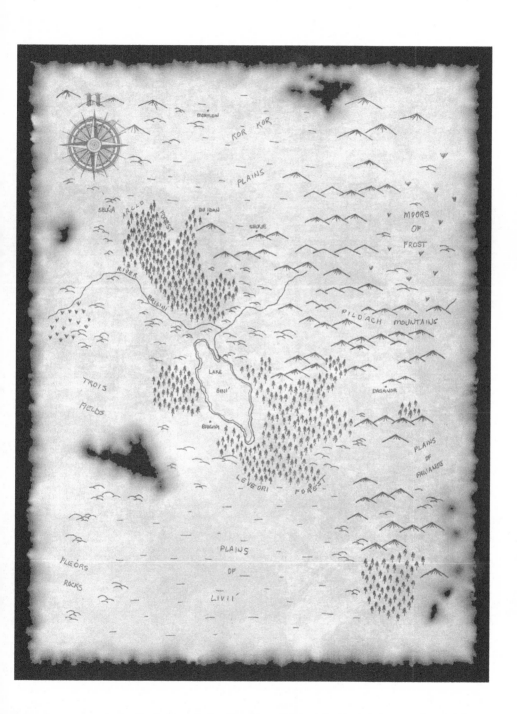

Chapter Fifteen

Dia and Caed moved through the forest, ducking the few bands of orcs trying to find survivors of Dia's now destroyed city. He could hear a few who had made it to the forest die under their swords, as their screams for their gods or help from warriors of Brigin'i echoed.

Quietly both made their way north until there were signs that they were near the foot of the mountains, as more rock formations began to break through the forest floor.

Caed motioned for him to stop and hide behind a large bush as the elf made his way up a large group of these rocks and disappeared over them, leaving Dia in silence. No bird chirped; no deer walked by. Nothing, not even butterflies, flew by, making the king wonder what was happening to the lands as he looked around, feeling a chill move through his body.

Pulling out the pouch of liquid Caed had given him, he took a small swig of it, feeling the power of it move quickly through his body, but the nervousness didn't stop until he saw the familiar sight of Caed coming back.

Waving his hand, the elf motioned for him to follow, which he did quite quickly, and when Dia finally got up the rock, Caed smiled at his ability to move as fast as he did.

"We're safe now, my friend," Caed whispered as Dia moved to stand next to the elf savior.

"Are you sure, Caed? I mean, we are still within your forest?" Dia looked back down at the forest floor, knowing that just over a few hills were those bands of orcs.

Caed placed a hand on the king's shoulder to reassure him that it was going to be fine. Quickly both made their way through the cracks of the rock formation and up a tiny trail when they crested the top of the trail, and Dia found that he was entering a glen wide enough to hold the city of Brigin'i at the bottom of it.

Dia gasped as he stopped to observe what was before him. Caed only smiled, but after a moment, stepped in front of him, saying, "Welcome to the Valley of Londona, King Dia. Here you will only find peace and protection." Caed's voice made Dia feel safe.

"Londona!" Dia whispered through his smile as he took in the beauty of the valley below him: lush trees, animals roaming open fields and water falls coming out of the sides of the mountains, falling into rivers that ran through these fields.

"I've never heard of or seen anything like this, Caed." He spoke quietly as he saw a bird fly just above him through the blue skies.

"And you will never speak of this place!" The voice made Dia turn quickly, as it was not Caed's voice but another's. The sight of the elf moving out of the shadow cast by the mountain cliff surprised him, but the sight of at least ten more brought a chill up his back, for they had been hidden so well that he had not noticed them.

"Dia, your people were never meant to know of this place. My people found this place many, many cycles before yours made it to these shores, and even during our wars, this place is a place of refuge for my people ... so Caed bringing you to this place means that we trust that you will not let your kind know of it. Do you understand what I am saying, King?" The elf had moved to stand in front of Dia.

Dia nodded quietly and quickly to show he understood what the elf meant. "Sir, my city and its people ... my people are ... they're all gone, so I have no one to speak to ... except your people." Seeing the elf's face show a bit of frustration, he quickly added, "But yes, sir ... I will never speak of this place."

The elf nodded slightly, and turning, he told Caed to take Dia and to make sure he was fed. Caed nodded, and smiling at Dia, he motioned for him to follow him down. "It is all well, my friend. We are safe here."

As Dia and Caed descended a trail into the valley, Dia could hear the older elf speak quietly to the others who had come out of the shadows, but he couldn't understand the elfish dialect they spoke in.

* * *

The sails flew out and caught the wind with a loud snap, almost instantly making nearly everyone on board grab something as the ship lurched forward. The crew, which numbered only 20, worked hard to get the ship as far away from Blath 'Na as possible. Each watched out of the corner of their eyes as the city erupted in flames behind them.

Shermee stood on the forecastle and watched the land move farther and farther away by the moment. She kept her eyes mostly on the people scrambling onto the ships and small boats that lay within the port of Blath 'Na City, trying to get away from the death that was moving through its streets.

Tears formed as she watched such a beautiful city dying so quickly. She had hoped to travel to the city of ships and shop its legendary shops. Friends who had traveled to her city in the past told her about the beauty of the city, but now all she saw was devastation, and she would never have a chance to see that beauty, as she saw building after building collapse and disappear in the smoke that was rising into sky along with the screams that echoed across the water.

Sending wishes that the people who were trying to get away would make it safely somewhere, she swallowed and blinked a few more times as the fog from the seas began to block her sight of the city.

Lowering her head when she heard a footstep behind her,

she closed her eyes and could only wonder what was in store for her now that they were out of sight of the city. She felt the presence of someone moving up to stand with her along the rail of the forecastle.

"I'm sorry you had to see that, my princess, but luckily we made it out before the city fell completely." She recognized the voice instantly, without having to open her eyes.

"Where are you taking me, Quinor?" Even though she knew the answer, she wanted to hear it again.

"You know where, my princess. Methnorick wants you to be … to be his bride." His voice suddenly told her something: either he was afraid or …

Quinor looked to where the city would be if the fog wasn't in the way as he swallowed silently. He wasn't liking this mission of his; he recognized that his voice told her something was wrong with what he was doing. He looked down, seeing that she was returning his gaze.

She saw that this man who carried himself as a strong warrior now looked like he was sorry for what was going on in the city they had just left.

"How long will this voyage take, Quinor?" she said quietly as a crew member walked by, grinning as he looked the princess over. She could guess what he was thinking and was starting to formulate a plan for how she could use this to her advantage. She would not be Methnorick's bride.

"It should be two, maybe three days, I would think, depending on the weather." He looked down at her, and she could just see a tear in his left eye. She began to wonder then as he smiled and turned to speak to the captain of the ship, who had joined them on the forecastle just then.

Captain Kochic was an ugly man with a long, blackish beard and scars everywhere on his face and arms, which told her that he was a seasoned warrior in his own right.   His large frame was enhanced by his muscles, which were everywhere, including his neck, but he only had a few teeth in his mouth, so once in a while when he spoke, he whistled his words.

The man wore a black outfit that could once have been the fashion but now was all ripped, but it was his smell that made her almost sick. It was like he hadn't bathed in a cycle at least.

She listened to the two speak but turned and watched the crew of the ship named the Reverter, a small ship, but strong to make it across the seas. Her father had always told her the seas were very rough since the gods didn't want their followers to travel on them in case they tried to travel to the gods' homeland, which legends say lay in the east.

The conversation between the two men about details of their route went on for some time, and then the captain turned to the princess. Acting like she wasn't paying attention, she said, "What was that, Captain?"

"My dear, if you keep to yourself and do'na bother me men, you can walk about this ship. If not ... understand ma?" His voice whistled as he spoke, but she nodded, understanding most of what he said.

He had shown her the hold when she first got on board the ship earlier. It was a dark, cold and wet place where she was sure she could hear and see rats running around — not a place she wanted to spend any time. She got the impression that the captain was now suggesting that would be her new location if she caused any issues.

So taking the opportunity that he had given her to walk around the ship, she slowly walked down the few stairs that led down to the main deck of the ship, where most of the crew worked. She slowly walked around the ship, watching the crew work, a few being whipped to clean the deck of the ship by a bald-headed man with only one eye (the other covered in a grayish-black cloth).

The Reverter wasn't a large ship. In fact a normal man could walk from one end to the other in a few moments, and that was what she found as she made her way to the room that lay at the rear of the ship behind a wooden door that only had a simple lock on it.

As she walked towards that door, two thin crew members stepped in front of her, grinning down at her like wolves looking at prey.

"What we have here, Normac, eh?" one man said through his grin.

Normac's eyes traveled up and down her body, making her feel uneasy, so she crossed her arms across her chest as a way to feel safe.

"Wha' we got heerre, you think, laddie? Cap'in must have brought us a toy, Syska. When can we have it?" Normac's voice was raspy and rough.

"You two ... back to work!" A scream and a snap of a whip made the two straighten up quickly, but they didn't stop grinning at her as they acknowledged the deck member that was yelling at them.

As they walked away, she looked behind her and saw that the man that had yelled was the one-eyed man with a heavy black leather whip. She stared at him and the two that were now working the ropes of the ship, trying to figure out if she could make this work to her advantage. Turning without another thought, she opened the door and quickly closed it, leaning back on it as she let out a loud gasp. Tears quickly ran down her face as she began to cry. All she could think about was where her father was, if he knew where she was, and if he was doing anything to save her.

"Cap'in says she's some kin'a princess or som'ing," she heard through the door, making her suddenly stop crying and move away from the door, thinking someone was on the other side, listening to her.

"A princess?" she heard as laughter erupted.

She knew she wouldn't make it to the other end of this trip. She had to do something, and fast, to turn this around. What was she going to do? she wondered as she leaned on the bed that the captains had given her for this trip. Swallowing hard, she closed her eyes for a moment and thought quickly about what to do. *Maybe if I get the crew on my side, they will fight for me and not turn me over to Methnorick,* she thought. She went on to think, *Maybe I can turn Quinor to my side. I think he might like me.* She smiled at that thought. *Maybe he could get them to turn the ship south and away from this Methnorick. But how?* She stared at the door as she thought, believing that at any moment the whole of the crew was going to walk through it. But nothing happened, so slowly she relaxed a bit, believing that the bald man and the captain must have gotten to them first.

The movement of the ship sailing on the seas made the cabin rock up and down, and soon Shermee felt sleepy and thought that maybe she could try taking a small nap. She lay back on the bed, and without knowing it, she closed her eyes and was fast asleep.

Outside the cabin the crew was doing its job, but the whispers were running rampant, as all had indeed watched this beautiful blond girl come on board. Normac and Syska whispered to each other about plans for the princess, and at least ten others were with them by the end of the day. Captain Kochic and Quinor stood on top of the forecastle and watched the sun go down as Quinor's thoughts moved to the princess now sleeping in the cabin below.

* * *

Bosstu walked silently with the group, as all he could think about were his friends, his city that lay behind him fighting for its life now. But his orders were his honor, and he would carry them out no matter what was happening back in Bru Edin.

The group, he also observed, was an interesting one. First off, the female elf he saw in this group he thought was the leader at first because of her beauty but also the way she carried herself and how she talked to the others. Blond with blueish eyes like the sky, she flew on the ground like the wind, leaving no sign that she had been there moments before.

The big half-orc, Bennak, seemed to walk quietly with one

of the warriors, who had not spoken a word since leaving the city behind. This man carried himself like he either was ashamed of what he had done or was experiencing some other feeling that Bosstu couldn't understand, but whatever it was, he didn't want to ask the man.

The mage who walked with them was very funny, always making those around him smile and laugh along with him. Bosstu couldn't understand it, but maybe the mage was just trying to make the others forget about the war and death that was around them for a while.

The dwarf and the small man or young boy — he couldn't tell which since he acted like a boy but sometimes said things that only a grown man would know — kept to themselves, but he could tell the two were friends since they smiled and laughed at each other's jokes or whatever they were talking about.

The two druids, who were not too far from him, were discussing the nature of this old mountain. Once in a while Bosstu caught some of what they were talking about. He wanted to correct what they were saying, but he also didn't want to interfere in this group that much; he was just taking them from one place to another.

It was the man he was told after starting this mission was the leader of this group who made him wonder.

Kalion, he had thought when he met him along the ramparts of Bru Edin, looked like he could fight even the worst that evil could throw at him, but now Kalion was quiet and seemed to be thinking of something else, or someone else, walking by himself at the tail end of the group. They walked on the rocky trail up the mountainside towards the two towers that would lead them through the northern mountainside to the fields that lay between Bru Edin and Chai'sell, which is what he was told was the group's destination.

When they got about halfway up the trail, everyone stopped suddenly when, under their feet, each felt a tremor. It only lasted a few moments and then disappeared as suddenly as it had happened.

Bosstu looked around the caldera of the mountain and then

back towards the city, whose towers he couldn't make out now, wondering what the tremor was, when Kikor walked up.

"You know what that was, my friend?" she asked quietly as she stepped into his view.

Smiling back, he shook his head slightly. "No, I am sorry, my lady. I know not what it was." He looked around a bit more and then thought that maybe it was just rocks falling somewhere within the mountain. "Sometimes this mountain speaks without warning. It's like its spirit is letting us know it's still here."

Kikor nodded back and smiled as Bosstu turned and continued to walk towards the towers, where he could leave this group and return to the city to fight the orcs that were hoping to destroy it.

* * *

Kalion burst into the room that lay behind the massive door at the bottom of one of the towers, as they had reached the far side of the trail. Having found the door locked and rusted, it took him only two tries before it burst open. Stepping back, he nodded to each member of the group but lowered his head slightly. "Let's see what is here before we move on," Kalion said to the group, who nodded quietly.

Bosstu had tried the key he had been given many cycles ago that should have opened the door, but it didn't work. He seemed a bit angered at Kalion's damage to the finely made door, but taking in a deep breath, he explained to the group what they should find inside.

"The first floor contains weapons, and ... well, it used to have food, but I know not when this place housed warriors last." His voice echoed in the room as Meradoth made his way through the doorway that led to some dark, cold and small stairs to another floor that indeed held everything a warrior would need in their travels.

Calling back down what he found, Meradoth walked over

to the small vertical window that lay at the northern wall. When he looked out, he saw a sight that made him smile: lush green fields of grass, a river he could just make out moving from the right to the left, and far beyond it all, the massive, snowed-covered Pilo'ach Mountains.

As everyone made their way through the rooms, Kalion walked up, seeing that Meradoth wasn't paying any attention to what was in the room.

"What do you see, my friend?" he asked, placing his hand on the mage's shoulder.

"Our destination, my friend. Take a look!" Meradoth stepped back, letting the ranger look through and lean back, smiling himself.

"There is a road down there that will lead us to the dwarven city, so I would think we will have an easy day's travel as soon as we are off this mountain," Kalion said as he turned and watched everyone leave.

Returning down the stairs, leaving the mage to explore more of this tower, Kalion found Bosstu leaning against the door that led back to the city with his arms crossed, watching everyone clean or arrange the weapons they had just found.

Walking up, Kalion looked over and watched everyone for a moment before whispering softly enough that only the man could hear him.

"I know your bringing us here, my friend, was something you didn't want to do," Kalion said quietly as Bosstu just stared at the ground. "If you like, you could travel with us."

"If you go down those stairs, you will find the door that will let you outside and to the north," Bosstu said, interrupting the ranger's invitation. Turning his head, Kalion saw on the far side of the floor stairs going down.

"Thank you, sir!" Kalion looked back at the man and could see that he was sad, and maybe mad, that he had to bring Kalion's people here. Bosstu then looked up and nodded at the ranger and then turned around and grabbed the door handle. Saying a quiet goodbye, he opened the door, bringing in light from outside, which grabbed everyone's attention and stopped all talk as they looked up and watched the man walk out and leave the group to themselves.

"Mysterious man, Kalion," Amlora remarked, showing a small smile, which made the others laugh at the joke within her comment.

"He must have family living in the city," Kikor quietly added. "I would gather that that is all he was thinking about as he brought us here."

Kalion could only smile at her as he thought about the man named Bosstu.

Chapter Sixteen

Methnorick stood watching the battle of Bru Edin before him on his tapestry with his arms crossed. The light in the room came only from the two torches that lay on the wall not far behind Methnorick, casting shadows before him. He had never liked his rooms to be lit much, and at this moment, the only fires he wanted to see were the ones he was watching develop before and within the city he wanted gone.

When he saw the death of Edin's general, he slammed his fist hard on his throne in excitement, causing the rock the throne was made from to crack under his hand, but Methnorick didn't care, as he celebrated, watching the man die under the assault of his army. Men's arrogance that they were superior in all things was what irritated Methnorick the most about humans.

He almost made his room explode from his excitement as he watched the ground collapse and envelop Bru Edin's cavalry, killing almost all of them.

"Die, Bru Edin!" he yelled at the tapestry, not noticing the door opening up at the far end of the room as he continued to yell at the wall, watching the mightiest army in the northern lands fall away from its outer defenses and hole itself up behind the largest and thickest of the walls that had made Bru Edin famous.

When a cough behind him caught his attention, Methnorick grabbed a piece of his now destroyed throne and threw it at the creature that was trying to get his attention. "Leave me, scum!" he yelled loudly.

Quickly the creature screeched and ducked as the rock crashed against the wall behind it. He scrambled quickly out of the room, leaving Methnorick to himself in his joyous cry that finally he would have the land of the north, as he knew that his armies were close to destroying the men that ruled across the lands. The land held the secrets, and the land is what he wanted — without men, without elves and even without orcs, giants or others that currently fought for him.

It took a few more moments for Methnorick to see that it wouldn't take long for the city to fall, maybe a day or two. Lifting a hand, he whipped it across the tapestry, which turned to mist before his eyes and slowly disappeared to show a new scene on the fabric. Methnorick again crossed his arms as he took in what he was now seeing.

The massive wall that circled the city that was known as the "City of Ports," Blath 'Na, was for the first time abandoned, without even the single guard that had once always walked along it. Banners still fluttered in the winds, but nothing moved under them. The massive gate that opened to the west was covered in marks of fire along the edge of one of the doors, Methnorick saw, as the image moved slowly around and into the city.

As the scene moved around the city, he saw a great number of dark clouds rise high into the air from fires that had erupted in buildings that had once stood proudly within the city of Blath 'Na.

As he searched, squinting his eyes slightly, he wondered where the bodies were, as the image moved around, showing dead horses, carts turned over, food lying on the ground and people's belongings scattered amongst all of this, but no bodies.

"Is it true?" he whispered loudly, thinking of what the scientist had told him about the creatures he had created: when they killed, the bodies would … mmmmm. Methnorick squinted his eyes as the tapestry's image slowly moved down a street.

"Masterrrrr!" a voice echoed within the room, making him look over, for it was not the servant that had come in earlier. He saw another creature standing in the shadows, leaving only its feet to be seen in the light. He could make out the small creature that had tried to get his attention earlier, standing slightly behind the creature, talking to him now, cowering in fear.

"What are you doing here? I remember sending you to the empire to get it ready for me," Methnorick quietly stated as the scene on the tapestry stopped moving but showed a large temple encased in high and powerful flames.

The creature stepped out of the shadows so most of it could be seen. Methnorick knew that Sunorak, his best general, who was not on the field like his other generals but worked from behind the lines, caused armies to fall apart when he ordered it. Methnorick held him at bay because he wanted the humans to suffer first.

"My master, the empire is yours to take. The high minister there has been convinced to follow your command. He will do what you order, but I am here to inform you that King Dia has disappeared." Sunorak's all-black eyes stared straight ahead, but Methnorick knew that they were staring directly at him now.

He blinked a few times as he wondered if he had heard that right. Tilting his head slightly, he reached up and pulled the hood back, revealing the long, black hair covering his grotesque features, which at that moment were wet with perspiration.

"What did you say?" Methnorick's question whisked through his teeth as his servant's words poured into his mind.

Nodding slightly, Sunorak stepped closer so his master could see that he was both not afraid and that he was serious in his message. "King Dia, master, has been able to escape that baron person and ally himself with elves that were still fighting within the forest east of his dying city."

Methnorick's anger began to grow by the moment, and Sunorak could see the redness form in his lord's face so quickly that he lifted his hands and waved them across his body to protect himself. He did so just in time, as Methnorick raised his arms high and exploded in anger, screaming out Dia's name, clinching his fists tightly as he screamed.

Suddenly the room erupted in bright red flames that quickly

encased Methnorick and set the tapestry along the wall on fire. Soon the two doors that were closed exploded out, engulfing anyone on the other side in fire, which melted them instantly.

Outside in the courtyard, orcs still training stopped what they were doing as they saw once again fire shoot out of the windows high above and heard their master scream out something in anger. As the fire receded, the orcs in charge turned and yelled at their warriors to continue training.

Up above, the fire disappeared as quickly as it had appeared, leaving only Methnorick and Sunorak standing within the chamber, not caring that the fire had killed the creature that had been hiding moments before and those standing guard outside the doors.

Methnorick stood, breathing hard, his chest rising and falling under the armor that he wore over his clothing. He stared at Sunorak, slowly gathering his voice back after having just released his anger.

"Tell me ... what happened?" Methnorick said quietly through his teeth again as he turned to walk over to the now blown-out window and stare across the castle grounds and towards the sea, looking at the land that he needed to conquer, and soon. "My spies informed me that he had been captured, and I was told in the last report that he was being brought here." Turning his head, he looked back halfway, waiting to hear an answer of some kind.

"They were correct, my master. Indeed, he had been captured while trying to escape Brigin'i as it was falling, but somewhere within the Levenori Forest something happened, and he was able to get away." Sunorak's voice echoed within Methnorick's mind, which of course didn't lessen his anger at hearing that his enemy had somehow escaped his plan.

"Where is that fat man ... that baron who was bringing him to me?" Methnorick turned back to the window, looking back out towards the seas as he thought quickly about what he needed to do now.

"There is no word on where the baron is, or if he is alive.

I found where Parnland lost him. There were only signs of orcs and those men that Parnland was using lying dead on the ground — I found no sign of the baron or Dia. I believe that either he was captured by those who took Dia, or he is hiding somewhere, knowing that you will search for him.

"Forget Parnland ..." Methnorick's mind raced as he thought about what he was going to do to that baron when he found him. "The princess is still coming, and when she gets here, my quest to control these lands will be complete, for she is part of the key to these lands." Methnorick smiled then, reassuring Sunorak that things were better now. Methnorick walked over and waved his hand so that the room suddenly appeared as it had been before, in perfect condition, including the replacement of the tapestry. Methnorick moved in front of the tapestry and waved his hand again to see an image erupt on the tapestry, which showed the city of Blath 'Na still burning.

"Your creatures have done more to that city than I had ever thought possible. It was visionary to use that scientist here to create such creatures in his lab." Methnorick looked over to make sure his servant was also watching the image.

"How is some little human girl going to help you, lord?" Sunorak whispered as he watched the tapestry for a moment.

Methnorick sucked in a loud breath, pushing his chest out as he looked over. Staring at the general, he thought for a moment about whether he should say how she would help.

"There is a legend that a girl of power — tainted by man, loved by the gods — shall rule all," Methnorick whispered as Sunorak looked over, hearing the answer now.

"Interesting, my lord. And you shall ...?"

"I shall rule her!" Methnorick declared, finishing his general's comment with a smile.

"My masterrr." Sunorak smiled and then bowed slightly. He turned and quietly left the chamber, moving away as silently as he had entered.

* * *

The warrior walked the high ramparts of the Father Gate without a sound, only hearing his footsteps once in a while as they landed on some bits of dirt or rock and a flock of birds crying as they flew over his position from the north, moving south.

He looked out and saw just beyond the trees the ravine that crossed the lands that made up the northern border of the empire, knowing that crossing it always brought him dread because he hated crossing the bridge that spanned the ravine.

He was tired of what he was doing. Ever since the massive gates had been closed, those in charge of this place had been on high alert that the orcs were going to attack soon. All were convinced that it was going to happen any day.

The day before, a score of cavalry scouts had taken the chance of going north and scouting out the region that lay northwest of where the gate was, as the general had received a report that something was moving, and he wanted to make sure that nothing was trying to sneak up on the towers.

"Chicken neck!" he whispered out loud and then suddenly stopped his curse when he realized his voice carried everywhere, making him look around to see if anyone had heard him. Luckily the other warriors on the wall hadn't heard, so taking a deep breath, he shook his head, telling himself he had to be careful next time, for the sergeant disapproved of his troops cursing in any way and enacted swift and strict punishment.

Next time ... of course there is going to be a next time. Commander Tevenic was acting like a fool, thinking that these towers could be attacked and then even conquered by, of all things, orcs! He smiled and laughed at what he was thinking. Of all the creatures that walked on these lands, the orcs were the least capable to doing something like that.

And sending cavalry north out into the open when they could have been protected behind these safe walls ... what a fool he is! the man thought again as he kept walking, doing his slow duty of keeping an eye on the lands that lay just north of the tower he was walking on, even though he considered it a waste of time.

Nodding to the warrior who passed him, he took another deep breath and continued walking slowly along the rampart, looking back to see that the compound was full of activity. Many men were training, and a few worked to get food prepared for that night's meal, but more were just standing around, not doing much.

An easy duty, the man thought as he walked, only stopping to peer over the edge of the wall to check out the bottom and make sure nothing was down there because he was sure he had just heard a noise.

Looking around to see if any of the other warriors had heard the sound, he noticed none had. "I've got to stop drinking the night before duty!" he whispered.

So adjusting the heavy spear he held, he continued walking slowly, thinking of his family who lived to the south in their home village. Many other warriors had sent their families away just to be sure they were safe because of the report about the whole of the north being on fire.

The shout from behind him brought him out of his thoughts, and he turned quickly, grabbing his spear with both hands, to see the warrior he had just passed pointing out north.

Seeing nothing as he looked in that direction, he ran over to the man, hoping this would give him a better vantage. They were joined by the other warrior on watch. As he got closer, he finally saw what the man was pointing at: the scouts who had left the day before were riding hard down the road towards the tower.

"The scouts have returned. Open the gates!" The words were screamed out as the gate door opened to let the cavalry ride through.

All the warriors along the wall watched as the cavalry got closer and closer, and all quickly saw that something was wrong. Their numbers were smaller than they had been the day before when they left.

"Send word below that the scouts have been attacked," the sergeant ordered another warrior, who turned and ran down the stairs to disappear within the tower.

"I count at least 40 missing, sir," the guard who had first seen the scouts reported.

"Men, I need you to continue your watch. If those scouts were attacked, whatever it was might try to hit us while we are watching them, so keep your eyes open." The man turned his head left and right as he spoke to make sure each warrior in his charge heard him.

Quickly they all turned and continued walking along the wall as the sounds of horses grunting and metal clanking echoed as the cavalry rushed through the gate, which closed quickly after the last horse had ridden through.

The sergeant in charge along the wall turned and watched. He saw Commander Tevenic run out of the right tower and speak to the leader of the scouts.

He could tell from the looks Tevenic had on his face that whatever the two were talking about was extreme; he was right to think that whatever had attacked the scouts was dangerous. Another horse was made ready, and within moments the rider who was listening to the general nodded, kicked his horse's side, took off and rode south.

As the man continued to watch the activity below, he could see warriors moving everywhere as the scouts were pulled out of their saddles and cared for by a few clerics who were working the gate. Another man ran up the stairs and informed the sergeant that he had been ordered to make sure all men along the ramparts stayed alert.

"What happened to those men below?" he asked before the

other warrior could run down the stairs.

Taking a deep breath, the man looked back down to see if he had a moment to talk. Turning his head around, he quickly explained what he had just heard.

"The scouts were patrolling along the Merninor Glen when they were attacked by ... by ..." The man suddenly couldn't answer, which made the sergeant very anxious. He quickly turned to look north, only seeing trees and green grass, so he turned his head again and stared at the man. He coughed slightly, hoping to get the man to continue his explanation of what had happened, but the warrior wouldn't, out of the fear of what he had seen.

"What attacked our men?" the sergeant asked, frustrated now but trying not to make it sound like an order, as he could see that this young man was scared of what he had heard.

"Trolggs ... it was trolggs that attacked our men, sergeant." The man took a long swallow and quickly ran back down the stairs to continue on his way, not saying another word as he descended.

The word made the sergeant straighten back up and mouth the word a few times as he quickly tried to understand what he had just been told. He turned and walked over to the edge of the wall and looked north to where that glen lay.

"Trolggs," the sergeant whispered loudly.

A commotion of movement near him made him blink a few times. "Sergeant ... sergeant ... what did he say? Does he know what attacked our men?" A warrior who had seen the two speaking stood not far away, and he could tell that, whatever the younger warrior had said, his sergeant now knew what had happened.

Swallowing as he cleared his throat, he turned to see the man looking straight at him with a question on his face.

"I want you to order each man on that side to carry a torch along with their weapon!" He pointed to where he wanted the warrior to go.

"Yes ... yes, sir, right away!" The man quickly ran off to

carry out his new orders as the sergeant turned and yelled at those working the other side to do the same thing. It didn't take long for the ramparts to be lit up with torches, as each warrior held a torch along with their spears.

"Trolggs ... here in this area. I can't believe it. How and where did they come from?" he asked himself quietly as he leaned on the rock and continued to stare north.

As the sergeant stared north, deep in thought, he didn't notice a pair of red glowing eyes staring back at him through the bushes that lay not far from the gate towers. As the sun disappeared in the west, the only thing that he could see if he looked south or north was the line of torches that moved slowly as the warriors who patrolled the ramparts carried them.

As the dark took over, the red glowing eyes watched the creatures that walked along the top of the structure. It knew it had to get past these creatures, and all night those eyes just hung there, watching.

Chapter Seventeen

$\mathcal{M}$ethnorick stood, leaning out the large window as he looked out onto the countryside outside of his castle. His anger from before had disappeared, and though his chambers were now in pristine condition, he decided to walk and clear his mind.

News spread quickly throughout his army that Bru Edin was finally in its final days and that General Kaligor had begun his final assault. Those members of his army within his castle worked harder in their training as word came that their lord might be wanting to move soon. Though the losses of orcs and goblins were high, Methnorick didn't care; all he wanted was for the "Shield of the North" to be destroyed at that moment.

After Sunorak left to carry out his orders, word reached him that his last general to lead a landing and attack the northern lands, a General Orle'ak, had landed in the north-western part of the continent and was destroying many villages and large towns, finding light resistance there. Quickly he had been able to block the passes of the northern borders of Brigin'i, and so far he had done well by capturing or killing many of those who had escaped Brigin'i, which pleased Methnorick even more.

Soon the landscape was littered with the corpses of the people of the northwest and Brigin'i, as they were pulled up high on poles everywhere. Fires were lit everywhere and those within Orle'ak's army fed on prisoners, making the smell travel for many miles beyond.

Only the very north and northeast areas of the land lay open for conquest, meaning the homelands of the elven hierarchy and their powerfully held forests and valleys were still unconquered.

These lay just west of Blath 'Na and east of Bru Edin. His plans were going perfectly, and his generals were expressing the same satisfaction in their reports. Corner and cut off the elves. Methnorick's greatest prize was getting closer. With the loss of Bru Edin, he could get the last of the objects within the elven homeland.

With the northern lands in his control, he would then turn his attention south. His thoughts were interrupted by the sound of a messenger running up behind him.

"My lord, my lord ..." The messenger ran up, stopping, almost out of breath. Methnorick reached out and grabbed the messenger by his throat and lifted the surprised creature up. The goblin-like creature's eyes expanded wide as he struggled to get out of Methnorick's grip, gasping for air as he struggled.

"What do you want!?" His anger could be felt by the goblin as he tried to answer his master. Methnorick decided it had suffered enough and released the goblin to let it fall down. The goblin looked up, and through his squeaky voice, he did the best he could.

"Ma– ... master ... I was ordered to inform you ... your navy, my lord ..." He gasped violently as he struggled to speak, but Methnorick knew what he was saying, so he quickly waved the creature away before he angered him anymore and he would have to kill him.

"My ships are at the ready. My army is ready. What could stop me? Nothing!" he joyously cheered out loud.

As he stood there smiling, a dark elf walked up a stairwell not far away, this time knowing that even if his lord was happy, he could still reach out and kill him just for the fun of it.

Methnorick watched him stand there for a while waiting, so finally he lifted his hand up, waving it to come closer. Quickly it stepped close enough for him to hear.

"Yes, what news do you have?" Methnorick's voice still haunted each creature that lived under his hand.

Bowing, the elf pulled back his hood to reveal his greyish hair.

"My lord and master, the creature that you seek ... it has been found." The elf'swords stung Methnorick, making him blink a few times.

"Repeat that, elf. Who did you find?" Methnorick whispered, wanting to hear it again.

"The creature that escaped from you many cycles ago, master ... it was seen," the elf repeated.

The news did not make Methnorick happy at that moment. "Where?" he asked quickly.

"Within the city of Bru Edin, my master. It was seen traveling with another group of warriors, my master, moving through the city."

Lifting up his hands, he slammed them together as he turned and walked closer to the elf that quickly knelt down to one knee and waited as his master stood over him.

It's been seen ... after all these cycles ... and now within Bru Edin. Could it be fighting for the men there? No, it wouldn't be doing that. It would find a way to fight without joining others. But who was it traveling with? Could it be this group from Brigin'i that I have heard about?

"Did you find who it was traveling with?" he asked quickly.

"No, master. We tried to follow but were stopped when Kaligor did something to cause a building to collapse between us."

Leaning down, Methnorick looked into the elf's eyes and said, "I do not want excuses from you. Find it. Follow it and find out who it travels with. Do you understand me, elf?"

"I will find it, my lord!" The dark elf turned to leave the room and carry out its master's orders, leaving Methnorick now wondering what the creature was up to as he continued his walk.

He walked into another chamber, this one larger than the one that held the throne. Though dark, it held many torches that made shadows throughout the room. In the firelight Methnorick could see armor hanging from the walls, ancient weapons lining everything and tapestries hanging from gold bars.

As he walked in, still reeling from the information he had just been given, he noticed standing off in one corner in the shadows one of his servants who had only been seen once in the world. Another stood near the large window, looking like a statue as it stared out into the night.

Methnorick walked up to the large table that had once held his maps and tools. Leaning down on it, he looked over the large map that showed him the northern lands that he was trying to conquer when his voice echoed. "I have something that both of you might be interested in." He watched them both smile as wings slowly expanded behind their backs and he told him his plans.

* * *

The princess had decided to use the threat to her advantage, so she called Quinor into the cabin and told him the story she had created about the captain and how she feared he would mistreat her.

"Princess, I am sure that the captain meant no harm to you. I will speak to him. I have known him for a while now and, yes, he is a bit ... ugly, but ..." Quinor smiled.

"Ugly!" she spoke a little loudly, making Quinor uneasy. She looked up at the warrior, smiling at him, quickly saying sorry with her eyes that she had spoken so loudly. "No, please don't speak to him. It may only make it worse, or he may take it out on you." She could see that the first part of her plan, making him fall for her, was working. The second part, drawing a wedge between Quinor and the crew, might be a bit harder.

"Listen," he said, placing a hand on her shoulder and looking deep into her eyes, eyes that he finally understood he was in love with now, "if you want, I can move my bed roll into your chambers if you're nervous about the crew trying to make its way in there or something. But I am sure that the captain will not let that happen."

His words were convincing her that she was right and her plan was on target in getting her kidnapper to trust her. She had not slept much that night for fear of the crew, and she was sure she wouldn't sleep well with him in the room; however, it brought her closer to her goal, so she would make it work.

"Yes, that would make me feel so much safer. I know you have kept me safe thus far and wouldn't let anything happen to me," she said as she looked back into his eyes.

Now Quinor walked out of the cabin. As she watched from the doorway, she saw the crew that was working nearby, pulling some rope out of the water, stop and give her a look that made her instantly scared. Quinor had brought her to this point and was now the only man she felt she could count on to ensure she got out of this situation before they reached Methnorick. However, the only way for that to happen was for her plan to work: to get Quinor to fight and kill the ship's captain and crew and take the ship.

A few moments later, she made her way into the stern cabin, where she knew Quinor and the captain were bunked. She found the captain and two of his crew members leaning over a table, talking. When she walked in, they quickly stopped talking and straightened up to stare back at her.

"Can we help you, Princess?" the captain asked quickly as the others smiled from the corners of their mouths.

Swallowing quickly, she looked around the cabin but didn't see Quinor. "I ... mmm ... I was looking for Quinor, captain ... sir."

"He was down below with his two men the last I heard, Princess." Captain Kochic nodded towards the hatch that would lead her down below.

"Thank you, sir." She smiled nervously and turned to close the door when she caught the words from the other two men who were with the captain.

"Let's get her whilst she's below, Captain."

"Shhhh ... no, tonight!"

Shermee stopped before she closed the door, turned on the captain and with a deep breath said, "May I remind you, sir, that I am traveling to be Methnorick's bride. I do not think he will take kindly on any intervention in this endeavor." With that she winked at them, slowly turned and walked out, swinging her hips more, hoping to entice the captain. As she shut the door behind her with trembling hands, hoping that her bluff played well, she almost ran over to the hatch, which opened just as just put her hand on the latch. Quinor walked out with one of his other men, who stretched and walked over to the edge to look at the water that was moving now pretty steadily under them.

Seeing the girl's face, Quinor looked around quickly and then grabbed her arm and pulled her off to the side, where now both were standing, talking.

As the two continued to speak, the door of the cabin opened and the captain and his two crewmen walked out. Seeing the princess talking to the big warrior, they shut their smiles down and only nodded at them both before moving on to their duties for the day.

Quinor pulled the princess closer to the rail and whispered for her to stay there as he called over his man.

"Akula, I'm moving my bed roll to sleep in the princess's cabin tonight. Can you please move it when you have a chance?" Akula had been steering the carriage that took them to the port. The thin but strong-armed man just nodded slowly as he looked the princess over quickly.

"Oh, and tell Fad to hurry and wake up. I have a feeling the next few days are going to be interesting."

"I had the same feeling when I overheard the crew last night." Akula turned to walk away, but Quinor quickly stopped him.

"Explain!"

"Over a few drinks, some of the crew were talking about ... mmm ... you know ... her." Akula nodded back at the girl standing behind them both now.

"What did they say?" Akula told him that a few members of the crew wanted to take the princess down to the depths of the ship and rape her. They felt it was their right for some reason, Akula whispered.

"What did the captain say to all this?"

"Well, he wasn't there, but some of the men, including the first mate, said they would not bother them as long as she was undamaged for Methnorick. They only stopped talking after they realized we had heard what they said."

Quinor leaned his head back, moaning slightly as he thought about what to do. "OK, go get my bed and both of yours. You sleep outside her door tonight while I sleep inside.

"Princess ... Shermee ... did you hear? The crew is planning something, but it does not seem to be the entire crew, only a few, so I'll confront the captain. But you need to go back to your cabin and wait, understand? Akula will stand guard until I get back."

She nodded quickly and started to walk away when Akula walked out of the cabin with a few blankets, and together they walked forward to the cabin that Shermee used.

When he walked out moments later, she quickly locked the door, though knowing that if any man really wanted to get to her, he could, as the lock was rusted from cycles of being upon the seas.

There she just waited and waited, thinking of ways to use her body to manipulate and convince Quinor to fight the captain when she heard a scream, and she instantly wished she had asked Quinor for a knife of some kind.

"Kalion!" she whispered, wishing the man were there.

Chapter Eighteen

The clouds that lay over Bru Edin made it very hard to see what was going on, but those outside the walls knew it wasn't going well for the human fortress; many could hear the booms and explosions of magic and rocks and even see the flashes that they were making erupt through the clouds.

Every once in a while, a large group of the populace could feel the ground shake from explosions as rocks hitting the walls and buildings of the mighty fortress made everyone scream or cry. The fighting itself was too far away, but everyone could imagine what was going on. Bru Edin, for the first time, was defending itself against an enemy that knew nothing except victory and death. This proud city being on the verge of defeat when it had only known victory reduced the people hiding to tears, for there was nowhere for them to go.

Men along the ramparts fought and died under the constant shower of arrows being released at them, and soon Marshal Tassalii was wounded when he poked his head over the wall to watch a few rocks slam into the gates and was hit by the shrapnel as part of the gate nearest to him exploded, sending shards everywhere.

He ordered any archer who still could fight to continue releasing everything they could, knowing that each one who tried to release an arrow was taking a chance at being killed, as the enemy had taken up positions along the inner wall that still stood to knock out his men who were defending the inner wall now.

His war machines continued to release their heavy rocks and stones, which were doing massive amounts of damage to the orcs and their allies, but he finally understood Bru Edin's weakness with regard to war machines like these as one of his machines was obliterated by a boulder, taken out by the enemy's bigger and stronger machines that had been pushed close enough. The enemy had giants running their war machines because their size was three times that of anything a man could control and carry, allowing them to release faster than his gnome-driven machines. They could also move theirs around, while Bru Edin's were stuck in place.

Before he could think, he saw three more destroyed this way. Their engineers and the men around them were disappearing in the clouds of dirt. Their screams echoed and then got quiet.

Tassalii screamed out orders for anyone who could to send what they had at the machines now showering the wall's ramparts with rocks and stones, killing everyone that came in contact with them as they landed hard, destroying parts of the wall.

He knew that it wouldn't be long before the last defense fell, so quickly he grabbed Captain Sanasis, ordering him to build up defenses inside the city and calling for the men on the wall to stall for time.

"In the city, sir? You believe they will make it in?" The captain, only 35 cycles of age, whose hands were covered in blood from helping the wounded, stood, showing concern to his leader.

"Not only are they going to get in, but each and every person within the city will die once this happens. Do you understand?" Tassalii screamed back in frustration.

Moving over to a map of Bru Edin lying on the ground, he pushed the dust and a few bits of rocks that had landed on it so he could give the man his ideas on the final defense of the city.

Both peered over it as the marshal went through idea after idea about what the man needed to do.

Pointing to the main road that led from the gates, he said, "If you go into these two buildings — here and here — go to the southern corners of each building. You will find a stone at each corner. Look for a cross marking on the stone and use whatever men you can to destroy that stone."

"Sir, are you suggesting that we knock these buildings down onto the road?" Sanasis asked, looking up after hearing the interesting orders that he had just been given.

"Yes, the builders of this city many cycles ago knew that, if the gates fell, this city could easily be taken. It is only in our arrogance of the last few cycles that we have forgotten this could happen. So they put in place buildings along the roads that, if knocked down, could potentially stop a breach from happening ... or least slow it down."

Sanasis's eyes grew large as he listened. Never in his life had he heard that this could be done. His marshal didn't stop upon seeing the captain's questions on his face but continued talking.

"Of course, when you knock them down, just get out of the way, but when you are done, go to this area and this area and do the same to this building ... and this one here." Tassalii pointed to the last few places and then leaned back to let the captain take it in.

When Tassalii was done, Sanasis nodded to his orders and started to move to carry them out when he heard a cough, making him stop and turn around.

"I'm giving you a generalship so you can carry these orders out with more strength. Understand ... General Sanasis?" Tassalii knew some might question a lowly captain giving out these orders.

Hearing that he had just gotten promoted made the man puff his chest out in pride as he nodded quickly. "Sir, it will be done!"

As the man left, Marshal Tassalii, blew out a large breath and looked over the map, knowing that if the man didn't do his job, then Bru Edin was finished. He didn't have much time to think about it, though, because a warrior ran in, informing him that orcs were pressing hard against the gates.

Marshal Tassalii, grabbing the cane he had been given earlier to help him walk with his injuries, quickly followed the man out of the room that luckily hadn't been hit by a rock or boulder when screams erupted as he looked towards the ramparts and saw that darkness was finally settling over Bru Edin.

* * *

The dwarf general marveled at the strength and hardness of his dwarven warriors, and when he called, they jumped, quickly gathering their armor and weapons and marching south to the human castle fortress that lay at the southern end of the Edin Plains, which were once called the Tongue of Chais by his people.

Now these 2,000 dwarven warriors ran at an easy but quick step to catch up to the Bru Edin cavalry that had passed them, charging around the mountain towards the battle beyond.

Odariam Skullcrusher only smiled beneath his white beard that swung under his face as he trudged through the grass. The dwarf was one of the bravest, strongest and wisest dwarves that led the dwarves of Chai'sell. With broad shoulders and thick arms and legs that were covered only in the best armor his people could make, he had long hair that flew behind him as he ran. Odariam never wore a helm like his brethren did; he had hated having his eyes covered since he was a young one, and now he was glad he didn't wear a helm, as running with one would only have slowed the old dwarf down.

When King Stokolma made the call for his shield wall to make its way south, he only had to nod. His people had been fighting the orc creatures since he could remember. Their own legends spoke of the time when the gods came and left their people to watch over the lands, but then as a game, left, and when the orcs moved in, the dwarves hunted them for entertainment.

Entertainment? Odariam smiled again. *That's a joke in the making.* Since he could remember, the orcs had not been entertainment but more of a force against which his people struggled to survive. Over the last few cycles, his people within Chai'sell had been fighting what seemed sometimes to be a losing battle, but he had to forget those battles that were happening within the deep darkness of his city. Their allies had made the call for help, and his king kept his promises.

His shield wall had trained its movements against the orcish charge that always seemed to them a mass explosion of teeth and swords whenever they battled, and he was sure that this time, even with his numbers, he could stop whatever was happening in Bru Edin, or at least die trying.

The dwarves all wore the armor of their king: a white- and red-covered armor. Each carried a shield and an axe or heavy sword. Whilst slowly running, many were dropping their helmets, as the weight was too much for them.

This run, all knew, would tire them out, so three times Odariam ordered a full stop for his warriors to take a breath. Each time he did, he sent scouts to run farther ahead and report if they could see anything. Each time they came back only reporting that the clouds were dark and the air was heavy. They had nothing to report in terms of sightings — only the sounds of heavy battle from the south.

As they stopped this last time, he and his warriors quietly talked about the battle to come while they waited for the scouts' report. Suddenly they all began to feel the ground underneath their boots shake slightly and hear what sounded like an eruption in the south.

Odariam knelt down and felt the ground as he closed his eyes and wondered what was happening at the fortress. He opened his eyes suddenly, as he felt something, maybe a worm or a mole of some type within the ground, touch his hand. He pulled his hand up quickly, wondering if he felt it wrong.

He stood up and stared at the others next to him, who were talking about family, battle, the plans for when they came around the final corner of the mountain, and the plans for how to spread themselves out, when they heard the cry from the last scout who had left a while earlier finally approach.

All turned to watch the warrior, who had stripped himself down to only his shirt, come running up, covered in sweat. As he arrived to stand in front of his general, breathing hard from the run but taking no water, he bent over to take a few breaths.

Odariam and his warriors waited until finally the scout bent up and took one more deep breath as his general looked on.

"Sir …" he began, swallowing hard, "sir, the Edin cavalry has fallen!" On hearing that, each dwarf that sat or stood by moved closer to hear what their comrade was speaking about.

Odariam looked at the scout with a face of confusion. "What are you talking about? They just passed us not long ago."

Nodding quickly, the scout said, "I know, sir, but when they arrived, something attacked them from within the ground, sir." The dwarf finally took a pouch of water and took a few long drinks of it as Odariam looked to the south, trying to understand.

After taking the water, the scout explained what he had seen when he came around the final corner, which all could see was within sight now as they looked south. When he rounded the corner, he was thinking he would either see a heavy battle between the cavalry that had passed them and the orcs or a total route of the orcs since all knew the power and skill of the Bru Edin cavalry, but instead all he saw were large openings in the ground and a few horses running away without riders.

None of the dwarfs that heard the tale could believe that the whole of the Bru Edin cavalry had been destroyed so easily and so quickly.

Odariam turned and quickly ordered his warriors to ready themselves in case the orcs were trying to circle the fortress and they would find themselves face to face with the orcs on this field sooner than he had thought.

As the call was shouted out, Odariam grabbed his captains who led his shield wall, and quickly they discussed what they should do.

"Return to Chai'sell" was one idea that came out.

"Fight to the gate of Bru Edin," another suggested quickly. Odariam could see that his warriors were wanting battle, but he worried now, as he could hear a few whisper in fear.

If the orcs had been able to destroy the cavalry so easily, what would they have in mind for his warriors when they entered the battlefield? By returning to their home, they could gather more warriors for if and when the orcs made their charge at their massive gates that had kept their enemies out for so many cycles.

Looking up as the others argued about what to do, he took a deep breath and stared at the scout, who was quickly snapping his armor that he had left earlier back on, and he walked over to place his hand on the dwarf's shoulder.

"Did you see what made the ground open up ... or what might be within it?" he asked, but the dwarf just shook his head "no," as he understood that if he did anything wrong, his warriors could fall into the same trap.

Turning, Odariam cupped his hands around his mouth to scream out his orders. He knew the orders would not make them happy, but he wanted to keep them safe.

"We will return to our home. The men at Bru Edin have fallen. I believe whatever opened the ground will attack us soon, and we have no way of stopping that. So quickly, my warriors, we return home NOW!"

Quickly screams of "No" and "Why" and "Honor" echoed in his ears, but he only shook his head as he walked through the crowds of his warriors to walk and then run back north. Soon he left his warriors all standing there, wondering what to do as they watched their leader move north with his personal guard running close behind. Slowly, and many with lowered heads, they began to follow Odariam, all wondering why, but they knew their general knew what he was doing.

Chapter Nineteen

Tassalii only gasped as he stood, watching but not believing what he saw. Almost like a statue, he just stood there with his mouth hanging open, not knowing what to do as he watched the scene before him.

Moments earlier, as the marshal had moved around the corner of the building he was using for cover, he had seen where the screams were coming from and felt a chill move down his body, as he couldn't believe what he saw.

Huge arms that looked like tentacles of some kind were reaching up from the far side of the wall and were grabbing his archers and warriors that stood along the wall, fighting off the orcs that were trying to climb Bru Edin's defenses.

Each time one grabbed one of his men, all he could hear was a death cry from that man as one of the arms wrapped around the body and threw him up high into the air and then reached out and grabbed another to repeat the process again and again and again.

Screams echoed everywhere as men ran off the wall, not caring that the orcs were climbing over their last defense to kill those close by with their blades. All wanted to get away from these tentacles that were flying in and grabbing easy targets.

As Tassalii continued to watch, he noticed a group of mages moving down the road. There were only three of them, but as he watched, he hoped they could stop this creature quickly. But before that thought could even get through his mind, he gasped and screamed out in shock, grabbing the top of the wall in front of him as one of these tentacles reached up and over the wall to grab one of these mages, who quickly screamed. Tassalii's eyes watched the mage rise up high into the air, his arms struggling to get himself out of the tentacle's grip, only to die as the tentacle let the mage go by flinging him high in the air to land far away within the forest beyond.

"Ohhh godsss!" Tassalii screamed as he watched the man disappear.

Screams echoed in his ear as his warriors ran up, asking what to do: run or fight. Tassalii looked at the man who was closest. For some reason he only saw the man's mouth moving, not hearing what he was saying.

Shaking his head a few times and even hitting the side of his head, he wondered why he couldn't hear when slowly the noise around him quieted, only slightly of course, but enough for him to hear this man and a few others screaming at him.

"Sound the retreat!" was all he could say as he turned and watched the two mages who were left release a fireball and a bolt of what could have been lightning to slam into one of the tentacles. He followed the fireball and watched as it enclosed one of the massive arms, but instead of it catching fire, all it did was wiggle roughly, and the fire disappeared as the arm moved over and grabbed a horse that was tied up next to a house. It repeated what it had been doing to his men, throwing the screaming animal up into the air to fall hard on the battleground now covered with orcs and giants, all trying to climb the wall and get in.

Chapter Twenty

The group made it across the field that lay between Bru Edin and the Pilo'achs, where the dwarven citadel lay, deep within its rocks. Kalion looked back at the group, each seeming tired from the journey since leaving the towers that were hidden deep within the rocks on the north side of the mountain that held Bru Edin. No words were spoken as they stepped through the grass. Kalion believed that an army of cavalry horsemen would greet them on the field, as they had been able to hear the sounds of armor and horses within the walls of the towers earlier, which seemed like days ago now. However, they found nothing there to greet them now.

Kalion could see signs of horses' prints everywhere on the ground, but nothing else. If they were not there, then they were in battle to the south, outside the gates of Bru Edin. This gave the group a little extra push to get away quickly. Kalion looked at each of the others and took off at a run.

The group ran hard, only slowing down once to get across a river that crossed the field. They took their time moving across the river, which luckily was only knee-deep for most. Holan and Chansor had to take a bit longer since their legs were shorter. Meradoth giggled as he watched the dwarf grumble about getting wet, and Chansor even splashed the dwarf to make him laugh, making the mage smile more. A few others also giggled at the dwarf.

As the entrance to the dwarven kingdom grew closer and closer, the feeling of cold stone made everyone shiver, except Holan of course, who whistled loudly, knowing they were close.

"Chai'sell has stood the longest of any of my people's cities or fortresses and has done very well for itself with the riches that they have found within the Pilo'achs." Holan spoke fondly as he remembered the stories of the large, deep fires that rose in the halls, the food that never ended and the strength of the warriors who protected and fought for it when others tried to take it.

Everyone listened but none spoke as they walked closer by the moment and the mountains themselves began to tower over them. Only Kikor noticed the dwarven warriors who walked along the tops of the rocks that lay on each side of the entrance. Not wanting to alarm the rest, the elf kept the sight to herself for the moment.

As they walked over the last rise, the sight made the entire group instantly stop. Chansor's eyes caught a sight that he had never thought he would see, and as he paused to look at each of the others, he realized he was not alone in this thought, for all stood staring wide-eyed at what they beheld.

Instead of the gates being open with huge fire bonfires to lead the way for travelers and make them feel secure, safe and welcome, as Holan had described to the group, the bonfires were larger than ever, and standing across the entry to the field that stood before the gates were hundreds, if not thousands, of dwarven warriors, all in heavy armor, all ready for battle, with banners flying in the breeze above their heads.

"What's ... what's going on here?" Kalion whispered to Holan who, not answering, turned and held his hand up, letting the others know they needed to stay put as he made his way towards the dwarven army. He was met by five dwarven warriors who approached.

As the others watched, Holan raised his hand as he got closer to his brethren. The group continued to watch as the dwarves started a conversation. Once in a while one of the dwarves would look up at the group and then return to the conversation.

"I hope he's telling them we are friends!" Meradoth said quietly with a slight smile on his lips. "I'd hate to have to run away from such small people!"

"Shhhh," Kalion said without looking at Meradoth.

Jebba was turning, slowly looking up the sides of the cliffs. Noticing the helmets of dwarven warriors that were now peering down at them made him nervous that he was being watched.

Chansor was getting a bit jumpy and edgy too because he couldn't hear what was going on with Holan. He jumped up and down, trying to see past Meradoth.

"Calm yourself, Chansor. Holan's with his people. He's probably just trying to find out what they have on the table tonight for us to eat." Meradoth's comment made the thief stop jumping to give him a weird look back. The mage only smiled at the little man.

Amlora looked at the two and smiled. She could understand why Chansor was nervous, but then again, Chansor was always nervous. However, this wasn't right and they all knew it. Dwarves were always very welcoming to travelers, but given what was going on just to the south, their unfriendliness was not totally unforeseen.

Whelor, as always, was standing not with the others but by himself. He wasn't one to travel into deep, cold rock like the others were hoping to do, and it made him nervous to think he might not see the sky for a while, so he closed his eyes and tilted his head back to feel the wind hitting it, taking in what he could before he went below.

His dreams were becoming more vivid now, and he knew something was very wrong with his mind. Since that battle within the stone circle, he knew his problem was going to only get worse and the others would begin to notice. He heard commotion that made him look over at the others.

"Here he comes!" he heard, so he turned his head and saw that Holan was walking back towards them.

Holan's face instantly told the group that everything was fine but as not as they had expected, for as the dwarf got closer, Kalion could see that his comrade was going to give them some unexpected news.

"My friends, all is well. My people will protect us whilst we're in their lands the best they can, but they have their own problems at this moment, it seems."

"What do you mean, Holan?" Amlora asked as she looked back at the dwarves.

Not answering the woman, Holan continued on. "Kalion and Jebba, you are to meet the king, who is waiting in his throne room deep within." Kalion nodded as he looked past Holan towards the massive gates that made Bru Edin's look like gnome doors in comparison.

"Why is their army waiting for us then ... or waiting on the field?" Jebba asked as he walked up, still staring at the bodies of warriors waiting for a battle.

"They're not waiting for us. There are things afoot within the citadel. The king will explain ... so please ... before they ... before they get uneasy ... follow me." Holan's voice sounded urgent, so Kalion nodded and took steps to follow his friend as Jebba turned to look up at Bennak, who was staring back with slight concern on his face.

"I'll be fine, my friend. Do not worry." Jebba followed Kalion and Holan down the road. Holan told the others to wait as he directed Kalion and Jebba down the road and past the dwarf warriors, who watched the three make their way towards the entrance with sharp eyes.

As they walked away, the others waited and watched their comrades disappear through the gates, leaving even Kikor and Niallee's sight.

Not long later, they came to stand in front of the dwarven king. Each bowed deeply to show their respect to the mighty king of Chai'sell. Kalion, knowing this place could and had held the orcs back for ages, stared at the dwarven king, waiting for him to say something.

Kalion took in the sight of the dwarven king, having never met him in the past. Like Holan and all dwarvenkind, he had a long, white beard. The king had his tied in four tails, each with a small medallion of silvery gold. The dwarf also wore armor, though not shiny or covered in jewels as the ranger thought he would have. This armor was that of battle, not ceremony.

When no one spoke for a few minutes, Kalion finally said, "King Stokolma Finfilli, we are thankful that your people have let us into your city." Stokolma raised his hand to stop him.

"I have no' let ya into my cit' yet, huuman!" Stokolma stated.

"King, you know of the happenings that are going on to the south at Bru Edin. They are not doing well fighting what could be a huge orc army."

"I kno mor than ya' what hap' to be going on to the south," the large dwarf grumbled.

Kalion continued. "My friends here and the group that we came with are on a mission for King Dia of Brigin'i to search out and find his daughter, the Princess Shermee." Stokolma raised his eyes.

"Hmmmm, I heard that one of my kind had also made it through the games of Dia's but was killed afterwards by a huuman. Is that true, huuman? ... And who are yea anyway, huuman?" Stokolma looked directly at both Kalion and Jebba for the answer. Behind them both stood Holan, who quietly listened, knowing not to say anything.

"King ... I am Kalion Sa'un Ukka. I am King Dia's forest ranger, and this is Jebba Plyhern and Holan Orcslayer of Cruachator. ... And, sir, what I know of your dwarven comrade is that, unfortunately, yes, he was killed by one of my people, but by a drunken human who was only celebrating the event. He has been quickly punished for his actions. Holan here took his place on our quest as a sign of good faith."

Kalion stared at the king, who was squinting his eyes for a moment as he thought. This seemed to settle the king as he nodded for Kalion to continue speaking. He looked down at Holan, who still didn't say a word but lowered his head slightly to acknowledge the king's stare.

"King, have you heard anything of King Dia's daughter being brought this way?" Jebba asked, piping in before Kalion could continue.

The old dwarf grunted and then looked down at the ground and thought for a moment, rubbing his beard. Then he looked at both of the men and said, "I hav' no' heard nor' hav' seen th'king's offspring. My warriors hav' no' mentioned such a thing ... though it has been a busy time for my people. I know of some other news that, my friends, you need to know." Both Kalion and Jebba looked at each other and wondered for the moment what the king was speaking of.

Seeing that neither knew what he intended to tell them, the dwarf king pushed himself up and off of the throne. Lifting his shoulders quickly so his royal robes would fall back, he slowly made his way down the stairs. As he walked up to Jebba and Kalion, both saw that, indeed, this dwarf was larger than most dwarves. Standing with his helm and large, muscular arms, he seemed to be larger than even Holan for a moment, until they stood next to each other.

The king directed them to come and follow him. As the two turned to follow the king, Holan came up and walked behind the three.

"I know no' if you have heard of what has happened to the west of here, but both the forest of Hathorwic and Brigin'i have fallen to orcish armies that now ravage the lands." This news made both Kalion and Jebba stop in shock as they looked at the king. Seeing their reactions, Finfilli waited for the news to sink in so he could continue speaking to the two.

"The Levenori elves fought hard and were able to slow the progress of the orcs, but they were unable to stop them due to the overwhelming number of orcish warriors sent to destroy them." Finfilli spit on the ground as he spoke the word "orc." Then he motioned for them to go sit on some soft chairs that had been gifts from the humans in Bru Edin many cycles before. Both Jebba and Kalion sat down slowly, still in shock from the news that now had been confirmed by many sources. Holan came to lean against the wall behind them, still not saying anything.

The battleground they had gone through east of Hathorwic had been just the first battle against the elves; it was so much worse than they could have thought.

"You spoke of Brigin'i falling as well. Have you heard of what became of King Dia, King Finfilli?" Kalion asked quietly. His king ... his city ... his people ... gone. The news almost killed Kalion, for even though they had heard rumors, he had chosen not to believe them until this moment. Taking in a deep breath, the dwarven king continued with the disturbing news.

The king's voice slowed down a bit so the men could understand him better. "The orcs burned the elfish homeland down, destroying, burning and flattening the forest where they could. The siege against the human city began three days later, after they had moved through the forest. My information says that it did not take as long to break through the human walls, and with giants, goblins and even some demonic-type creatures within their ranks, the orcs were able to break the siege and get inside." Seeing the sadness on Kalion's face, the king stopped speaking for a moment to look at his kin, who looked shocked but nodded when he saw that the king was looking at him.

"This is all I know, my friends." It was enough for the three to hear at that moment as they stood with nothing on their faces except the recognition of the loss of everything that they had fought for to that moment.

"Do you know if King Dia was killed or captured?" Kalion's question made the dwarf tilt his head up as he looked at the ceiling far above, thinking.

When he looked back down, his look suggested to them that Brigin'i's king had, indeed, been either killed or captured by the orcs, but his look also indicated he could not confirm which. They looked at each other to see what they were thinking; none said a word, but this gave Kalion hope.

Finfilli waved over a servant, who leaned over towards the king and listened. Nodding, he ran off. A moment later the dwarf came back with a tray and four glasses on it. Taking one, the king waved at the others to take theirs as well.

Raising his glass, the king whispered a small prayer to his god on behalf of King Dia, wishing the king well in the other world, as Kalion and Jebba did the same to their gods. Holan wished the best for his people as well. For a while no words were passed between the four as they sat there, thinking to themselves. Finally King Finfilli spoke up, first by coughing slightly to get the attention of the others

Suddenly the room shook slightly and a boom was heard as something echoed down the hallway. Dust came down slowly from above; each looked at the others and then at King Finfilli, who wiped some dust off his shoulder.

Standing up straight, he looked over and saw them looking at him. Smiling, he continued on like nothing had happened. "Your group is more than welcome to stay within my kingdom, but only for the night, for I know you have a lot to consider, and there are some decisions to be made." Looking at Holan, he continued, "You must also be aware of what has already occurred outside of Bru Edin, which my people are ready for, as you saw when you came up to the gate. It may affect the route you take. The cavalry that was to attack from either side of the mountain has been taken by something from deep within the ground. The way my scouts described it, the ground just swallowed them up.

.   "I must also share something else with you," the king added. Kalion could only shake his head, wondering how things could get worse, when he saw King Finfilli offering a reassuring smile.

As the king started to continue, he was interrupted by a cough. Holan coughed again and asked the king if he could speak for a moment.

"My king, I know what you are about to share. Are you sure?"

"I am fully aware of what I am doing."

"How many of your warriors do you have within Chai'sell? Those rumbles we felt are not from above but from below." Pointing to the two sitting down, he said, "These men are able fighters, sir, and can help us here."

Finfilli's beard moved slightly as he grimaced at Holan and then turned to Kalion and Jebba. "I have kept the word silent that we have been also fighting a war here within our kingdom for a long time and now will face a battle on multiple fronts."

This surprising news brought Kalion back from his sorrows as he looked over, concerned, at Finfilli. He raised himself up slightly out of the chair and leaned on his knees to listen more closely. Jebba saw Kalion move to hear more as he himself did the same. They both looked over at Finfilli.

"Sir, what do you speak of?" Jebba asked the dwarf king quietly, almost in a whisper. He was as surprised as Kalion, not having heard a word of this place being at war.

"What I speak of is an attack from within the darkest parts of our kingdom by our ancient enemy." Seeing the slight confusion from the two, he tried to explain. "We dwarves are a proud, very proud race, and as one of the two prime races of this world of ours, we feel very deeply for what happens above and below our lands, so when we started to get attacked from within our own lands by our own people, we felt that we had to deal with them ourselves ... with no other's help, as it was no one else's business. We provided assistance to Bru Edin, and with the fall of the cavalry out there, my warriors returned. However, we now face this new challenge from Bru Edin.

Kalion understood. He had known many dwarves and always knew of their proud heritage and feelings towards the lands, wherever they lived.

Finfilli interrupted Kalion's thoughts. "My people have fought back these attacks time after time, but by doing so, we have lost a large part of our city, having to abandon it due to the destruction of buildings and more."

Jebba took a drink and wondered what the king was getting at. *Sometimes dwarves,* he thought, *are creatures that talk too long and only circle the real meaning of what is really happening ... and this is one of those times.* He had never liked being underground too long, and at this moment, he really wanted to get above for fresh air, for he was really unsure where this was going.

"Did you know that there are two of my peoples?" Finfilli finally asked the warriors sitting in front of him. Seeing them both shake their heads "no" back to him, he wasn't surprised; most did not know this. He saw Holan give him a look of concern as he stood up and walked over to stand near a column.

.   As the king spoke slowly, another shake of the floor occurred, and dust fell down, making Finfilli stop speaking ... but only for a moment. "All I can say is that my people have been cursed since I can remember." He waved his hand over to Holan, who looked at the king with some anger, which Kalion suddenly noticed.

Silence suddenly made the room very loud as the four stood there, looking at each other and not saying a word, until finally the sounds of footsteps approaching broke the silence. To Jebba, the footsteps sounded like a parade of giants. Out of the corner of his eye, a dwarf ran in and quickly bowed in front of his king.

Seeing the two men, the dwarf quickly switched to dwarven to relay his message so these quests couldn't understand him.

"My king, the first barriers ... they have fallen. Our warriors are fighting off the assault, but with heavy losses, sir. General Odariam ordered me to inform you." The armored dwarf looked at the two men as he finished his message.

"Curse them! ... Curse them all!" King Finfilli screamed in dwarfish, slamming his fist down on the chair that was near him. Kalion and Jebba stood up quickly, as the anger made the king curse a few more times. They stood back slightly to watch.

"Where is the second battalion making its stand?" he quickly asked the messenger angrily.

"My king, they are at the Crying Gate, as you ordered last week," the messenger stated quickly. These gates had been built many ages before. The dwarves who had been digging found a metal that made them cry, so in honor of this, they built a large gate called the Crying Gate.

Finfilli turned away from the messenger, who stood nervously looking at the guests and then at his king, who walked towards his throne. He grumbled to himself as he thought about what to do. So far he had lost two whole legions of warriors fighting off these attacks and ones from his own people. Outside, Bru Edin would probably fall sometime soon now. The 2nd Battalion, made up of his oldest and most able warriors, might be slow compared to his regular warriors, but they knew ways to fight their old enemy. *Soon we will be fighting on two fronts: with these orcs as well as these … these cursed ones!* he thought.

Staring over at the messenger, who was standing there, breathing hard under his armor as he waited, the king ordered, "Take more warriors from the main gate to assist."

"Yes, my king!" The dwarf bowed slightly and ran out, leaving the others to stare up at the king.

The king sat down hard on this throne. He thought for a moment, using his fist to hold his chin up, when he realized that the travelers were still in the room. Turning, he looked at his guests still waiting by his throne. "I do believe it is time for you three to leave." He looked away before they could answer.

Jebba turned then and said, "You have yet to tell us what you wanted from us. I mean that whole story … what was it about? And why tell us now?"

Kalion shifted his feet for a moment, wondering what was going on as he looked at Jebba and Holan, only seeing that they were confused as well.

Suddenly Finfilli's voice echoed loudly, making all three step back for a moment as they heard the words. "Guards, escort these humans out!"

Before Kalion or even Holan could say a word, out of nowhere a group of guards, who almost seemed to have materialized out of the stone walls, appeared, each carrying a heavy spear with a deadly tip, which was bent slightly down as they walked towards the group. Kalion was wondering what was going on, so he quickly walked up to the throne and stood near the king.

"King Finfilli, you said that we could stay for the night. What's going on here that you would now order us out, sir?" Finfilli just stared at the ranger but didn't answer as his personal servant walked into the room, carrying battle armor in his arms. The guards moved in and quickly escorted the group back outside. They saw that the warriors who were standing in order had been marching back through the gates, only leaving one large contingent of warriors to stand ready at the gate, who in turn watched the group walk out and up the road towards their friends.

As they got far enough away to not be heard, Jebba grabbed Holan's shoulder and roughly turned him to look directly into his face. "What just happened in there, dwarf? What's going on here? He invites us to stay and then tells us to leave!? We both know that you know. ... So tell us!" Jebba's grip tightened as he spoke, but Holan quickly twisted his body to get the man's hand off him.

Holan saw that Kalion was showing the same frustration at what had just happened, so swallowing, he stopped walking, which made the others stop as well to look at the dwarven warrior.

"I am sorry for what just happened. It seems that my people are in a direr situation than I thought." As he spoke, the other two looked at each other with curiosity on their faces.

Holan coughed slightly as he continued, "My people, as the king said, are cursed ... but not like you think. Not cursed with some disease or sickness. ... The gods, all those cycles ago when they ruled these lands, decided to curse my people, bringing death to my kind. It has become a legend, but over the last few cycles, these creatures of legend ... they have been coming at us from the darkest and deepest parts of our realm."

Kalion raised a hand to stop Holan from speaking for a moment. "Wait ... wait ... are you saying that what is attacking this place is a group of cursed dwarves? How many can there be?" Jebba nodded at the ranger, wanting to know the same thing.

Holan looked down for a moment as he thought about how to reveal his people's greatest secret. "Our greatest enemy is known as the Qlorfana — the "Dark Ones" in my people's language — and they are now approaching what we call the Crying Gates for the first time in a millennium, from what I was told. They are not just hundreds in number, but hundreds of thousands."

Hearing that number made the two warriors whistle quietly as they both looked at the dwarf with wide eyes. Then Jebba asked the question he wanted answered. "What did the king want of us then, Holan? It was obvious he wanted something when he invited us in."

"Maybe he was going to ask for our help ... but I am not totally sure."

Turning to Kalion, Jebba then said, "If we can't move through this citadel, what now?"

Holan looked south and east to where he saw the arm of the mountain disappear into the ground where he knew the road turned and led east towards the City of Ports and through the elfish homeland. Then lifting his hand up and pointing, he said, "We need to take the road east and leave this area. If the orcs take and destroy Bru Edin, these fields will be covered with their kind soon after, and unless you want to stay and fight them with a closed gate behind you ... I'm going to inform the others about what has happened and tell them the same."

At that, Holan pushed past the two men and continued up the road to where the others were waiting, leaving the two to watch for a moment longer, when Kalion finally broke the silence between them.

"Are you staying then, Jebba?" Kalion secretly wanted the man to stay because of their argument earlier.

Jebba tilted his head back slightly as he watched the dwarf walk away. Then he turned to see that Kalion was staring at him. "You want me to leave, don't you?"

"To leave? ... no ... but for you to understand that I am leader of this group and that our mission is to find the princess and nothing else. If you desire to fight, then stay here and fight." Kalion put his hand on his sword pommel as he finished speaking, letting the other warrior know what he meant.

Jebba thought about ending their argument right then and there and fighting the ranger for dishonoring Birkita, but he felt an urge to do it somewhere else, so he turned without saying a word to the ranger and followed Holan up the road, leaving the ranger to be by himself for a moment.

Looking back at the dwarven warriors, who, though out of hearing of the ranger, were watching his people intently, Kalion looked at the massive gates with the bonfires that stood outside of them, burning hard, covering many of the dwarves who stood nearby with a glow. He looked up at the sides of the canyon to see that many of the dwarves he had seen earlier were entering the dwarven fortress. The ones who had been watching his group from above were also gone, leaving no sign that they were ever there.

He turned and looked up the hill and saw that Holan was explaining to the group what had happened in there and the group was asking questions. Jebba walked over and spoke to Bennak, whom he could see nod a few times and once look back at him, letting him know that the two were talking about what to do now. Somehow Jebba was convincing the big man to come with him, and Kalion might have a problem stopping him.

His thoughts raced to the princess, trying to remember her and his feeling towards her, as he began to walk himself back up at the hill. He thought of the first time they met while he was searching for a horse that her father had lost while hunting in the woods, the first time they met secretly in the castles gardens, the first time he kissed her and told her he loved her ... the thought of her made his chest hurt as he approached the group and saw that they had decided on what to do.

"Kalion, Holan's information on what's happening with Chai'sell and the fact that there is probably nothing living west of here ... and, of course, Bru Edin ... I believe we are all hoping and wanting now to enter the elven homeland, which Kikor here says is the best-defended forest in the lands," Meradoth stated quietly as Kalion crossed his arms to listen.

"Of course I'm all up for the fun of staying here, but you know moving east is where we've all wanted to go anyway. Going through a dwarven city ... not really my top choice." Meradoth smiled at his joke.

Kalion looked at each member, seeing them slowly nod in agreement with Meradoth's comment. Sucking in a deep breath, the ranger then looked south to the mountain still covered in dark clouds, knowing Bru Edin was falling as they stood there. Then he turned and looked north towards the dwarven gates and then east, where he saw the road travel.

Nodding slowly in agreement, Kalion looked over to see Jebba and Bennak standing off to the side together, not saying a word as they stared back at the ranger. Only Whelor seemed to be smiling, but for reasons Kalion didn't understand or care about at that moment.

"Then we travel east along the road!" Kalion finally declared. Without a word, each member reached for a pack or weapon they had left on the ground as they rested, and then slowly the group turned and walked east.

Chapter Twenty One

The council stood, looking out as they watched the battle erupt on the fields that lay outside the massive walls and gates of the city. One of them crossed his arms and stood, watching. He heard a scream of someone in the battle once as the wind moved his way, but mostly the battle to him was silent since he was so far away.

The only sounds that he heard were the arguments of the other councilmen and women who ruled Bru Edin behind him, trying to decide what to do.

"We need to leave this place NOW!" one of the men shouted repeatedly; his voice told the others that he was scared. Scared is what they were feeling, but only he was saying it at the moment.

Sucking in a deep breath, the man turned and walked back into the chamber to see that the ten or so councilors of the city were debating what to do, so standing at the doorway, he listened for a moment until he couldn't take it any longer.

"My friends, we have done well in keeping this city safe, strong and moving well, but," he waved his hand back towards the battle behind him, "as you all see, this city will fall soon, and I for one will not be here when it happens."

"You're leaving?" one of the councilwomen asked quickly from behind a long table.

Nodding slowly, he said, "Yes, lady. I for one do not want to end up at the end of an orc dinner table. As soon as my servants get things in order, I'm leaving here!"

"Where will you go?" another of the council members asked, wondering what their leader would do.

"If this place ever falls, then I have a tunnel that will lead me out of Bru Edin to safety." The man spoke, knowing that he was spilling his plans to people he didn't really care about ... but he wanted them to know that he was going to live while they weren't.

Hearing that he had a tunnel, the chamber filled with loud and quick arguments, all calling for the councilman to tell them about this tunnel and his plans for escaping the city, but hearing their pleas only made the man smile as he refused to answer anything else.

Finally he thought of an idea as the group moved closer to try to understand him better. Pushing the hands that were grabbing him, he walked to the other side of the chamber and looked at the group that should have been leading the city in this desperate battle, but instead, like him, were only thinking of themselves.

"Pay me, and I will bring you all!" He felt that it would be worth helping them escape if they did that.

His greed brought many to anger as they threatened him and pushed him hard against the wall, yelling at him to tell them where this tunnel was.

Trying to get their hands off him, the councilman and the others didn't notice the door to the chamber open and close, and they also didn't see the man walk in and lock the door behind him and then move over and sit in a chair that was not far from the door.

Sitting there watching the leaders of the city scream, cry and argue over what was going on instead of leading the city made Bosstu only feel hatred for their weakness. When he had arrived back in the city after leaving that group, the general had ordered him to get to safety. He walked down the road to find the city in almost chaos, with the populace running almost everywhere, trying to find a way out.

When he asked where the council was, a wounded warrior who was part of the council's private guard gave him the answer he knew couldn't be true: the council was hiding in the tower that they used to conduct business and more for the city.

The feeling of anger took over Bosstu as he finally understood that his city was going to be lost since they were hiding, so he walked up the road that led to a storage house with items that the mages used, knowing that its doors were probably open. He found, luckily, that it was so. He easily walked in and walked down the aisle to find what he wanted.

Now he pulled out what he had found and juggled it in his right hand as he watched the leaders of his city plead with each other, thinking how to escape. How could these people be the leaders? he wondered. Leaders would be along the wall below fighting and leading the army in its defense of the city. All he saw were the people that he felt had led his family to their deaths.

When the door next to him suddenly moved, causing the room to echo with the loud crack of wood as the door tried to move open, the council members who heard the sound turned to see who might be trying to come in, but instead, they only saw a man sitting on a chair, staring back.

Quickly they cried out that they had a visitor, making everyone, even the council-man trying to leave, stop screaming to stare at the man looking at them with his eyes squinted and face drawn tight.

"Who are you? How dare you come in this chamber? Answer me, man. Who are you?" He pushed past the few members who had been holding him against the wall to walk towards the man.

He stopped at the other end of the table and squinted at the man as he realized that he recognized him. "Answer me, man. How did you get in here?"

Bosstu stood up slowly, sucking in a large breath as he did so, not caring that the door was still being pushed and pulled by someone on the other side trying to get in. Everyone could hear the council guards on the other side screaming, trying to find out what was going on inside the chamber.

When one of the members stepped forward, thinking he would try to surprise this intruder, Bosstu just shook his head "no" at him as he stepped back and moved to stand in front of the door, making the man stop in his place and step back. All wondered who this man was.

"To find you all here, hiding, arguing about how to escape the city while your people below ..." He took a breath as his anger rose more. "While they are dying by the moment, you ..." Bosstu's voice came out through his gritting teeth.

The councilman who a moment earlier had gotten greedy lifted his hands as he spoke, trying to calm the man down. "You do not understand what is going on here. We are not trying ..."

Bosstu's voice erupted loudly, making the lord step back. "YOU LIE! You are trying to leave this city and forget it like you have already done to the villages and towns in the area ... like you did my family!" Bosstu's anger rose as his face turned red, making the council members wonder what the man was trying to do.

"I am not lying, but you need to leave this place, or I will have the guards arrest you and ..."

"Arrest me? ... Go right ahead, have them arrest me. But I think you should know that if any of you scream or try to leave this chamber, I will kill you all here!" Bosstu reached into his cloak and pulled out the device he had been playing with moments earlier.

Lifting his hand, he quickly got everyone to gasp, and one of the women even whimpered as they wondered what he was holding. Not caring about what they were saying, Bosstu just smiled at the lord and the others.

Swallowing hard as he focused on the device in this intruder's hand that was now stretched out for everyone to see, the lord asked, "What ... what do you have there, my friend?" His voice told Bosstu that he was afraid.

"Before you all die, know this: I'm not doing this to save the city. You have all made it possible for the orcs to get in ... talking and talking about nothing while the countryside burns around you all. I'm doing this for my family!"

The man swallowed hard again as he watched Bosstu lift his other hand to cover the first. He screamed and jumped towards the man as everyone watched Bosstu close his eyes and smile.

"Boooosssssstttttttuuuuuuuu!" the councilman screamed again as he desperately tried to grab the device, hearing the intruders through the others' screams.

"For my wife!" Bosstu whispered as he twisted the top of the device.

Instantly it exploded in a bright blue flash of fire, making Bosstu and the man who was only a foot away turn into fire and disappear. As the explosion grew, it blew out of the doorway that led to the balcony outside, giving the flames a way to escape as the door leading to the halls and chambers imploded outwards, killing the guards who were trying to get in. The fire raced down the hallway and into other rooms and chambers that were nearby.

Down below in the city of Bru Edin, people were running everywhere, trying to escape the now conquered wall and outer gate. They stopped as they heard a loud explosion above them. Quickly everyone lifted their heads to gasp as they all saw the bright blue flash of fire blow out of council tower.

Screams erupted everywhere within the city as everyone watched in shock as the balcony cracked and fell from the tower. The tower itself quickly melted away and crumbled apart to fall down onto the city below.

* * *

King Finfilli walked quickly down the ramp that led to the under dark of his city. When he walked through the gateway that led to this part of the city that had been abandoned a few months earlier when the attacks began, he passed many dwarves being treated by his people's clerics.

He could see that many had been wounded not only by swords and axes but also by mage fire. Whole bodies, he was told, had been melted by strange fire that engulfed their armor, turning it red as the warriors under screamed from the pain.

"We lost over three score, my king, in the last attack." The warrior who captained the wounded being cared for had walked up and waited for the king to gather what had happened.

Hearing about the loss, Finfilli shook his head as he looked left and right at the wounded lining the hall. Not saying a word, he just nodded at the captain and then continued walking down the hall until he reached a corner that he would have to turn. There he stopped again as he saw the wounded lining this hall as well.

"My people," he stated loudly to get everyone's attention, "we will win this. It will be hard, but our people have never lost ground to anything in the history of this kingdom. We will WIN!" He screamed the last word, seeing those who could nod and smile back at him.

At that he grabbed another captain who was walking up, and together, along with his guards, they continued down the hall until Finfilli began to hear the eruptions of explosions and screams, as well as the familiar sounds of battle, drift up the halls.

As he ordered the captain to continue the fight, the dwarf only nodded and ran ahead of his king to carry out the orders. Finfilli breathed harder by the moment under the weight of his prized armor as he made his way to the part of the city that now had become the forefront of his people's battle against their dreaded enemy.

* * *

While walking silently along the dirt road that led east and around the southern tip of an arm of the mountain range they had to walk by, each member of the group quietly thought to themselves about the last few days and the things that had happened both at Bru Edin and within the dwarven fortress.

Only Chansor seemed not to be really concerned. He

skipped along, kicking some small stones and even throwing a few in a creek that they passed, trying to get them across it. When he got one to skip at least eight times, he smiled and looked over and saw Meradoth wiggling his fingers and then instantly stopping as he saw that the thief was staring at him.

"Were you ... were you just ...?"

"Who, me? No, not at all, just watching you, my friend." Meradoth smiled widely then turned to continue on with the others, leaving Chansor to stare at Meradoth's head for a moment. Then he shrugged his shoulders and caught up to the others.

A way down the road, Amlora could see that the dwarf was deep in thought, but she had to know what really might have happened within the underground kingdom, so she strode up to walk beside the warrior, who looked up to see her smiling at him.

"Holan, why wouldn't the king help us get through his city?" Amlora asked quietly. "I'm sure he would love our help, do you not agree?" Holan lowered his head, shaking it "no" to her.

Bennak, walking not far away, heard her question and smiled, wondering the same thing, but then he turned his head to look down at the man who, since leaving the fields in front of the dwarven fortress, was beginning to make sense about leaving the group. Upon seeing the frown on his friend's face, he placed a hand on the man's shoulder and leaned over slightly, whispering to Jebba, "We can survive this, my friend."

Niallee, who walked just behind the huge half-orc, heard him and nudged him in the ribs, motioning for him to say it again. She agreed with him, though she didn't understand that Bennak was speaking about something else. He had more muscle than she did at that moment, so she nodded for him to speak louder, which he did.

"We can survive, my friends!" Everyone turned to look at the big half-orc, who smiled down at Niallee.

Meradoth shook his head, for the others made it sound as if they were considering going below, with or without the king's permission, after hearing this news of the battle under their feet. "Friends, you know that I wouldn't have been the best if we had gone down there." His voice carried across to everyone's ears.

Chansor giggled, wondering what the mage was saying. "You are such a joker, Meradoth. Why would you not have been at your best if we had gone below?" Chansor was confused. Why would a mage be weaker the farther underground they went?

Meradoth smiled. He knew not many knew of his kind's weaknesses. Why would they? No mage had ever told an outsider of this weakness: that most mages needed sunlight for their strength to be used. He straightened himself up as the others looked at him, confused.

"The leader of my order told me once that it was because of a curse that the gods gave us long ago. 'Those below cannot use above; those above cannot use below,' as the legend goes," he stated, trying to find a way to explain his weakness.

"I know not of this curse, as I have never been below. I am letting you know now before we meet anything: I will be of no help." Amlora walked over and laid a hand on the mage's shoulder. She understood that there are limitations to any powers and that to hold power means you can't cross that line, for it would mean certain death.

"It seems to me that your king was worried about another potential army that is tough enough to destroy dwarves. While traveling through the dwarf kingdom would be faster if we knew the way, staying outside, going around the mountain ..." Whelor said, smiling to himself that he was free of going under the mountain, as another mind almost sent a large smile across his vision for a moment, hearing the same words.

As the group began to discuss the new plans of travel while they continued walking, Chansor walked over to the edge of the hill they were walking along, some distance from the group, to stare south at the mountain that held Bru Edin. He could see the light from the fires that were burning within it. He had noticed a bright blueish light rise from the city, but then it quickly disappeared. Before he could tell anyone, he heard Whelor's voice interrupt his thoughts.

"I think we need to leave, my friend. The situation is not good down along the fields, and I for one do not want to be here longer than needed." Chansor turned and saw the big man standing behind him, looking across the lands.

Smiling at Whelor, getting a weird feeling that the big man's voice was different in some way, he adjusted his pack and walked off the hill and towards the road that led east with the others. Whelor stood there for a moment longer, taking in the scene. He saw, just like Chansor, that Bru Edin was burning: somewhere he was glad to no longer be within ... he hated fire.

If Whelor had stepped forward just a moment earlier, he would have seen the little thief nod at something within the bushes. Luckily, Chansor thought, the man is slow.

Meradoth was going through a pouch when Chansor ran over to him, giving him a look of hello that brought him out of his thoughts, seeing the thief smiling up at him.

"What did you do now?" Meradoth asked, looking back and only seeing Whelor standing at the edge of the hill, back down the trail.

"Me ... why do you think I'm always getting in trouble?" Chansor's voice sounded innocent, which made Meradoth almost laugh as they walked together.

"I've got the feeling you're a troublemaker, my friend." Hearing that made Chansor laugh, hoping that the mage didn't suspect him. His laugh made a few of the others who were quietly arguing about Holan's comment about his people's enemies look back to see the two laughing and smiling at each other.

Whelor heard the laughter as he continued scanning the lands. Turning slowly, he saw his group walking farther away by the moment. Pulling in a deep breath, he looked up to see what might be happening in the sky as he stepped forward to follow the group that he was beginning to enjoy being with now as they walked out of the area that was dwarven country towards the mountain and, on the other side, Blath 'Na City.

Chapter Twenty Two

The screams and yells from outside told him that things were not getting better as the cleric came in to finish his work on his leg. Hrliger knew that his leg was not going to be saved, that it would have to be cut off. The green and bluish coloring of his skin around the cut wasn't leaving, and the cleric whispered that it was giving off an odd smell. When it was decided that his leg wouldn't last, the cleric worked with precision to extract Hrliger's leg.

When he was done, the cleric left and told him he should leave the city as well. Hrliger only half-smiled and said, "How am I to do that with this leg? A I wasn't aware of any way to leave the city at this point." Even though he knew his friends had left by a secret passage, he also knew that not many in the city were aware of this route. But at that moment he wondered why not; the city's council should have said something cycles before just in case.

The room empty, Hrliger felt alone suddenly, and he could hear commotion outside the house he lay in. So being the stubborn gnome that he was, he grabbed the staff that the man had left him, saying it would help him walk. Hrliger grunted through his teeth as the pain shot up his now much smaller leg as he hobbled outside.

When he pushed the door to the balcony all the way open, he stopped and looked around with wide eyes, gasping at what he saw.

The war machines within the city were working hard, swinging huge boulders towards the orcish army that was still outside of the wall, but the screams of those who ran by told him differently: the orcs might be within the city walls soon.

Falling back against the wall, Hrliger couldn't believe that this city was falling. He remembered how this place looked when he had come in through its gates — the largest and most powerful gates he'd even seen, outside those he knew that the dwarves had built in nearby Chai'sell — and seen the army here.

"What is going on?" Hrliger whispered, wondering how in all the heavens the orcs could do what they had been doing recently. First Brigin'i, now this fortress ... these humans didn't fight that well, the gnome thought quickly.

He called out to a boy running by, getting his attention by swinging the staff in front of him. The boy ran over, seeing the small gnome leaning on a staff, looking pitiful to his eyes as he approached him.

"Sir, you should leave our city!" the boy said quickly as the echoes of screams moved past their ears.

"I will try, my friend ... but please tell me ... are there other ways out of the city?"

"There's a rumor, sir, that there's a way out through the mountain, but ..." the boy stated. Hrliger could see the fear on the boy's face as he spoke.

Thanking the boy, Hrliger hobbled himself over to get to a position where he could look down on the city below so he could see for himself what was going on. He shook his head slightly when he saw buildings were burning. He watched boulders and rocks still being flung inside by the orcs' war machines, causing buildings to collapse under their attacks. When he saw the movement from where he stood of tentacles reaching over the walls, he gasped, hopping up to the edge of the wall he stood behind.

The only creature that I know of with arms like those is a Lingropand, but those creatures do not live in the area. Lingropands are creatures that only live within the warmest of areas of the empire that lie many, many miles to the south, so what are they doing here? If Methnorick is able to call those creatures to his service ... how can anything survive his armies!? Hrliger thought as he watched arm after arm grab a victim and throw him or her high into the air to die as they hit the ground.

252

His people had fought these large creatures for many cycles when they tried to enter his homeland. The only thing that he knew had stopped them was water in large amounts, like a flood, as they couldn't survive in the liquid. He remembered the time they had flooded the tunnels that one of the creatures was attacking from, killing it. However, he now wondered where he could get water ... here in the middle of the plains.

How could it survive the massive rainstorm we just had here? Unless it was so deep underground at the time of the rainstorm that the water didn't reach it. I must think of a way to create another rainstorm, stronger than what the gods could send, to drive it back underground.

Hrliger looked around. *In my condition I could not survive outside these walls; I'd be killed within moments. But if I could find the tunnels the others took, I might stand a chance. I first need to tell someone what they could do stop that creature. ... Maybe there are druids within the city still alive.* Hrliger fell against a stone wall and breathed hard as he looked back towards the battle and then back to where everyone was running, believing the farther away they were, the safer they were.

Knowing then that he would have to do this by himself and seeing the massive crowds, knowing he'd never make it through them, he hopped slowly around and made his way back down the hall towards the balcony he was just on to give him the best sight of the dying city below and around him. Once there Hrliger took a few deep breaths and closed his eyes, thinking of the words he needed to get what he wanted. Finally he remembered everything he needed, and as he opened his eyes, he searched for what he was looking for. Many war machines still stood now at the farthest edge of the orcish army, working hard along the tree line, being pulled back and loaded by huge giants; a few were within the orcish army as well, and of course, the Lingropand at the wall was killing what it could reach.

Lifting his arms up as he leaned against the wall to support himself for what he was about to do, he spoke quietly, "Wake up, my friends ... creatures of old." He repeated himself three more times, hoping that they would hear him. Lowering a hand down, he grabbed dust that was in a pouch. Quickly grabbing the ashes of animals killed by orcs, one of his druid secrets, he threw the ashes before him. He knew doing this in the current situation he was in health-wise, he wouldn't survive, but he had to do what he could for this city.

Instead of falling back down to the ground quickly, the ashes started to form a cloud and shimmer, slowly turning into a dust whirlpool flying up into the air. Hrliger smiled and told the dust what needed to be done. The dust swirled before him in response as forms of animals materialized from the cloud, everything from horses to snakes to birds, quickly disappearing to be replaced by another. Within a breath, the cloud quickly left the spot to take the action requested by Hrliger.

As Hrliger watched, he quickly put his hand back on the rail as the ground under his feet shook hard. He could see the main gate being ripped apart by the tentacles as screams rose from it.

As he stood there watching, he began to feel what he knew would kill him for going too far with his powers, as his chest began to tighten, making it hard for him to breathe. Sharp pains shot from there down his body, making his good leg weak. Grabbing the staff with both hands, the gnome knew this was it for him as he formed a weak smile with his mouth and watched the storm move through the city streets and over the wall, killing orcs that had once destroyed them in life. Their screams soon overtook the screams of the tentacle's victims who being thrown into the air.

The smile quickly left as his one leg gave out, making him fall hard to the stone floor, still holding the staff for support. Hrliger let out a gasp as pain shot through his head.

As he lay there, he imagined what was occurring from the screams and explosions, weak but familiar sounds to his ears. While Hrliger listened, he looked up at the sky, which had turned red and cloudy from the fire within the city. Closing his eyes, he asked for the gods to give him peace as his body was racked by pain. Hrliger shook a few more times and then lay still, having wished he could have told the people of Bru Edin the best way of dealing with the Lingropand.

✳ ✳ ✳

The man he leaned back, blood pouring from his stomach, as Shermee gasped weakly at what she had just done to the man. She pulled the broken piece of wood out of the man's stomach, leaving him to gasp in pain and fall back in total surprise at what his victim had just done to him.

The princess cried as she backed off. She continued to observe the man gasp, looking at her with wide eyes as he held his stomach and blood poured out of the wound.

Just moments earlier this sailor had tried to attack her in her chamber, catching her by surprise as he crawled into the room from a side window, avoiding the protection detail outside her door. Quinor had just stepped out of the room to check in with his two men when the sailor caught her by total surprise, grabbing the clothing strap that held up the dress she wore and ripping it, hoping he could get further before she reacted.

Quickly covering her mouth, he growled for her to shut up as he used his other hand to move the now ripped clothing off her shoulder and bring him closer to getting to her body when he suddenly cried out loud in pain as the princess had taken a knee and smashed it hard between his legs, crushing his groin. Quickly he fell off her to stand and then collapse to his knees, weak from the pain, as Shermee reached behind and under the pillow she used for the shard of wood she had broken off of a chair in the room. Wrapping her hand around it, she jumped off the bed just as he launched himself at her again and just as Quinor burst into the room.

The sailor finally fell to the ground to die in a pool of red blood that caused the wood of the deck to turn black. She looked at the cabin door to find that it was open and Quinor was standing there with a blade in his hand, breathing hard as his eyes went from the sailor back to her.

"Are you ok, Princess?" he gasped, seeing her nod, still looking at the now dead body of the sailor. "The crew, I believe, is making its move, so my men are here with me to stop them. Just stay here ..."

Quinor was cut off by a voice behind him that made him turn as Shermee heard yells farther away. Reaching back quickly, the man grabbed the handle and shut the door hard as the princess fell back to lean in her bunk to listen to what was going on outside.

Had she been outside, she would have seen Quinor's two men and Quinor as they stood their ground against the rush of ten or so sailors, who broke out from below the decks and rushed the trio as they blocked the cabin where the princess was now.

Each sailor held either a curved blade or a short sword, weapons that were used in closed quarters such as ships, and there were a few with medium axes moving out of the hatch that they used to get below, into the hold.

Quickly Quinor and his two men fought off these sailors, blocking and swiping across many, knocking them back as the sailors tried to use their mass to kill the three. As they all tried to swing down or cut them in half one by one, the sailors were each killed by Quinor or his men, who easily fought them back.

"These sailors are terrible warriors!" Fad laughed as he pushed his blade deep into the chest of a sailor who wore only pants. As he pulled the sword out, the man fell back hard onto the deck with a surprised look on his face, grabbing his stomach as it burst open, letting his innards spill out.

Smiling to himself, Quinor nodded as he blocked the one-eyed man's heavy curved blade from cutting his head in half, and using the man's force, he knocked the blade off to his side to slam into the deck just to Quinor's right, causing it to get stuck in the wood.

As the man tried to pull it out, Quinor reached out, and pushing hard, he knocked the second in command of this ship off his feet to fall back and slam into three of his men, who, in turn, all fell back onto the deck.

Shermee almost cried as she heard the metal sounds of battle ring into the cabin. Each time she heard a cry of pain she wondered if it was Quinor. Not like she really cared, she thought to herself. He had kidnapped her. ... He should pay for that ... but her plan was working. Her beauty and slight advances towards the crew had convinced them to try to fight each other and maybe Quinor.

She just didn't expect the surprise visit of the sailor who now lay dead on the deck before her.

Outside the battle quickly ended when, out of the crew of twenty, only 10 were left, the rest lying dead or dying around Quinor and Fad. The remaining sailors retreated to the aft end of the ship, leaving Quinor to care for the wound that Akula had received. Seeing that the wound wouldn't be the end of the man, Quinor quickly pulled him inside the cabin to lay on the floor near the princess, who stood looking at the man as Quinor knelt down to care for him.

"You, my friend, need to protect her. ... You know what we need to do, yea?" Quinor pulled the cloth tight around the wound, making the man wince loudly in pain, but he nodded and gasped a yea to his leader.

"These men are lousy warriors and probably even worse sailors. Look, the sails are loose and those ropes aren't tight enough, but ..." the man grunted through the pain of the sword cut on his leg.

Quinor rose up and looked outside to see that, indeed, the sails were loose. Suddenly a cry made Fad lean in to get the attention of Quinor, who left and closed the cabin door as both men raised their blades, believing that another attack was on its way.

"You need to surrender the princess, Quinor. ... Why fight for her?" the voice called out from somewhere, but Quinor knew who it was.

"Captain Kochic, what you want is something I cannot give. She is my prisoner!" Both searched for any surprise that might be moving at them.

"Maybe, Quinor, but we can all share her. Let my men have her for an hour, that's all I ask of you!" Kochic answered, but Quinor could hear a slight hesitation in his voice, making him wonder what the captain had promised his men.

"My men and I will fight to the end if need be, but your crew will never get to her!" Quinor's voice echoed down the deck as the ship rocked back forth on the seas.

"Then all we have left is for you and your man to die!" Kochic cried back. "We have killed one, and we still outnumber you!" Quinor lifted his sword up, knowing that they had to be getting ready, when he and his man were knocked off their feet as the deck and the ship suddenly groaned loudly, causing Quinor to slam hard into a mast that moved toward them and hit his head, knocking him out.

As he fell to the deck, the ship quickly began to break apart as it crashed hard into large rocks that lay in its path. The masts fell, and the men on the deck screamed in terror as wave after wave of water quickly rose over the rails and washed across the deck, grabbing many of the bodies of the dead and alive, sweeping them out into the seas.

* * *

Hrliger's dust storm continued its destruction, bringing down war machine after machine that the orcs used. Those giants that were left ran for cover among the trees as the tornado moved itself across the field, catching many within its path, sucking them into its cone. Screams rang everywhere on the field of battle as it left the tree line and made its way back to Bru Edin's walls, not stopping as it moved over each wall that was still in orc hands. Those who could stood or cowered down under something as they watched the tornado, now with many forms of animals and unknown creatures, move up and stop directly over the creature that had given the orcs the ability to get within the castle.

Quickly the wind around it whipped faster and faster as it grabbed the huge creature, which tried to burrow itself back into the ground to get away. But it was not quick enough, as the tornado grabbed the massive creature, and those able to watch saw for the first time the Lingropand that Hrliger knew would cause the destruction of Bru Edin if it wasn't stopped be lifted up into the air and whipped around time after time. Finally the winds did what the creature had been doing for a while, and with one big whip of its strength, it threw the massive creature high into the air and beyond even those elves who still fought, disappearing and leaving nothing but a huge area of destruction and death. In the area that had once been crowded with orcs, giants and the huge machines were lying everywhere. Dead orcs were killed by being slammed against others, and giants trying to kill the storm hit each other or were slammed against others. The machines — the ones no longer standing — were also everywhere.

General Kaligor sat upon his horse and watched the destruction with amazement, not believing that there was a mage left within the city who could do such damage. As he watched the creature that had given him the opportunity to destroy the famous gates of Bru Edin rise up and disappear, he thought that he had lost this battle, but then quickly he saw his opportunity: the city itself was in disarray and didn't mount a counterattack or defend itself.

Lifting himself to stand on the straps of his mount, he screamed loudly, causing every creature around him to cower as he did, expecting him to be furious. When none moved to carry out his orders to charge, he grabbed the head of one orc that cowered nearby, and in one movement, Kaligor threw the orc out towards the battle front, screaming for the rest to push forward.

Looking back at the loss of the machines, he grabbed a spear that lay nearby and threw it towards the city he wanted. As it landed, it slammed into the back of an orc running forward, pinning it down to the ground. Some around it looked back but then continued charging at the humans.

As his orders were sent out, those in the orcish army that had survived charged forward to finally push into Bru Edin. As he heard the loud roar of anger, Kaligor moved to grab his weapons and kicked his mount to go forth himself into the battle. "These stupid things," he cried out as a Blingo'oblin not far away moved up to hear its orders.

Pointing up at the burning city, he looked at the giant creature that stood as his second in command. "Send your warriors into the city. Its gate is wide open; kill everything within it!"

Nodding to his new orders, the armored creature bowed and then turned and screamed for those of his kind to do Kaligor's bidding. Then it turned around to see the Cyclops grinning back at him. "I do as you command me, my lord," the Blingo'oblin stated, and at that, he turned and rushed with two other Blingo'oblins through the masses of orcs and goblins that were charging the city, leaving Kaligor by himself.

Kaligor reached back and grabbed his huge shield that lay on the side of his saddle. As he looked around and saw nothing else he needed, he kicked his mount, which cried out loudly itself, and quickly maneuvered it towards the gateway that led into the city.

Looking to his right, he saw that the dark elves were doing well, finishing off the last of the cavalry that had somehow been able to gather itself together to make a last stand. He saw explosions and bright lights from where he was, which caused horse and rider to die as these elves finished them off. Smiling, he grumbled something that none of his guards could make out, but they followed their master forward as his creature stepped over the dead and made its way forward.

Chapter Twenty Three

Weeing the loss of so many orcs, Marshal Tassalii rallied his troops, sending them in a counter attack to sweep the destroyed gate area of any orc. Whatever that storm was gave his people a slight break, the marshal thought. Blood and brains went everywhere, but Tassalii didn't care; he needed to kill as many as he could. He could see many orcs and goblins dying as they struggled to stop his men, but it wasn't enough.

He had decided as the gate had disappeared that, even though badly injured earlier, he would fight to the end, letting the people of his city retreat behind the buildings he knew would collapse soon and hopefully get out. He ordered his men to take a last stand.

Tassalii saw a horse nearby that would give him better view of what was going on. He called for help, and a warrior assisted the marshal in getting up onto the saddle, quickly strapping him on tight, knowing that the man wouldn't be able to stay on long without help. When the warrior was finished, Tassalii pulled on the reins, making the horse rise up and move forward. As they got close to the front, he began letting the large beast land hard onto a large goblin that was trying to get past him. The sound of bone cracking made Tassalii smile as he looked around to see the field clear of orcs behind and directly ahead of him. He turned to the others under his command and said, "Go now back into the city; protect those who still need to get moving."

"Yes, sir, but what about you?"

He smiled. "I'm right behind you," he said as he considered what he had set out to do. He watched as his group turned back towards the inner city. Turning his head around, he looked and charged his horse at full gallop out the front gate. As he passed the now destroyed gate, he was amazed that one of the towers still stood, having seen that weird creature's tentacles rip it apart. Shaking his head, he looked across the field and pulled the reins of his horse to stop it. What he saw as he rode out the gate was something that he had never seen in his living life. Entering the field with more orcs than he could believe were still alive, he saw a Cyclops carrying a huge axe pole and riding a nightmarish creature of a horse in front of the army of orcs.

* * *

Quinor opened his eyes but quickly shut them as bright light sent pain into his eyes, making him groan as it moved through his head. Moving himself, he felt weight on his body and, after a moment, understood why he couldn't move. He opened his eyes slowly, blinking hard. The bright light slowly dimmed as he got them opened to see that he was lying on the ground and was looking up at the sky, the light coming from the sun shining down on him.

Groaning again, he looked slowly around and saw that he was lying on a beach. The sound of waves hitting the beach entered his ears loudly but then quieted down as he got used to it.

Looking down, he couldn't make out what was on his chest but could tell his hands were bound tightly. He also made out that his clothing was ripped up and wet.

Looking around, he blinked a few more times as he tried to understand where he was and wondered who might have bound his hands. Finally he could make out a figure not far away, but his eyes were still a bit blurry from being unconscious for who knew how long.

He shook his head slowly, trying to get his eyes cleared. When he was finally able to see the figure, he gasped slightly, recognizing the princess, but then he saw that she wasn't standing alone. He worried that it was that ship's captain and that it was he who had tied him up.

He blinked quickly and hard as he lifted his head and watched the two figures talking to each other. Shermee had her arms crossed as the other figure, who stood about the same height as she did, wore a long, flowing blueish robe coat. He noticed that the figure didn't wear boots like the princess, and then he saw him move his head to look over at him, nodding as he saw that Quinor was staring back.

The princess turned and looked at him. Lowering her arms, she strode slowly over with the other figure. Quinor quickly gasped, recognizing who the man was as they both walked closer and closer.

"You survived the wreck, Princess!" His voice cracked as he spoke, but he knew she heard him as she watched. She looked at the man she had been speaking to and then back at him.

"Yes, I survived, but we were the only ones to survive it, Quinor." Her voice sounded stronger than it had been when he had last seen her, right after killing that sailor. Now she looked how he remembered her looking when he first grabbed her from the dark elves: strong, independent and capable.

His eyes went to her new friend, who was staring down at him with crossed arms, but he could see that he was right. The face, the build ... everything reminded him of an elf.

"Who's your friend, princess?" he asked quietly. It took her a few moments to think and figure out a way to answer, but she moved her mouth open and closed and then stared over at the stranger.

"He ... he's one of the sea elves. He saved me when the ship crashed on those rocks, and after I told him what you did for me on the ship, he allowed you to live as well." She nodded at his hands.

"Why?" He lifted his hands up to check them out.

Kneeling down, the elf, whose grey hair swung down to cover his chest, looked directly into Quinor's eyes, where he saw that they were silver in color. Quinor swallowed as he stared back, wondering what the creature was thinking, when he saw him open his mouth and, like a whisper, heard him speak.

"My people don't take kindly to kidnappers, but she pleaded for you and told me about your help in protecting her on the ship, so I decided that you needed to be held until I decide what to do with you." The elf's voice was like music, almost singing, to Quinor, but he understood every word; he was the prisoner now.

"I told him what happened to me and where you were taking me!" Shermee quietly said as the elf just knelt there, staring at him. "His people know who Methnorick is and what his plans are!"

"And who are your people?" Quinor asked, staring back at the elf who sat above him.

The elf smiled as his eyes closed slightly to stare at Quinor, who got the feeling that this elf was going to kill him, so hoping she would listen, he pleaded quietly with the princess.

"Princess ... Shermee ... I understand what you have gone through, and I am sorry that I had anything to do with it, but I was given orders that I couldn't disobey." He closed his eyes and took in a deep breath, making the girl look at him harder as he thought about his next words. "Methnorick has my family, my parents. I had to do what I did for him." Quinor lifted himself up slowly so at least he was sitting and could look at her eye-to–eye now.

Taking a deep breath, he took his opportunity to quickly tell her the truth. "I fell in love with you, my princess, long before we arrived in the City of Ports, and I did what I could to make sure you were never hurt, but I couldn't tell you how I felt about you."

Shermee closed her eyes, almost not believing what she heard, but considering the plans she had enacted on the ship and wondering if the man was lying to her now just to get free. But for some reason, as she thought back about the way he spoke to her and how he looked when he did, she realized she was right that her plan to make him fall in love with her had worked, but now she had to consider whether she needed him any longer.

She thought a moment longer and then decided that he might still come in handy. "If you're lying to me, Quinor, I will have him kill you instantly or have him leave you here to let Methnorick deal with your betrayal, because he's taking me away from this place to a faraway area where I'm told I will be safe from this war." Shermee looked down at Quinor, crossing her arms as he looked over at the elf.

"What do you think ... leave him here?" the elf asked, looking back at her and then back at the man he knew was fearing for his life now, probably for the first real time.

"I will take you with me ... but know this: you are under my command and will do my bidding now, no matter the outcome ... understand?" Quinor quickly nodded, letting out a tiny breath of relief, knowing he could live a bit longer.

Shermee walked past the warrior as the elf stood back up. Quinor moved himself to his feet and looked at the princess as he suddenly realized that the weight that was on his chest was now gone — he had finally told her his feelings.

"Where are we going then, my princess?" Quinor asked, looking over to see the elf kneeling at the ocean edge, placing his hands in the water, which Quinor thought was odd.

"He's actually communicating with his people," Shermee whispered as they watched silently.

When he was done, the elf stood up and turned his head slightly to speak to them. "I am taking the princess away from this island that we are on. Methnorick is close, very close, and if he finds us here ... We must leave this place soon." The elf's words told Quinor they must be on the island that he was told to sail to as he watched the elf begin to walk into the water, leaving the others to watch.

When he got up to his chest, he turned around and looked back. As they looked at him apprehensively, he explained, "Our kind has the ability to protect those near us, enabling them to breathe under water. Come ... come with me and under my protection.

You will survive the sea. Just stay close by my side." He turned around and, in one quick motion, dived into the water and quickly disappeared under the waves, leaving the two to stare at each other.

"Well, I guess there is nothing to do but follow!" Quinor smiled at Shermee. Lifting his hands up, he asked, "Do you mind untying these? Kind of hard to swim like this."

Shermee looked at the rope and then back into the eyes of her former kidnapper. Knowing if he tried to kill her that the elf would return and return the favor, she said, "I'm taking the chance that you know what's best for you and will not harm me." She leaned down and lifted a piece of metal from the ship that was lying nearby and slowly cut through the rope. When she was finished, she threw the metal on the ground and quickly made her way to the water, leaving the warrior to rub his hands and wrists to get the blood flowing again as he watched her disappear into the water.

He looked back towards the island, seeing the dark clouds upon it and knowing that the man or creature that had ordered him to grab the princess was nearby. He considered the idea of walking to where Methnorick sat and telling him of his failure, but he knew better. ... He would die.

Pushing his chest out as he sucked in a deep breath, he turned and followed the one person he had to trust now as he dived under the water to follow the princess.

* * *

Jebba did his best to look around in the dark. He hated that he couldn't see in the dark like an elf could, for he hated depending on others in moments such as this. Niallee and Kikor had gone ahead to check out the area while the group stayed where they were. Holan stayed behind, as he was the only one now who could see their surroundings as the rain lightly came down. That didn't help Jebba, though, as he stumbled around until he finally found a rock.

He slid down and waited for word to come back that the road ahead was safe.

Holan could see Jebba getting nervous, so he walked over and slid down beside the human. "Jebba, it's fine; it's all fine here, my friend. I see nothing here that will harm us." He spoke quietly so that his voice didn't echo.

Jebba didn't say anything. He just looked around, trying to imagine what the area looked like. He sat like that for a while, with Holan sitting next him, keeping an eye out, until both heard the echo of feet moving towards them coming from where the two elves had gone.

Whispers were heard as the two elves came into the clearing. Jebba pushed himself up and stood, waiting to hear what they had found. Someone whispered for Meradoth to open up a flame quickly. The mage whispered a few words, and instantly a bright glow appeared before the group.

"It is fine, everyone," Kikor stated. "We can stay for a while." As she spoke, Niallee walked over and nodded to Kalion, who waited next to a tree. She then turned and walked over to where Bennak and Whelor stood, whispering to each other. As she came up, she heard the two men arguing about something, but they quieted when they saw the druid coming up.

"What are you speaking about, my friends?" she asked. Whelor didn't look happy at her approach. Not saying anything, he even turned away as Bennak answered, "Oh, we speak of nothing. What did you find ... anything we need to know?"

Before she could speak, Kalion and Jebba walked up to the group, and then they started to share what they had found. "We found nothing ... nothing except an old group of buildings, fallen down and unused." Kalion looked over at Jebba and then to Holan, who looked back to the ranger.

"Hmmmm, nothing else, you say?" Meradoth asked. Niallee and Kikor both informed the group that, in that area, all they found were large buildings, many of which had fallen down. "But

I think it might be a place we could stay for the night, too," Niallee quietly whispered.

Kalion, who listened, had crossed his arms quietly when he saw movement out of the corner of his eye and looked over to see Whelor, who still hadn't turned to look at them. He wondered what was wrong, but he would ask later when they could be alone.

A while later, with Meradoth in the middle of the group with his light and Kikor at the front letting her eyes see where they needed to go, the group moved silently down the trail until they came to the buildings that they had spoken of, all damaged and abandoned.

As they entered what used to be the courtyard, around them stood huge buildings. Many of these had fallen down from cycles of disrepair or worse. Holan walked over and stood next to one of the largest in the area, just looking up at it as he reached out and touched it.

When a slight shadow came up from behind, the dwarf turned around and looked at him. Bennak could see the sadness in Holan's face and wondered for a moment why, until Holan explained.

"These buildings ... my people made them long ago, and now they stand here ... alone ... in the dark," Holan said quietly as Bennak listened, looking up at the building.

"Your people made wonderful things, my friend."

Holan interrupted him. "Now my people are dying." Bennak understood, letting the dwarf walk past him. He looked up at the building again, turning around and following the dwarf back to the rest of the group and the refugees.

"Where do you believe we should go from here?" one of them quietly asked. Jebba, taking a deep drink of water from his pouch, pointed with the other hand to where the road went.

"We should keep moving. I'm getting a feeling like what

Holan spoke of before. This area is going to be filled with orcs soon, if and when Bru Edin does indeed fall."

"Let us go then!" Holan said as he walked by the group. "We need to keep moving quickly, my friends." The dwarf walked past Bennak, who stepped forward and began to walk down the road behind him. Meradoth, who moments before had sat on a stone for a moment's rest, stood up and followed, and slowly the rest of the group, one by one, did the same, leaving the ruins behind.

They made their way down the road, moving along the buildings and rubble with only Meradoth's light guiding the way for them now.

With Niallee marching up from behind and Kikor in the front as a point to keep an eye open, none noticed a small figure coming out from one of the buildings to watch the creatures that had entered its realm walk past. Curiosity took it over, and being careful, it followed the group as it made its way down the once great road built by the dwarven kingdom cycles before.

Chapter Twenty Four

Back within the empire, Vana had finally arrived with his army, who quickly dispatched themselves into building a large camp just south of the towers and gave relief to those in need as he and Commander Tevanic looked over the ramparts of the gate as the sun crested the trees to their right; they both were silent as they observed what was below.

After Vana ordered more warriors to the ramparts to keep an eye out for the trolggs, everything began to go wrong.

The howls and cries echoed from the tree line, making everyone along the wall believe that a whole army of orcs was moving at them, which caused a few to get nervous.

Vana gathered his commanders and told them that the patrol hadn't been attacked by orcs but by creatures they hadn't seen for many cycles. The trolggs were making their presence known, he told them, in this war in the north, and he guessed that their position was the closest and easiest, so they were not attacking them. Vana reminded them that trolggs, or trolls as they were more commonly known, were not the brightest and would attack whatever caught their eye.

Before any archer had been able to gather additional packs of arrows, the attacks began as the roars got louder and the warriors on the ramparts screamed down that movement was seen coming south towards them.

Trolggs were ancient creatures that had once been elves that had been attacked by an ancient god, who, in his anger, had made them disfigured and ugly with total hatred for everything, even for themselves, if the legend was true.

271

None had been seen since Vana had been a child, for they lived deep within the ground or in swamps that lay northwest of this very gate. But that was only rumor, for they were thought to be extinct.

"It's up to you, archers, to keep them back!" he ordered as each warrior who could stood on top of the wall and released everything they had at the attacking trolggs.

It wasn't like they could do much damage. The legend said that if you were ever bitten by one, then you were doomed to become one. The only way to kill one was to destroy its head, cutting it off its body, or use the sun before it went down, as they were blinded by its light.

This continued for two days, and each day these trolggs attacked the wall, Vana wondered why. Even though they weren't the smartest of creatures, they should have known that they couldn't get past this place with its high walls and defenses.

As he looked down at the bodies lying on the ground, the sun beaming its light down on them, he wondered what their plan was. He lost count of how many lay there, but he was told that the archers had emptied their bags of arrows. Quickly he ordered the fletchers to make more arrows as he and his commanders gathered and decided what to do: open the gates and destroy the bodies or leave them where they lay. If he believed the stories, they would wake with the setting sun if their heads were not destroyed.

It was quickly decided to open the gates and destroy them. This was the decision that could secure or lose the gate, Vana thought, as he and his warriors, carrying torches, slowly cracked the gate open as the sun was starting to set.

* * *

Bru Edin's Marshal Tassalii knelt on the stone ground with his hands behind his back, looking around with his one eye at the grinning orcs and goblins, as well as a few giantkind, that had gathered around him. The Cyclops quietly spoke to a dark elf that stood with crossed arms, nodding once in a while as the giant creature spoke. The headache Tassalii was experiencing was nothing like he had ever felt before, but as he faced the wrath of his enemy, which was heightened by their inability to take his city or get it to surrender, it was the furthest thing from his mind. He couldn't believe this had happened; he had chosen to die in battle, but not like this.

He looked at the Cyclops, knowing it was deciding his fate, but he knew he wouldn't be alive long, as he looked around to see the spear poles and the heads that now adorned them: heads of his friends, his comrades ... his men.

The dark elf looked at him and then smiled slightly. Nodding, he turned and walked into the crowd of orcs, who closed ranks behind him as the Cyclops walked towards Tassalii. Tassalii took in a deep breath, knowing that this was it. His life was done and over. He dropped his eyes to the ground, but when he saw the boots stop in front and not move, he looked up at the creature.

"Marshal Tassalii is it?" The voice seemed almost like a man's, making Tassalii's forehead tighten as he looked up at the creature to stare at its one blood-red eye.

When the man didn't answer him, he tilted his head, letting out a wisp of breath as he thought for a moment. "No matter if you are him or not ... this city is mine," Kaligor said quietly while Tassalii knelt below him. Kaligor then leaned his head back slightly, closing his eye for a moment, remembering his conquests. "I have stood over cities across the lands, in faraway places, as I am now ... looking over each one as they burn and fall apart as my armies destroy them. The Levenori Forest ... Brigin'i City ... I have fought and taken each of these places. Soon even Blath 'Na City in the east will be ours!" He waved his arms up and opened them as he spoke. "But Bru Edin ... the Shield of the North ..." Kaligor smiled at that saying. "Your city fell like all others — quickly — believing that you could not be destroyed." The general knelt down so their faces were close enough that only the two could hear each other.

Defiantly, Tassalii spoke through his teeth. "It has not fallen yet!"

"Give it time. In not much time, I will be within the gates, and all will die."

Swallowing, Tassalii whispered so only Kaligor could hear his words. "Are you proud that each place you have destroyed is in ruins ... or is that what you call paradise for your kind?" Tassalii lifted his eyes as he spoke, wondering.

Kaligor huffed and ground his teeth slightly, moving his jaw a bit as he stared at the face covered in blood from the wound on his head. He changed the subject quickly, though, as he was growing tired of looking at this man.

"I know there is resistance still in this city, but that will not last long. Surrender, and I will let them live. Your precious cavalry you were expecting to come to your rescue are gone. The elven warriors — gone. Even the dwarves from the north have retreated back within their mountain. There is no help for you."

Tassalii looked up in surprise as he finally realized the fate of his city. After a moment's pause, he got enough of his strength back to speak again as he looked up at the creature still kneeling next to him. "Surrender? Like the ones I see adorning the tops of your banners did?" He nodded over and saw the many heads of men he knew had fought with him and against the orcs; he saw generals, captains and friends, all gasping in pain as they lost their heads to be used as trophies.

Smiling, Kaligor followed the man's eyes and saw what he was looking at. Returning his stare, he coughed slightly to get the man's attention back. "Ahhh ... those men fought against me, yes ... but I had to do what I did to them. If I had not, then these orcs might have turned on me."

"Then why not add my head to theirs? I fought you ... what

makes me different?" Tassalii could see some of the orcs were getting restless as they talked; many snarled, looking at him like he was a piece of meat.

"You are no different than they, true. ... But I need you, and that is why you are still alive."

"So when you don't need me anymore, you're going to kill me anyway, are you not?"

Kaligor smiled again, shaking his head, as he couldn't believe he was trying to convince this man to do his bidding. When he came to the understanding that this marshal would not do it, his anger rose, as did his legs, leaving him to look down.

"I do not have time to deal with you, man creature. Do my bidding or die here along with all your warriors who tried to stop me. Decide now!" Kaligor's voice turned dark and deep, sending a chill down Tassalii's back as his jaw shook inside his mouth and he blinked a few times, quickly trying to think of what to do.

He knew of no plans for if the city fell. ... But he did find out just before the gate had fallen that a tunnel that had been used by the council had been found, with many of the populace struggling to get into it, though many had died trying to make it out of the city, being crushed as they were rushing through the small tunnel.

"Tell me where your council is, and I will let you live!" Kaligor's voice echoed in Tassalii's head, making him smile.

"They died. Did you not see the council tower implode?" Tassalli said quietly. "They never leave that tower. They must have died within it."

Kaligor's forehead lifted above his eye as he did remember seeing a large tower explode with blueish fire before his army had even destroyed the last gate. He looked over to where he thought it would have been standing and found that all that stood there was rubble and stone that used to be part of a large tower.

"Mmmmmm ... who destroyed it?" he whispered out loud as he stared up at the cracked and melted stones.

"Whoever did it, I'm sure, killed the council that was inside it, sealing the fate of this city with it," Tassalii answered, swallowing hard as his throat became dry at that moment. He thought that this creature must have done it to distract his people during the battle, cause panic and cause everything to fall apart.

Kaligor, smiling, stared down at the marshal, who, he could tell, wasn't going to do what he wanted. Crossing his arms, he turned, and crying out loudly, he ordered a Blingo'oblin that was standing nearby to grab the marshal and bring the man creature with him.

The huge creature nodded and walked over, grabbing Tassalii, who struggled under the strong hand of the creature who lifted him up and over his shoulder like a sack of flour. The orcs and other creatures cheered and yelled at seeing the man struggle.

As Kaligor walked up the road with Tassalii in tow to where the two large buildings had fallen earlier, stopping the orcs from moving further up the road, he made sure he was seen by the archers poking their heads out of the rubble and looking at his army.

"Drop the human!" he ordered his Blingo'oblin, who grunted with a smile, throwing the wounded marshal to the ground as the Cyclops reached down, grabbing the man tightly around the neck and making him gasp and struggle slightly as the dark-skinned creature stood up to look over the wall.

Deflecting an arrow that was released quickly at him with ease, he huffed a laugh and lifted his arm up with Tassalii to get the archers to stop their assault.

"Here is your marshal. I order you to surrender, or he dies!" Looking at Tassalii, who gasped and squirmed within his tight handgrip, Kaligor nodded his head and stared at the men defending the area before him. "You are trying to defend something you all know is a waste." When he heard no answer, he called out again. "What say you there along the rubble? Surrender or see this man soon adorning my banners!"

His eye scanned the archers along the quickly made wall.

He could see them talking amongst themselves, and men moved to get themselves ready, but soon he saw a new face move up and stare down at him, someone he could tell was one of the commanding men based on the cloak he wore, red like the blood that men held within their bodies.

"Kill him and my people will never stop until our last breaths!" the man screamed down at Kaligor, who quickly smiled at the man's words of resistance.

Kaligor quickly turned his smile into a loud, strong laugh as he grabbed Tassalii's hair with his other hand, bringing his head up sharply to show the man along the rubble what he was about to do. Tassalii cried out from the pain, but that was all he was able to say before Kaligor mumbled for him to be quiet.

"To the last breath then!" At that he reached down, pulling out the small sword that hung at his side. He let the sunlight hit the metal as he brought it up to the marshal's throat, but stopped at the last moment.

"Order them to surrender, Marshal Tassalii ... or die here!" His words echoed up to the man, who now had others with him looking down to see the scene below.

Tassalii had recognized the captain who had answered the Cyclops and knew that he was a great warrior and that he would do what he had said: fight until the last breath. The blade dug into his throat, making blood seep out slowly and adding sharp pain to his already terrible headache as he swallowed to get a deep breath so he could speak.

"Captain Rabmer," he said, knowing his words would be his last. "Captain ..." Pulling in a deep breath, he screamed "FIGHT TO THE LASTTTT!" but it was garbled and cut short as Kaligor pulled back his head and, in a quick swipe of his sword, cut through the neck of the man, instantly killing him.

Those standing and watching from the rubble screamed as they heard their marshal's last words and then had to watch as the Cyclops cut the man's head off and raised it above him. Quickly they released arrows at the creature, hoping to kill him, but instead their arrows only found orcs rushing past their leader as they charged to fight the last of the populace of Bru Edin. Kaligor yelled in triumph as he held the now decapitated head of Tassalii high in the air.

* * *

Dia walked into the glen surrounded by high cliffs and walls of stone as he was led past the largest army of elven warriors he'd ever seen gathered together in one area. The elf who had rescued him continued walking through the glen towards a pavilion adorned with blue and gold banners flapping in the breeze that moved through the glen. As they approached the tent, Dia could see many guards, covered in what had to be royal armor or something close to it, who turned to see him approaching.

As he walked towards the opening, these warriors separated to let him and his savior pass. As he looked inside he could see, sitting on a wooden chair, an elf king waiting.

Moments later Dia stood, listening to the elf wearing both armor and blueish robes. "You see, my elves gather in the hopes of fighting Methnorick's army." The king looked down at Dia as he continued to talk. "I am sorry we were not in time to save your city." He saw the sadness in the man's face, so in almost a whisper, he leaned forward and said, "Do you know of the status of your daughter and wife?"

Dia looked up at the elf king. "My wife is dead, and my daughter has been kidnapped."

"I am sorry to hear that; Shermeena was a wonderful woman. Do you know who took your daughter?"

"I do believe that Methnorick had something to with it, but I sent a group from the games after her."

"Do you think with all that has happened they still search for her?"

"All I can do is hope."

The king went on to explain what he knew, including reports he had received that the dark lord, Methnorick, ruled from an island far away off the east coast of the mainland and used it as a base to send his armies against Dia, the city states and the elves.

Soon both leaders discussed how they were going to counter the evil lord, as they watched hundreds, maybe thousands, of elves working hard to prepare themselves for the battle all knew was coming.

Looking out towards the northern edge of the glen, he could see movement that looked slightly familiar coming down from the snowy mountains to gather with the elven warriors.

"Ice Giants!" he said under his breath as he watched the huge creatures lumber into the glen. He lost count, seeing each carrying a large weapon, big enough to cut through 100 bodies at once, and he heard some elves laugh not far away.

As far as he could see, he was the only human in the glen with these elves, and it made him angry to realize that his people truly had been slaughtered by Methnorick's army, for the elf king shared a few reports that Methnorick had, indeed, destroyed the beloved city, villages and towns he had once called his and now were moving back east to attack Bru Edin.

As he crossed his arms and watched, cavalry rode by, each carrying a sharp spear and a highly polished shield as their helms gleamed in the sunlight and their horses galloped with great strength.

Dia could only observe this army, as he was told that he would leave soon, but the next day he was to sit in on a meeting of leaders to find out their plans.

* * *

Shermee held her breath as she ducked under the water's surface with Quinor close beside her. As they made their way slowly down the underwater slope into deeper water, she started to panic. Looking over at Quinor, slowly she started to move towards the surface as the need for air overwhelmed her. However, something had her ankle and would not allow her to rise any farther. She looked down to see the sea elf below her. She panicked and actually started to take a breath as Quinor reached out to grab the elf. Shermee suddenly realized that there was no need, as she looked down to the elf who released her ankle as he saw the look on her face. She looked over at Quinor, who had the same realization and released his grip on the elf as well. They all continued to make their way down the slope. Both Shermee and Quinor stopped, smiling as fish floated by and taking in the new sights around them. To the two of them, this was a world they had known only in their fantasies. Shermee reached out to touch one of the fish, only to giggle as it whipped its tail and shot away before she could.

Looking at Quinor, who had made it past some boulders, she could see him staring at something far away. She moved up to the man, touching his shoulder to get his attention.

Turning his head, he saw her staring at him. Not saying a word either, he just nodded to what he was staring at.

Far away, deep in the water, Shermee began to see something large moving through the water. She concentrated on the movement of the figure. Her mind was filled with questions as she watched the shape move closer and closer, until she saw what it was, but just then she looked over at the elf and saw his arms lifted above his head and his mouth moving like he was speaking at the same time.

This shadow, the darkness they both saw, was not just one shape but three creatures that floated through the water like it was air, whipping their tails back and forth.

Almost like ... horses, she thought as they came to rest in front of the elf, who reached out and patted the neck of the closest creature, which moved its head up and down in response. *Like he is talking to it,* she thought.

Quinor blinked a few times as the creatures floated up and stopped before the two, not believing what he was seeing as he took in each creature.

About the size of a war machine, he thought, maybe 20 feet in length with the body of a ... a dragon? He shook his head as he thought, *This has to be a dream, or am I truly dead, and this must be where all go when they die — to the seas — and these creatures are my gods' messengers of some kind.*

"You are not dreaming. My friends are here to help me take you away from Methnorick's reach to a safe land far away." Both looked at each other and then back at the elf, who was staring at them ... and talking to them.

"You are safe. As long as you are both with me, no harm will come to you!" The eyes of the elf blinked as he smiled at them.

He's talking ... but his mouth isn't moving, Quinor thought to himself. *How can I ...*

"My people have no use for our mouths like those creatures above do. We only use them when we converse outside the waters, which rarely happens." The elf walked slowly towards them, and Shermee grabbed Quinor's arm and held on to the man as the elf approached them both. She watched him walk on the rocky surface like it was grass.

"Come ... I can feel Methnorick's mind trying to find us. We need to leave ... and quickly!" The elf reached out with his hand that lay open, making the princess feel safe. She let the elf take her hand, and together they moved towards the three creatures that waited for them.

"My friends here are not going to harm you. Feel at ease," Shermee heard the elf say softly as he helped her onto the back of the creature, which she could see was watching her with two almost-black eyes.

She reached out and grabbed the hair, or what she thought

was hair, floating in the water as she moved upon its back and sat on it as she would a horse. She turned to see the elf help Quinor do the same, and soon both were tightly holding on to the creatures as they watched the elf jump up and lean in, speaking to his mount, which slowly turned its head back and nodded.

Shermee almost screamed out in fright, and even slight delight, when suddenly her mount whipped its tail, and the three shot through the water like arrows, quickly leaving the island behind them.

Chapter Twenty Five

The group quietly walked along the dark, wooded trail, not speaking for fear their voices might echo. Kalion caught up and joined Kikor on the trail.

"Our friend Whelor ... I think something might be wrong with him." Kalion looked at Kikor, who didn't answer, so he continued, "Since entering the depths of the mountain, the warrior hasn't spoken a word unless someone speaks to him, and then still hardly anything."

Kikor, who was also wondering about the large man, replied, "I do not know either, but something seems to be bothering Whelor."

Kalion nodded and looked over to where the human walked slightly ahead of everyone in the dark and said, "Maybe I need to find out." They both looked at the warrior.

Whelor walked cautiously along the road. The three times their group had stopped to rest, he had caught a scent and thought he could hear something as well. He didn't mention this to the others, for he just was not sure. How could he sense this when the elves and druids couldn't?

As he continued to walk down the trail, the smell caught Whelor's nose once again, and it was getting stronger the farther they went. Kikor came up along his side, and they continued to walk.

"Whelor, are you ok? You haven't said much since leaving Bru Edin."

Kikor has always been nice to me, he thought as he looked up and responded quietly.

"I am fine, Kikor. ... I am fine," he whispered. Looking away from her, he took out a water pouch, taking a small drink as they walked.

Kikor looked back at the others as she and the big warrior moved ahead.

"Whelor ..." She looked at the others to make sure no one heard her. "You smell something that, well ... something that shouldn't be here?" Kikor asked quietly. Her question caught the big human by surprise. He looked at her and took a moment to respond to her question.

"I have smelled something for a while now, Kikor, but I do not know what it is yet," he said as quietly as she did. He pushed his water pouch back into the pack and rubbed his shoulder for a moment.

"When did you pick up the smell first, Whelor?" Kikor knew somehow that Whelor's nose was stronger than the other humans'. She couldn't understand it, but somehow he had picked up things that the others hadn't before, which was why she came to him.

Looking over to Kikor, he answered as well as he could. "I started smelling something about a league back — since leaving the dwarven citadel — but have wondered if or what might be following us and whether it has been behind us even before the fortress." Kikor remembered it and thought for a moment, nodding her head to him.

"There's something else, isn't there, Whelor?"

"There always is," he replied quickly.

Kikor smiled at the human's humor. Whatever might have been bothering the man, at least he still had a smile, but Kikor felt the need to press on. "Whelor, I've found you to be a strong but quiet man, but one I can trust when things become bad. What is it that you know?"

Whelor looked at the ground below his feet as they walked for a moment, thinking about what to say to her.

"I have the feeling that we are being watched. By what, I

am not sure, but by something with intelligence ... something that shouldn't be within these mountains or even these lands."

Kikor looked around, seeing Amlora, Jebba and Kalion, who walked behind them and stared at her with a look like "So?" Meradoth stopped for a moment and leaned against a tree with his eyes closed. The poor mage had worked hard to keep a blue flame going all night, for the blue flame allowed them to see in the dark but not attract unwanted orcs. It had made him quiet tired, however, and now the others could see the toll it was taking on him. Kalion whispered for them all to stop and talked to Meradoth about options. Kikor couldn't see the thief, Chansor, but knew he was nearby, probably getting into trouble.

At the far end, she could make out both Niallee and Bennak keeping a watchful eye behind the group, so as far as she could tell, she and Whelor were the only ones who thought something was amiss.

"I'll go tell the others that we both believe we're being followed or at least watched by ... by something." Kikor turned to the others as Whelor looked up at her and grabbed her arm.

"Careful. We don't know what is out there, and it might attack if it knows we are onto it." Nodding an answer, Kikor quickly walked over to where Kalion and Meradoth stood.

Kalion looked up and smiled at Kikor as she approached.

"So, what does our big friend say is wrong?" the ranger whispered, looking back over Kikor's shoulder to see Whelor standing like he was watching for something.

Kikor pulled in a deep breath. "He believes we're being watched." Meradoth, hearing that they might be being watched by something, opened his eyes and looked over at the warrior and then back to Kikor.

"We have at least two days until we hit the eastern edge of the Pilo'achs and get into elven territory," Kalion said softly, seeing Kikor getting settled. "What did Whelor have to say about what he thinks it might be?" He nodded towards the big man he knew was standing silently in the dark.

She looked at Kalion and the others now resting. As she leaned in a bit, she recounted what the big human was feeling and thinking and how she agreed with Whelor's thoughts. The others listened, looking around in the dark as she whispered and then turning back to where Kikor stood.

"Do you want me to see if I can find out what it might be?" Amlora piped in, looking at the others as she stepped forward.

Kalion nodded quietly, looking to Amlora to ask the animals of the forest to see who was keeping tabs on the group.

As Amlora got up, Jebba whispered, "We should get moving then," bringing Kalion's attention back.

"Let Amlora do her work first," Kalion said, cutting Jebba off. "We must know if something is following us and what it is."

Jebba got up with a disgusted look and turned to walk away from Kalion as Kalion watched Amlora, who had closed her eyes and begun to whisper quietly.

Amlora finished and opened her eyes. "It seems we are being followed, but by what, my forest friends can't or won't say. It seems they are either not sure what it is, or they just can't get close enough to sort out what it is. They say it does not smell or move like anything they are aware of. Whatever it is, they say it is not an orc."

Kalion looked at the group and whispered that everyone should get up and start moving in a moment.

The sound of groans and bodies moving echoed slightly around the group. A few regular torches were lit to help the group and allow Meradoth more time to rest. Kalion figured they were already being followed, so what was the harm in regular, tough fire at this point?

Chapter Twenty Six

*H*olan quietly ran down the road, at least as quietly as a dwarf could. He had been watching the deer for who knew how long now, and even though he knew the deer could smell him, he was determined to kill it.

Most deer, he thought, would have run away after catching his scent, but this one looked strong and smart and even had the appearance of knowing what the dwarf was thinking.

With Kikor moving around to his right, he was sure the two of them could corner this creature. When he made his way around a large group of boulders that lay among a grouping of trees, he suddenly stopped to see that standing at the other side was a cloaked man.

Pulling himself back, he was sure that whoever it was had heard him. *Who wouldn't have?* he thought. A dwarf never was a quiet creature in the forests. Lifting his axe up, he wondered if he should try to attack this man, but then he thought better of it. *Could be a mage of some kind!* He'd seen what Meradoth and Harbin had done in the past; this man, or whatever it was, could be or do the same. He decided to stand and peer around the boulder and watch when he heard a snap of a branch behind him. He turned quickly, thinking it was a trap, to see Chansor smiling back at him.

Grinning, Holan shook his head, not believing the thief had snuck up on him like that. But he motioned for the man to be quiet as he turned around, peering back again to see that the cloaked figure hadn't moved, but just stood there.

Chansor, confused, quietly moved up and slowly peered around his friend. He saw the cloaked man and gave Holan a look, shrugging his shoulders to show that he didn't recognize what he was staring at.

Holan grabbed Chansor's cloak, pulling his ear up close so he could whisper, hoping that whoever this was hadn't heard them.

"Go tell the rest. Be quick. ... Be quiet!" Holan nodded at the thief, who smiled and nodded as he did what Holan asked, leaving the dwarf alone again to observe the man, who, he could see now, was moving his covered head like he was looking around for something.

"I know you are there, dwarf. Come out and let us talk!" the voice said loudly to Holan.

Holan thought for a moment. Could he turn and run? No, he saw that this man had planned this just right. The sides of the road were thick with bushes and tree trunks. The boulders also made it hard to move away quickly. So gripping his axe tightly, he swallowed deeply, knowing this could be it for him. He stepped out, walking as quietly as he could towards the figure and keeping at least a spear's length between himself and this cloaked man. As he walked around, he squinted his eyes, trying to figure out who this figure was, as for some reason the voice sounded familiar.

When he finally made his way around to look directly at the man's face, all he did see was a lowered hood that covered his face. He did see that his hands were young and held a staff, letting the warrior know that, indeed, he was correct in thinking this was a mage.

"Who are you?" Holan whispered as he held his axe, ready to strike down on the mage if he tried to move quickly.

"Ohhhh, Holan ... you know me!" At that a hand moved up and pushed back the hood to reveal a smiling face, making Holan drop his axe quickly and gasp angrily back at the man.

"Harbin ... where ... who ... we lost you back in Bru Edin. Where have you been, mage?" Holan lowered his axe, letting it fall to the ground as he spoke clearly now.

"Sorry, Holan. I had to go and find out some information ... and it drew me here to get the answers." Harbin smiled as he looked around. The dwarf, confused, also looked around.

"You found answers ... here ... in this forest? A bit daft, do you not think there, mage!?" Holan gave him a smile, knowing he was picking on the mage, who huffed and smiled back at his friend.

"Not here, my friend. No ... not far from here is where my kind train and become ... I knew that if I went there, I could find out who this Methnorick is!" Harbin walked over and leaned against the same boulder that Holan had been leaning on a moment earlier.

Holan was curious now as he walked closer to look directly at his friend's face. He saw Harbin had grown older somehow. Maybe the strain of being what he was had something to do with it ... or something else.

"What did you find, my friend?" Holan asked quietly, concerned that maybe his answer would make the group's situation even worse and make it harder to find the princess.

Pushing out his chest as he took in a deep breath, Harbin looked up at the sky. Seeing the bright blue and white clouds moving across it, he smiled slowly, but then returned the look that the dwarf was giving him.

"When the rest get here, I'll explain everything I can, my friend. But in the meantime, I am glad that you made it out of Bru Edin. I saw what happened there ... but why not go to the dwarven citadel? I am sure that it would be strong enough to hold off orcs and their like." Harbin could see Holan's reaction, and he knew this would be interesting.

Holan walked over and leaned against a boulder next to his friend as he quickly tried to explain what had happened when they escaped Bru Edin and the dwarven city. He told him that the dwarven people were deep in battle with their dreaded enemy deep within the mountains and that the king did not want their help and would not help them.

Harbin looked at the ground and thought as Holan spoke about the dwarves and their battles. "That would explain the quakes that I felt a while ago," Harbin whispered and then smiled when he saw Holan staring at him, wondering what he was talking about.

"No matter, my friend. We are safe now!" His words made Holan tilt his head slightly. They both began to hear the movement of branches around them and feet hitting the ground hard.

"Ahhhh, our friends are here!" Harbin pushed himself off the boulder, leaving the dwarf to look up at him like he was losing it or something, when he heard the familiar sounds of boots moving through the forest and looked to see Chansor and then Kalion move around the boulder. The ranger had his bow, ready to release an arrow at Harbin, but he quickly lowered it when he saw who was standing there with open arms.

"Harbin?" Kalion smiled as he relaxed, seeing the dwarf leaning against the boulder not far away. "You're well, I see. Where have you been?"

Seeing the rest of the group make its way into the clearing, Harbin looked and nodded at each. Whelor was the last to enter the clearing. As he did, he gave the mage a half smile and nodded as he placed his sword back in his back scabbard.

"Where's Kikor?" Harbin asked as he looked at the group and realized the elf warrior wasn't amongst them.

"I am here, Harbin. I've been watching you for a while!" Her voice made the mage turn around quickly to see the blond-haired elf jump down from a tree not far away. As she landed, she replaced the arrow that she had been holding on the string, pointed at the mage, moments earlier while she watched him and Holan talking.

"Always ready. Mmmm, Kikor ... good!" Harbin turned and looked at the rest, who were looking at him all confused. Even Meradoth looked a bit out of touch as he watched his fellow mage.

"Holan asked me where I was and what I have been doing since I left Bru Edin. As Meradoth could attest, I went to the one

290

place I believed would tell me what or who Methnorick is — I went home!" He thought about what he had told Kalion back in Bru Edin about the spy amongst the group but chose to keep that piece of information quiet for the time being. He would address it with Kalion when he was alone with the ranger.

"Home ... to this forest?" Jebba snickered, looking around. Harbin smiled at the man's joke.

"Not here, my friend." He turned and pointed up the mountain. "Up there!" He turned and watched everyone look up, except Meradoth, who just shook his head slightly back at Harbin, who gave him a quick smile.

"What's up there, Harbin?" Chansor asked quickly, wondering how anyone could live in the Pilo'achs Mountains.

"It's hard to explain without showing you, my friends, but we will be safe. We will find answers there ... and maybe more if you let me take you there!" Harbin looked at each of his friends and then at Meradoth, who gave him a tired look as he leaned on his staff, returning Harbin's stare.

"How long to get there?" Kalion asked, looking back at the mage he thought had abandoned them a while ago.

"Not long. Maybe a few hours' hike up ... isn't that right, Meradoth?" Harbin calling out the other mage made everyone look at the other man, who leaned on his staff, wondering what Harbin meant.

Seeing everyone staring back at him, Meradoth breathed in deeply and nodded slowly. "Yes ... it's not far from here." Meradoth walked over to stand next to Harbin and gave him a look saying they needed to talk before he shared too much more.

"See that deer trail there, Chansor?" Harbin pointed to an opening between two large trees.

Chansor saw what Harbin was pointing at and nodded quickly. Then hearing his instructions to take everyone that way, not knowing that Harbin had just used his ability to let the others see the opening, which was normally never there, he led the others down the path.

As the rest began to make their way, Harbin turned to his fellow mage and waited until the rest were far enough away. Then he answered the question he could see on Meradoth's face.

"I know ... I know ... bringing them there is against everything that our people hold, but I found out who Methnorick is by speaking to our elder ... and it was he who asked me to bring the group there!"

Meradoth squinted his eyes a bit as he stood there, listening, but then lifted his forehead, as he knew that if their elder had made the request ... "Nothing I can say then about it."

Harbin smiled quickly and followed the rest of the group, with Meradoth bringing up the rear. As they walked through the forest opening, it quickly disappeared, leaving it to look like it always did before: a tight group of bushes.

Chapter Twenty Seven

Finishing off the last of the trolggs, Vana and his men walked the field that lay directly below the massive towers of the "Father Gate."

Here and there they found a trolgg hiding under a log or tree and quickly dispatched its head with ease, but this didn't sit well with the general.

Why would these creatures, ones that haven't been seen for many, many cycles, just throw themselves against this gate, knowing that they can't get up and over it, or through it? There is more at work here, he thought.

Vana watched as his men walked around the field, their armor shining in the sunlight. A few had large smiles while some showed signs of exhaustion from fighting all night long. An even smaller number were still showing signs of worry. Vana considered that they were also thinking this wasn't the last they would see of these ugly creatures.

Turning, he walked past the opened gate and back into the courtyard that was between the two large towers. He stopped to order the warriors out on the field back within the safety of the walls now that the sun was coming back up.

Another warrior ran up and handed him a pouch of cool water, and quickly taking a large sip of it, he lifted his head back and saw the horseman riding up from the south being stopped by one of his men. He noticed that the rider was a scout since he wore nothing like armor.

Watching, he saw that his men talked briefly to the rider and then turned and pointed to where he stood. The rider nodded back, and kicking his horse, he moved quickly across the field and into the courtyard, where Vana waited for the man to approach.

"Sooo ... what is so urgent, my friend?" Vana asked as another warrior ran up, telling him that the field was finally cleared and the warriors were moving back behind the protection of the walls, as he had ordered. Nodding, Vana saw the rider jump off his horse and stand there.

"What say you, boy?" he asked again.

Swallowing, the boy pulled in a deep breath and explained the need for his hard ride to the tower gates. When he was done, Vana shook his head and then slowly lowered it as he took in the news: the trolggs were indeed just a diversion to get his warriors to look another way — away from the south, it seemed.

The scout shared that orcs, goblins and some other creatures were attacking farms about half a day's march from where he stood, and from what the scout said, it was a large enough contingent to take on the warriors Vana had here at the Father Gate.

Vana considered the news further and wondered how they had gotten to the south without passing through his gate, for there was no other way across the great ravine close by. The closest bridges across the ravine had been smashed and decayed by cycles of nonuse. As Vana considered this further, he turned to the scout. "Get yourself some water and food, boy. You look tired from your ride." The boy nodded as Vana turned and screamed for his second in command to come hither.

As the old warrior ran up with a smile, thinking that they were done, he saw his general's look quickly turn serious.

"Close the gates. Make sure we have enough archers and men to man them, and then gather the rest here in the courtyard. I want a full inspection within the hour. ... We're marching." Vana spoke clearly and sharply to make sure his second in command understood.

Nodding, the warrior with over 25 cycles of experience

turned and cried out the new orders. Soon the courtyard was full of yells as orders were sent out to get moving. Not long after Vana had given his order, the massive gates were moving to close.

Turning, the man gave Vana a look that asked why and what was going on. Vana watched for a moment and then placed his gloved hand on his friend.

"I've received a report that orcs are attacking and moving across the fields south of here, assaulting farms and killing as they move. Those trolggs were to get us to look one way while they did their job and attacked us from the rear."

"All the gods together!" the old man gasped, looking south as though he could see the orcs. "How did they get across the ravine, sir?"

"I do not know, but we must address the threat to our people. Have that mage of ours try to send a message to the other gates to see if they breached one of them. But meanwhile, you're in charge of the gate while I'm gone." At that Vana walked past the man and up into the tower, where he had the rest of his gear stored.

As he went into the tower, the courtyard below him soon got crowded, as men, along with their equipment and arms, gathered and waited. Sergeants screamed orders, and many began to whisper and talk about what was going on, but this quickly stopped when they saw Vana appear at the doorway that led into the tower.

He walked out, stopped and looked over the men gathered below. Banners fluttered in the wind gently as the sun shined off armor and weapons.

"Men, I've received a report. ... Orcs have made it past our gate and, at this moment, are attacking farms, families, friends. Family members of ours are dying. We must save as many as we can and destroy each and every orc that believes it can roam our empire without us knowing." He took a breath and then waited for the news to sink in for everyone who was gathered. He could see the anger on a few faces. A few looked nervous as well, but he trusted that each and every one of his men would fight to the death if he so ordered it.

"We leave here within the hour. Gather your mounts. ... Make sure you are ready for what is coming this way. We will fight. ... We will win this field of battle!"

Screams echoed out from the courtyard as the men all cheered at his words, and quickly the order was given for them to disperse and get their mounts ready. Within the hour, Vana, whose horse had been prepared, was leading his small army of warriors slowly out of the courtyard and onto the field that lay south, with banners and spirits flying high. Vana knew they could do the job.

"Tevanic, keep this place safe. I suspect more is at play!" The commander nodded his head and lifted his hand in a salute as the general moved out with his warriors.

* * *

After breaking through what he thought was the last defense of the men guarding and living within this fortress, Kaligor found that there were many still holding out in the small upper level that lay deep within the castle.

Now with 20 orcs running up behind their commander, they made their final approach to the human fortress. There they found the large building that looked more like a palace than a castle, with what looked like at least 20 score heavily armored humans waiting in front of the closed gates.

Kaligor pulled the reins of his horse and stopped smiling, as this final victory was close at hand. Lord Methnorick had given him overall command of the northern armies, and with this final destruction of the humans here, he would be almost done with his mission.

As Kaligor sat upon his mount and stared at these warriors left on the wall, looking almost like statues to him, he could see that, if anything, they didn't show fear like many of the men he had encountered. Seeing their leader staring back at them, scores of his orcs that had fought their way through the weak human defenses ran up behind him and stared up at him with blood-shot eyes and blood even leaking out of their mouths, waiting for their general to give the order to charge.

Kaligor lifted his massive weapon up over his head as he screamed and snarled at the humans. He was about to yell for his troops to complete the final assault when suddenly he heard a voice behind him.

"My lord, why do you hesitate?" Kaligor turned in his saddle in anger, thinking an orc or another creature had the nerve to speak to him, but instead saw a black-robed figure with its head covered walking up the hill, making its way through the parting orcs.

Kaligor was about to scream at the figure when he got the deep feeling not to, seeing that it was Chenush walking up. However, it was not this but the sight of what was coming up behind the black-robed figure that gave the chill to the Cyclops. Sitting on top of black horses were five similarly robed figures, each with eyes that glowed red from under their hoods, like the figure that was now standing next to him.

Walking past the Cyclops and coming to the front of the orc lines that slowly closed behind him, the black figure walked to stand a few feet from the human armored warriors. No arrow shot out, nor did any spear fly at the robed figure as it stood there.

"Humannnssssss ...." its voice echoed. The voice of the black figure made many humans lower their spears, but yells came from their soldiers to stand ready. "Thisss iss yourrr chanceee to leave her' nowwwww!" Kaligor was sure he could make out many of the humans soiling themselves, as his nose picked up an unusual smell that their kind made when that happened and he was sure he could see liquid forming around many of their feet. At the sound of the figure standing in front of them, even a few of his warriors moved back, feeling the same fear.

No sound or word came from either side as a few birds flew overhead, looking for food, and a brief, cool wind moved up the street, bringing the smell of death to the men. Suddenly, as Kaligor watched the humans begin to part, one of the small gates opened and a lone human came walking through the line of the warriors guarding the gate and castle beyond.

The human made his way to stand in front of the robed figure. Kaligor found that he could make out what they were saying as the human ordered them to leave this place. This made Chenush laugh.

"You think we came here to just leave?" The laughter echoed everywhere in the area as he continued, "Surrender now, or I finish this here ... now!" This time the voice echoed, so it could be heard by Kaligor and his orcs, who quickly grinned and snarled, knowing that victory was at hand for them.

When the man didn't answer, Chenush rushed forward, making the man scream madly. Chenush grabbed the man, and as Kaligor and his warriors, along with the man's companions behind the wall, watched, Chenush quickly killed the man and in one motion ripped his head off his body. Chenush screamed as he leaned his head back, making blood within his mouth fly out everywhere.

This quick and sudden attack made those humans standing guard fall back, quickly melting away to disappear from sight. In one motion they disappeared, and the orcs saw that the gate had been pushed open. As soon as the orcs standing around Kaligor saw this, they started unleashing loud screams of victory. The small courtyard they all stood in suddenly erupted as the screaming orcs charged forward, running past Chenush, who just stood, staring at Kaligor, giving him what Kaligor thought was a smile.

As General Kaligor watched, his warriors pushed the gates open and charged in. Quickly his ears picked up the now familiar screams of women and men that echoed out from inside the castle as his warriors quickly massacred everyone inside. As he sat upon his horse, he watched as the last of the humans within Bru Edin were thrown from windows to die before him, leaving him to stare at the creature in the black robe that now was standing in front of him.

"Master wanted this done. I was ordered to come end this,"

Chenush told Kaligor, who knew not to anger the creature. Chenush held the head of the man he had just fed on in his hand and, like it was a toy, soon just dropped it on the ground and kicked it away like a ball as he talked to the general.

"I had things in order here. This was their final resistance, and now Bru Edin is finished, and it is mine!" Kaligor's mount could feel the anger in its master as the Cyclops spoke.

"Bru Edin is our master's, Cyclops. But enjoy your victory. ... He has new orders for you." Chenush looked up at Kaligor.

"And what does Methnorick ask of me now?" Kaligor turned his head and watched with pride as his warriors were destroying everything around them.

"He orders that you lay waste to the elven homeland to the east to show all the races of this land that they are finished. Then march back towards Stych and await his coming." Chenush's voice suddenly sent a tiny chill down the Cyclops' back, making him suddenly worry. No creature had ever challenged him. Not even Methnorick had tried to take the Cyclops on in battle, knowing that the large creature was strong, wise and cunning ... but this creature was now doing just that.

"I will do what the master asks, of course, but do not challenge me. I am not one to ..."

"I am not here to challenge you, Cyclops. I am here to give you orders that our master has given to me," Chenush interrupted Kaligor, who closed his eye slightly, staring down at Chenush, knowing he was lying to him about something.

Chenush nodded and, without a word, strode off, passing orc warriors, who quickly stepped out of the way, leaving Kaligor by himself as the black-cloaked figure left, along with the other riders, who turned and followed the vampire.

As Chenush walked down the road, he put his hand inside his cloak, pulling out two small metal objects that just recently had been in the basement of the once proud-looking tower of the council. Now that the council was gone, it was easy to search for and grab these things.

Not that Chenush cared for them. He knew that his master wanted them, and that was all he cared about as he disappeared, along with the other black-cloaked figures among the crowds of orcs.

Kaligor, meanwhile, screamed for his next in command as he slid off his saddle and patted his horse, who snarled. Giving Kaligor a look of approval, the large red eyes stared back at him, but then suddenly it moved its head back towards where the castle lay as an orc approached.

Kaligor turned to give his command. "Send out the word: destroy this place. You have two days. I want everything torn down. Nothing is too survive ... not even the rats!" Kaligor moaned down at the orc, who quickly answered back that his orders were to be carried out.

As Kaligor watched, the orc jumped up and ran back into the castle, quickly crying out orders, which made everyone inside cheer and yell. The general watched as fires soon erupted from the castle to join in with the fires that already were burning within the city.

Pulling himself back onto the saddle, Kaligor turned his horse around, and slowly they made their way back down the main road that wound through Bru Edin, passing orcs, goblins, giantkind and even dark elves having their fun killing, raping, eating and destroying the city, not even stopping as their general rode past.

When Kaligor finally passed the main gateway, or what was left of it, he stopped and turned to look up at the burning city. Knowing that the smoke from it would be seen for many leagues, he let a smile show on his face.

Bru Edin was dead ... destroyed by him and his army. He turned his eye to look east towards the area where he was ordered to march. Maybe his master knew something he didn't, but to hear that he could finally destroy the thorn in his side ... Everything Kaligor had fought for was finally in his grasp.

Holan had been walking quietly for a while now, his feet touching the ground as he went up the trail — a trail that looked more like men or elves had made it, not deer.

Behind him the rest of the group silently walked, taking their time as the trail led up the steep hill, winding itself back and forth. Once in a while, Harbin's voice could be heard saying that they were doing well and soon they would be where he was taking them.

Holan gripped his axe even though Harbin had said it was safe for them all. Chansor, meanwhile, was enjoying the trail, bobbing up and down, skipping and laughing as he and Harbin spoke quietly about where the mage had been and how the thief had been doing.

Kalion and Kikor walked next to each other. Neither spoke, but the elf could sense that the ranger was nervous about this trail as well. She had tried to give him a smile of confidence, but so far it hadn't worked.

Niallee showed her anxiety on her face. So far she had been able to hear creatures moving in the forest as they walked, but since entering this new trail, she couldn't feel or hear anything.

Jebba and Bennak walked together as well. Both warriors held their weapons at the ready, looking left and right for a surprise both thought might jump out at them.

So far Meradoth hadn't spoken a word, but he looked at Harbin, who just smiled and nodded back at the other mage, which didn't make Meradoth feel any better. He was worried, and Harbin could see that.

Whelor, meanwhile, had made sure he was far enough away from each member of the group. He walked slowly but with effort as they ascended the hill, which turned into a mountainside as they left the tree line.

When they finally hit a cliff, the group stopped and looked back and down at the forest and fields that lay below. Harbin moved to the front of the group, where Holan was leaning against the rock wall, breathing hard from the climb.

"Almost there, my friend," Harbin whispered loudly as he approached the dwarf.

"Almost where, Harbin? I do not like this!" Holan eyed the mage, who nodded slightly as he leaned against his staff.

"Just up this last part of the trail, and you will see. No worries, my friend ... all is safe here!" Harbin could see Meradoth, who also was leaning on his staff, stare at him as though he disapproved of what he was doing, but Harbin had his orders.

Niallee was staring across the forest and fields with the others, and she could make out the mountain of Edin pushing itself out of the fog that had gathered behind them when something caught her eye. She pointed directly at the mountain.

"Look ... Bru Edin is completely in flames!" she said calmly but with sadness.

Everyone stopped what they were doing and stared out towards where the druid was pointing. Each moved to the edge of the cliff and stared at the mountain, knowing that what they all saw was, indeed, the fortress burning.

"That's not fog. That's smoke from the city," Kikor said softly as she watched the smoke move. She looked over at Kalion, who returned her look and nodded slowly.

"Where are you taking us, Harbin? We have been on this trail for hours now, and you said it was close by." The ranger turned to look directly at the mage, who was staring at the mountain beyond.

"To a safe place, my friend. Meradoth knows where we are going. ... We will be safe, yes?"

Meradoth stared at his fellow mage and then, sucking in a breath, he nodded slowly as the others stared at him, waiting for his approval. "Yes ... we will be safe there!"

Chapter Twenty Eight

The journey was something that Shermee would never forget. They had just entered the water, and as they floated through it, they passed numerous creatures that lived within the sea, all going about their own business, from massive creatures that looked to be the size of several ships to tiny creatures that swarmed up to her, floated still for a moment and then quickly turned and swam away.

Shermee stretched out her hand to let some water float through it as a school of tiny fish that parted around her hand moved by. She muffled her laugher as the tiny fish tickled her skin.

The excitement of the journey had Shermee looking left and right as new creatures appeared and disappeared around her. This new and exciting world was something she had never imaged, and she wanted it to never end as she continued to watch the sea life around her with excitement.

The two floated endlessly through the water, always behind the sea elf who never spoke or even looked back at them, which made Quinor wonder what the elf really had planned for him.

Quinor considered, *He mentioned that I was his prisoner, so why not try to escape him? ... Well, he also said we have to stay with him to breathe underwater, and since we are a few leagues under the waves, it might be difficult, and I can't leave the princess now, but ...* He answered his own question as he tried to pull the reins of the creature to the right to maneuver it away, but nothing happened and the creature resisted. *Well, that settles that,* he concluded.

They had been traveling for a while at a rather slow pace, and Shermee, not far away, was starting to wonder how long this trip was going to take, when a few moments later, her eyes started to get heavy, and she could barely keep them open. She looked over to find that Quinor had fallen fast asleep. She continued to look at the wonderful creatures around her and fought the heaviness with each passing moment; however, it was too much for her as she started to doze off and fell slowly down to lie on the neck of the creature. If they had been awake and aware, they might have noticed the elf look back and smile, seeing that both of the humans had closed their eyes.

Raising his hand, he motioned to the sea creatures to hurry towards the area they were headed. Each creature quickly whipped its tail and shot through the water like an arrow, leaving nothing behind to follow in their wake.

* * *

Manhattoria was busy like never before, getting itself ready for the war the population thought either would not come in their lives or, as many had hoped, would never happen at all, believing that the empire was finally at peace.

People spoke about how High Minister Halashii hadn't being seen for a few days, but the ministers, in his absence, worked hard to get the army prepped and ready. On the outskirts of the massive city, the cavalry was being armed and fed while all weapons needed were brought out of storage, sharpened and strengthened, and given to each able man and elf that joined the ranks.

The main army soon formed itself and camped outside the city on the northeastern plain that lay flat a few miles away from the border wall of the city. The grassy plains that used to be covered in wildlife were now covered in campfires and the sounds of metal and feet marching. The lights from the city shined out onto the field at night, but the fires from the camp returned that light to be seen by those living within it, giving many eerie feelings about what was going on in the north.

Michelc silently walked the small lanes that were built

306

between the tents as he listened to men laughing at jokes and stories, making the elf smile and feel proud that the empire still hadn't lost its sense of superiority, and so far from what he could hear, none spoke of fear or being nervous, not even the newest recruits, many of whom had never even encountered an orc in their short lives.

"You think we should ready by morrow's eve?" the elf that walked beside him asked. His words brought Michelc out of his thoughts to look over and see the elf looking at a group of archers stringing their arrows together, many making jokes about something as they strode by.

"From what I've been told, only the machines need to be brought into the camp. After that, I believe we are ready. ... But why? What are you hearing or thinking, my friend?" Michelc brought his arms behind his back and held them together, nodding at a warrior as he walked by.

"Mmmm, no, I have not heard a whisper, in fact ... but it will take an army of this size a while to get to the Father Gate or even the Gate of the Hand, so I hope that whatever might be happening within the north doesn't march south before we arrive at the bridge." The elf smiled at his joke, as did Michelc.

"I would hate for any orcs out there to have to wait for us, too, my friend, but even if the orcs do try to get past any of the gates and towers, which they would be hard-pressed to do, all they will find is death ... from us of course." Michelc smiled at another warrior, who was sitting on a stool, sharpening his long sword. The man quickly stood up, saluting the elf, who nodded back with a large smile.

Michelc, who wore the bright, but strong, armor over his blueish-gold robes, having changed from his regular minister clothing earlier, coughed a moment as he remembered something. "Ohhhh ... please make sure that the musicians are rested. I would hate for them to be tired when we leave tomorrow. No drinking for them, my friend!"

The elf walking next to him, wearing the same armor, stopped to turn and look at the minister before answering. "Of course ... I will make sure of that myself, sir, but ..." The elf looked back at the city for a moment and then turned his gaze towards the elf who had been given the leadership of the main army. "... is there any word on the high minister? Is he still in seclusion?"

Michelc looked back at the city himself, towards the tower that held the high minister's chambers. As he looked up at it, his mouth tightened as he thought for a moment. Then breathing in deeply, he shook his head slightly and, speaking almost at a whisper, said, "None ... I have heard nothing from him since the call to arms."

✳ ✳ ✳

At that moment, if the elves could have seen into the tower where the high minster, Halashii's, chamber was, they would have seen Halashii lying on the floor of his chamber, squirming in pain as he gripped his chest. His mouth was moving but no sound was coming out as he squeezed his eyes tightly from the pain.

"Never ... never ... never ... I will never betray ... never !" he quietly uttered as another spasm shook his body hard, making him bend his back as tears landed on the stone floor.

The agony of his betrayal of his empire was nothing compared to what Methnorick was doing to him. He was unaware that it was Methnorick's mindslayer who was at this moment reaching into his mind, causing the pain that he was now experiencing. He had woken early that morning from the third night of nightmares — ones in which his people found out that he had made a deal with Methnorick to save himself, only to turn on him and either kill him or torture him. This nightmare was the worst so far. So now he resolved to find a way to protect his city and his people. He was still contemplating how when Methnorick reached out to him, causing him to fall down to his knees as his mind screamed.

"You betrayed me, Halashii!" was all he heard echoing through his mind as he lay there. "You betrayed me, Halashii!" Each time the voice spoke, his body was racked with pain, and just when he thought he was getting over the pain, it would begin again.

"Never ... never!" he finally screamed out loud as he got a moment of strength, which quickly disappeared, leaving him to squirm again on the floor.

How could he ever have thought he would get away with the any plan against the dark one? "Follow my orders, and you and your people will be saved, and you will become emperor over all the lands within the empire," were the words Methnorick had said to him a long time ago.

As Halashii lay there in pain, he remembered a tale, a legend that spoke of a warrior from a faraway land who would come to his lands and of the evil that would be destroyed at its darkest moment by whoever held the hand of the warrior. And now Halashii, who had led the empire for many cycles now, knew that this could be its darkest hour and that he could be the one the legend spoke of since he was from the southern reaches of the empire. But to hear that Methnorick was also searching for a princess from the north ... he just had to get the princess before the dark one did ... but where was she?

He knew that Methnorick did not have her yet, or he would have bragged about his victory in getting the girl, and his spies a few days earlier had been able to tell him nothing beyond her boarding a ship in Blath 'Na that left for lands beyond just before that city fell.

As he lay there, though, the words shot again through his mind, again making him scream as he struggled to get rid of the pain as words echoed again and again: Shermee ... Shermee.

Chapter Twenty Nine

The group was rounding a corner on the trail when Kikor came to a stop and pulled her bow string a little and quickly notched an arrow. Her ears were picking up something inside the smoke — something she had never felt or heard before. It made the skin on her back tighten as she looked slowly through the smoke for whatever it was.

Kalion could see Kikor stiffen up and notch the arrow, making him concerned as his senses moved quickly. If she was like that, then something was out there, so he slowly pulled his bow out and strung it quickly but then stopped when a hand landed gently on his shoulder. He turned to see Harbin looking at him.

Harbin shook his head "no" at him as the feeling that something was wrong disappeared from Kalion. He lowered his bow stave and turned slowly to look at the mage with a confused look. Then he moved his eyes towards Kikor, who stared outwards, on alert. Kalion felt something was still waiting for them out there, but he felt a bit more at ease with Harbin next to him. The three stood there quietly, without moving, as the ranger began to hear the familiar sounds of his group moving up the dirt trail. Soon he could see the rest of the group moving within the smoke not far away from where he, Kikor and the mage stood.

Harbin let go of the ranger's shoulder and lifted his hands up, looking at the man as he did. "Observe, my friend!" As Kalion turned his head slowly to one side, he quickly saw that the smoke was dissipating from around them. He turned completely around with wide eyes as he watched everything become clear once again.

The group watched in amazement as the fog lifted and

moved away from the group, as if waters were parting to reveal what lay before them. They slowly, as one, took in the view and lifted their heads as they saw what looked like a massive structure towering before them.

Off to the edge of the small clearing that the group now stood within, Meradoth looked down at the ground, leaning on his staff, as the rest of the group took in the sight of the structure. The group let out a quiet gasp, for the structure stood so high that its top couldn't be seen from where they stood, still being covered in clouds.

Shining as if it were armor used in battle, the structure was wider than any tower any of them had seen before and was silvery in color, with many areas covered in moss and rust. None could see an opening to get inside; Kikor, lowering her bow, looked around it quickly, trying to see if there were any openings where maybe archers could aim at them. She found nothing — no balconies, windows or doors as far as she could see — when a voice boomed out of nowhere, causing her to bring her bow back up.

"Welcome, my friends. You are all protected within this sphere of safety. Here we will find answers ... and together we will hopefully stop the evil that is raging around us all."

Hearing the new voice echo from nowhere, everyone grabbed their weapons in surprise, fearing the worst, when they saw a figure emerge out of the fog just to their left. Jebba brought his sword up, and Harbin quickly whispered, "There is no need to show arms, my friends."

"Kalion ... all ... you are safe here, my friends. It is well. Trust me!" Meradoth finally said quietly. Kalion, hearing his friend's reassuring voice, looked over at the mage to see his friend return a smile and nod. The ranger thought quickly but knew that if his friend was fine with the situation, they should be too.

Slowly the group replaced their weapons as the figure pulled back its hood to show a smiling man, maybe 30 cycles of age, looking back at them all with a face that showed wisdom and strength, making them suddenly feel secure.

The man slowly walked closer. As he passed each member of the group, he smiled and nodded at them. "Hello, Jebba ... Bennak ... my friend, Chansor ... ahhh, Kikor, you are safe here ... Niallee, hello to you ... Holan, friend ... hello, Amlora, all is for you, too ... and Kalion, the leader of this group, I say hello to you." As the man slowly moved through the group members, smiling at each, he failed to notice both Jebba almost snarling at his words about Kalion and Whelor waiting among the trees, far enough away to remain out of sight.

As he finished walking around the group, the man stopped to stand in front of the ranger, who looked him directly in the eyes and took in the feeling that they were, indeed, finally safe and sound.

"Who are you, friend?" Kalion asked, saying the words that had crept into the minds of each of the members as he had mentioned their names, but he kept his hand on the pommel of his sword, just in case.

The man smiled and turned to look at the two mages. Harbin smiled in return, but Meradoth shook his head and looked at the ground before slowly looking up at the man. "Hello, Father!" Meradoth said, quietly bringing everyone's attention away from the man now standing within their group.

"Father?" Chansor said excitedly. "That is ... wait, how can he be your father, Meradoth? He looks like your brother!" The thief looked confused as he glanced back and forth at the two.

"Hello, my son, welcome home!" the man said, ignoring Chansor's comment. He smiled and put his hands on Meradoth's shoulders as he spoke. Turning, he walked back to stand in front of the group as Chansor stared back and forth between the two men, trying to figure out everything.

"My name is Nicolorr Boyrnor, and all questions will be answered within. But please ... Harbin, my friend, take them inside. We need to get them fed and rested before we begin to answer all the questions that I am sure you all have had since the beginning of this adventure. Quickly, now. We have not much time." Meradoth's father spoke quietly as he looked out beyond the group towards the forest. His voice made the rest feel secure now as Harbin bowed slightly and, obeying the man, walked through the group and made his way towards the shining structure that lay before them all. He waved a hand, and an opening appeared in front of him, which he moved through, with the others closely behind him.

As each member walked past Meradoth's father, they nodded and smiled, as he did in return, not speaking to them, only giving Chansor a tight look when the small man walked past, smiling up at him. When he finally saw Whelor walk out of forest and move up behind the group, his smile quickly disappeared, and he squinted his eyes slightly like a hawk would as he observed the big man moving up.

He didn't say or do anything as Whelor walked past. Neither spoke to or smiled at the other. As the man watched Whelor's large frame disappear into the opening that had appeared in the side of the structure, Meradoth slowly moved up and stood with his father.

"What is it, Father?" he asked, looking at Whelor and back at his father.

"Who is that man, Son?" he quietly asked as the man left their field of vision. He knew the answer to this question, but he didn't want his son to know just yet. He had to be sure.

"Who ... Whelor? He's a warrior who was in the games in Brigin'i. I was told that he came from the northern reaches. Why? Is there something wrong?" Meradoth looked confusedly at his father.

Turning, Meradoth's father smiled quickly. "No, Son ... just a feeling. Come, it is good to see you. Your mother will be happy to see you as well." He placed a hand again on Meradoth's shoulder as he mentioned the man's mother. His son took a deep breath, feeling the hand on his shoulder.

"Father, I didn't want to come here ... but Harbin was insistent that we come. He said he had orders from you. Well, he didn't name you specifically, but you are the head of our order and

..." Meradoth and his father slowly walked side by side as they approached the structure. The smoke behind them slowly closed around the area that, moments before, the group had been standing in.

"Yes, for a number of reasons. One, to see you, and two, I believe we will need to work together, my son, to fight this evil that has come from the east. Only together, I believe, can we do it." The man followed Meradoth inside the structure. As Meradoth walked inside the hall, he saw the others looking around in amazement, for they had expected to be standing in tight and closed-off quarters, but when bright torches erupted on the side of a large hallway with a high ceiling, the group stared with wide eyes. Meradoth turned and looked back at his father as the opening that led outside slowly shut behind him.

Quickly a torch appeared on the wall behind the mage, and to the unseeing eye outside, the opening disappeared completely as the two mages walked down the hall to join the group that had gathered now inside the structure.

As the door shut, returning to its normal appearance, two tiny reddish eyes moved out of the shadows. The eyes had been watching the group, tracking it since Bru Edin from a distance. Very slowly the creature pushed itself out of the brush to look up and around the structure, making sure it was alone, before it almost hopped up on its two tiny legs, standing a few feet away from the structure.

Its long but thin tail whipped around behind it as the two wings that hung on its sides flapped slightly. The creature began wondering what to do as it watched the fog that had moments before cleared away slowly move back down to cover the silvery building, making it hard for the creature to take in anything else.

"Massssttteeerr, nooo, noottt thiisss pllaaacceee," the tiny mouth spoke quietly as its eyes moved back and forth, trying to understand what it was looking at.

"Dooo weee teelll massssttteeerr?" another tiny voice piped

in from behind the first, making it turn its head backwards to observe another creature just like itself move out of the brush not far away to hop up and stand next to it.

"Maassssttteeerr waanntedd uusss too waattchh theemmm," the first stated as the fog began to cover even them now.

"Weee shhoouuldd waattchh theemm!" The second hopped closer as it spoke.

"Chaannnssoorr willl telll usss moorreee!" The first smiled and looked at the second one, who returned a smile full of tiny, sharp teeth. It lifted a tiny hand that held a parchment roll as it spoke.

Turning around, both hopped back into the shadows and brush to wait and watch. They had time.

Chapter Twenty Nine

Both had been lying on the shoreline of Lake Brigin'i what seemed like cycles before, enjoying a picnic as the cool breeze moved through her hair and she smiled over at the man lying next to her.

"What are you thinking about?" Kalion asked calmly.

"Just us!" she whispered when a sharp but loud ringing in her ears woke her from the dream. She groaned slightly as she turned her head back and forth, trying to get the ringing to quiet down. A bright light hurt her eyes, even as they were closed. She lifted a hand and covered her face for a moment to let her open her eyes up, only to moan as the light caused her extreme pain, making her shut her eyes for a moment longer.

She cautiously turned her head and peeked out from under her hand to see nothing but bright light, but slowly as she looked around a bit more, the light dissipated, and she could see structures begin to form. Black formations in the distance made her blink a few times as her eyes adjusted to see that the formations were just trees and bushes, and her ears finally understood that she was listening not to singing like she would hear at a party but to birds chirping from the tops of the trees.

She lifted herself up, groaning a bit as she felt the pain in her head slowly disappear, and found that she was lying on a beach. She then heard the rush of a wave move up onto the shore and retreat as she blinked to watch the waves move.

She looked towards the trees and wondered how she had gotten there. She remembered being on the ship and then waking up to find that she was on a beach almost like the one she lay on now.

But what about that feeling that crept in — the memory of being underwater with a sea elf?

A sea elf? "Must have been a dream," she whispered out loud.

"It was no dream, my princess!" A familiar voice made her turn her head around to see where it came from. Standing not far away was the man she had been a prisoner of before ... before their ship had crashed. But now he smiled at her.

Her eyes said the same as the man's did as he spoke quietly. "I remember floating within the deep of the water as well. The feeling is so strong that it could not have been a dream." Quinor walked towards her and knelt down to offer his hand.

"Here, let me help you up!" he said, nodding his head at his hand that was reached out towards her. Slowly she reached out, wondering if he was going to tie her up again or do something worse. Gently he helped her up, and together, they stood looking at each other.

Quinor tightened his lips as he thought of the right words to say, and then he smiled down at the girl. "Princess, I am sorry for what I did to you. You are ... you have ... you are ... too special to me, and I cannot harm you ... or let another do the same. So please, Princess ... my princess, let me protect you now!" He swallowed deeply, hoping she would hear the sincerity in his voice.

She stared up at the warrior, who returned a gentle smile. She felt his body heat and realized the grip on her hands was not tight like he was going to harm her. Had her plan worked, then? she wondered. Had she been able to get her kidnapper to have feelings for her?

"Do you know where we are?" she asked in a loud whisper, dismissing her plans for the moment.

Looking around, Quinor took in the scenery around them as he concentrated for a moment, trying to see if he knew where they were. "From the way I feel — warm from the sun above — I would say we are far to the south of the northern reaches ... maybe even in the deep south ... maybe within the empire." He turned and looked once again before returning his vision to the princess.

"The empire ... of all the gods' places for us to be. ... Is it safe here, Quinor?" Her nervousness made the warrior smile as he felt it as well in her hands.

"Safer than I think it would be up north. At least Methnorick hasn't reached these shores. From what I have heard, the empire is stronger than ever. So, yes, I do believe we are safe here." She nodded as he answered.

"So now where ... can we just stay on the beach?" He smiled at her joke, shaking his head "no."

"I think if we move to the west, we will find a farm or something, where I believe we can get food and maybe information. But first ... do you trust me, my princess?" Quinor needed to know that she did before they left the beach.

"Am I a prisoner still?" she asked quickly, returning her thoughts to her plan to win over her kidnapper.

Shaking his head, he smiled again at her question. "No, and not only are you not my prisoner, but I am your prisoner ... or your servant, if you so agree." He hoped that he would get to be beside her as they walked.

She squinted her eyes as she looked up at him and said, "No, you are not my prisoner, Quinor ... servant maybe. For now, let us just say you are my protector, yes?" Quinor smiled quickly and nodded a "yes" as he had hoped she would say those words to him.

Shermee smiled and let go of his hands as she turned to look at the tree line and the skies above as well as to where he was hoping they would walk. Then she looked back at the man, and noticing something missing, she spoke quietly.

"I do believe you need to get a weapon. Hard for you to protect us when you do not have the means. Then food and information are needed as well. But first, you can call me by my name, Princess Shermee, when we are alone, but when we encounter others, for safety, just call me what my father calls me: Shermee. I have to face the reality that my father and my city are gone, so a princess is no longer what I am. I am Queen Shermee, understand?"

Quinor smiled and even laughed as she spoke. She had grown up before his eyes ... and his feelings for her had grown. "Shermee ... Princess Shermee ... Queen ... I am proud, very proud to be your servant and protector!" he said as he walked up and past her to stop and look at the same tree line.

Shermee looked at the man's back, shaking her head slightly. She really cared nothing for this man. He had kidnapped her, tried to bring her to her father's enemy. Though, yes, he had protected her a few times, he still had taken her away from her family and her city. *I have nothing but disgust for you,* she thought.

"From this moment forward, I will protect you from anything. Even Methnorick will not be able to touch you!" Quinor boasted as he turned his head to see her nod back at him slowly. He moved towards what looked like a deer trail as both began a journey, neither knowing where it would take them.

As she followed her former captor, her thoughts went back to her city, her father and the man she missed. She walked into the trees and followed the warrior, who quietly stated that he believed this was the way. They began walking on what must have been an old deer trail of some kind, as it was easy to walk along, but she only smiled when her thoughts went back to the face of the man she missed.

"Kalion!" she whispered to herself, "I miss you!"

* * *

King Stokolma Finfilli stood behind the shields of his warriors as they faced their deadliest enemy within the deep. So far his warriors had fought and withstood each assault that their dark cousins had sent towards them, and each time they had been able to repulse them. He knew his dwarven warriors were killing their dark cousins, but he was losing warrior after warrior, and his shield line was showing the losses now.

Even the return of the reinforcements he had sent to help Bru Edin hadn't changed the situation, and he knew that sooner than later, he was going to have to order a full retreat to the gateway behind him. That would be two gates that their cousins had been able to take from his people, and this angered the old dwarf.

So far he could not understand how their cousins had been able to get this far. Dark dwarves were not the smartest creatures, having lived for so many cycles within the dark. They had to have gotten help, but there was no word on or sighting of who or what it was, and this made him worry more that something was lurking behind their formations.

If the Qlorfana were, indeed, getting help, from what he had seen so far, his kingdom would fall within a fortnight's time, and all he would be able to do would be to watch it from where he was.

"My king, here they come!" a captain screamed out to his right, bringing his mind back to the situation before him as his eyes quickly saw the helms of the Qlorfana moving through the caverns and up the road where his warriors had placed their shield wall.

Quickly the battle exploded with light as mages on both sides threw what they could at each other and archers within Gusfana's ranks released arrows and cross bolts, killing their dark cousins in waves, not stopping as their screams echoed over the explosions around them. In return, many arrows flew through the dark, quickly killing Finfilli's warriors and leaving openings wherever he looked.

The fighting lasted for more than an hour until a Qlorfana horn blasted, signaling a retreat, and as they had time and time again, the dark dwarves melted back into the deep darkness of the cavern, leaving Finfilli's warriors to lick their wounds and care for their wounded. Many within the dark dwarven ranks lay moaning in pain as well, but they were left to die where they fell.

The old king quickly ordered clerics to move forward, pull

the wounded back and take them above as some reinforcements moved in to relieve those warriors who had just fought the hard battle.

"My king!" Finfilli looked over to see a dwarf with half of his face covered in a bloody bandage. It was one of his mages, he could see, who had been on the line for most of the time and had not left even when ordered.

"Yes?" he said, quickly having to move to the side as clerics walked past the two dwarves, who waited for the opportunity to speak clearly to each other.

"My king, I know who is attacking us!" The answer made the king shake his head hard, bringing up anger and making him wonder if his warrior was out of his mind from the wound.

"Of course you know who is attacking us. There's nothing new about that information ..." He was quickly cut off by the warrior, who shook his head.

"No ... no ... no, my king. I know it is the Qlorfana that we fight, but it is what is behind them that I speak about — the ones giving them orders. I believe I saw a Buwan Amnach and something larger ... looking almost like a human from above. I saw them when we gave that final push before they retreated. I saw them standing behind that pillar down there, sir." The dwarf pointed to the large pillar that held up part of the cavern, which would give cover to anything behind it. The king saw it was a good spot for anyone to observe the battle from the other side.

"Interesting!" he whispered. Squinting his old eyes so he could look beyond the pillar, he thought to himself, *So the Buwan Amnach have joined this war as well ... but what would a human be doing amongst them?*

As the old king thought about what it all meant, he didn't realize that his observation was being returned. The dwarf ordered the mage to find a way to destroy the pillar as a pair of eyes looked up at him, squinting hard.

Kaligor sat upon his mount as he pulled a large piece of meat off the bone of some unlucky woman who had died trying to stop a few of orcs from getting into her house. It was torched to get her to run out, and when she did, she was cut down along with a few other family members who tried to escape.

When it turned out that she was a council member who happened not to be in the tower when it fell, Kaligor's second in command, who saw her robes as he was moving by, had her body dragged down to the fields below to be served up for the general, who now sat looking at the fires being used to cook prisoners and others killed to feed his army.

Now Kaligor pulled and gnawed on the meat, smiling as the blood leaked out and dripped down his chin. He threw a piece of the meat to his beloved mount, which of course ate it faster than he ever could have but also agreed that the meat was perfect.

"Human ... the best meat!" he laughed out loud. The orcish cook and a few warriors that were standing by on guard for their general overheard him and also laughed in total agreement, having just eaten themselves.

Looking up as he ate, he watched the city burn and collapse before him. His orders now were to march south and east, but he wanted to watch the "Shield of the North" die. Watching prisoners being killed and cooked made his army happy, and that's what he wanted. Orcs were hard enough to control when they had full bellies, but without food ... orcs would eat their own if they could.

When he was done with the meat, he threw the bone down for his pet and patted its neck, whispering to it to savor the bone, knowing that it was one used by a creature that had tried and done everything it could to destroy his kind.

The reports that many groups of the populace had been able to retreat did not seem to bother the Cyclops; they would die out in the wild sooner than later. But it was the populace that was still inside that he was told was resisting and fighting back, and in a few areas, they had even been able to force his orcs to retreat.

"My lord, your orders?" the Blingo'oblin commander asked as it walked up. Chewing the meat, the general looked over and took in the shield it held with its muscular hand and arm. Kaligor could see scalps that it had taken from within; a few heads of those it had killed also decorated the large spear it was leaning against when it stopped to hear its newest orders.

"At night's beginning, send word out that sections one through three are to begin moving the machines south. I want us to bring everything we can with us. I have a feeling that, where we are going, we will face our biggest battle yet." Kaligor leaned on the horn of his saddle as he spoke.

"Then have sections five and seven continue the push to destroy everything within this city. The rest I want to march by night's end."

He always enjoyed watching his victories, and not having the chance to see the last three — first, the Levenori Forest; then, Brigin'i City; and now, the biggest of them all, Bru Edin — angered the big Cyclops deeply. How could his master deny him this glory?

"Sir, I will have the reserves brought to order as soon as I can and have them join the movement with all the war machines that are able to move. What of the Buwan Amnach, sir? They will not listen to me." Hearing that, Kaligor smiled at the stubbornness of the dark-skinned ones.

Nodding as he looked over at the dark elves, who were also celebrating the victory, but at the edge of the forest to keep themselves out of the light of the sun that was luckily coming down now, he replied, "I will take care of them, my friend, but make sure my orders are carried out. We need to be on the road this very night, Joocc!"

Leaving his Blingo'oblin to bow slightly, he did not wait for an answer as he grabbed the reins, turned his mount to the left and slowly made his way to where the Buwan Amnach that had helped in his victory had camped themselves. As he got closer, he could hear them laughing and shouting about their deeds and more, but they quickly stopped when they saw him walking towards them.

Kaligor saw the elf that was their leader turn around as he was joking with another of his kind and nod towards Kaligor. Then he walked until he was at the very edge of the forest line to wait for the general of all generals.

"Your people have done a great service for me, and of course, your rewards will be plenty!" Kaligor declared loudly and with pride as he got closer. The dark elf warrior bowed deeply as he spoke.

"Thank you, sir. This was ... fun!" The elf smiled back as he watched the Cyclops swing his leg around and jump off his mount, which snarled slightly at the dark elves, making them take a few steps back. A few dark elves jeered, hearing the joke.

Kaligor stepped up. He looked directly into the eyes of the elf and spoke in a commanding voice.

"I have been given new orders by the dark one. We are to travel south and east this very night, so I am leaving this field of battle. I had hoped to stay and enjoy my victory, but I need you and your warriors to travel with me." The Cyclops put his hands behind his body as he took a few steps to look over at the dark elven warrior's smile and listen to what he was speaking about. Turning around, he looked down at the thin but quick warrior, who stood, chewing on a piece of meat he had been eating. "I want your people to travel like a picket force as my main army marches." Kaligor indicated what he wanted on his hands, showing the elf what he was thinking.

"Are you expecting something to attack you?" the elf asked, lifting his eyes after taking in the movement orders. "What would have the courage or even the strength, General, to attack you ... after what you have done here?"

"I always suspect, my friend. These lands might be ours soon ... but not yet, and I suspect that there are many creatures out there in the dark that would love to assault my army if they could."

The dark elf huffed and smiled at the Cyclops as he stated with pride that no creature — elf, man or even dwarf — would attack. "I will do this for you, sir!" He smiled at the opportunity to take on the adventure out in the wild.

Kaligor smiled and nodded slightly as he thought about the idea of his army marching. The dark elves ruled the darkness ... and along the right of his armies' column, he believed nothing would ever attack him.

Nodding to the elf and then to the others, Kaligor turned and jumped back on his mount, which snarled and puffed loudly again as Kaligor grabbed the reins and looked down at the elves once more. "Remember this day. The human is no longer going to be able to kill or hunt your people. Take pride that you were the ones that made that happen!" As he turned, he listened to the elves' cheers and yells celebrating what they had just done to the creatures that had caused so many cycles of pain for their kind. The big Cyclops smiled as he slowly galloped over the field of battle, taking in all the dead, dying and wounded that lay everywhere.

The number of those lying on the field did not bother him; he suspected that he had lost three to four thousand warriors in the battle of Bru Edin, leaving him an army of five to six thousand. This was not enough for the battle he knew was coming, so he hoped that he was going to get reinforcements soon.

* * *

"What are you speaking about, sir? Meradoth could not be your son. Brother maybe ... but son?" Jebba smiled out of the corner of his mouth as he sat in the plush chair, looking at the man who had brought them inside the enormous tower he said was his home.

Meradoth had sat himself in the corner of the room, leaning back in the chair with his leg over the arm as he relaxed, reading a book that he had forgotten about many cycles before. Hearing the group talking, he looked up and smiled as he realized many in the group were talking about him and his father.

"Jebba, my friend, it is a story or tale that I want to tell, but I do not know if you or any here except Harbin and my son would understand." The man smiled as he leaned on the table before him and looked the others in their eyes.

"Try us, sir!" Kalion said calmly, believing that his group could take in the information.

"I'm sure whatever you have to say, sir, this group is more than ready to hear." Kikor smiled up at the man as she sat cross-legged, eating some lettuce he had brought in earlier.

"Father, tell them what they need to know. If you don't, I'm sure they will nag you and nag you." Meradoth smiled, making Holan grumble nearby. Amlora huffed a laugh as she nodded to Meradoth's father, who stared at each member of this group his son traveled with.

When the group had entered the chamber a while earlier, they could see that this room was huge — not just huge, but ... huge according to Chansor, who began walking around, browsing what was along the walls. There was a huge collection of books and parchments, and the furniture, though covered in dust slightly, made the chamber look relaxing and inviting. The thief slowly walked around, taking everything in. He stopped to look up when a shadow crossed his path. Massive statues that looked almost as tall as the towers of Bru Edin and Brigin'i City were looking down at him.

Each statue showed not warriors, mages or anything close to that. Each stood representing the gods, each standing with their hands clasped before them, looking down with closed eyes. Each, he felt, showed the strength of what they represented: the first of their kind.

As the group behind him spoke quietly about things he didn't care about, he slowly walked past each one, touching the feet of each to get a feel of the strength these statues might hold.

When he came around a statue that represented one of the elven goddesses of beauty, he saw what had to be the largest one, which depicted a man who wore strange-looking trousers and a cloak and hood over his head, looking down from under it. His feet were covered in boots that Chansor wished he had — they looked expensive.

The elven gods, of which there were two, according to Kikor, stood across from each other, looking at one another in silence, but smiling, unlike all the others. The male elf, which Chansor could see standing to his right, was wearing robes such as a cleric might wear, while the she-elf standing opposite wore a shorter robe that showed her legs, each the size of a giant's head. Holan had snickered earlier when he saw them.

Her hair fell down over her chest while the male's was a bit shorter but still showed his leadership. Chansor could see that, whoever these two were, they led their people with pride and strength.

The other statues he saw represented the dwarven gods and the gods of a few other races that had lived upon the lands many cycles before, but Chansor began to wonder. This tower was not one that a druid or cleric would use; why would mages have statues such as these? He blinked when his ears caught the old man speaking quietly and calmly about this place and turned his concentration to what the man was saying.

"You, I would believe, know of the legends ... the tales of the gods and how they came to be?" he asked, looking around and seeing a few nod "yes."

"Many, many cycles ago, before even Kikor's people walked the lands, the gods lived beyond our world ... beyond even where we could see in the night skies ... beyond the stars."

"I heard that the gods once lived in a world they each ruled parts of until it died around them," Niallee said quietly. Her voice almost echoed in the chamber, making everyone look at the druid.

The man nodded slightly at her comment. "Yes, my dear.

They once lived in a world far beyond, but not together as the legends say. They lived in their own worlds, ruling over their own peoples, until they came to ours. Here they fought on the lands and in the sky." The man saw everyone looking at him and paused to let them take all the new information in.

Amlora, leaning forward on the table to look directly at the man across from her, said, "Wait ... what does this have to do with Methnorick? What do the gods have to do with him?" Many looked at Meradoth and each other, and a few nodded, wondering the same thing, as the man smiled back.

"If you would please let me continue ... You see, there was a terrible battle outside our world that left our world almost destroyed. But the gods decided to leave their own here. Why, I know not, but each of us — elf, man, gnome — we all came from another place."

"Impossible!" Jebba stood up looking at the mage before him. "No gods have ever ruled these lands. None!"

"Father ..." Meradoth stood up and walked closer to the group. Everyone looked at the mage and then back at the man who called himself Nicolorr.

Nicolorr nodded as he leaned back, smiling, to let his son speak. He didn't stop his son as he spoke clearly about what this place was. They knew his son better and might understand him more clearly.

"Methnorick is not the one that leads the armies of orcs and other dark creatures." Meradoth strode over to stand next to his father, as did Harbin. The three stood, looking at the others, as everyone gasped at this news.

"He is human like myself, like Chansor, and even like Whelor over there, but he uses magic of some kind to slow his aging. There is more I believe you should know about our enemy." Kalion looked at his friend with a confused look, believing he was trying to pull something on them all. Methnorick ... human?

"Methnorick is destroying everything in these lands," Holan declared, thinking of his dwarven comrades.

"Birkita died fighting those orcs that he leads. We need to find a way to stop them," Jebba stated as Bennak nodded in agreement.

"Hrliger probably is dead fighting within Bru Edin. We need to do something," Amlora whispered loud enough for the others to hear as they all piped in, trying to understand what Meradoth and his father were speaking about.

Meradoth crossed his arms as he listened to a few other comments, and then he looked at his father, who waved for him to continue.

"In many ways this place has something to do with the fact that my father, Harbin and I look so young. Harbin and I are over 80 cycles of age. I am sorry to deceive you by not telling you this before, but we are that old." Meradoth smiled when Chansor finally got it and clapped his hands together, letting the mage know that at least one of them was going along with what he was saying.

Meradoth looked around the chamber as he opened his arms up. "Let me explain. This place has godly powers. It is where my people, and yours, Amlora and Niallee, get our abilities. How we do not age while your people do, I know not."

Kikor got up to stretch her legs and walked over to a column that was holding up another floor. She leaned against it as she listened, remembering what her father had taught her about the ancient tales of where their people came from.

"From across the eastern seas, our people came. Before there, they lived with the gods within the night sky." Her father's voice rang through her head as she looked over at Meradoth, who had stopped to listen to a comment from Niallee, who cleared her throat.

"There is a legend told among my people that says we are almost as old as the gods and that they were the ones that caused my people to suffer their wrath during a battle within the stars. Are you saying that this place has something to do with that?"

"This place, yes. But there are places such as these around the lands, where over time, the powers within have ... well, done things to those that live near them," Nicolorr said after listening to the elf warrior's comment.

Jebba coughed to get the others' attention. When they looked at him, he said, "I do not care why this place is here or how old you all are. What I want to find out is how to stop and kill Methnorick. He has caused us all so much pain and destruction. What do you know about him and how to stop him?" Jebba's comment made a few nod in agreement as they stared back Nicolorr.

Pulling in a deep breath and slowly blowing it out, the mage gathered the words together in his mind, hoping they would all understand.

"Far beyond our lands in the east, where legends say life began in this world, there is a land where the gods are believed to ... well, experiment on their peoples."

"Experiment? What?" Amlora asked, shocked to hear that her gods would do such a thing.

"I know not the right words, but all I can say is that I was once told that they want to try to perfect themselves through us. One of those perfections was, or is, Methnorick."

"Ohh, gods." Kikor scratched her head as she thought about what that meant.

"Meradoth, are you saying that Methnorick is some creature that is human but not human?" Kalion asked, even though he somehow knew the answer.

"Yes. The gods or something experimented on him and made him what you hear about today, but there is something I know none of you would understand unless I explain. Methnorick is destroying the lands not just to destroy everything around him, but for two reasons. "

Nicolorr took a moment to take a sip of water as he cleared his throat.

"Sir, Methnorick has destroyed everything. What he's doing it all for?" Niallee asked, trying to understand what she was hearing as she looked over at Meradoth's father.

He looked at the elf and smiled gently. "My dear, one reason is that he is searching for objects of power — objects that would give his overlords the ability to travel to the gods."

"What objects would they be, sir?" Kalion asked quickly as he turned his stare from Kikor to the older man.

"Objects that to this day have changed these lands. To the very peoples that walk above and below these lands, down to the flesh of your blood, these objects are very dangerous, but needed."

Hearing that made the group hang their heads. A few whispered that maybe they should just leave and go home, but Kalion cleared his throat to get the rest to hear what he had to say.

"Methnorick is leading an army of evil creatures no one has ever seen upon this land and using them, I guess, to search for these objects. But Nicolorr, that really isn't the reason he makes war. It seemed to me that he had hatred towards Brigin'i and other cities. Did Dia hold one of those objects you speak of?"

Nicolorr walked over to the ranger and laid a hand on his shoulder, looking down. "My friend, if he gets all these objects, then the world we know will disappear forever. That I know."

"Did he have hatred towards Dia, sir?" Jebba asked the question again.

"Dia, I am told, knew Methnorick many, many cycles ago." Nicolorr sucked in a quick breath. "He experimented on Methnorick and made him the creature we know of today."

Hearing this made everyone stand up quickly and shout out loudly, wondering what to do. The chamber echoed loudly as they spoke about how this small group could ever stop the armies that Methnorick had on the fields. They did not see Nicolorr turn and walk slowly to where Whelor was leaning against one of the elven statues, thinking beyond what the others were at the moment.

332

When Whelor saw the mage move closer, he let his crossed arms fall as he pushed himself off the statue and waited for the man to get a few feet from him. He stared down at the man who was staring up at him.

"What do we have here? Whelor, I am told. Is that your name, friend?" Nicolorr's question made Whelor squint a bit as he looked down to slowly nod "yes."

Nicolorr smiled gently as he thought about how this man felt different from the others and why he always seemed to be standing far away from the rest of the group.

"Where are you from, friend?" Nicolorr asked, trying not to sound threatening.

Whelor stared at him a moment longer and then pulled in a deep breath. "My people lived in the northern reaches, near the coldest north," Whelor said calmly in return, not feeling totally at ease with this man's stares.

"'Lived.' Are they still living there?" Whelor shook his head "no" as Nicolorr tilted his head back slightly. He thought about where this man came from, making him wonder more. Nicolorr wondered why he was feeling uneasy about the massive man, but before he could speak, he heard Meradoth's voice.

"Whelor, come and join us. We would like to hear what you think about all of this!"

Whelor nodded towards Meradoth and stepped forward when Nicolorr put his hand on the big man's forearm, making him stop and look down at the mage's stern look.

"I have the feeling that you and I, friend, will be discussing what you have inside you before you leave this place." Whelor didn't respond as he stepped forward and walked over to where Meradoth stood, laughing with Chansor and Amlora about some of the answers the group was coming up with. Meradoth's father followed the warrior to join the rest.

"So Methnorick attacked and probably destroyed Brigin'i

because Dia experimented on him in the past?" Niallee was speaking when Nicolorr joined the group. As he did, Nicolorr kept an eye on Whelor, who now stood behind the rest with his arms crossed, trying not to return the mage's glare.

Harbin piped in then. "I think he attacked the city for two reasons really: to take revenge on Dia by kidnapping his daughter, the princess, and to somehow find those objects we spoke about."

"What is so important about those objects, sir?" Holan quietly asked, having been wondering what the dark lord would want with silly things.

Nicolorr smiled quickly and then sucked in a breath as he answered.

"Those objects, when put together, generate power for something much larger than anything I could think of ... and Methnorick's overlord wants them badly."

"How do you know who wants them and what they do?" Jebba asked, speaking a little louder than the rest.

"My father has known things about this world for many cycles before you all were born, sir. So if he says there is something pulling Methnorick around, then there is," Meradoth said, coming to the defense of his father, who placed his hand on his son's shoulder as he fought off Jebba's attack.

Jebba lifted his hands up in surrender, seeing that the mages were standing together. He turned to look up at Bennak, who so far had also been quiet, but at least he was interested in what was going on.

"So how do we counter the might of Methnorick if he has reinforcements from beyond the seas helping him, Nicolorr?" Kalion asked calmly, trying to bring down the stress being felt in the room for a moment.

The mage looked slowly at the faces before him, returning their gaze before answering the ranger. "With strength, cunning and skill, sir. Aside from that, the luck of the gods!"

✳ ✳ ✳

The fires erupted across 30 to 40 percent of Blath 'Na's northwestern sections, but to the populace, it felt like the whole city was burning as they rushed to get away to the famous port area of the city.

Overnight, those who hid in their homes or in dark areas on the streets heard screams of both victims and the creatures attacking and moving through the streets echo in the night. Families shook in fear, holding each other tightly and praying to their gods that the evil that had entered the city would move past where they hid and disappear soon.

The army did its best to stop the assault by pushing over carts and stacking heavy boxes across smaller streets, hoping that, by doing so, the creatures wouldn't be able to get through. On the larger streets, shield walls were put up, and so far these had held up with minimal losses.

Those wounded were left on the street as they noticed that those attacked and bitten died sooner than later and somehow returned to attack. The army could see that many of the barriers wouldn't hold up for long since those attacked were growing in number. Nothing was spared.

Small and large ships were quickly packed to the rails, causing a few to sink from the weight of the people in their hulls. Orders were put out that the populace needed to board orderly and slowly. Luckily those orders were kept throughout the nights as the smaller island just east of the bay was packed with survivors and small ships returned to get more people trying to leave.

Far away in the forest that lay west of the mighty city, eyes had been watching the city. Peering through the leaves of the huge, ancient trees were five elven scouts sent by their king when a rumor came into the ancient elven kingdom that the human city was under

335

attack by something never seen in the lands before.

As each of the scouts watched, fire and smoke rose over the high walls, and the screams echoed across the grassy fields to their ears, making the elves look at each other with wide eyes as they whispered, wondering what was within.

Quietly these elves left the observation points and returned to inform their king. Blath 'Na City, the City of Ports, seemed to be a loss, as none of the scouts had the courage to investigate because of the ominous feelings each got.

Methnorick was standing on the balcony when he got the feeling that someone or something was close at hand. When the Blingo'oblin walked in and told him that the princess's ship had not arrived, he crossed his arms silently as he stared out towards the water that lay far away, wondering what this feeling was that he'd had for a while. He closed his eyes to move his mind past the movement around him. His mind drifted like a crow would across the island's landscape and out towards the water and the mainland beyond.

As he got about halfway across the water and was just starting to see the land, Methnorick got the feeling that he was going the wrong way, so turning his vision around, he came back to the island. The feeling got stronger as he did, and he suddenly realized that it had to be the princess. She was finally there ... but where was her ship? It had to be her, he thought, as his vision moved across the rocks and the waves until he saw something that made him stop.

"Noooooo!" he screamed in his mind when he saw the floating parts of wood smashing themselves against the rocks as the waves brought pieces in and out. A few dead bodies also floated with the debris, but none looked like a woman. He moved himself to look over the whole scene, and slowly he could see that, indeed, it used to be a ship — a quite large one, he could see, from the amount of litter that was below.

A mast, broken in two, floated in the white foam, as did some sails, and here and there, he could see the body of a sailor lying facedown in the water, floating. He screamed again, knowing that this was her ship. The princess's ship ... that one object that he had to have ... gone!

He opened his eyes, grabbing the railing of the balcony as he gritted his teeth tightly. His anger made it hard for him to understand anything. The object of his desire, killed while at sea. He couldn't believe it.

A cough behind him made him lift his head slightly to stare at the sky as he gripped the metal tightly, slowly bending and warping it as he tightened his hands on the metal.

"Yes!" he grunted.

"My lord, you are being asked for!" the voice answered. He knew that only Sunorak would disturb him at this moment. Without a word he pushed himself away from the railing. He turned and saw that the mindslayer was standing there, looking back at him with his watery black eyes.

Only nodding as he walked past, he went down to the chamber that he used as his throne room and walked in, seeing the goblins that had been repairing and replacing the two massive doors standing there.

As he walked by, he motioned for them to leave. They quickly bowed and disappeared before he even got to his blackened throne, where he turned and sat down to look at the tapestry he used to observe his campaign of war.

Looking up at it for a moment longer, he waved his right hand across it and watched as the fabric began to waver like it was water and change the sewn scene of a castle surrounded by a battle into a dark void.

"Meeetttthhhhhhnnnnnoooorrrriiiicccckkk!" a voice erupted out of the blackness, making the man who, up to that moment, had felt as though he was the lord of all swallow and shake under his clothing.

"Yes, master. It is I!"

Made in the USA
Monee, IL
04 January 2022

87074802R00204